JAISHREE MISRA

Secrets and Lies

FSC is a non-profit international organisation established
to promote the responsible management of the world's forests.
Products carrying the FSC label are independently certified
to assure consumers that they come from forests that are managed
to meet the social, economic and ecological needs
of present and future generations.

Find out more about HarperCollins and the environment at
www.harpercollins.co.uk/green

AVON

AVON

A division of HarperCollins*Publishers*
77–85 Fulham Palace Road,
London W6 8JB

www.harpercollins.co.uk

A Paperback Original 2009

First published in Great Britain by
HarperCollins*Publishers* 2009

Copyright © Jaishree Misra 2009

Jaishree Misra asserts the moral right to
be identified as the author of this work

A catalogue record for this book is
available from the British Library

ISBN-13: 978-1-84756-168-8

Set in Minion by Palimpsest Book Production Limited,
Grangemouth, Stirlingshire

Printed and bound in Great Britain by
Clays Ltd, St Ives plc

With apologies to Housman, with gratitude my heart is laden for golden friends I have. This book has been written for them – friends who so richly people my life, providing love, laughter, food, absorbent shoulders and nuggets of irresistible material they will spot scattered through the book. Here, then, is my tribute to you: Qubra, Vini, Chinks, Rach, Ranju, Mukti, Ushma, Shalini, Geetika, Rads, Theo, Sunanda, Shrabani, Nicki, Aradhana, Renu, Kusoom.

Then there are those who, over and above being great friends, *also* allow me to twist their arms into reading unfinished drafts: Nisha, Karen, Smita, Anshu, Raja. Thank you all for being so diligent and discerning and, largely, polite.

Big thanks too to Sujay and Ant for the website.

Heartfelt gratitude too to my agent and publishers: Judith, Keshini, Maxine, Karthika, a band of extremely skilled and dedicated professionals who are the hidden power-house, with very special thanks to Keshini for the most brilliant editorial notes I've ever seen.

Although the character of Victoria Lamb is entirely fictional, she has naturally been inspired by a certain sort of teacher, my chequered education across India having brought me before many such. Great teachers and mentors all, although some have now, sadly, passed on: Mrs Gadadhar and Miss Fritchley at Baldwins Girls' High School in Bangalore, Miss Dawson at Mater Dei School in Delhi, Kaushi Ramdas at the Convent of Jesus & Mary in Delhi and Professor Madhukar Rao in Cochin. Here's evidence of how far, in place and time, some ripples from your pebbles have spread.

Good thing I write books or I'd never get around to thanking my family for the many things they do for me. But for unstinting love (and air-freighted home food), thanks to both Mummies and the clans on both sides. And, of course, Rohini and Dicky, my immediate two; for allowing me to float off into other worlds whenever I need to, for keeping me safely tethered on those flights and for happy landings when it's time to come home. All that, *and* an uncomplaining 24-hour IT service. Writers should be so lucky.

This book is dedicated to all my girlfriends, but most especially Qubra, who never minded that I regularly swiped her lunch back at school . . .

With rue my heart is laden
For golden friends I had,
For many a rose-lipt maiden
And many a lightfoot lad.
By brooks too broad for leaping
The lightfoot lads are laid;
The rose-lipt girls are sleeping
In fields where roses fade.

A.E. Housman

Prologue

DELHI, 2008

Victoria Lamb sealed the last of her letters and placed it on top of the small pile. Then, steadying herself on the arms of her wooden swivel chair, she eased herself up from the writing bureau where she had been sitting since dawn and walked across to the French windows. Flexing her stiff hand, Victoria parted the old curtains at their faded central strip and blinked as Delhi's sharp summer sunshine flooded in. The rose garden, denuded of flowers, lay thorny and colourless, dust stubbornly clinging to everything: the leaves, the trees, Lily's stone grave at the bottom of the garden. Beyond the hedge and through the smog haze, the mansard roof of the school building with its squat clock tower was just visible. Emptied of its student population, the old Edwardian building had lain silent for the last six weeks, with only the occasional flitting figure of a nun disturbing the dark peace of the convent's corridors.

Tomorrow the new term would start in its usual clamorous manner, beginning with the distant rumble of school buses approaching the gates. A pleasant enough sound, but one that unfailingly lapsed into belligerence as the bus drivers competed with the private cars that brought the more affluent

3

pupils to school. That was when the ear-shattering revving and grinding of engines invariably began. The bus drivers were mindful of Miss Lamb's strict 'No Horns' policy but, despite the occasional sternly worded home-circular, there was little she had been able to do about the strident car horns, the expression of self-importance that flowed from Delhi's wealthy to their chauffeurs.

Far more forgiveable were the children's shrieks that would assail Victoria's ears at precisely half past seven, when the first of the school buses would disgorge its passengers just as she was sitting down to her breakfast of one poached egg and a slice of unbuttered toast. But the girls knew well enough to keep their voices hushed once they were inside the school building, or when they saw Miss Lamb passing through the grounds from the cottage at the edge of the school. That was indeed the best time of the day for Victoria – and had been for many years – the moment at which she cut across the quadrangle, saying hello and sometimes stopping to speak to a passing student, while the aroma of coffee wafted in the air alongside muffled laughter from the staff room. Victoria felt a small rush of gratification at the thought that she would be experiencing that familiar glow at roughly this time tomorrow. And then she reminded herself that tomorrow was to be the very last time she would be at St Jude's to see the start of term.

Victoria sighed, not for the first time in the day, before turning away from the window. How could she pretend it would not be hard to leave all this? Fifty years at Jude's; it had become her life! Her smile was rueful as she walked slowly around the living room of her little cottage, making mental notes about what she would need to give away or pack. Not that she would miss *everything* about the life of a school principal, of course. The job had been robbed of some

4

of its joys along the way, not least because St Jude's – with its very old reputation of turning out stylish and well-spoken young ladies – had in recent years become the choice of noveau-riche Delhi business families who merely wanted their daughters to speak English properly, thereby acquiring a sheen of sophistication. The school population had certainly enjoyed a more healthy mix when Victoria had first arrived here, college professors and government servants then seeming more able to afford the fees for their children than these days. But competition from those exclusive day-schools springing up in South Delhi had led to St Jude's management deciding to install air-conditioning in its gym and library ten years ago, and now a gleaming indoor swim-ming pool was being built on the site of the old chapel. Victoria had tried to argue that the soaring fees would invariably lead to falling academic standards, but the only concession management would make was to increase the number of scholarship students from one a year to two. Her point had been amply proven over the years, but it brought no satisfaction to Victoria whenever she saw how the quality of Jude's alumni had fallen. Running a finishing school was not what Victoria had had in mind for herself at all!

Back at her bureau, Victoria riffled through her small stack of letters, studying the names and addresses. She had tracked them down more easily than she had initially thought possible. Her girls. Somehow she continued to think of them as her special girls, despite the thousands that had since passed through the school. They had, in fact, been dubbed 'Miss Lamb's *crème de la crème*' the year the school had performed *The Prime of Miss Jean Brodie* as a play. She corrected herself: '*Lamboo*'s *crème de la crème*', for that was what the girls had always called her. Never to her face, good God, no! Far be it for her to allow that kind of familiarity.

Besides, her popularity notwithstanding, the students respected her too much to take those sorts of liberties. She had never particularly minded being called Lamboo. It wasn't malicious, merely an affectionate twist to the Hindi word that aptly described her tall and willowy figure. Victoria Lamb had, in fact, discovered her nickname from one of her first batches at St Jude's, once they had passed out of the school and returned en masse to pay their respects one day. Yes, one way or another, they always came back. Even if only to seek admission for their own daughters.

Victoria tapped the envelopes on the wooden surface, her face turning pensive as she remembered her batch of '93 and the dreadful events of that year. She had another night to decide whether to post these letters or not as the school peon would turn up on his bicycle at nine o'clock to take her mail to the post office. Agonising over this decision for days, she had tried imagining how the letters would be received by those four girls who had so deliberately never returned to the school.

Victoria still saw them in their grey-crested blazers and knee socks, even though they would be in their early thirties now, women of the world, married . . . some with children, she knew, and husbands and jobs. Every so often, a snippet of news about one of them would arrive, either via one of their old classmates, or in the pages of those glossy gossip magazines she leafed through while sitting in the dentist's waiting room.

Victoria understood perfectly why they had never come back, of course. The reason lay in that lonely grave at the bottom of her garden. Why, she herself had nearly left St Jude's after Lily's death, unable for weeks to step into the rose garden without remembering that terrible December night – and the sight of Lily as she lay on the damp earth speckled with freshly fallen petals. The picture had been imprinted on Victoria's memory forever: Lily's sequined dress pooling around her body like water and her face, her beautiful face, not yet drained of colour, turned up to the sky as though admiring the stars.

It was Lily's unblinking eyes that had first given it away.

That, and the blood seeping over the side of her head.

Chapter One

LONDON, 2008

The letters arrived at their destinations almost fifteen years after the death of Lily D'Souza.

The first to receive hers was Bubbles Raheja, as she sat curled up on a divan in the morning room of her palatial Belgravia home. She was in a state of unusual tranquillity that morning, as none of the family were at home and, consequently, she was painting her toenails a cheery post-box red when the maid brought in the mail. Generally it was Sooki, the silent but ever-smiling Thai pedicurist at the discreet little salon tucked away in a Mayfair side street, who tended to her nails, but, sometimes, doing little tasks like this for herself gave Bubbles an odd sort of pleasure that she struggled to explain. On one level it transported her instantly back to her teenage years in Delhi when she and her sisters would squabble over the last congealing dregs of Toffee Pearl, sometimes having to mix it with Cinnamon Brown and a few drops of nail-polish remover to get it to spreading consistency. But, these days, Bubbles manicured her own nails as a form of rebellion; the only kind of rebellion Bubbles ever mounted against her husband and in-laws: quiet and private and completely inconspicuous. She knew how deeply Binkie would loathe the sight of his wife sitting in as public a space as the living room performing such an ungainly task for all the house staff to behold, but that was *exactly* what made it so agreeable. Of course, her timid insurgence was a bit wasted, given that Binkie wasn't around to witness it – but then Bubbles had long grown used to making do.

She smiled at the maid and ordered a cup of elaichi tea before gesturing for the pack of mail to be left on the inlaid marble foot-stool at her elbow. Then she returned to the unfamiliar job at hand, frowning as she concentrated on getting the second coat just right. It was only ten minutes later, when the maid carried the tea-tray in and tried to make room on the small stool crowded with bottles of varnish and thinner and balls of cotton wool, that the pack of unread mail fell to the floor and Bubbles spotted the plain white envelope. The sender's address typed onto a label in the lower left-hand corner instantly caught her attention. How could it not? The nail-polish brush was hastily discarded as Bubbles reached down to pick up Miss Lamb's letter. She did not notice until much later that a drop of varnish had fallen onto one of the cream silk cushions, forming a permanent testament to her guilt – a round red blotch that rather fittingly resembled a small splash of blood.

A little later that same morning, Samira Hussein also looked disbelievingly at the envelope in her hand. It had her Kensington address and postcode absolutely right, which in itself was surprising. Was it her imagination or had her fingers actually started trembling as she read the contents twice over? She looked at her reflection in the hall mirror and was startled by her own stricken expression. The cloying, sickening smell of the Gallica roses in their cut-glass vase

10

suddenly filled her nostrils. She cast a baleful look at their perfect velvet folds. Sam never normally bought roses – there was good reason for that – but this bouquet had been given to her by Akbar's boss who had been invited to dinner last night, and the maid must have thought she was being useful by replacing the more customary gladioli with them. Sam picked up the telephone. If there ever was a time to break the old pact of silence, it was this. She did a quick count on her fingers even though she already knew – fifteen years this winter. She waited, desperately willing Bubbles to answer the phone, but by the seventh ring Sam knew it was useless.

'This is the Orange voicemail service. The number you are trying to reach is currently switched off. Please leave a message after the tone.'

Why did they always use such annoyingly nasal voices for automated messages, she thought illogically, and where on *earth* was Bubbles; she had usually risen by midday. Sam looked at her watch and guessed that her friend was either in the sauna or having a massage, or aromatherapy, or whatever she was on these days. Bubbles hardly ever turned her mobile phone off, the damn thing usually an ever-present appendage to her left hand or ear, but now Sam had no option but to call Anita. She was normally most reluctant to bother anyone who had an actual career on a weekday morning, but this was important.

'Sam,' she heard Anita's habitually brisk voice a mere second after the phone rang, 'can it wait, darling? It's coming up to the hour and the bulletin . . .'

'I know, I know, I wouldn't have, but I just wanted to know if you've had the letter too.'

'Letter?'

'I've just had a letter from Lamboo.'

She heard the silence before Anita spoke, her voice incredulous.

11

'*Lamboo*? After all these years! Whatever for?'

'Oh God, I'm so sorry, Anita, I know I shouldn't have rung when you have to be on air in . . . what is it, ten minutes? Shall I call back later?'

'Yes . . . no . . . Sam, wait! Just quickly, what sort of letter is it?'

'It's an invitation to some kind of reunion at the school, I think. Doesn't say very much . . .'

Anita let out a long breath. '*Fuuuck*,' she whispered.

'I know. I haven't stopped shaking since opening it,' Sam replied.

'Look, shall I come around this evening? Or, if you can, would you pick me up from work? Five-ish? We'll get a drink around here somewhere.'

'Okay, I'll get Bubbles too. Speak later . . . and don't think about it if you can help it.'

She heard Anita emit a short laugh before hanging up. Sam marvelled when, ten minutes later, she heard her friend's clipped and measured accent deliver the lunchtime news on her kitchen radio as though it were just another day.

At exactly three minutes past the hour, Anita Roy pulled down the faders on her newsroom console and clicked the button that would transfer listeners to the continuity announcer. Luckily she knew the routine so well that she no longer had to concentrate on what she was doing. She pushed her headphones off and they lay against her neck, crackling with the tinny faraway voice of the girl who did the programme trails as Anita sank her head into her hands. Fifteen years on and the memories still lacerated her on certain days. Not, oddly, when she'd had a bad day and was tired and tense, but the very reverse. It was invariably when-ever something tremendous happened: a promotion, a new man, even the day she got the keys to her first flat. It was exactly in those brilliant, luminous moments, when life seemed filled with the sweetest prospects, that Lily unfailingly returned. Not just a passing memory of her, but the sight – as clear as anything – of her pale face and the way she had looked at her that night in the rose garden, moments before she had died.

MUMBAI, 2008

Miss Lamb's letter to Zeba Khan had been delivered to the film star's Juhu address the previous week, but it would be another few days before Zeba herself would see it. The letter had nearly got lost, nestled as it was alongside many others in the customary gunny bag. The local post office, accustomed to receiving fan mail addressed sometimes just to 'Zeba, Bombay', had taken to using a pair of large sacks to deliver her mail. That day's load had been an exceptionally heavy one and Zeba Khan's secretary, Gupta, had already spent an extra hour trying to clear it. He resisted the temptation to throw the last rubber-banded clutch into the bin so that he could finally leave to catch his train to Ghatkopar. It was his main task every day to wade through his employer's fan mail, answering each one with a standard letter of appreciation, a photograph of the film star showing just a hint of her famed cleavage and a carefully forged signature. Gupta sometimes wondered about that signature of his, the carefully crafted Z, the flourish as the A ended in a small cross, musing over its many grateful recipients. One persistent correspondent had even written back to say that he kissed the signature every morning before leaving for work as a porter at Victoria Terminus, convinced that it gave him strength.

Gupta picked up the last letter, eyeing the cheap envelope and handwritten address, resisting once again the urge to hurl it into the trash can unopened. Madam received all sorts of invitation cards: premieres, parties, even weddings and baby-naming ceremonies, as though her fans really thought she was as sweet as her roles made her out to be, and very eager to drop by their family function if she happened to be passing. He knew, of course, better than anyone else, that Madam rarely stirred out of bed for anything less than five lakh rupees these days. He sighed deeply as he slit open the envelope. She had maintained an uncanny knack of finding out if he had shirked any of his tasks and, having no wish to receive one of her verbal lashings, he surveyed the letter before deciding how to respond. This was an unusual one, not the kind of thing Gupta had ever had to deal with before. Certainly not a request that could be fobbed off with a signed photograph showing some cleavage. He held the letter briefly in his hand, reading it again more carefully. The address and postmark looked authentic, and this Miss Lamb apparently knew Zeba Madam well. He could not assume that Madam would not want to reply to the letter herself, or perhaps despatch a box of her trademark spray of orchids to its sender, for that was what she sometimes did when she wanted to turn someone down without making it too blatant they were being turned down.

It had become obvious to Gupta over the years that Madam was not in touch with anyone from her Delhi childhood, not even her family, so this was rather intriguing. And she was, in fact, due to be there in December for the annual Film Awards, for which they already knew she was receiving the Best Actress prize. This might be the kind of distraction from her routine that she would enjoy, it would perhaps even present some good PR and photo-shoot opportunities.

Gupta remembered having once, in his early and more enthusiastic days, suggested to Zeba Madam that her fans would probably love to know more about the kind of school she had attended and people she had studied with, that being the kind of insignificant information that usually thrilled her silly admirers no end. But she had flown at him in a sudden rage, dismissing his idea as being 'stupid' and 'thoughtless'. Gupta had never again strayed into what was clearly sensitive territory.

He looked at the letter again, deciding to leave it casually on Madam's bedside table. She would not miss it lying there when she returned later tonight from Zurich, where she had gone to shoot a song sequence.

Chapter Two

LONDON, 2008

Despite the tumult of painful memories that had been sparked by the arrival of Miss Lamb's letter, Sam managed to get through the rest of her day maintaining her normal placid demeanour. It was nearly two when she finally managed to speak to Bubbles, but her friend was uncharacteristically reticent about explaining why she hadn't taken her calls. Bubbles too had received Miss Lamb's letter, and Sam could tell, from what sounded like a blocked nose, that Bubbles had been crying. Not wanting to discuss it on the phone, Sam merely told Bubbles the time and place that had been agreed with Anita before hanging up.

Luckily it was time to collect Heer from school, and Sam left her house with relief, pulling on a cashmere cardigan as protection against the stubborn chilliness in the air. She looked up at the watery sun as she closed the gate behind her, trying to take pleasure in its rare appearance. What a dismal summer it had been so far, even the daffs that had struggled to emerge in the back garden a month ago had turned brown and soggy and collapsed within days. It was as if life itself was fighting to cope against all odds.

Sam turned as she heard a familiar voice hail her and saw her neighbour emerge from her driveway.

'Hey, Franci,' she said pleasantly, although she couldn't help taking in the sight of Francesca's trim legs beneath her summer dress with a rush of envy. Francesca had clearly worn such a short dress on a cold day only to show off her tan. She was maniacal about her fitness regime and had certainly earned every inch of her fabulous figure, but it was enviable to Sam, whose battle to curb her burgeoning weight was now taking on epic proportions.

Francesca took Sam's arm in her usual friendly fashion and they walked down their leafy road together, meeting up with another pair of mums who were also school-bound.

'Oh goodness, I've got to show you something,' Francesca said as the group reached the school. She fished out her iPhone from a small Purdey shoulder bag. 'Piccies from our half-term hols,' she explained, giggling as she clicked through a few photographs. Francesca turned her phone around to show the one she had picked for Sam and the others to see. They peered at a picture of Francesca's husband, Tom, normally an immaculately clad banker, wearing a pair of baggy swim-shorts and beaming inanely as he struck a ridiculous muscleman stance with a surfboard on a Mustique beach. The women fell about laughing but Francesca said, 'That's not the half of it. There's a real corker here somewhere. Ah, this one.' The next picture was of Tom standing in the kitchen of their villa, still bare-chested and this time holding a large gleaming cucumber up against the crotch of his swim-shorts. The droll expression on his face made everyone scream with merriment and Sam forced herself to join in, feeling something catch at her heart. How greedily she always gathered up particulars of the kind of relationship Francesca took so much for granted and that would never be hers to have. It wasn't that Akbar was a *bad* husband, but they certainly seemed to have a lot less fun than couples like Francesca and Tom did. Sam could not, in fact, recall Akbar ever having done something absurd purely to make her laugh, and had put it down a long time ago to her own taut demeanour; to the fear that lurked deep inside her, always half-expecting things to go wrong if she enjoyed herself too much.

Fortunately the school bell was now ringing and everyone was distracted by the emerging children. Sam didn't think she could bear looking at more of Francesca's happy holiday pictures.

They walked back home together, nevertheless, chatting companionably and carrying their load of colourful jackets and bags, the children tumbling ahead of them.

'Coffee?' Francesca asked as they reached her gate.

Worrying at the prospect of having to look at more photographs of Francesca's boisterous family having fun, Sam made a hasty excuse which, thankfully, wasn't entirely untrue. 'I'd have loved to, Franci, but I'm going into town a little later to meet a couple of old school friends for a drink.'

'Those two mates of yours from your school in Delhi?' Francesca asked, adding, 'I remember them from Heer's birthday party, they were the only women there who came without children!'

Sam laughed. 'That's them all right. Couldn't keep them away if I tried! Anita doesn't have her own kids yet so Heer's a sort of surrogate daughter for her whenever she gets maternal or broody. Which doesn't happen very often. And Bubbles' two are now far too grown-up for kiddie birthday parties!'

'I'll tell you what I do remember about your mate Bubbles – the fabulous croc-skin clutch she was carrying. Just gorgeous! Bea Valdez, she said it was. It's not like me, but I just couldn't *help* asking.'

'Oh, Bubs would never mind anyone asking her anything. Sometimes I wonder how she retains her niceness considering the kind of stratosphere her family moves in,' Sam replied.

'Golly, yes, you did say once that they were pally with the likes of Lakshmi Mittal and Tamara Mellon.'

Sam smiled. 'Lakshmi Mittal's a family friend of theirs, I think. But Bubbles' only connection with Tamara Mellon is that their daughters go to the same school. Oh, and that she buys every other Jimmy Choo shoe ever produced!'

'Seriously?'

'Absolutely seriously. She must have at least fifty pairs at any one time, dear old Bubbles. I mean, the sales girl at the Chelsea store personally calls her whenever a new design comes in, for heaven's sake! Oh, and you should see her shoe closet – to die for!'

'Ohhh,' Francesca breathed dreamily, opening her gate. 'Some people do have such dream lives, don't they?'

Sam recognised the irony of the situation. Here was Francesca – whom Sam had always envied slightly – madly envying Bubbles, who was, all things considered, really just the archetypal poor little rich girl, the fat pimply teenager she once was still lurking just beneath the surface. But Sam would not dream of gossiping with Francesca about Bubbles and so, as Heer was now pulling her away, eager to get home, Sam waved her neighbour a hasty goodbye.

Punching in the numbers to open her electronic gate, Sam allowed her daughter through first, following her down the steps that led to the kitchen door. She unloaded Heer's schoolbag, jacket and ballet slippers onto the kitchen table before grabbing her daughter, whose hands were already raiding the biscuit jar, giving her a big kiss before she wriggled away.

'I bought those for *me* from Konditor and Cook today! Well, no more than one, Heer, if you want to be the world's best ballerina. And early dinner tonight, okay?' she called out after the small figure that was already bounding up the stairs to her room brandishing a large wedge of chocolate-chip shortbread in one hand.

Sam exchanged a smile with her maid, who was brewing up some fragrant masala tea. 'Oh, a cup for me too, Masooma,' she said, pulling off her trainers. 'And then we can do the month's accounts, yes?' Not that the accounts needed doing as they weren't into July yet, but Sam knew she had to stay busy and keep herself distracted until she was with Anita and Bubbles. Miss Lamb's letter had been carefully put away in the bottom of her lingerie drawer where Akbar would never find it. She could never discuss it with him. Only Anita and Bubbles would understand her pain and guilt.

By evening there was a light drizzle falling. Sam pulled up at a parking meter as near to Anita's Aldwych office as she could manage. The space was tight and it took a couple of shunts before the bulk of her Audi was comfortably contained in its slot. Odd how expertly she could do that, without Akbar's presence in the car making parallel parking fraught with all kinds of perils. After turning the wipers off, she sat for a few minutes watching raindrops make their journey down the windscreen, some unhesitant and quite certain of their destination, others – like her, she couldn't help thinking – tentatively stopping and starting before finally rolling reluctantly towards the bonnet. When the rain had eased a bit, Sam emerged from the car, pulling her handbag and pashmina from the back seat. Then she zapped the central-locking system, which responded with its familiar reassuring beep. Akbar usually did that while striding purposefully away from the car, without even glancing over his shoulder, but Sam preferred to be sure the locks were down and flashing their little red lights before she could walk away.

Shivering, she wrapped her stole around her bare shoulders and assessed the gaps in the traffic before darting across the road. Even a passing summer shower could instantly turn London back to a wintry grey, the city seeming to return with relief to being its favourite avatar. She looked at her watch as she quickened her steps for Bush House. She'd told Anita four o'clock and already it was a quarter past. Her super-efficient journalist friend often despaired over Sam's rather scatty time-keeping abilities, recently joking: 'Imagine if I were to open up the news bulletin with . . . *It's – oh crikey, so sorry everyone – just a* couple *of minutes past ten. But does it matter, for heaven's sake, just a* few *minutes this way or that?*' Anita had mimicked Sam's lazy drawl as she said that last sentence, eliciting a good-natured smile from Sam, who would have been the first to admit she had airily carried over the concept of 'Indian time' into her life here in England, unlike Anita. Constantly amazed by Anita's brusque professionalism, Sam often found it hard to imagine that they'd managed to stay friends since they were seven.

She went through the tall doors of the BBC that were invariably surrounded by dripping scaffolding, and waved when she spotted Anita standing at the top of the stairs joshing with an elderly security guard. Anita would chat to anyone, and had once claimed that casual conversations were the sources of her best stories.

They hugged as Anita reached the bottom of the stairs. 'Are you okay?' she asked Sam, who nodded. 'Sorry I couldn't speak when you called . . .'

'Don't worry, but I couldn't get hold of Bubbles either and really needed to hear one of your voices.'

'Is she coming?'

'Of course, she said she'll meet us at Heebah at five.'

'Make that six then,' Anita said wryly, pulling up the hood of her gilet as they stepped outside the building.

'She won't be late today. She just has to drop her mum-in-law somewhere before getting the car and driver to herself.'

Sam ignored Anita's eye-roll. Anita was the only one of them who still travelled on the tube – which was fine until she started making a virtue of it. Occasionally, if she went on for long enough about carbon footprints and off-setting emissions, Sam would feel guilty enough to walk across the park or hop on a 98 bus to get into town. But that wasn't really an option on a day as rainy as this, and for Bubbles to even dream of travelling anywhere but by car was ridiculous, given her millions. Well, her pa-in-law's gazillions, to be more accurate.

Sam took her friend's arm as they walked over the zebra crossing, hastening their footsteps for the politely waiting traffic. The drizzle was turning heavier and the café was still half a block away. As usual, she'd forgotten to carry a brolly and pulled her stole over her head. She was ruining another good pashmina, but Akbar had told her to get her hair done in honour of his boss's visit yesterday and that hadn't cost very much less.

A few minutes later they ducked with relief under the awning of the hookah café, squeezing their way past brass tables that had been placed on the pavement for smokers. Since the introduction of the smoking ban, Sam had taken to feeling sorry for all those smokers who had been relegated to muddy pavements as they bubbled into brass hookahs and stared moodily out at the rain. Sam had spent years going uncomplainingly to places like Heebah for the sake of her two best friends as, going by the law of averages, it had seemed altogether fairer that they should go to smoking rather than non-smoking establishments. She had tried not to think of it as a sacrifice anyway, having long ago got into the habit of taking shallow breaths when she was around her friends. Anita had been smoking since they were fifteen, claiming then that it helped her concentrate on cramming for their exams, although Bubbles had taken to it only after her marriage, citing her reason as stress induced by, alternately, her mother-in-law, father-in-law, children and husband.

The women were ushered to the table that Sam had sensibly thought to book earlier in the day, and settled onto a pair of commodious white leather banquettes. Sam noticed that all the Persian hookahs and filigreed marble ashtrays had gone, replaced by artful bowls filled with colourful glass beads. Anita ordered their drinks: a full-bodied Shiraz for Sam and a vodka tonic for herself. After their waiter had left, she said, 'Well, let's see Lamboo's letter then', and as she shrugged off her damp gilet she saw that Sam was already holding it out in her direction.

Bubbles looked fretfully out of the car window – they had left Belgravia at least half an hour ago, taken fifteen minutes to get to the art buyer's office on Curzon Street, where her mother-in-law had disembarked, and were still only just approaching Grosvenor Square. The traffic snarl-up around the American Embassy wasn't helped by the ghastly concrete road blocks that seemed to have become a permanent feature of the square. She could see a metal passageway with a makeshift placard saying 'Visas' that was occupying half the road and snaked all the way around the block. The passageway was empty of people, the embassy probably having shut at five, although a hulking guard with a jutting chin stood holding an impressive piece of weaponry while gazing at the

24

passing traffic. He caught Bubbles' eye briefly through the car window as she drifted past, but there wasn't the usual flicker of interest on his impassive features. He had obviously not registered the fancy car and liveried chauffeur in the way most people did, sneaking unashamedly curious peeks at the occupants of the rear seat to catch a glimpse through smoked glass of such blessed beings that could afford to ride in a Maybach. They were hardly likely to know that she, Bubbles, rode in it only when accompanying her imperious mother-in-law like some kind of handmaiden. Nor would they know that there were things money and Maybachs couldn't achieve, such as being able to get through the London traffic faster on a day like this. There was no point getting tetchy with the poor driver, as her mother-in-law had done a few minutes ago. He was doing his best with the bulky car that had purred *again* to a standstill. To distract herself, Bubbles delved into the magazine rack behind the seat and found copies of *Tatler* and American *Vanity Fair*. She leafed through the first and then the second, trying to absorb the gossip and the fashion tips. But her concentration was terrible today. She hadn't been able to think straight since the arrival of Lamboo's letter this morning, unable even to speak to Sam when she had seen her name flash repeatedly on the screen of her phone. Slapping the magazines down on the seat, Bubbles opened her bag and took out the envelope for the umpteenth time. She gently ran her fingers over its rough paper, in some inexplicable way relishing the painful tug she felt in her heart. Just when her psychotherapist had confirmed that she was finally learning to put futile memories away, this! Someone – it must have been Anita – had once said that people remembered happy things like their childhood days and first love and first taste of ice-cream in a cone only when they were *unhappy*. If that was so, then it was clear to Bubbles that she was condemned

25

to be surrounded by her memories despite the best psychotherapy Harley Street had to offer. And how they had rushed back this morning, faces and voices emerging thick and fast from some kind of wintry mist, even the tiniest details etched with sudden frightening clarity before her eyes. Bubbles shoved the letter back into her Mulberry tote, nervously rubbing her other hand over the cold hardness of its metal studs, warming them against her palm as she looked out at the rain.

It had rained in Delhi too that morning long ago, complete with lightning flashes and thunderclaps, which was not so unusual for late December. The downpour had made the roses in Miss Lamb's garden drop their petals all over the winter earth, like red spatters of blood. Or so Bubbles had thought, until she had actually seen what blood looked like after it had fallen on wet earth – virtually invisible to the eye. She shuddered. 'Where are we now, Mottram?' she asked in a high voice, for want of anything else to say.

'Old Burlington Street, Madam,' the chauffeur replied. 'I'm trying all the back roads to get out of this mess. Not long now, hopefully.'

Bubbles recognised the shops of Regent Street as the car turned a corner and she saw shoppers burdened with raincoats and bags, crossing the road and waiting at bus stops, looking as though they carried the weight of the world on their shoulders. She wondered sometimes at the sorrows that might afflict other people, occasionally feeling pangs of guilt at her own rather pampered existence. The cafés were all brightly lit and buzzing with people taking shelter from the rain. She could see a couple kissing in the large window of Starbucks, a mug of shared coffee steaming in between them.

The car crawled over the lights at Piccadilly Circus. They

weren't far from Heebah now, thankfully. Suddenly Bubbles longed to see her two old schoolmates more than anyone else in the world. Anita could be such a pain sometimes, carping on about left-wing stuff and recently making her feel personally culpable when her in-laws' company bought up an airline. As though those were things she had any control over at all. She'd tried sarcasm ('I'm not exactly Binkie's dad's business advisor, y'know') but nothing could stop Anita once she had mounted her soapbox. Sam was different, good old Sam. Unfailingly tactful and diplomatic, always playing peacemaker. In truth, though, Bubbles loved them both, even Anita, whose energy and intellect she could draw upon when required, which was frequently. Sometimes she wondered whether it was the combined presence in London of her two oldest friends that had kept her sane all these years. In that respect, at least, she had been lucky.

After the chauffeur had pulled up alongside the maroon and gold awning of Heebah, Bubbles stepped out gingerly, careful not to get her new Manolos wet. A couple of men gave the car, and then her, appreciative glances as she wended her way past the pavement tables into the restaurant, pushing her heavy mane of auburn hair back from her face. Her linen trouser-suit was probably crumpled, but she could tell from Heebah's fawning mâitre d' that she still looked expensive. She had never figured out how people uncannily smelt affluence emanating from her person, but they invariably did, even when she hadn't bothered to dress up.

She made her way across the room as she spotted her two friends. They were deep in conversation and saw her only when she was ushered into her seat. After she had ordered a champagne cocktail for herself, she turned to them. There was none of the usual preamble about clothes and hair and weight today. Instead, she nodded at the letter that lay on the table between Sam and Anita and said sombrely, 'What the hell do you think Lamboo's doing?'

'I was just saying that it's amazing how she managed to track us all down,' Anita observed, adding, 'well, that's assuming she has sent letters to everyone. I haven't had mine yet.'

'It must be waiting for you at your flat. She wouldn't leave you out. Wonder whether she's written to everyone, you know, the whole batch of '93?'

'Something tells me it's just us, actually.'

'She must have met someone who knew our addresses,' Bubbles suggested. 'Or maybe the internet makes all this easy now. My Ruby was talking about some Facebook website thing where her school friends meet and chat or something . . .' Bubbles stopped rambling. The last thing any of them wanted was to be chatting to their other school friends, their little circle having snapped firmly shut the minute they had left school.

'It wouldn't have been that difficult to trace us,' Sam was replying in her usual pragmatic manner. 'Why, Lamboo might just have called one or the other of our parents in Delhi. I think we're worrying too much. Maybe it's just as her letter says: she's retiring from Jude's and wants to see us before she "disappears into the deep hush of a convent".'

'Mmm, I don't know . . . typically poetic, but something tells me it's more than that,' Anita said dubiously. 'It's clear she's holding something back . . . like here, where she says, "*I have so much more to tell you girls before I go, but perhaps it is best to wait until you are all gathered here together as before*".' Anita tapped the letter with her forefinger. 'How the fuck does that not indicate she really wants to say something else, huh? Would she really summon us 4000 miles just to say goodbye?'

It was Bubbles who first said the unsayable, uttering the name not mentioned between them in all these years. 'Do you think they might have found some new leads in Lily's case?' she asked in a small voice.

'Nonsense. After fifteen years?' Anita scoffed, although she sounded more nervous than incredulous. 'I can't see the Delhi police being that efficient somehow.'

'It's possible she just suddenly got a bit maudlin or emotional or some such. After all, the date she's suggested will be exactly fifteen years since Lily died,' Sam offered before trailing off.

'Lamboo emotional? Don't think so somehow. It just isn't part of the Brit psyche, stiff upper lip and all that.'

'Oh God, it just doesn't make sense,' Bubbles said, picking up her champagne flute from the table and taking a long swallow. Sometimes the very act of thinking made her head hurt.

'D'you know,' Sam said, wrapping her shawl around her shoulders, 'I met Aradhna Singh at a lunch party the other day. She was just back from her school reunion at St Jude's. Makes a point of it to go every year, apparently. And she was saying that ours is the only batch that has never had one. A reunion, I mean . . .'

Anita thumped her glass down on the wooden table with some vehemence. 'Well, that must've been a happy thought for Aradhna,' she said.

'What do you mean?'

'Well, don't you recall how miffed she always was at us being the top dogs at school? Their batch, coming straight after ours, would never have matched up, I reckon.'

'Her "*crème de la crème*", Lamboo called us. Remember?' Sam said softly.

'Don't think that meant anything particularly. She just

picked the term up from the Brodie play we were doing that year.'

'Oh that's not true, Anita,' Sam protested. 'Lamboo just *doted* on us. She really did believe we would go on to do special things.'

'Well, how the mighty have fallen then,' said Anita.

'Oh don't say that,' Bubbles cut in, trying to offer comfort. 'At least *you're* doing useful things and meeting interesting political types. Y'know, like Boris Johnson and all . . .' She trailed off, knowing how unconvincing that sounded, before making another attempt. 'I remembered that expression – *crème de la crème* – just the other day actually, when Binkie got an invite to the Gorbachev concert which said that London's "*crème de la crème*" was being invited. Somehow it felt much more special when Lamboo used to say it . . .'

'We *were* special to her . . .' Sam insisted.

Anita leaned forward to pick up the menu. 'Well, only until her precious *crème de la crème* took so violently against Lily D'Souza. That could never have been lost on someone as canny as old Lamboo, even though – to be fair – she never once did let on. But I was always sure it was the reason why she never had us back for a reunion. I mean . . .' she paused, keeping her eyes on the menu, 'surely it would have been anathema for someone as morally upright as Lamboo to jolly around with us after Lily's death . . .' Anita's voice dropped as she kept her eyes down, unable to make eye contact with her two companions as she continued in a mumble, '. . . especially seeing how plainly we benefited from it.'

Anita had aimed the comment at herself, but in the silence that followed it slowly dawned on her that Sam and Bubbles might have misunderstood such a clumsy expression of remorse. Discomfited, she looked at her friends and saw appalled expressions on both their faces. Realising suddenly how wounding her words must have been, she leaned forward and clutched Sam's knee, her expression now mortified. 'Heyyy, Sam, I'm *so* sorry, I didn't mean to sound so sharp, nor be so terribly thoughtless. I've just been feeling so tetchy all day.'

'God, me too. Even my *father-in-law* noticed,' Bubbles said, taking another long sip of her drink, the flute trembling slightly between her fingers.

Sam was looking into her own wine glass, now stained pink from the Shiraz. 'I can't deny . . .' she whispered, her face suddenly full of lines and shadows. She took a deep breath before continuing, 'You know, even today I can't think of that year without my heart squeezing itself so hard in my chest, it's as if I can't breathe for a few minutes. I know we never speak of it but . . . Lily's death on the night of our Social. I honestly don't know how we ever . . .' She turned back to Anita, but her friend could see that Sam's dilated pupils were unable to focus on her own. A glass of wine was usually all it took to make Sam a little drunk, but this, Anita knew, was something else altogether. Poor Sam was clearly trying to gather herself together, her voice trembling as she continued speaking in a low voice, now seeming unable to stop her thoughts. 'You know, it was only much, much later that it really sank in. The enormity of what we had done. I know I just wasn't myself that winter . . . death seemed almost to be stalking me like some evil beast . . . but still . . . I shouldn't try to find excuses for myself . . .' Sam stopped abruptly and shivered. The women sat in silence for a few minutes before Sam squeezed Anita's hand, which was still in hers, indicating forgiveness for her earlier remark.

'Such a terrible time. I still dream of it sometimes. Not just think of it, but *dream* of it. There's a difference, you

31

know. My Emotional Freedom therapist once said so,' Bubbles put in.

Normally, Bubbles' array of therapists was meat and drink to Anita's sarcastic sense of humour, but today she didn't have the heart to rise to the bait. The friends fell quiet again and Anita looked away. Her stomach churned with guilt as she saw Sam press a tissue over her eyes and put an arm around Bubbles, who had also started to weep.

MUMBAI, 2008

Night had fallen in its usual glittering manner over the pulsing city of Mumbai when Zeba Khan lay back in the claw-footed bathtub of her sumptuous designer bathroom. She took deep breaths of the Yves Rocher bath oil recently purchased from Zurich, sighing with relief and pleasure as her tiredness melted slowly into the tepid water. She had asked for all the Jo Malone scented candles to be lit, and now she half-opened her tawny brown eyes, seeing the flames flicker quietly, turning the cream Italian marble of the walls and floor to molten gold. It had been a long, long day. Despite her superstar status these past ten years, she knew better than to mess with up-and-coming directors like Rohit Mirchandani and had stayed the course, out in the midday sun with the rest of the crew, despite being desperately jet-lagged from her European trip. As the son of a legendary director, Rohit had no doubt enjoyed a head-start in the industry, but his last two films had both been massive hits and Zeba had heard about a new one due to start filming this winter. She had done her damnedest today to find out if the casting had been done but couldn't get anything out of the canny young man, who was obviously enjoying the power he could suddenly wield over her.

Zeba felt a few tendrils of hair escape the luxuriant pile on the top of her head, and reached out for the silver seashell that housed an array of clips. She sighed as she slid a few more bobby pins into her hair and sank back into the water. Rohit had always secretly loathed her, having grown up with the knowledge of her decade-long liaison with his father and, as a result, immersed in his mother's bitterness. It was to Rohit's credit, though, that he had never advertised his abhorrence, careful to stay not just on his father's right side but Zeba's as well. It wouldn't do for an up-and-coming director to upset Bollywood's top actress. And so they continued to play this ridiculous cat-and-mouse game with each other, dodging and side-stepping but never confrontational, and always, always most carefully and deliberately civil to each other when they were on film sets. Was it any wonder she felt so exhausted today?

Zeba leaned back again, massaging her temples. Rohit was one of a whole new breed of directors that were changing the landscape of Bollywood unrecognisably these days. Now they were all American-educated and slick and media savvy. And, consequently, far less inclined to be worshipful of her own star status. The older boys had been so much easier to read and seduce, but they were all fading into obscurity in their hillside mansions, seemingly content to feebly hand the directorial reins over to the next generation while they totted up figures in ledgers and kept a tight hold on their purse strings. Half of the new crop of directors were gay too, and that didn't help one bit.

Zeba knew the time had come to tread carefully. She was thirty-two this year, it was most unusual for a heroine in Bollywood to have stayed at the top for so long. At first people said that her popularity was because she looked equally sexy in both Indian and western clothes, but as she had got older and her attractiveness to audiences had not diminished, she was gradually acquiring the makings of a legend. Despite an astute unspoken self-awareness regarding her own meagre acting talent, Zeba could not help hoping she would become as iconic as Nargis or Madhubala someday. After all, like those two actresses, she was equally beloved to audiences whether playing mother, sister, lover or even prostitute. It was almost touching how her fans just couldn't seem to get enough of her, and the only reason why producers and script-writers had kept running to her door these past ten years, trying to keep up with the demand and putting a steady supply of roles her way. Indeed, her popularity in India was of such a scale that she could quite safely turn up her nose at Hollywood, a place that – as journalists sometimes liked reminding her – had never shown any interest in her. Oddly, it was India's great unwashed that particularly adored her – the market vendor, the paan-wallah, the coolie – doggedly spurning the new stick-thin, size-zero girls flooding the industry from modelling agencies in favour of her own more traditional curves. It was they – those sun-darkened, wizened figures that thronged the city's streets and sometimes tapped piteously on the smoked-glass window of her Mercedes – who had made her what she was. She had never forgotten that – hence her recent idea of founding a charity for street children.

Zeba sighed, reaching out for the loofah. She scrubbed her elbows, thinking of what hard work it was constantly thinking up new ways to climb that very shaky pedestal marked 'legend'. Firstly, there were a hundred others clawing at her ankles, trying to pull her down, upstart teenagers with bigger bust-lines and tighter butts and, of course, new top directors to be their godfathers. Sometimes in Bollywood the latter was the only attribute required to become a legend. Which, if she was to be honest, had worked out rather well for her. Old Shiv Mirchandani had, after all, been completely loyal to her all these years, both professionally and in a personal capacity, *and* despite being aware of her other occasional dalliances. He had even said something sentimental the other day about growing old together which had quite terrified her, given the ravages of age he already wore so cheerily on his cheese-grater face.

Zeba raised a long, shapely leg from the bath water and eyed it contemplatively as it shone wet and gleaming in the candlelight. Perhaps she should call for Najma to scrub and exfoliate her heels. Feet and hands were what first gave away a woman's age, her Ammi had always said. Additionally, Zeba had spent all afternoon in an excruciatingly uncomfortable pair of stiletto heels, playing the role of a corporate boss in Dubai. But she had to be up again early tomorrow morning and was on the point of dropping off right here in the bath. She sat up in the water, her ample breasts glistening as they floated among the shiny bubbles. Perhaps she would treat herself to one of Sylvio's famed pedicures at the Taj instead, after tomorrow's shoot. They were wonderful there and always used their private suite at the back of the salon to assure her complete privacy. Zeba reached out for the bell by the bathtub to summon Najma who would help wipe her down and fetch a fresh silk nightie. She hoped that the hot bath and her familiar bed would dismiss jet-lag and aid a good night's sleep.

After Zeba had been carefully patted dry by her maid and massaged with Crème de la Mer, another recent acquisition from Zurich, she padded her way through her dimly lit, cavernous bedroom. Someone – Gupta probably – had left

35

a little stack of papers for her to go through under the bedside lamp. She picked up the rubber-banded bundle after she had climbed into her white leather water-bed and pulled a silk razai over her legs. Freeing the pack from their band, Zeba scowled, her sweeping eyebrows meeting in a furrow above her nose. The first letter was from a cousin, asking for a loan – that would have to be a 'no' – it wasn't as if she hadn't helped him before and he would merely surface again after another few months with some new tale of hardship. She had much better things she could think of doing with her hard-earned money than passing it on to blood-sucking relatives. Her newly founded charity, for one.

Discarding the letter onto the floor by the side of her bed, where it would be picked up and binned by the sweeper in the morning, she reminded herself to stop frowning so much and swiftly cleared her brow. Luckily, the next letter offered much pleasanter fare – a request from *Vanity Fair* to be cover girl on their inaugural Indian publication – a definite 'yes'. The next was an invitation to a private party being thrown by liquor baron Ramsy Fernando on his Madh Island home – hmmm, probably a 'yes'. At least there wouldn't be much of the film crowd there, Ramsy was too much of a brown-sahib snob for all that. But . . . what was *this*? The unseemly scowl returned to Zeba's beautiful face.

Zeba scanned the words quickly: . . . soon going to retire as principal of the school . . . needed to meet her girls . . . a reunion . . . a *reunion*?! Was this someone's idea of a bloody joke? Zeba turned the letter over as though searching for clues. Gupta must have got rid of the envelope . . . there was nothing else but a suggested date in December and a small scratchy signature at the bottom. She ran her eyes again over the spidery writing that was both familiar and yet uncharacter-istically weak, becoming virtually illegible in the last few lines. Goodness, it was crazy to think of St Jude's old Princy still alive and kicking and rattling around in that cottage next door to the school. The woman was probably in her mid-seventies now. It was no surprise, of course, that the convent had not retired her yet; school principals like Miss Lamb were hard to come by these days – the archetypal English spinster, willing to dedicate her whole life to the school. Victoria Lamb. What was it they used to call her back then? . . . Lamboo! Lamboo, for her long, noodle-like appearance. But then girls were cruel creatures under those coy exteriors.

And that niece of Lamboo's . . . Lily. 'Doan't be silly, Lily', they had tittered behind her back on her first day at the school, quoting the villain in that ridiculous film. But they found out soon enough that Lily wasn't silly at all. Not in the slightest. But that she was very, very manipulative and go-getting indeed. In fact she was clearly trying to become the star from Day One – not the best course of action in a girls' school that was already full of stars like Zeba. This had always puzzled Zeba: that clever little Lily had not been clever enough to see how many enemies she had made in her short time at the school. She should have considered treading more carefully, but on the other hand she had seemed genuinely not to care about earning anyone's approval. It was almost enviable, that kind of self-satisfaction.

Zeba put the mail away on her bedside table and smoothed her fingers gently over the middle of her forehead. She had recently noticed the deep furrows that her mother had between her eyes, a permanent record of the stresses she had suffered in bringing up three rambunctious children under the watchful eye of an autocratic husband. So far the skin on Zeba's face had remained taut and unlined, but she did have to watch out for bad genes – letters from the past

37

that set off dark thoughts weren't likely to help. She slipped off her silk camisole and tucked her legs under the sheet, wiggling her toes and taking a few deep breaths.

Lily D'Souza, good God, what a chest-thumping blast from the past. Even though she hardly ever stopped to remember her old classmate, Zeba did have to admit that, over the years, she – the great film star Zeba Khan – had in fact taken a useful leaf out of Lily's book when it came to developing a supreme nonchalance to one's detractors. Enemies were an undeniable part of working in an industry like Bollywood; perhaps they were an undeniable part of life itself, particularly when one was beautiful and accomplished. So what was the point of treading around so carefully that you never got anywhere? Still, even though one never made any real friends in a place like this, it was at least worth knowing who your enemies were. Zeba pulled the sheet over her shoulders, feeling a sudden chill.

The world probably saw her as supremely controlled but, suddenly, Zeba could feel something inside her quail and shrink as an almost visceral memory tumbled back unbidden, reminding her of how deeply she had hated Lily, virtually from the very first moment the girl had set foot in the classroom. Zeba let her head sink into her pillow, trying to relax her shoulders. She felt a small shiver, born from either guilt or satisfaction as she realised that she was now all the things that Lily had probably imagined *she* would one day be – an acclaimed star, the adored darling of India's teeming audiences. Heroine to millions of people willing to queue for hours outside those crummy tin-pot cinema halls in slum areas on the night of a Zeba Khan blockbuster release. Now *that* was the real thing, an ambition worth fighting for. Quite unlike a stupid, inconsequential little school play. But that was what all teenagers were like, surely, narcissistically allowing the silliest things to take on the kind of significance that was impossible to comprehend in later life. Zeba scrabbled around in her bedside drawer and, finding a phial of Valium, swallowed two tablets with a little water from the crystal flagon that was always kept on her bedside table.

Two hours later, Zeba awoke from a ragged sleep, sweating profusely. Either the air-conditioning had broken down or she was having one of those ghastly night-sweats one heard about. She lay on her bed, listening to the roar of the sea outside and the lapping inside her own water-bed. Even on quiet nights, the combined watery sounds drowned all else. It was strange how people were willing to pay so much extra for properties lining the Arabian Sea, never thinking that its crashing waves provided such great cover for the city's stalkers and burglars. The alarm system Gupta had tried installing a few years ago had caused all sorts of problems, tripping and going off every time the voltage fluctuated even slightly, leaving Zeba to rely on the time-tested method of security guards. She employed a whole army of them, but remained unsure of how much she could really trust such dangerous looking men who undressed her so unashamedly with their eyes.

Something cracked loudly in the garden outside, making Zeba jump. She lay frozen for a few minutes and contemplated ringing her panic button for the servants. They were probably all sleeping the sleep of the dead (or the drunk, more likely) on a hot pre-monsoonal night such as this, the useless dolts. What did they think she paid them over the odds for? She turned over and tried to close her eyes but the clamouring in her head was too much. Perhaps she hadn't taken enough Valium, although she had promised her doctor she would try to cut down. Tonight it was the fault of

39

Lamboo's bloody letter. What was Gupta thinking, leaving it on her bedside like that? Almost willing these nightmares on her. Would she even contemplate going to something so ridiculous – a school reunion, for heaven's sake! Reunions were meant for ordinary people, not *stars*; for bored wives to enviously eye up each other's husbands and empty-headed mums to compare notes about their little darlings' teeth and teachers. Zeba knew she would have absolutely nothing to say to any of her old classmates now – although, tossing her sweating body around again, she suddenly recalled having bumped into Samira Hussain (now Samira Something-else, of course) at Heathrow a few years ago. They had exchanged phone numbers and said all the glib things old classmates did when they met, about how *marvellous* the old days had been and how they really *must* stay in touch. Neither of them had mentioned that traumatic final year at school, of course, and they had parted knowing that both of them had grown too far apart in their respective lifestyles and sensibilities to maintain all but the briefest of contact.

Sam had, with typical dependability, attempted the occasional phone call after that meeting, and Zeba had tried her best to reciprocate, but they had lately drifted once again into sending each other only an occasional card or email, many of which Zeba, rather guiltily, got Gupta to deal with anyway. Even back in school, Sam had been the antithesis of Zeba, one of those annoying good girls who never got into scrapes of any sort and whom all the teachers adored. But at least she had not been the tattling sort, Zeba recalled, and so an unlikely bond had formed between them as they had travelled together from kindergarten to high school. However, from the short conversation inside the first-class lounge at Heathrow, it had seemed to Zeba that Sam had grown dull and vapid with age. Perhaps it was just the mumsiness that some women took on so earnestly with the acquisition of husbands and children, but Zeba could tell that even the little they'd had in common as schoolmates had now shrunk to virtually nothing. Sam had provided news of some of their other classmates, though: Anita, predictably still single, working with the BBC in London and, oh God, who didn't know that Bubbles was married to the son of international textile tycoon Dinesh Raheja. Zeba had once seen Bubbles in the pages of *Verve* magazine, attending a flash corporate party at the Grand Maratha and clinging to the arm of a thin, nattily-dressed man.'*Binkie and Bubbles Raheja, golden couple from London, gracing Bombay's shores*' the accompanying caption gushed, going on to divulge that Mr Raheja's suit was Armani while Mrs Raheja was in Zac Posen, a Boucheron piece around her neck. Zeba had pored over the picture, examining Bubbles' clothes and shoes, or whatever she could make of them in the grainy photograph. She sure looked good, Zeba couldn't help noting with a twinge, although she had not been able to put her finger on whether her envy was over the rich husband and private jet that had been mentioned in the small accompanying article, or the ease with which wealth had come to the woman. Bubbles Raheja had almost certainly not had to do a day's work in her life, and probably didn't even know the meaning of the word 'schedule'. But who'd have thought that the spotty fat kid at school was the one who'd end up snaring a millionaire. She wasn't even from a big business family herself – a chain of sari shops was all her parents had, as Zeba had seen when Bubbles had got married and the whole class had attended her wedding. There was nothing interesting to say either about how she'd done it: snag the millionaire, move to London and transform herself from plump and pimply teenager into an international

41

jetsetter. It was all, in the end, just a matter of luck and timing; Zeba knew that better than most.

Well, if that lot were going to attend Lamboo's planned reunion, it might actually not be a bad idea to go along, Zeba thought suddenly, surprising herself. She climbed out of her bed, now wide awake, and padded barefoot across her collection of antique Persian rugs to the large bay windows that ringed her room. Drawing the heavy tussar curtains aside, she looked out at the Arabian Sea, calm and black and lapping gently against the white sands at the bottom of her vast garden. Sometimes fans of hers managed to get to the beach and loiter, hoping to catch a glimpse of her until chased away by one of the guards. But tonight there were surely neither fans nor burglars prowling around those neat shrubs and flowerbeds lying peacefully in the moonlight below her bedroom window. Through the trees Zeba could see light in the guard's gate-house shining dimly and she pulled the curtains shut, feeling a bit better. She smiled suddenly. It might actually be fun to spend an evening with old class-mates exclaiming over how well *she'd* done for herself. Minus a husband too!

Her gaze fell on the stack of film magazines that Gupta had placed on her replica Louis XIV desk. Every page that carried a photograph or news piece about her would be obediently marked with a Post-It note, and Zeba could see the usual profusion of yellow bits of paper sticking out from the pages even in the faint glow of the night-light. She turned on the table lamp and sat before the pile of magazines, drawing them towards her with satisfaction. Leafing her way to the first marked page in *Cineblitz*, she thought of how her old schoolmates must pore over her pictures in the society pages of magazines and newspapers, admiring the rocks she wore on her hands and her chain of male escorts, with as much envy as she had felt when she'd read about Bubbles' private Learjet.

Zeba opened the drawer of her dressing table, searching for her old BlackBerry. She remembered having keyed Sam's details in there. Even if she couldn't find it, Gupta would probably be able to fish it out for her in the morning from one of his dusty old diaries. Zeba squinted at the small green screen. There it was: Samira Hussain, and a London phone number. She reached out for her telephone.

LONDON, 2008

While Zeba sat sleepless on that hot Mumbai night, telephone held to her ear, night was falling on the other side of the world, turning London's rainy skies to a cold slate-grey. The three girlfriends had been drinking steadily for the past two hours and Bubbles was by now quite drunk. As was usual, the third Kir Royale had plummeted her into the most abject depths of despair, and she was now weeping in such earnest that she had even managed to scare off their fervent Lithuanian waiter to the far end of the restaurant.

The letter had started it off, of course, bringing back memories with a force so powerful that each of the three women had, at different times in the evening, looked into their glasses of alcohol and felt a little sick. They had obviously never forgotten anything, even though their old pact had forbidden speaking of it. Bubbles had, predictably, allowed the collective reminiscing to plunge her back into dwelling on her more immediate territory of grievances against Binkie and his parents. Anita, slumped on her pouffe, was only half-listening as she knocked back the vodka tonics in an attempt to recover from her 5 a.m. start. Luckily, she could rely on Sam to pay attention to Bubbles, and saw through her drunken haze that their ever-reliable friend was nodding sympathetically and occasionally passing Bubbles scented tissues from her handbag.

Bubbles' life had never seemed *that* dreadful to Anita. Her dear friend had a dire mother-in-law, without a doubt, and the father-in-law, Dinesh Raheja, was a horrendously unethical capitalist who couldn't give a toss about the environment: the kind of person Anita normally reserved her deepest bile for. However, Anita had found it hard to dislike Dinesh Raheja from the day he'd uncomplainingly turned up at short notice for a BBC interview at her request, for which, as a rookie news-room journalist, she'd received a rare pat on the back from her editor. The funny thing was that it had not been at all difficult to get the old man to come to Bush House. Like many self-made men, Dinesh Raheja wore his success rather like a matador would use his cape, probably petrified that everyone would forget how hard-won it had been. So despite his predilection for strutting, his inability to tone down the Punjabi accent he had carried over from India and his rough-edged manners made his millions seem somehow more deserving.

His son Binkie, married to Bubbles, was another matter altogether. Having made his first million while Binkie was still in high school, Dinesh Raheja had been proud to send his only child to England when he turned fourteen – to Harrow or Eton, Anita could never remember which. But, having had a relatively late start at the whole business of becoming staunchly Anglophile, Binkie had taken to it with alarming relish, changing his name by the time he got to university from the admittedly dull Rajesh to the positively preposterous Binkie, speaking in a strange faux-Wodehousian tongue, and buying himself a metallic mauve Bentley

Continental GT as soon as he was old enough to drive. From what Anita could tell, he seemed to be worsening as he approached his forties, getting his battery of butlers and valets to perform the most ridiculous tasks, such as ironing the morning papers and trimming their edges so that the pages were perfectly aligned before he would deign to glance at the day's news with his eight-minute egg (not seven or nine minutes, but exactly and precisely eight). His only concessions to Indian-ness lay in the kind of things that apparently made life hell for Bubbles. These boiled down to two main things: an utter and complete devotion on Binkie's part to his dragon of a mother, and maintaining the promise she had extracted from him that, despite all their money, he would always and only stay in the same house as her. Some house it was too, in the heart of Belgravia and with miles of corridors and multiple floors, each square inch of which would be worth thousands of pounds according to Anita's calculations. Raheja Mansion had in fact been formed by knocking together two palatial town-houses that had belonged to a pair of Kuwaiti brothers, which explained why the pool house looked like something out of the sets of *Caligula*, complete with Piedmont urns, artificial palms and bare-breasted marble nymphs with golden nipples. But, unsatisfied with such largesse, Mrs Raheja had even bought the lower ground floor flat *next door* to the main house and installed the kitchen in there so that there was no risk at all of Binkie's delicate nostrils being assailed with the smell of curry. Then there were the houses in Paris and Cape Cod, the country pile in Bucks and the baronial manor in Scotland . . . but it was almost laughable that, despite such a profusion of global real estate, poor Bubbles had nowhere to call her own, nor any place where she could really get away from her mother-in-law.

'It's like I'm married to *her* rather than him, Sam!' Bubbles was wailing again, taking another slug from her flute, whose edge was now encrusted with almost as much lipstick as was left on her mouth.

'I know, I know, darling,' Sam consoled, 'but couldn't you persuade Binkie to take you to the Paris flat when the schools close next month? The children will be going up to their summer camp in Switzerland as usual, won't they?'

'Bobby will be at camp in Montana, although Ruby's still trying to make her mind up. But, you see, Ma's already arranged for me to be in the Bahamas with her and Auntie Poppy and Poonam Maasi . . . I told you about that cruise for Papa's sixty-fifth. She's hired a 300-foot yacht and is taking her whole family, and obviously I have to be there.'

'Oh yes, of course, you did say,' Sam said, subsiding back into silence, remembering how they had dissolved in giggles at the thought of a bunch of Punjabi matriarchs sunning themselves in voluminous one-pieces when Bubbles had first mentioned it.

'How about we go somewhere together after the summer then? Just us girls,' Anita offered, rousing herself briefly. 'We've only ever talked of it so far, and now that both your kids are old enough to be left with their nannies, it should be fine, shouldn't it?'

Sam's face wore a doubtful expression. 'I don't know . . . Akbar doesn't much like the concept of girlie holidays . . .'

'Oh, fuck Akbar,' Anita replied crisply, 'about time you told him where to stick those fine concepts of his.'

'I'm not sure Binkie would like it either – you know how he seems to think my main role in life is to keep his mother company. Unless . . .' Bubbles' face was starting to clear. 'The only place I can get away to without any of them in tow is my parents' house.'

'Delhi,' Anita exclaimed, 'now there's a plan.'

'No one can stop us from going to see our parents, I guess,' Sam said slowly.

'Be too bloody hot till November though.'

'You weren't thinking of December, were you? I mean . . . Lamboo's invitation . . .?'

The three women looked at the letter, still lying on the table before them, and then at each other in the candlelight. Bubbles' eyes suddenly looked like hollows in her head, and Sam, wrapped in her cream pashmina, was a sad and portly ghost. Anita shuddered, feeling uncharacteristically nervy. She was dying for a cigarette. 'I've never been back there since we left school,' she muttered.

'Nor me,' Sam said softly after a pause.

'I've been past those gates, oh, I don't know, at least a hundred times,' Bubbles said. 'Every time I go to Papa's Connaught Place shop, in fact. And, you know, it's like a bad habit, but I still cross my heart and mutter "Our Father" when I see the school church. But I've never once stepped through those gates since we left. I'm not sure I'll be able to take it, actually.'

'Look,' Anita cut in, sitting up and trying to sound more brisk, 'I know there's good reason for us never having gone back. But I'm not sure it's really helped, y'know. Sometimes things just seem to get worse the longer you leave them.'

Her two friends were silent for a few seconds before Bubbles spoke up. 'My therapist sometimes says I'll only make real progress when those old issues are resolved . . .'

'It's more than that for me,' Sam said. 'More like . . . atonement.'

'Well, if we don't do it now, we never will,' Anita said, taking Sam's hands in hers. 'I get some leave around Christmas, so shall we try to go together by, say, mid December? Let's see what it is that Lamboo wants. We owe her that much. Time to try and lay some of those ghosts to rest.'

Chapter Three

DELHI, 1993

'Have you heard? We're getting a new girl in class,' Sam said, putting her satchel down on her chair to take out her lunchbox and flask of iced lime juice and position them carefully in the inner recess of her scuffed wooden desk.

Even Anita, slumped lifeless over Flaubert at the back of the classroom, looked up, shoving her glasses back up her nose as various classmates started instantly to quiz Sam.

'Who?'

'Where's she from?'

'I hope she's not pretty, yaar.'

'Or over-smart.'

In her usual calm manner, Sam ignored them all until she had hung her satchel on one of the hooks on the back wall and started arranging the exercise books on the teacher's table into a neat pile. Finally, she said, shrugging, 'Dunno, I haven't met her yet. But Lamboo stopped me in the quadrangle to say that a new girl was joining our class to do her final year here. She wants us to be nice to her because she's been recently orphaned, I think.'

There was another flurry of interest:

'Orphaned! Bloody hell . . .'

'Who's an orphan?'

'The new girl we're getting, man, why don't you listen!'

'Christ that's bad, poor thing.'

'Where's she coming from, Sam?'

'One of the hill schools, Lamboo said – Mussourie, I think?'

'I hope she's nice. Some of these hill-school types think no end of themselves.'

'Yeah, almost as though they're little English missies . . . they wear stockings and hats and things. Imagine!'

'Those hats are called "boaters", Anita offered. 'Actually it's the hill stations that are the real relics of our colonial past.' She looked around and saw that, as usual, her classmates were all ignoring her to concentrate on the crass and the mundane.

'Whatever,' Zeba growled from the bench next to Anita's, 'she had better not try lording it over us.'

'Yeah, I really hope she's nice.'

'Of course she'll be nice,' Sam said, adding, 'well, more importantly, we have to be nice to *her*. Must be awful to have lost both parents.'

'Both *together*?'

'Must have been a car accident or something.'

The conversation was brought to a halt by the clanging of the office peon's iron rod on the brass bell in the quadrangle outside. The class shuffled to their feet as Mrs Menon, their teacher, sailed in, orange and black sari pallav fluttering after her.

'Good morning, Mrs Menon,' the class intoned.

'Morning, morning . . . good weekend?' The teacher smiled briefly before sitting down to unlock the desk drawer and pull out the class register. A few indistinct mumbles

50

greeted her query but she had obviously not been expecting any replies as she looked up with a blank expression to take the roll call in a brisk voice.

'Anita Roy?'

'Present, Miss.'

'Arpana Singh?'

'Present, Miss.'

'Ashwathy Pillai?'

'Present, Miss.'

'Bubbles Malhotra?'

Mrs Menon looked up and scanned the class over her reading glasses before repeating, 'Bubbles Malhotra? Not here?'

A voice piped up from the back. 'I think she's coming, Miss. Must be late . . .'

'She wasn't on our bus this morning,' someone volunteered.

'Well, she's always missing the bus. Last week we had to wait while she came running down the road with her two servants following her, one carrying her bag, the other her water-bottle,' someone else said to general titters.

'Enough, enough, let's move on. Maybe she'll come later.' Mrs Menon returned to her ledger. 'Damini Mehta?'

'Present, Miss.'

As predicted, there was soon a kerfuffle at the door as Bubbles Malhotra stumbled in, red-faced and sweaty from her exertions. 'Sor-ry, Mi-ss,' she puffed, 'missed the bu-s, Miss . . .'

'Really, Bubbles, you must try harder than this to be punctual. This must be the third time already this month that you've been late.'

Bubbles performed a small apologetic shimmy, still standing uncertainly in the doorway while trying to catch her breath. Her indecision only seemed to annoy Mrs Menon further, who snapped, 'Okay, come in, come in, what are you waiting there for now?'

Anita rolled her eyes as Bubbles flopped onto the bench next to her. Bubbles was in a right old state, her tie askew, socks sagging over grubby trainers and a pair of new zits ballooning on her chin. Anita listened to Bubbles wheezing for a few minutes as she recovered from having run up two flights of stairs to the senior school before rather unkindly scribbling 'Lose Weight!' on a note that she pushed across the table towards her. She and Bubbles had been bench-mates for a few years now, both choosing to inhabit the last row for completely different reasons – Bubbles so she could hide behind girls cleverer than her, and Anita so she could read novels during the maths and science lessons. They had eventually managed to overcome an initial mutual suspicion of each other to become unlikely friends, mostly because it massaged Anita's ego no end to have Bubbles so desperately need her crib-sheets to keep from flunking every exam.

An hour later, Mrs Menon was droning on, drawing geometric shapes on the blackboard that made scant sense to most of the sixteen-year-olds seated before her, when they were interrupted by a knock at the door. All heads were raised as the principal walked in, a girl wearing a patterned smock and sandals following a few paces behind.

'I am so sorry to interrupt the lesson, Mrs Menon, but I wondered if I might take my session early. I'd like to introduce a new girl to the class.'

'Yes, of course, of course, Miss Lamb,' Mrs Menon said, hastily putting her chalk stub down and backing away. 'I was just finishing anyway. Please, please do come in.'

Anita had often wondered at the nervousness Miss Lamb seemed to evoke in most of their teachers, speculating on whether it was merely because she was principal or whether her being British had something to do with it too. Old Lamboo had always seemed to Anita to be like someone who had fallen out of an E.M. Forster novel, her foreignness accentuated in a curious way by her not having left India when most of her countrymen and women had. The first time Anita had the opportunity to use a carefully learned big word had, in fact, been with reference to Miss Lamb, when – soon after winning the St Jude's scholarship as a seven-year-old – she had informed her amused father that the new school principal was 'quintessentially British'.

Anita now watched while Miss Lamb waited politely for a harassed Mrs Menon to collect her books and bags. The new girl stood behind Miss Lamb, wearing an impassive expression on her face. She was tall, like Lamb herself, and athletic and astonishingly pretty, Anita thought, sneaking a glance at Zeba and her best friend, Natasha, sitting in the third row, who had always fancied themselves as the school beauties. It satisfied her to see that they were gazing at the newcomer in open-mouthed wonder too. This girl was much lovelier than either of them, her skin tanned to the kind of gold that was rarely achieved by white skin, quite unlike Miss Lamb's florid summertime pink. Anita saw too that the girl's eyes were a strange blue-grey colour, their only flaw being that they were set a little too close together in a heart-shaped face that ended in a pointed chin. She didn't look pure British, more likely Anglo-Indian, as someone had surmised earlier. Their eyes met for an instant and Anita was shocked at the sudden frisson she felt run through her, which was followed by instant revulsion. She knew a lot of girls at school often developed crushes on other girls but, even as a junior, she had prided herself on never having been at either end of such ridiculous infatuations, saved from them – she would

53

have been the first to admit – by being scrawny and bespectacled and not sporty at all.

Mrs Menon departed in a flurry of apologies and chalk dust and Miss Lamb now stepped forward, clearing her throat in the way she did when she wanted their total attention. This was not a problem today as the class sat rapt before her, silenced by their curiosity. The last new girl this particular batch had received was Natasha Walia, whose father had been posted back to India after a long stint abroad in the diplomatic service – and that had been a good six years ago.

'This, my dear girls,' Miss Lamb said to them, 'is Lily D'Souza. Lily is new, not just to our school, but indeed to Delhi, having just moved here from Sacred Heart convent school in Mussourie. I know some of you are quite familiar with Mussourie, travelling up there for your summer holidays, so I do not need to tell you what a big change this is for Lily, who has never been to Delhi before.'

Anita noticed that the girl next to Miss Lamb remained unsmiling, plucking absently at the canvas strap of the bag she was carrying slung across her torso as though it were a guitar.

'My dear girls,' Miss Lamb continued, 'I know I don't need to tell you to make Lily comfortable and welcome. Now, where can we find room for Lily to sit?' Miss Lamb scanned the room and nodded approvingly as she saw the dependable Samira move up on her bench in the front row to make room. As the principal gestured, Lily walked hesitantly towards the rows of girls, unslinging her bag and holding it ahead of her. Anita observed Sam smiling warmly, even using her tissue to clean Lily's side of the desk, but she could now no longer see the face of the new girl, only a ponytail of straight brown hair that hung down her back all the way to her waist. The girl sat down, shoving her bag between herself and Sam, and, as the bell went, Miss Lamb opened her tattered copy of *Macbeth* to begin her lesson.

Anita's concentration was poor in the hour that followed, even though Lamb's classes were always the high point of her school day. Today the principal was wittering on about the nature of ambition and did not seem to be quite herself either, gripped by a preoccupied air that was infecting the whole class with a kind of listlessness.

When the bell finally rang for the lunch-break, Miss Lamb looked as relieved as everyone else, setting the group an essay on the banquet scene as homework, before leaving for the dining hall. Anita got up and stretched with a loud groan. She scanned the room. Sam seemed to have taken the new girl under her wing already, opening up her foil pack of cheese sandwiches and offering her one.

Anita and Bubbles joined the small group that had already gathered around Lily and Sam's desk.

'Are you related to Miss Lamb?' Natasha was asking the new girl.

Anita saw Lily hesitate for a minute before a set of invisible shutters descended over her face. She pursed her lips, suddenly acquiring a mean expression as she said with more vehemence, 'No, we're not related. I'm nothing at all to that horrid old bat.'

There was a collective horrified intake of breath. No one ever spoke about Miss Lamb in that tone of voice. Even the nickname of Lamboo, used by generations of St Jude's schoolgirls, was only ever employed affectionately.

Sam hastily changed the subject. 'Oh, Bubs, one of your pimples has just burst,' she said.

Attention turned to Bubbles, who clamped a piece of tissue, spotted with blood, back to her chin. 'Oh God,' she mumbled through her clamped jaw, 'I had just two pieces of cashew burfi last night, y'know, and see the reaction!'

'Let's have a look,' Zeba said, 'I may have some Clearasil in my bag.'

Bubbles gingerly removed her hand, eliciting a chorus of moans.

'Christ, that's a prize one,' Natasha said.

'And look, there's a new one sprouting right next to it.'

'Clearasil won't work, those need Dettol.'

'Or DDT even!'

Sam's ruse had successfully drawn everyone's attention away from the new girl and Anita noticed that even Lily was now smiling, although she couldn't tell if Lily's subsequent attempt at humour was malicious. 'Etna and Krakatoa, that's what those two are,' she said.

'Who?' Bubbles enquired, nonplussed, but Lily shook her head, smiling to herself.

Anita stepped in to rescue her friend. 'Okay, everyone, stop treating Bubs like a prize exhibit. We're off to the dining hall now, if anyone wants to join us for some five-star world cuisine.'

Victoria Lamb decided not to join the throng in the dining hall, as was her usual custom. Instead, she walked down the southern corridor and past the music room, where the sound of a trombone was blaring tunelessly over the lunchtime hubbub. She had this morning given Lily money to buy a hot lunch in the canteen but would herself return to her cottage, which lay on the far side of the rambling school grounds. Lakhan would rustle up a sandwich for her, which she would eat quietly in her study overlooking the rose garden. She deserved a little peace and quiet after the traumatic events of the past few days, not made any easier by Lily's difficult behaviour.

Victoria unlatched the small wicket gate that led to the rose garden and walked to her cottage, dipping her head to avoid damaging the flowers of the madhumalati that were dangling crimson over the door. She turned on the cooler, still thinking of Lily's obstreperous conduct since her arrival. The rusty old machine sent a welcome blast of cool air through the cottage and Victoria exhaled in relief, relishing the respite, not just from the heat but also from the past few days of argument and tears. Who could blame the poor child, though? What Lily had undergone lay beyond the bounds of most people's imaginations, certainly her own, and what the girl most needed now was stability and quiet, unquestioning acceptance. Love and other such things would gradually follow in their own time. Victoria certainly hadn't thought it prudent to tell Samira more than what was absolutely necessary this morning, of course. Heaven knew what the girls would make of the whole thing, if they found out. Or, for that matter, their parents! An exclusive and well-reputed school such as Jude's really couldn't afford a scandal of any sort.

Victoria popped her head into the kitchen, startling old Lakhan who was pottering at the stove, probably brewing his fifteenth cup of tea.

'*Mere liye bhi ek cup chai, Lakhan,*' she said, '*Aur sand-wich. Kya hai fridge mein?* Tomato? Ham?' She paused, waiting while her Nepali cook rummaged around inside the cavernous old fridge, emerging finally with a rather shrivelled cucumber. '*Accha, cucumber sandwich theekh hai,*' she said resignedly.

Victoria Lamb walked into the cool of her darkened study and, rather than turning on the light, opened the drawn curtains slightly. Harsh sunshine poured in through the crack and for a moment she closed her eyes tightly shut. Slowly opening them a few seconds later, she blinked uncomfortably, letting her vision get used to the glare. Her eyes wandered over her shorn rose bushes and empty flowerbeds. May in Delhi was a bleak time in many ways. Not the best season to have Lily brought here but there hadn't really been a choice. Still, in another few weeks it would be the summer holidays. She ought to think of going somewhere with the poor girl – a short vacation. Not to the hills, of course, that would be most injudicious. But anywhere else would be far too hot. Perhaps staying in Delhi would be best; giving Lily time to find her feet and get used to each other and the city.

Victoria sat upright on her armchair, unable to physically relax when there was so much on her mind. She absently polished the glasses that hung around her neck. How unusual it would be this summer to have someone around during the long holidays, when everyone else, staff and students, went off with their families to all sorts of jolly destinations. The school building and playing grounds were almost ghostly when emptied of their noisy population. Victoria Lamb looked up at the distant gulmohar tree, the crest of which was aflame with red flowers. Suddenly she felt a little blessed. The dear Lord had strange ways, but it was as though He had understood that, with the passage of the years, she too would need someone to help fill the lonely evenings. And so Lily had been sent to her so unexpectedly, someone to love again, so late in life. Of course, the poor child was savagely angry and resentful, especially at the secrecy that would be required for the time being. The row last night had been quite unbearable, but it was best not to reveal the past – Lily would simply have to understand that.

At the end of her first day at St Jude's, Lily stood at the first-floor window of her empty classroom, looking at the droves of girls heading down the drive for the cars and school buses that would take them all to their homes. She imagined them being received by their mums at the door and the smell of food that would be emanating from their kitchens. Whenever Lily conjured up images of family life in her head, she saw them like those television advertisements for rice or talcum powder that both fascinated and repelled her, and sometimes broke her heart. Weren't those the kind of families most people had: mums in pretty saris and aprons serving up steaming bowls of rice, dads driving up to neat little houses in their shiny cars, coming in from work holding briefcases, while children with plump, scrubbed faces sat laughing around dining tables? That was what all those girls streaming out of the school gates had. And they didn't even consider it as being out of the ordinary. 'Everyone but *you*, Lily D'Souza,' she muttered under her breath, feeling that by now familiar twist of anger and bitterness in her stomach. All she had was School Principal Victoria bloody Lamb – and there was no way she could think of that scrawny old bat as being even remotely related to her. Certainly not *now*, when it was too late; much, much too late.

Lily twisted the handkerchief in her hand till she could feel its embroidered edge snap and tear. She turned from the window and blew her nose loudly as angry hot tears fell from her eyes and rolled off her chin. Leaning on the windowsill, Lily wiped her face roughly, wondering how long she could skulk around in the school building before being either turfed out or locked in. She surveyed the empty classroom, the rows of scuffed and ink-stained wooden desks and chairs left all awry, bits of paper littering the floor. To calm the horrible wobbly feeling inside her and have something to do, she walked between the rows, noisily straightening the desks till they formed neat lines, then proceeding to clatter chairs under them until everything was tidy and orderly, the way it was meant to be. She looked at the names and graffiti that had been carved into some of the desks, seeing initials of girls, some coupled with what were probably initials of boys surrounded by heart shapes. Such things were the normal concerns of most girls, she thought as she picked various exercise books and pens off the floor and placed them on a desk. Surveying her handiwork, she wondered if she ought to go to the next classroom and do the same thing there as well. There was something faintly comforting about bringing order where she could. Besides, there was no way she was going back to the cottage where she would have to put up with all that solicitous fake familial behaviour again. Just a week and already it was choking her to death. She wished she could run away from St Jude's and this horrid noisy city and go back to her beloved Mussourie. It was the best season to be there, when wildflowers came bursting out of the grassy banks and the pine tree outside her window would be heavy with cones . . .

Lily started to cry again. One thing she knew for sure was that she would never, ever forgive Victoria Lamb for what she had done.

Chapter Four

LONDON, 2008

Sam drove nervously through what was now very heavy rain. She'd volunteered to drop Anita off at her flat in Borough as they left Heebah's and, perhaps because of the downpour, Anita hadn't demurred. They were both unusually quiet on the drive south, each sunk in her own thoughts, Anita occasionally providing directions to get to Blackfriars Bridge.

As they drove over the bridge, Sam glanced at her friend's profile, trying to think of something to say to lighten the atmosphere.

'Oh, I've been meaning to tell you. I saw a really good film the other day. You and Hugh will really like it,' she said.

'Really?' Anita roused herself. 'Which one?'

Sam racked her brains. This was the trouble, she had got to a stage where she couldn't even remember the things she *liked*. At thirty-two!

'Oh God, it had whatshisname in it . . .' she said, lifting one hand off the wheel to click her fingers frustratedly.

'You don't mean *whatshisname*!?' Anita laughed. 'Oh, I just adore him! Left at the lights, Sam.'

'Yeah, I know where we are now, thanks,' Sam said ruefully, swinging to the left and pulling in at the door to Anita's loft apartment, 'although it probably won't be long before I'll be forgetting more than just the names of films and actors!' She turned to her friend and added apologetically, 'Oh, what's wrong with me. The name will come to me the minute I've driven away from here. How annoying!'

'Never mind, darling. Coming up to my flat for a glass of wine?'

Sam shook her head, smiling. 'I need to get home before Heer turns in, sweetie. Is Hugh coming tonight?'

'He's on the night shift all week, but I'm going over for dinner this weekend. He's cooking!'

'We didn't mention him at all tonight,' Sam noted apologetically, turning off the ignition and looking directly at Anita.

'Hardly surprising, given what was on all our minds.'

'I hope it's going well?'

'With Hugh, you mean? Yeah, I guess. He does seem awfully nice, but then I've only known him a couple of weeks. Sounds awful, but I keep waiting for him to put a foot wrong. So far he hasn't, I must say, but I do worry that it might just be by careful intent!'

Sam considered this for a moment before replying, 'Well, even if it is by careful intent, isn't it rather nice that he cares enough to do that?'

Anita's grunt only sounded half-convinced so Sam continued her counsel. 'Listen, don't keep watching and waiting for something to go wrong. Just relax and enjoy getting to know him.' Sam stopped, vaguely aware tha˙ it was a bit rich for her to advise anyone on matters of the heart.

Anita nodded. 'You're right, Sam. I'm too much of a cynical old cow for my own good sometimes. Listen, call if you need to talk, okay? Any time. You know that.'

Sam reached out over the gear-stick to kiss her friend's

cheek before she got out of the car. 'You too. Call me whenever you can.'

She started up the engine again but waited until Anita was through her door before reversing and heading back for Borough High Street. She jumped as a motorbike courier flashed by, inches away from the side mirror, and cursed under her breath. That second glass of wine had been a bad idea, taken only because Bubbles had insisted that the police would never be prowling on a night as wet as this. How stupid of her to have taken advice from someone who never drove! The last thing she needed after such an emotional meeting with her two friends was a brush with a policeman waving a large breathalyser. If that did happen, she was sure she would collapse right into his arms in a flood of tears.

Sam nervously edged her Audi into the stream of traffic heading for Waterloo Bridge, earning an angry toot. Well, she hoped this was the way to Waterloo Bridge; even the road signs were virtually invisible in the rain. Sam cursed again. Akbar had told her weeks ago to get a sat-nav device fitted in her car, but, as usual, she'd forgotten. She didn't usually travel south of the river as Anita was the only person she knew who lived there and she was generally happy to meet in town. Sam had made every attempt to refrain from postcode snobbery, but no matter how hard she tried to be comfortable south of the river, she invariably felt a little lost and threatened the minute she got past the South Bank Centre. Even at the start of the twenty-first century, these grubby narrow streets managed to look faintly Dickensian to her.

As she neared a large green sign, Sam peered upwards trying to read it – ah, Westminster Bridge, that would do nicely. She started to breathe easier as she drove under the blue railway bridge that she recognised as being the old

Eurostar line. Now she knew where she was and pressed her foot on the accelerator with more confidence, heading for the bridge. Glancing out of the window, she saw that the river was a sludgy brown, the rain having chased all tourist traffic away from the choppy dark water. The Houses of Parliament looked as secretive and mysterious as ever, their narrow Gothic windows sending thin golden slits of light piercing through curtains of rain.

Perhaps it had not been a great idea, Sam thought, meeting the two people who shared those dark memories that had been triggered by the arrival of Lamboo's letter. Instead, she ought to have gone somewhere bright and busy like Harvey Nicks, distracting herself as she so often did with a platter of *moules frites* at the rooftop café, and enjoying the anonymity of the summer crowds. Even if she had stayed at home and played Heer's favourite tennis game on the Wii console, she might have ended the evening feeling less wretched. Luckily, Akbar had left this morning on a business trip, accompanying his boss to Frankfurt and Berlin for three days. She had come to rely on little breaks like this ever since Akbar's firm had merged with the German practice, and she was grateful that she wouldn't have to endure his sarcasm tonight: 'What's agitating the acidic Anita these days then?' or 'Ah, the bimboesque Bubbles Raheja – now if she had one more brain cell she'd be plant life.' Sometimes the sarcasm was preferable to the more direct hits, though: 'What's with the glum face? Some of us have been hard at work and have earned the right to be morose, you know.'

Sam would never in a hundred years be able to explain to Akbar about Miss Lamb's letter and the despair it had brought upon her. She'd mentioned Lily's death to him once in the early days but he hadn't seemed to take it seriously, and she had assumed that things like that were probably commonplace for someone in the legal profession. She hadn't wanted to dwell on it anyway – not at a time when she had just got married and her life suddenly seemed to be blooming again. Later she had told herself it was just as well she'd never revealed any of the details to Akbar. Without a doubt, he'd have subsequently used the knowledge to make her feel even more remorseful than before. She could almost hear his sneers, especially seeing that he'd always harboured a special resentment towards her school friendships: 'What sort of a Social ends with a kid being found dead?' 'So that's what your gang was like at school, sure explains a lot!' He never noticed that he was usually the only person enjoying his remarks, so busy sniggering at his own wit that he invariably failed to look around and see the stricken expression on her face or, worse, the embarrassment of whoever was in their company observing Sam's mortification.

Sam slowly relaxed her fingers on the steering wheel as she passed the bright chaos of Knightsbridge and the traffic eased a bit. Hyde Park was covered in wet darkness, its black and gold wrought-iron gates closed for the night. She drove along with Classic FM playing softly on the car radio, trying to remember when Akbar had changed from being the charming, suave man she had fallen in love with to the remote stranger she was now married to. She couldn't understand why his main source of entertainment seemed to lie in belittling other people, especially her.

Sam recognised Elgar's 'Nimrod' as it swelled through the speakers and felt a familiar prickle behind her eyelids as it slowed and turned soft and poignant towards the end. Elgar invariably caused sad memories to unspool and undulate through her head, but today even the soothing tones of the radio presenter was making her want to weep. It came to her as it always did in her lowest moments: it wasn't Akbar, it was her. It was *she* who had changed her husband, embittered him in some way by letting her own misery seep into their life together. She had never quite measured up to Akbar's brilliance anyway, even in the early years of their marriage, doing a part-time job in a library briefly before giving it up, embarrassed by the growing disparity in their salaries and the sheer inanity of carrying on working when he was earning such mega-bucks and needed her to be a support to him. Then, sitting around at home all day or meeting other non-working wives for lunches at Nobu and Zuma and attending the weekend parties thrown by the Kensington banker–lawyer set, she had slowly started to put back on all the weight she had lost at college, almost without noticing it.

It was almost certainly her growing size that had first put Akbar off her, and perhaps it was that which had started off the sarcasm too. Maybe Akbar had thought that jokes were a less hurtful way of letting her know that he did not like being married to a fat woman. But early on she hadn't taken the hint when he disparaged other overweight people, even those he didn't know, declaring in that superior way of his that they were all indubitably either 'weak' or 'lazy'. But their sex life had started to dwindle at some indefinable point and then there had been his gift of an exercise bicycle on her thirtieth birthday.

Sam turned down her road and drove past her neighbours' familiar handsome town-houses, some advertising plush interiors through uncurtained windows. She wondered at that sometimes; she herself always drew the curtains before the lights were turned on – not that she didn't have expensive contemporary art on her walls or designer custom-made sofas to show off, but there was something comforting in silently declaring that not everything had to be publicised and made known.

Fishing out the electronic buzzer from the glove compartment, she watched the tall metal gates to her house swing slowly open. The maid had drawn the curtains of all the upper windows and only the kitchen was visible from the garden as she pulled into the drive. She could see Heer's small black head bobbing around inside and felt her heart melt as she turned the ignition off. At least she had her daughter's love – although who knew for how long. Heer was growing up to be the spitting image of Akbar, and might inherit – dear God – his sense of humour too one day.

Sam gathered her things from the back seat of the car and ducked under the dripping honeysuckle. Heer let out a reassuringly delighted shriek as she walked through the kitchen door. 'Mamma, Mamma, look what Masooma and me have been making for you!'

Sam smiled as she peered at the pale brown sludge in the bowl. 'Masooma and *I*, *beti*. But what on earth is it?'

'Chocolate mousse!'

'Oh dear, perhaps it needs a bit more chocolate then. What have you put in it?'

'Two bars of Dairy Milk and some cocoa, an egg whipped up and . . . here, try some.'

'Actually, Mamma's eaten, sweetheart,' Sam said hastily as Heer held out a spoonful, feeling bad at the disappointed moue her daughter's mouth instantly formed. Even though she had only nibbled on some pita sticks and olives at Heebah, she did in fact feel rather ill and couldn't face the thought of food. She turned to the maid and spoke in Urdu. 'No dinner for me tonight, Masooma. Has Heer eaten?'

'Yes, memsahib. I gave Heerbaby dinner at six. Daal meat with rice and salad, as memsahib said.'

Sam nodded. 'Thank you, Masooma. Heer, darling, I'm going to get changed . . .'

'Oh memsahib, there was a phone call from India. It was Zeba Khan madam. She wants you to call back. I have written phone number down here.' Masooma could hardly contain her excitement. 'Memsahib, it is *Zeba Khan*, film star, your old friend you told me, no? I know her voice so well I immediately recognised.'

Sam nodded blankly as her heart sank. So Zeba would have received Lamboo's letter too. There had been no contact from her in months, and the only reason for a call out of the blue would be that letter. Sam felt quite sure she could not stand talking about the letter and reunion any more. Despite Anita's conviction that they would all benefit from 'laying old ghosts to rest', as she put it, Sam now felt exhausted at the very thought. Reunions were for people who wanted to stay in touch, and she had done that with Bubbles and Anita because they had both been in London as long as she had, and because they were, after all, the closest thing she had to family here. Since that chance meeting at Heathrow, there had been the occasional email from Zeba who, for all her starry airs, had evidently never forgotten that she had to thank Sam for never revealing her affair with Mr Gomes, despite being class monitor and Lamboo's favourite. But that had been the sum total of her old school friendships. And given everything that had happened, that was probably the best way to keep it.

Sam changed into a tracksuit and lay down for a few minutes, recalling all manner of things from her schooldays. Then, suddenly, she swung her legs off the bed, sitting up abruptly as she decided to pick up the phone and return Zeba's call. Perhaps she would know more about exactly what Miss Lamb had in mind for them all.

The ringing tone on Zeba's mobile was distant before she heard the click and Zeba's famously husky voice, thick with sleep, mumble an indistinct 'Hello'.

'Oh goodness, how stupid of me, I'd completely forgotten about the time difference, Zeba, it must be past midnight there – *sorry*! Were you asleep? I only just got in and just wasn't thinking . . . it's Sam here.'

To Sam's surprise, Zeba sounded relieved rather than annoyed. 'Oh, that's okay, Sam, no problem. I'm so glad you called. Wasn't really sleeping as I'm totally jet-lagged.'

'Been travelling?' Sam asked, unsure whether to mention the letter until Zeba brought the subject up.

'More than I'd like,' Zeba replied. 'You got Lamboo's letter too?' she asked in her habitual abrupt style. Luckily, there was no beating about the bush with Zeba. Sam recalled there never had been.

'Yes, this morning, Zeba. What is she up to, do you know?'

'I have absolutely no idea. But I must say I get a very bad feeling about it. As though it's a . . . a *plot*.' Zeba tried to joke. 'A plot in a really bad Hindi movie.' But neither she nor Sam could bring themselves to laugh.

'I've been feeling pretty spooked myself, to be honest,' Sam replied.

'What about Anita and Bubbles? Have they had letters too? Have you seen them?'

'We just spent the evening together, to talk about it in fact. Anita wants to go. In fact, she wants us all to go. Brave it out, she says.'

'She has a point. I'll go if you guys are coming.'

Sam, trying not to sound too surprised, responded with a nervous laugh, 'Safety in numbers, huh?'

'Well, something like that . . . I hope you guys don't think it too weird for me to join you out of the blue, but we had grown very close that year, remember? Us four, that is.'

'Of course it's not weird, Zeba, we've been classmates since we were tiny,' Sam said, trying not to sound doubtful but quite uncertain of whether someone like Anita would care to have Zeba suddenly back in their inner circle.

'Well, in that final year we were drawn together mostly by our common hatred of Lily.'

'Oh, Zeba!' Sam remonstrated mildly.

'But it's true, Sam, we might as well admit it. What on earth did I ever have in common with someone like Anita? Or Bubbles even?'

'We may have grown apart now, Zeba, but back then we were all pretty much the same, weren't we?'

'Just a bunch of Delhi school kids, I suppose . . .' Zeba's voice suddenly sounded less crisp. After a small pause, she spoke again. 'When do you think you'll come to India, Sam?'

'Mid December, when the schools here close, I expect. I'll bring Heer, but I don't know what Bubbles will do with her Bobby and Ruby. They'll probably prefer going on one of their exotic holidays.'

'I notice Lamboo's suggesting the third weekend in December for this reunion, just like the Socials used to be.'

'And the anniversary of Lily's death,' Sam pointed out.

'Exactly what I was thinking. It's so weird, Sam! As if she knew all along what we did that night and is now intent on reminding us of it.'

'That wouldn't be like old Lamboo. She wouldn't hurt us, that I'm sure of. It could be some kind of memorial thing for Lily.'

'After all these years? I don't think so somehow.' Zeba's voice rose as a new thought occurred to her. 'Do you think they might have found some new evidence, and they're doing a kind of reconstruction thing?'

Sam couldn't help a small laugh at that. 'What, like they do on TV? Hoping someone will crack?'

'Don't laugh – what if someone does crack, as you put it,

or remember something and it all comes out? Ugh, so macabre.'

Sam considered the possibility. It wasn't entirely non-sensical and Zeba had a public reputation to consider. This was the kind of story those film rags would fall upon with relish, poor Zeba. Poor *all* of them – nobody needed something like this when life was already so complicated. 'Murder will out,' she said softly, remembering Miss Lamb explaining the nature of guilt in one of her *Macbeth* lessons.

'Don't! You're really scaring me now,' Zeba implored. 'But, really, if you think about it, Sam, we'll all be gathered together in almost exactly the same circumstances. It's a well-known ploy used by the police the world over. Agatha Christie always did it.'

'But why now? All these years on?'

'Maybe she wants to see justice done before she dies, see the guilty brought to book once and for all.'

Sam, unable to keep up her casual tone any more, started to weep at that, lunging for her bedside tissues and pressing a wad against her mouth. Sam had always been one of Miss Lamb's favourites, never achieving the top marks Anita achieved in Lamboo's subjects of English and History, but unfailingly making class monitor year on year, simply because the principal had trusted her so implicitly. Now, with stinging recognition, she realised how grievously she had betrayed old Lamboo's trust in those last few weeks at school. Worse, she had not even attempted any sort of reparation, never once returning to visit either the school or its old principal.

'Sam? . . . Sam? You okay?' Zeba's voice echoed distantly down the line.

Sam gathered herself together. It wasn't just Miss Lamb and Lily. There had been so much to deal with that terrible winter, but perhaps Zeba had – in the midst of her present glitzy life – forgotten the dreadful events of that year. What Sam needed now, quite desperately, was to end this conversation. 'Yes, I'm fine, Zeba. Look, I gotta go now. I've been out all evening and need to put Heer to bed. I'll call you tomorrow . . .'

'Oh God, I've upset you now, haven't I? You aren't crying, are you? Sam?'

'No, no, I'm fine, Zeba,' Sam mumbled, managing to keep her voice steady. 'Look, stay in touch. I've told Anita and Bubs that we need to keep each other's spirits up.'

'Too right,' Zeba agreed. 'Yes, I'll stay in touch too. You'd better go and sort Heer out now. Call me when you can. And try not to think about this if possible, Sam. We've all got our lives to live.'

MUMBAI, 2008

The following morning, Zeba managed to drag herself out of bed and get to work on time, despite having caught only five hours of sleep. Getting out of her car, she straightened her back and walked into the studio, knowing she was already getting full marks from the assembled crew for not making them hang about all morning like some of the other stars did. There were some things about her father's strict upbringing that she did have to be grateful for.

She looked around the Filmistan sets in amazement. This was good even for Shiv Mirchandani, whose hand was clear in the attention to detail. The fake marketplace had everything: the ration shop, the post office, the vegetable vendor with his trolley full of shiny aubergines and damp bunches of spinach. Zeba suddenly realised that she had not actually seen the inside of a real market for years, merely expecting the fridges and fruit bowls in her Juhu house to be well-stocked at all times. She'd even forgotten who in her domestic retinue had been delegated to oversee all that! But, from her childhood memories of accompanying Ammi to INA market every Sunday, the set designer had got this exactly right.

What a pity that it had all been put together only to be blown apart. Today's shoot was the bomb-blast scene, which she wasn't looking forward to at all. The mess and noise, the acrid smoke and smells – horrible. Then she'd have to be rushed to make-up for them to put the grime and blood on her face and clothes for the rescue scene. Zeba stopped short, remembering that her co-star on this film was Neel Biswas, a man with the most horrendous bad breath. She shuddered, imagining submitting to halitosis fumes as she lay in a swoon ready to be gathered up in her distraught lover's arms.

Zeba sensed someone sitting down gingerly on the seat next to her and turned to see a grinning young girl – probably one of the extras. She felt her hackles rise. She *really* did not want to be bothered with useless chit-chat when she was sleep-deprived and trying to gather her thoughts for her scene. She had learned method acting the hard way, living as she did in a world where no one else even knew what the term meant. Perhaps she should cock an eyebrow at her maid or assistant to signal to them that they ought to be keeping fans at bay. There was a time and a place for adulation. But Zeba could spot nobody familiar in her immediate vicinity and reluctantly turned back. She'd be cool and distant – Zeba knew from experience that would send the girl scurrying off. No harm in being polite, though – you never knew when the press would descend in disguise, and those *Starworld* journalists were always looking to find something on her that would bring all her hard-won success crashing down.

'Yes?' she said with a plastic smile that she knew was not quite reaching her eyes.

'Madam Zebaji, I am your biggest fan,' the girl breathed.

Zeba nodded. She couldn't help softening at the sound of those words, but she'd heard them so often that they had long ceased to really thrill. 'Hmm, how nice to know that,' she said, trying to sound pleasant but with scant success.

'Madam, if you don't mind . . . I am writing a book about our Bollywood industry and want to ask you . . .'

Zeba had been offered that excuse so many times that it wearied her. Did these people really think that writing books about the film world was easy? How silly they were to imagine that actors would ever stop acting for long enough to reveal their real selves to anyone? It was *all* an act, she wanted to shout at them sometimes, even the casual chats and confessional-style interviews. How on earth could anyone imagine otherwise? And who was this chit of a girl to offer the world her wisdom on Bollywood anyway? When people like herself, Zeba Khan, had slaved for years to make their way up its labyrinthine, treacherous corridors. Zeba's beautiful face closed up. 'Why don't you make an appointment with my secretary for an interview. He will . . .'

'I will most certainly, Madam. But I saw you sitting here, and if I can just ask you one or two things now. Just some basic questions . . .'

Zeba darted another look around her before nodding reluctantly – where was bloody Gupta, or her PA, or Najma even. Her status allowed her to have as big a retinue as she wished on set, but what a strange way they all had of vanishing when you most needed them. 'Well, you know, I have just one or two minutes before going on the set . . .'

'Don't worry, Madam, I will not take up much of your time. Just *one* question . . .'

Zeba took a deep breath. This was one of those brazen ones who would not be shaken off. Some of these people had no shame, really, no sense of *privacy*. There were laws to protect the rich and the famous in other countries, but here in India, no bloody chance! Zeba put on her polite but resigned expression and nodded again.

'Okay. Thank you, thank you,' the girl gushed, pulling out a bright yellow notepad. 'Madam, Zebaji – may I call you Zebaji? Okay, Zebaji, please tell me when you first took up acting? I mean, when did you first think to yourself, "I am going to be a superstar". A Bollywood thespian. Maybe Hollywood even!'

Zeba parted Bollywood's most famous luscious lips to dish out the usual reply . . . *ever since I was a child . . . my parents, recognising my unusual talent, used to . . . la di la di la la la* . . . Her patter had been perfected over the years. And the old Hollywood question too – she was sick to the teeth of it! As if all her hard-won success in India amounted to nothing if she failed to get the nod from Hollywood. Which Hollywood star could claim to have a fan-following that stretched to a billion people, for God's sake! Weren't journalists supposed to be intelligent people? But, just as Zeba was formulating her reply into polite language, she spotted Gupta hurrying across to her.

'Madamji, you are being called onto the set. Immediately please!' he said, taking his cue from Zeba's glowering expression.

Zeba threw a falsely apologetic look at the girl, who looked like a child that had suddenly had her lollipop snatched away from her. 'I am *so* sorry,' she said, getting up and smiling sweetly before turning to Gupta and saying, 'Gupta-sahib, *please* take this author's details and arrange a time with her for a proper interview. She is writing a book and we must help her. Okay?'

Gupta nodded, his face a mask. Madamji's acting was so good that he sometimes had to check later with her whether she really meant what she said in front of other people. Zeba had already turned away from the girl, thinking it best not to wait for a reply. Security in this place was not what it used to be, Zeba thought crossly as she hurried back to her rooms, carefully picking her way over the network of cables and wires that lay strewn across the floor of the studio. In the era of the big stars, journalists knew their place and never wrote badly of the celebrities, no matter what they got up to – bigamous marriages, name changes, even changing religions to suit their convenience. Nobody questioned anything. They were like Gods in those days, lording it over ordinary mortals from the big screen. Now everyone thought film stars could be their *friends*, thanks to their TV sets that took them right into people's living rooms. But why journalists considered it their job to expose film stars and find something – anything – to destroy them, Zeba had never been able to work out. Didn't they have politicians to chase any more?

She closed the door behind her in relief, throwing herself down on the bed. Suddenly remembering the hours it had taken her hairdresser to get her seventies-style beehive hairdo just right, she hastily sat up again. Casting a quick look at the mirrored wardrobe, she breathed a sigh of relief. No damage done, thankfully. Zeba angled her face to examine herself in the mirror. Her skin glowed alabaster white, just turning a pale rose over her cheekbones. Her neck was smooth and curved downwards quite marvellously to shapely shoulders. She looked into tawny brown eyes that, she had on excellent authority, were capable of making hardened underworld dons swoon. Then she fluttered her lashes, trying to see what it was that other people saw, smiling, lips together, then lips carefully parted, revealing a sparkle of fine even teeth inherited from her father.

The journalist wanted to know when she had taken up acting. Well, Zeba knew *exactly* when she had: aged two, when she had first become conscious of her ability to make people coo over her merely by pouting coquettishly and swinging her little hips. But she wasn't exactly going to divulge all that, was she? Nor that there was one particular day when she had realised that she would kill – yes, *kill* – to be the star. An image of Lily D'Souza clad in a white robe, declaiming for all she was worth on the school stage, flashed into her mind. Zeba could even remember the words . . . '*Oh God, that madest this beautiful earth, when will it be ready to receive thy saints? How long, oh lord, how long?*' She remembered the electricity of that moment: the pain that seemed to drip off Lily's beautiful face, the silence pervading the school hall, and, most of all, the awed expression on the old drama teacher's face as he gazed up at Lily with the kind of expression none of Zeba's own histrionic efforts at school had ever elicited. Oh yes, if a knife had been handy at that moment, Zeba would have happily leapt onto the stage, killing St Joan right there in the middle of her bloody audition. She could imagine the reaction if she ever told a journalist all that. Wouldn't they just love it? The story of how Zeba Khan, aged seventeen, had fought for her role in the school annual production with a new girl, Lily D'Souza. Beautiful, brilliant Lily D'Souza, who was later found dead in the school's rose garden. Oh how the press pack would love it, dementedly carrying the story on all their networks, reporters standing outside her house, breathlessly exclaiming over the unsolved case in which top star Zeba Khan was clearly involved! She remembered the time a careless remark she had passed about a local politician had made the morning news, thereafter being repeated all day on an endless loop in red ticker-tape at the bottom of the TV screen. They were *starved* for stories, these 24-hour news channels, and fell upon the smallest scrap of celebrity news as though it were manna from heaven! This story would not be a scrap of news, though. It certainly would not be difficult for a reporter to find interviewees – old schoolmates jealous of her success, teachers she had been rude to, any number of people who would no doubt delight in giving chapter and verse on how stuck-up Zeba Khan had been at school. There was a lot of stuff from those days that was well worth keeping hidden, after all.

In the mirror, Zeba saw fear and guilt darken her face at the memory of Lily and reminded herself angrily that *nobody* had liked the new girl. 'Thinks too much of herself,' someone had said, and, 'What does she think, that she can just walk in and take over from us?' But, even after it had been well established that Lily was the most conceited little bitch they had ever met, Zeba had been astonished to hear that Lily had had the nerve to put her name down for the lead role in the play that year. It wasn't just that Zeba always, always played the lead – everyone knew that – but Lily was *new*, an outsider, for heaven's sake! A new girl didn't ever show such impudence if she knew what was good for her. It was no less than arrogance to think she could waltz in and steal things that had always belonged to others. Besides, it was Zeba's final year at the school and the part of Joan of Arc had been virtually written for her. Why, old Moss, the drama teacher, had even adapted parts of the script to suit her accent as he had heard that scouts from both film school and the National School of Drama were going to be in attendance. Zeba had toiled all year for the role, neglecting her schoolwork to prac- tise for hours before her bathroom mirror till each line had been perfected like a carefully chiselled jewel. Did everyone think she would quietly stand by and let some cocky brat from the sticks just waltz in and rob her of all that? All that effort, all that work, her ticket to film school and her dreams of stardom? Well, the bottom line was that it was not Lily D'Souza who shone in the limelight at the annual production that year. It was Zeba. It was Zeba Khan, as it always had been and was always meant to be. And, despite the circumstances surrounding that fact, Zeba could still – even after all these years – take some satisfaction from it.

Chapter Five

By the time Lily D'Souza had been at St Jude's for two weeks, there were not many classmates left still trying to befriend her. She had, on her very first day, managed to upset half the population of the class by declaring that Delhi was a crass city because of its Punjabi business population, not stopping to consider that half the girls in Class XII were the daughters of Punjabi businessmen. Then, granted exemption from studying Hindi on the basis of having come from another state, she airily dismissed what was the mother-tongue of most of her classmates as 'the language of politics and corruption'.

Even the normally peaceable Sam and uncomplicated Bubbles had retreated hurt, burnt by Lily's acid tongue on too many occasions to persevere any more with amiable overtures. No one wanted to befriend the new girl, for that was what Lily was still persistently called.

'It's because she's so horrible that we can't stop calling her "new girl", I think,' Bubbles remarked as their group sat under the gulmohar tree sharing their lunches one day.

Startled by her bench-mate's unlikely astuteness, Anita agreed. 'Absolutely. It's not like I *haven't* tried seeing it from

81

Lily's point of view. I mean, it's never *easy* to break into an established group. But we've done everything to make her feel welcome, haven't we? Well, at least Sam has.'

'And me!' Natasha chipped in. 'I even offered her my Mont Blanc pen set, you know, when her crappy ball-point ran out in Biology the other day. But would she take it? Like heck! Just too nose-in-the-air, that's what.'

'Essentially, Lily's done nothing to *try* to belong,' said Anita firmly.

'It's like she's in another world, floating way above us. Just because she's *pretty*.' Zeba spat out the word.

Only Sam was still faintly doubtful. 'Maybe we should give her more time ... I mean, we don't know yet exactly why she was brought here, but it's almost certainly because something bad has happened in her past.'

'But then she should *tell* us about it. We can only sympathise if we know.' This was Nimmi speaking, a cheery sort of girl whom Sam knew was usually quite reasonable.

'Definitely. *We're* all so open with each other, aren't we?' Natasha was starting to sound quite indignant now.

'Maybe she will be too, once she's settled down and starts coming out of herself,' Sam replied.

Natasha spluttered on a mouthful of ham and cheese. 'Coming out of herself! You're not suggesting *shyness* is her problem, Sam? Have you seen the way she looks around the classroom? Looking without seeing, that's what she does. As though we're all too far beneath her to be noticed. You're the only one she'll deign to talk to, Sam, and even that is only when she needs something.'

'Yeah, and have you seen how she only ever sits in the front row? Because that way she doesn't need to look at anyone else,' Zeba grumbled.

'Oh, I don't know,' Sam murmured, 'maybe we're reading

too much into all this. The front bench is just the place she was given. I sit in the front row too.'

'But you're different, you're class monitor,' Bubbles said, adding, 'you've always sat in the front row. And you keep looking back at us at least.'

'Yeah, only to say "ssshhh . . . quiet" and suchlike!' Sam replied.

'Oh, for heaven's sake, Sam – even you should be able to see that Lily's just a stuck-up, arrogant little bitch,' Zeba demurred, nibbling delicately at the edge of a shammi kebab.

'Perhaps she thinks she's above us because she's the Princy's relative and lives in her cottage,' Bubbles offered.

'But she said on her first day that she *wasn't* related to Lamboo, remember?' Nimmi queried.

'Well, that's clearly a lie, isn't it? Why would Lamboo take her into her house if they weren't related, huh? And didn't Lamboo describe Lily as her relative to you, Sam?' Zeba asked.

'She did, actually, I'm sure I didn't mishear that. Something about her being Lily's nearest relative after the loss of her parents,' Sam said, getting up and dusting sandwich crumbs off her navy pleated skirt. She scanned the playground, empty except for their own little group occupying the only shady area under the trees. Delhi in June was as hot as hell and she could see dust lifting off the basketball courts and hanging in the still air. Luckily these were the last two weeks of term before the summer holidays and she would soon be off to the hills with her family. Much as she loved Delhi, she hated the coming season of sandstorms. Already there were days when her throat and nasal passages felt clogged with dust, and she feared greatly for both her father and brother, both asthma sufferers. She cast a look at her watch.

'C'mon, girls, we don't want to be late for Gomes. There's

83

just five minutes left until the bell, and I need to fill my water flask from the cooler on the way to the lab.'

'Oh it's only our Gomesey,' Zeba said lazily, stretching her lissom legs out from under her and tying her long brown tresses into a loose knot at the nape of her neck. 'He never gets cross. I'll take care of that.'

Everyone tittered uneasily but Sam's forehead creased into a small anxious frown again. She had been waiting to have a serious conversation with Zeba about her relationship with their Chemistry teacher. 'I've been meaning to say, Zebs . . .' Sam adjusted her tone, trying to sound less sanctimonious. 'You really must stop this absurd thing before it goes too far. I feel so terribly scared of what might happen, you know.'

But Zeba merely smiled cheekily up at her, amusement making her pretty brown eyes twinkle and dance. 'Listen, Sami, this "thing", as you describe it, has been going on for a couple of months now and nothing has happened, has it? Has it?'

'What do you mean, "nothing" – you mean, like, you haven't had full-blown sex, yeah?' Natasha clarified.

Bubbles squealed at the sound of the word 'sex', clapping her hands over her ears and giggling uncontrollably. Zeba threw her a disparaging look as Sam tried gamely to continue her counsel. 'Even if it's not . . . *sex*,' she cleared her throat, 'you have been doing . . . all kinds of things you just *shouldn't* with a teacher, Zeba.'

'Only waist up, Sam, nothing waist down,' Natasha said in a reassuring tone, adding, 'and he only went past her bra just the other day.'

Bubbles squealed again but Zeba regally ignored her this time, nodding in appreciation of Natasha's defence. 'Anyway, it was Gomes who made the first move, not me,' she said.

'Yeah, like that makes a *real* difference,' Anita said sardonically.

Natasha put in another mild entreaty on behalf of Zeba in her phlegmatic American drawl. 'Hey, listen, we all know of Zeba's irrepressible desire to flirt. Can't we just let it be?'

'And what can I do anyway if *he* keeps flirting with *me*?' Zeba asked, emboldened by Natasha's defence and trying now to sound wounded.

'Well, if you're such a victim you could try reporting him, couldn't you?' Anita enquired caustically.

Sam cut in hastily, 'I don't know about that. We'll have to think things through before taking such a course of action. Reporting a teacher is a big deal. Gomes will go and lose his job and there'll be an enquiry and heaven knows what else. Can't you just try to put an end to it yourself, Zeba? Just tell him he's too old for you or something.'

'But right now it's just so amusing, Sam,' Zeba giggled. 'Last week he was leaning over me, to use the pipette, y'know, and, when his hand slipped it landed on my thigh . . .'

'If I were you, I'd have screamed my lungs out at that point,' Anita said sharply.

Zeba looked pityingly at her as though assessing the unlikely prospect of anyone, Gomes or otherwise, making a pass at someone who wore glasses and pigtails.

'You let him grab your thigh?! Really, Zeba, how can you be such an idiot!' a horrified Sam exclaimed, ignoring the sound of the bell clanging in the distance, which announced the end of the break.

'When you're Zeba, being an idiot is the easy bit, Sam,' Anita put in drily.

Sam could not bring herself to smile, despite Bubbles and Natasha going off into gales of giggles at that. 'Just don't *encourage* him, Zebs, please!' she implored.

Zeba got up along with the others, now looking slightly more shame-faced than before. 'It's actually not so easy to put Gomes off, you know, Sam . . .' she said as they dusted down their uniforms.

'Why not?' Anita demanded, picking up her satchel. 'Give me one good reason.'

'You see . . . well, okay, I'll tell you because I eventually would have anyway. But, listen to this – Gomes says he might be able to get the Chemistry paper for me before the Board Exams. A friend of his is the person who's going to be setting it. Just think of it . . .' Zeba looked around at the group, half pleading and half excited.

There was a sudden silence as everyone stopped walking to look at her open-mouthed.

'He *what?!*' Anita screeched.

'Oh Zeba, how could you . . .' Sam breathed.

'Listen, I was going to *share* the paper with you guys, so don't look at me like that!' Zeba said.

'Oh God, Zeba, like that would make it all better. Oh, I just don't know what to say,' Sam wailed.

'Listen, without it I'll just flunk. And there'll be no getting to the film institute without a school leaving cert. Then my parents will ground me and there'll be no outings and no fun, and life just won't be worth living,' Zeba said, her voice rising dramatically.

'We'll talk about this later – okay? God, there's the *second* bell! Now I won't even have time to go to the loo,' Sam wailed over her shoulder as she hurried away from the group of friends. Leaving them to wend their way across to the Chemistry lab, she ran towards the water-coolers, nodding absently as she passed a gaggle of seventh graders on their way out of choir practice. They had temporarily suspended their trilling to say hello to her but Sam's thoughts were miles away as she hastened past them with a serious look on her face. Normally she made it a point to talk to her many fans among the juniors, but today she had not even noticed that she had left them gazing disappointed at her retreating back.

How horribly muddling all this was, Sam considered while filling her water flask. As head girl she really ought to do something about this ghastly mess, but what? Perhaps she ought to let Gomes know somehow that the girls all knew what was going on and that his dirty secret could not be contained any more. Anyone could stumble upon Gomes and Zeba in the lab, which was where – as far as Sam knew – most of their trysts took place.

She ran down the corridor and reached the lab just as her group of friends were walking through the door. By now Sam was perspiring profusely, both from the heat and out of fear. Fortunately the Chemistry lab was the coolest and darkest room in the school, shaded by ancient trees. Set back from the Edwardian building that housed all the classrooms, it had once been the outside kitchen of the old convent that had since acquired a brand-spanking-new stainless-steel canteen indoors. Converting a kitchen to a lab must have been easy, Sam had observed when she had first set foot in this building. The shelves of colourful spices had been replaced by bottled chemicals and the sink now bled the pink juice of potassium permanganate crystals rather than the blood from meat. The faintly unpleasant smell of hydrogen sulphide hung over everything now, though that apparently hadn't been much of a deterrent to either Gomes or Zeba.

Sam tried not to feel nauseated when she saw their Chemistry teacher simpering openly at Zeba while the group took their places on the stools surrounding his desk. Gomes was a tall, slim man with a mop of oily black hair, and would not have been bad looking were it not for an underhand kind of manner that Sam had often found quite sly. Even the way he walked around made it look as though he were sliding around the lab rather than walking. The incorrigible Zeba looked nonchalant as she perched herself on a stool right under the teacher's nose amid all the clattering and shuffling. She placed one foot on the stool next to her, a position that caused her skirt to slide a few inches up her long legs. Gomes whipped out a handkerchief and wiped his forehead with it, his small black eyes flicking momentarily towards the shadow between Zeba's thighs before he struggled to look away. Sam took up her station at the counter as Gomes came around lighting the Bunsen burners, keeping a wary eye on Zeba who was whispering with Bubbles and saying something so hysterical that it was making both girls shake with laughter. As Gomes approached the pair, he dropped the matchbox, scattering matches all over the floor. This made the girls crease up some more and then, while he was scrabbling around on his knees, Zeba stood up behind him to make a thrusting gesture with her hips, wearing a droll expression on her face. Sam flashed a warning look at Zeba as the whole class started to titter and Gomes staggered back to his feet, red in the face. The laughter didn't seem to bother him, though, and he merely looked adoringly at Zeba as she readjusted her facial expression to one of faux respect, leaning forward on the counter so that he could see right down the V of her open-necked blouse to where her cleavage nestled temptingly. Sam shot a look around the classroom and saw that while most of the girls remained oblivious to the drama of Zeba and Gomes, busying themselves with today's silver-making experiment, Lily D'Souza had her eyes carefully fixed on the pair. Sam saw those pale blue-grey eyes narrow in recognition before Lily looked as though she were calculating something in her head. Sam shivered and looked pleadingly at Zeba, who was still behaving as though she'd inhaled a whole canister of nitrous oxide. Oh, she was going to get *such* a telling-off when the school day finished.

Zeba was, however, her usual insouciant self when Sam cornered her after their lab session.

'You should have *seen* the way Lily was looking at you when you were flirting with Gomes,' Sam hissed, squeezing Zeba's elbow hard as they walked to the gate to emphasise her point.

'First of all, Sam, it's not me flirting with Gomes but the other way around, okay? And secondly, I'm not scared of Lily. What can she do to me, hanh?' Zeba replied brazenly.

'What can she do? She can tell Lamboo, that's what! And then we're all in big trouble.'

'She'll never tell Lamboo, yaar,' Zeba dismissed airily.

'Oh, and what makes you so confident?'

'Well, because they never talk to each other at all – we all know that. Whatever goes on in the Princy's cottage after school, happy chit chat between Lamboo and Lily doesn't seem to be part of it.'

Sam recognised the truth of what Zeba said. The principal and Lily certainly did not seem to get on very well. On some days they barely made eye-contact with each other when Miss Lamb was taking their English lesson, or so Sam had observed. So it was a relatively safe deduction that Lamboo was the last person Lily would go snitching to. But that didn't take away from the fact that Zeba was still dancing with death, playing with fire – no hyperbole would suffice to express Sam's terror.

But to Zeba she merely said, 'You could be right about Lily not telling Lamboo. I do hope for your own sake you are. But someone else could sneak . . .'

'Who? No one in our class would tattle, you know that.'

89

'Hmmm,' Sam conceded reluctantly. 'Look, we'll talk about this later, Zeba, and I'll help you figure out a way to get rid of Gomes. But I gotta go now. I have Haroon coming to pick me up today.'

The conversation was dropped as Bubbles joined them in the exodus to the school gates. 'What are you two talking about?' she asked.

'Nothing much,' Zeba said. 'Well, I'm off to my bus. Bye – and *stop fretting*, Samira Hussain! I'll look after myself. I promise!'

'What's she talking about?' Bubbles asked.

'Oh, just that damn Gomes thing. I really, really want her to put an end to it before it all goes horribly wrong.'

'Do you think – just maybe – she actually loves him?' Bubbles asked. 'I mean, it must be serious if she's thinking about having *sex* and all . . .'

'Oh Bubs, how can you be so naïve?' Sam said, throwing her head back in despair. 'There's only one person Zeba will ever love and that's herself. Thing is, she's so beautiful she'll always have men chasing after her, and I guess she'll just use that to get what she wants.'

'Maybe Gomes loves her?' Bubbles offered, undaunted. 'After all, he's risking his job and all that too.'

Sam finally smiled in sheer exasperation. 'What is it with all these theories of love, Bubbles Malhotra? And, pray, are you being kind enough to walk with me to the gates only because a certain Mr Haroon Hussain is expected? I know I foolishly mentioned in your presence during lunch break that my brother was coming to pick me up.'

Bubbles blushed and Sam squeezed her arm, laughing, 'You're just hopeless at hiding your feelings, you know!'

Bubbles had met Haroon at least a hundred times, having been a regular visitor to Sam's house since the age of six.

But her comfortable old relationship with Sam's big brother had recently undergone a curious shift that she had magnificently failed to conceal. Sam wasn't sure yet how serious it was, but it would have been impossible to miss Bubbles' newly developed curiosity about Haroon's life, or the ineptitude with which she conspired to be in his presence, only to become all gauche and awkward when she was.

Sam spotted her brother's head in the crowd and waved. She made her way through the car park, which was crowded with parked cars and school buses, Bubbles still glued to her side. She couldn't bring herself to ask Bubbles why she wasn't searching for *her* car. That would be too rude, and poor Bubbles had already lapsed into tongue-tied silence at the distant sight of Haroon anyway. As Haroon spotted the girls, he raised a lanky arm and grinned lopsidedly. The other thing Sam hadn't figured out yet was if Haroon reciprocated Bubbles' feelings. He certainly liked her, but then he had always treated Sam's friends nicely. Not that Sam would mind at all if her brother did start going out with her best friend. Bubbles was pretty much already a part of her family.

'Hey there, gorgeous girls,' Haroon said as they neared.

'You only said that because Bubbles is here,' Sam complained, throwing her bag into the back seat of the car. 'On my own, I'd never ever get a compliment.'

'That's not true!' Haroon protested. 'Is it true? Bubbles, you tell us. Am I not always showering my sister with compliments? I order you to arbitrate!'

Bubbles smiled shyly from under her lashes, her voice little more than a whisper. 'I don't think it's true at all. Haroon's always saying nice things about you, Sam!'

'Yeah, right, turncoat!' Sam said.

'Good girl, high-five,' Haroon yelled, slapping palms with Bubbles. 'Need a lift?' he asked, reaching out for her bag.

'No, no, it's okay,' Bubbles replied.

'Really, it'd be no trouble at all. Hop into the car,' Haroon insisted, not noticing his sister's exasperated eye-roll.

'Come on, Bubs, do you or don't you want us to take you home?' Sam asked.

Hearing the irritation in her friend's voice, Bubbles started backing away. 'No, no, my car must be here somewhere. I just came to see off Sam and to say hello to you, Haroon . . .'

'You sure, Bubbles? A lift wouldn't be a problem. You're right on our way . . .' Haroon wasn't letting go and now Bubbles was looking ever more confused.

'Yes, she's sure, Haroon! Didn't you hear her say that her car's here?' Sam yelled, climbing into the passenger seat. 'C'*mon*, let's get going now, I'm starving! Okay, bye, Bubbles!'

'That wasn't very nice,' Haroon said to his sister as they finally pulled away, Bubbles waving forlornly at them from the car park and barely noticing that she was blocking the path of a bus.

'God, if you must romance each other, at least have the decency not to carry on under my nose,' Sam snapped.

'Romance? What – me and Bubbles? You can't be serious!'

'Well, I think she is. And I think she thinks *you* feel the same.' Sam was seriously annoyed but squawked in fright as her brother, who was gazing astounded at her, nearly ran into the back of a taxi.

'You mean you hadn't noticed about Bubs?' she asked after Haroon and the taxi-driver he was overtaking had stopped gesticulating rudely at each other.

'No! Since when?' Haroon asked, adding an agonised, '*Why?*'

'Beats me,' Sam replied impolitely, before accusing Haroon, 'Must have been something you said. You must have led her on in some way.'

'Me? Lead Bubbles on? For God's sake . . . I've known the kid since she was a snot-faced six-year-old!'

'Oh, poor Bubs! So you don't fancy her,' Sam said. 'She's never had her heart broken before. And it'll all be *your* fault! I hope you're happy with what you've gone and done now, Haroon Hussain.'

'But I haven't *done* anything. Look, just tell her tomorrow that she's got it all wrong, okay?' Haroon wheedled. 'Please?'

'Why should I be burdened with breaking her heart? You're the one breaking it. *You* tell her!'

'Have a heart, Sam. I can't say anything to her if she hasn't said anything to me, can I?'

There was some logic to that, Sam had to agree. 'Well, okay, I'll try to say something to her,' she said finally. 'Not tomorrow, necessarily, but whenever I get the chance. And I don't know when that will be, so don't keep pestering me in the meantime, okay?'

'Thanks, sis,' Haroon said with relief, 'I owe you one.'

Sam sighed, looking out of the window as they approached India Gate and the roads became quieter. The lawns flanking the road were brown from the summer sun and ice-cream vendors were plying a brisk trade along their edges. 'Trouble is, Bubbles isn't very good at picking up non-verbal cues. I'll have to virtually hit her over the head with this information. Then she'll probably start crying and – aaaaarrrrrgggghhh – why did the idiot have to go and fall for *you*, of all people, Haroon!'

'Well, some people just can't help their magnetic good looks and overwhelming charm, I guess,' Haroon said, twinkling and then hollering 'Owww' as he earned a sisterly slap on his thigh.

Chapter Six

Bubbles sniffed her forearm appreciatively. Bergamot oil would help unwind her tense mind, the therapist at the Mandarin Oriental had assured her. The diminutive Chinese woman had been unfailingly sympathetic and gentle but, while being ministered to, Bubbles had not been able to help speculating that this woman was thinking, as all her therapists no doubt did: 'What the hell do *you*, you beautiful, lazy, pampered wife of a millionaire, have to be *stressed* about?' The staff at the Mandarin Oriental spa had emitted a collective sigh when Bubbles mentioned her recent cruise in the Bahamas, but little did they know how stressful it had been for her to play dutiful daughter-in-law throughout her two weeks trapped on the *Minerva,* not just to Binkie's mother this time but to all her cousins and best friends too! There was no point trying to explain. These people would never understand anything,

The Bahamas cruise had been particularly difficult for Bubbles, because added to the usual stresses had been the effect of Lamboo's recent letter. It wasn't merely that the letter had been a shocking reminder of Lily and Haroon and all the terrible events of that winter. Bubbles had not been

95

at all prepared for the manner in which Lamboo's words would transport her back to her school years in Delhi and make her think of all the things she could have done to change her fortunes. She had spent much time on board the yacht thinking of the place she was in now, married on sufferance into a family to whom she was at best a convenience, rather than a loved and respected member. Of course, Bubbles could never say anything like that to anyone because she knew that no one in their right mind would ever look at her and think, 'Oh, *poor* you!' Not when they saw the houses and cars and jewellery and expensive holidays that ran almost seamlessly one into the other. Not even her two best friends completely understood, although they were the only ones who tried. At least Sam had some idea of what it felt like to be an impostor in one's own marriage.

After her massage and sauna, Bubbles strolled through the elegant hotel lobby, calling her chauffeur on his mobile phone as she reached the door. When Rob drove up a few minutes later, she sank into the cool leather back seat of her Mercedes and felt the friendly August sun playing on her face as she donned her sunglasses. She looked through pale pink Versace lenses at people crossing in front of the car where it had stopped for a pedestrian light. There was a woman in a smart office suit and soiled trainers walking into Hyde Park, while two young mothers in skinny jeans were going the other way, holding tightly onto three toddlers on harnesses who were behaving like excited puppies. A gaggle of Japanese tourists wielding maps and cameras were strolling along with no urgency, while an irritated commuter tried to get past them into the tube station, laptop slung across his shoulder and a paper cup of coffee held before him like a weapon. It was strange, her world-through-a-window view, leading Bubbles to feel almost dissociated from the life she saw unfolding all around. The only occasions on which Bubbles saw what she thought of as 'real life' was when she was being driven like this around London, and she looked now at the faces milling about on the streets, some happy, others anxious and stressed. All this stuff in the newspapers about the credit crunch seemed not to have changed her own life in any way, and clearly any one of these people would swap their life with hers in a heartbeat if they could. How could she explain that it really, really wasn't as fabulous as it looked?

'The guv'nor wants to be collected en-route, Ma'am,' Rob said as the car started purring forwards again. Bubbles knew that the household staff adopted a more familiar tone with her than they did with the rest of the Rahejas and had always been rather flattered by this, seeing it as a kind of acknowledgement of her being much nicer than the rest of them. She was sure, for instance, that Rob would have used the words 'Mr Raheja' rather than 'the guv'nor' had her mother-in-law been in the car.

'Who needs to be collected, Rob, my father-in-law?' she asked.

'Mr Raheja Junior,' Rob clarified.

'Oh, did he say why?'

'No, sorry, Ma'am, he didn't say.'

'Okay, let's go to the office first then. I'm in no huge hurry to get home.' There was no one waiting for her at the Belgravia house anyway – Bobby had gone to summer camp, the nanny would take care of Ruby's needs when she came in from school and her mother-in-law was most likely playing cards at the house of her best friend, a large lady who went by the universal monicker of Auntie Poppy.

When they arrived at the tall, gleaming structure on Park Lane that was the Raheja International headquarters, Bubbles called her husband on his mobile.

'Coming,' he said briefly, in lieu of greeting.

'Shall I wait in the car?' she asked.

'No, come up, it won't look good. I might be another ten or fifteen minutes.'

Bubbles got out of the car and walked across the chrome and glass lobby, smiling briefly at yet another brittle blonde receptionist. This front desk seemed to sprout new clones of that type month on month, so she had long given up trying to remember their names. People were walking up and down the corridors, carrying folders and files – some nodded in recognition as Bubbles passed, although no one stopped to speak.

Bubbles wondered sometimes if Binkie's employees liked him. He certainly made more effort to be popular than his father did, insisting the previous year on having a family day out for the London staff, hiring Kengrove Hall and erecting carousels and bouncy castles in its grounds alongside a great marquee serving sandwiches and cake and tea. Binkie had also wanted to hire a few of those Bolli Darling girls he had seen at Lord Lyndon's birthday party, dressed like flamingos and butterflies to wander the gardens and entertain the guests, but his father had quite firmly drawn the line at that. Bubbles had gamely tried taking the children along to the office party but, within half an hour, they had both promptly declared it 'naff' and demanded to go home. All Bubbles could now remember of the day was that it had been hot and sticky and that hardly anyone had come up to speak to the two Mrs Rahejas who had sat under the shade of a tree, wearing the matching Givenchy sunshades Binkie had bought on a business trip to Rome, fanning themselves vigorously with paper serviettes. Perhaps the Raheja employees maintained their distance due to the glowering presence of Mr Raheja Senior, who had parked himself with his wife and daughter-in-law, unable to cope with the idea of socialising with his staff and continually grumbling under his breath at the unnecessary expense involved. Luckily the idea of a staff outing appeared to have been dropped this year, probably at Binkie's father's insistence, though Binkie had tried to save face by saying that they had decided that the company would have a family day out on *alternate* years.

Bubbles took a seat in the lobby outside Binkie's penthouse chambers, where she sat dwarfed by an enormous vase full of long, black orchids. A few more Raheja employees walked past, but as no one stopped to talk, Bubbles glanced idly out at the park that lay bathed in summer sunshine eleven floors below. Tiny people and cars looked like those little digital images she sometimes saw on her son's Nintendo screen, except that these were not being controlled by his speeding thumbs. Starting to feel bored, Bubbles peered through the translucent walls of the waiting area and recognised her husband's shape through the glass bricks. Binkie was with James, his old schoolmate from Eton, whom he had employed as his personal assistant. Hailing from an aristocratic but impoverished family that Binkie had once described as being 'all breeding and no bucks', James was a rather toffee-nosed young man who wore pink bow-ties and had the limpest handshake Bubbles had ever known. She'd assumed he was gay when she'd first met him, but Binkie had dismissed her remark instantly and rather crossly, telling her of the regular Friday night trips that the younger members of management made to Spearmint Rhino, James apparently leading the group. Bubbles was aware that he had persuaded Binkie to go along too a few times. Of course she had a pretty good idea of what Spearmint Rhino was – she'd seen enough Hollywood films in their home cinema to gain that insight – but the idea that Binkie might be making regular visits to gawp at buxom lap-dancers failed to trouble her too much, mostly because she knew how fastidious Binkie was about allowing *anyone* to touch him, even his own wife. The idea of him submitting to some raunchy fake-breasted woman's flirtations just seemed too ludicrous to be disquieting.

Bubbles could see that both men appeared agitated about something today, James's face and tie looked like twin pink blurs through the glass bricks as he gesticulated with both hands. She didn't see them quarrel very often, Binkie usually appearing content to have either his parents or James run his life, but luckily the argument resolved itself quickly enough and Bubbles sat up as the two men emerged from their cabin.

'Oh *hellow*, my dear Bubbles, how very lovely to see you again,' James said in his plummy accent, pale grey eyes looking at her from under long lashes as he performed the usual trout impression with his damp palm. Bubbles allowed her hand to rest limply and briefly in his, quelling the desire to pull out a pack of wet-wipes as soon as she had retracted it. It was curious that even though James had been nothing but charm and graciousness to Bubbles, she still harboured an inexplicable distrust for him. Perhaps it was the extent to which Binkie relied on James for everything. Or shared some of his quirks: like holding his head at a certain angle, or drawling some words out in that funny camp way.

She waited while the two men agreed in unusually curt tones to finish their discussion the following morning. Then, when Binkie started to walk down the corridor to the lifts, she hurried to follow her husband's footsteps. He seemed preoccupied and she wondered if the disagreement with James had been a serious one. 'Is everything okay?' Bubbles asked her husband as they silently waited for the lift.

Binkie appeared not to have heard her as the lift doors opened and they were engulfed in the sound of muzak. He jabbed the button for the ground floor with some ferocity and, as Bubbles felt her stomach lurch slightly with the motion of the speed-lift, she tried again. 'You seemed to be having an argument with James?'

'Nah, nothing important. Just a philosophical divergence on a management matter.'

Binkie often resorted to abstruse terms like that to shut Bubbles up so she would not question him any more. It wasn't that Bubbles particularly minded Binkie having secrets. Besides, as the child of a businessman, she knew that the very nature of business involved having to keep certain things undisclosed. But Binkie was a particularly enigmatic person, and not just when it came to his finances. Even in the early years of their marriage Bubbles had seen how, if asked at a party or social gathering what he did, Binkie would merely say rather vaguely that he was 'in business'. Specifics were never offered and, if demanded, could usually be put paid to with a modest shrug. The British were never as pushy as Indians anyway, especially when they had already spotted the Patek Philippe watch and the cut of Binkie's bespoke Ozwald Boateng jacket. They probably put his secrecy down to modesty but Bubbles had wondered if Binkie's secretive manner was just habit inculcated from having such domineering parents.

However, what Bubbles could not help recalling, with the tiniest pang of envy, was how much access her mother had always had to her father's business secrets. Even as a small child, Bubbles had seen her father return home and hand over briefcases or cotton satchels stuffed with notes to her poker-faced mother, who would swiftly transform them into gold and diamonds at the jeweller's the following day.

Her mother always knew exactly 'what was what'. In fact, if asked, her mother would surely say that knowing 'what was what' was a woman's main job after marriage.

Bubbles sighed, getting into the back seat of the car again, next to her silent husband. Together they wafted out of the gates of Raheja International, the chauffeur steering the car expertly into the traffic on Park Lane. Bubbles took in an envious look from a woman driver who overtook their gleaming Mercedes in a beat-up blue Corsa. 'Don't be jealous,' she wanted to call out to the woman as the tiny blue car nipped around other vehicles and disappeared in the direction of Victoria. 'I don't even know how to drive!'

Bubbles settled back into her seat, wondering whether everyone – Binkie included – would respect her more if she had at least one skill or qualification to her name. The problem would be trying to explain to everyone why on earth she needed to enrol at a driving or secretarial school, for surely those would be the only places that would take someone without a basic college degree. Even if she could afford private lessons, people would still think her quite mad for wanting to learn anything. Bubbles had also long decided there would be no point in asking Binkie to find her an opening in his business. Why, her husband did not even trust her enough to explain why he was arguing with his assistant.

The journey home was slow, the evening traffic just starting to build. Binkie did not speak at all in the car, looking pensively out at the falling dusk instead. When they reached the house he trotted up the stairs, going straight into his study. After a while, Bubbles, attempting to use the intercom to ask if he wanted a cup of tea, heard the strains of *La Traviata* floating down the stairs. Poor Binkie was definitely feeling stressed. Even though many aspects of her husband's character still remained a mystery to her, Bubbles knew that when Binkie was worried about something he always listened to opera.

She pulled off her sandals and walked barefoot down the corridor to her room. Ruby was probably back by now but hated being disturbed while she was chatting to her freinds on the internet. Perhaps she ought to see if her mother-in-law was home. Even after all these years abroad, Binkie's mum was still a stickler for all that good *bahu* behaviour – pretending not to see her arrive at the breakfast table until *she'd* said good morning first, expecting Bubbles to go and check on her welfare every evening, or to participate in her kitty parties and bridge sessions, even if all Bubbles could possibly do at them was sit around and look pretty. Over the years, the role of supervising high tea at these sessions had fallen on Bubbles, the mathematics of bridge proving too complex to master. There was no support from Binkie in this matter either, given what a relief it had seemed to him to be able to relinquish his role of keeping-Mamma-company to Bubbles as soon as they had got married. Though still quite intimidated by her in-laws, Bubbles tried to find consolation in the idea that the only person who did take some genuine interest in her day-to-day activities was her mother-in-law. In fact, so interested was Binkie's mother that her enquiries were not restricted just to Bubbles' day-to-day activities but sometimes even her minute-to-minute movements.

'Aaaaarghhh,' Bubbles thought, turning around and pulling on her sandals again to walk down the other corridor to her mother-in-law's room. It was best to announce her return before enquiries were made.

She knocked on the door and gingerly pushed it open with her toe. Her mother-in-law was lying on her orthopaedic bed and cocked a baleful eye in her direction. 'Your massage session took a long time,' she said accusingly.

103

'I went to pick Binkie up after that,' Bubbles explained, letting herself into the cavernous and heavily curtained room.

'Why, where was his car?'

'I don't know, taking James somewhere I expect.'

'And where is his father?'

'Papa? I don't know,' Bubbles said, not intending to be unhelpful although she knew her response would probably be viewed as such.

Today, however, Mrs Raheja was more engrossed in immediate matters. She groaned and stretched. 'Ooffo, I am having such body aches,' she said.

'Oh, why? Have you been exercising?' Bubbles asked politely, thinking of the new gym machine that had been acquired for her mother-in-law that moved one's limbs up and down without one having to put in any effort at all. Before its purchase, the only exercise Binkie's mum would ever subject herself to was a slow waddle through Fortnums with one of her lackeys pushing a trolley along behind her.

'Exercising?' Mrs Raheja Senior uttered the word as though it were an expletive. 'Don't be silly,' she snapped. 'I think that new Swedish massage girl is not good at all. Poppy's friend Mala Thapar's recommendation, but I should have realised that she knows nothing about anything.'

'The Swedish girl?'

'No, Mala Thapar!' Mrs Raheja Senior was feeling very snappish indeed.

'No, no, I meant was it the *Swedish massage girl* you found not good,' Bubbles clarified patiently, abhorring her own tendency to sound apologetic even when she had nothing to apologise for.

'Oh, I don't know, Swedish, Swiss, whatever. Tall girl with red-red dyed hair. Very poky hands. I must find someone else. She has done I don't know what over here.

See, behind my shoulders. You can feel some bumpy thing here under my shoulders.'

Bubbles reached out for her mother-in-law's bump with a tentative forefinger, wondering how much more solicitous talk would be required of her before she could change the subject.

An opportunity soon presented itself. 'MAAA!' The war-cry at the door was thirteen-year-old Ruby Raheja announcing her presence. 'Where the hell have you *been*, Ma, I've been looking everywhere and your bloody mobile's turned off!'

Bubbles sighed. Her daughter's summer holidays were beginning to seem interminable as the headstrong child had flatly refused to go to the summer camp in Switzerland with her brother this year. 'Mind your language, Ruby! At least in front of your grandmother,' Bubbles said, even though Mrs Raheja was beaming fondly at the truculent scion who was now flouncing in.

'Yeah, but I *needed* you. Urgently!'

'Well that's most unusual – and very nice to hear, Ruby.'

Ruby rolled her eyes at her mother's gauche attempt at humour. 'Stop joking! You have the number for that woman at Fendi who *promised* that my boots would be sent today.'

'Well, today isn't over yet, honey,' Bubbles said in a pla-catory tone, looking at her watch as if to confirm there were still some hours of the day left. 'If they said the boots would come, they will come. It is Fendi, after all.'

'It's all very well for you to say that! *When* will they come?! I need those boots for Arabella's party. It's *tonight*! Like, in three hours!'

'Surely you have something else to wear, darling, just in case they don't arrive in time,' Bubbles replied.

'Yeah, like shoes my friends have all seen a *hundred* times before!' Ruby's loud voice was now filling with angry tears. 'Besides, I wanted to wear *boots* with that Cavalli dress!'

'Well, if they're real friends, they won't even notice what you're wearing. Anyway, it's too warm for boots if you ask me . . .'

This time Mrs Raheja spoke before Ruby did, sounding no less fractious than her granddaughter. 'Just *call* the Fendi shop, Bubbles, and tell them to send the boots. That's all Ruby is asking!'

It was clear where young Ruby Raheja had inherited her exacting nature from and Bubbles was not pleased to see a triumphant look come over her daughter's face as she rewarded her grandmother with a kiss. 'Thank you, Daadi, only *you* understand me in this house,' Ruby said, causing her grandmother to swell slightly with pride. Then Ruby turned back to her mother. 'Well, call the shop then!' she demanded.

Bubbles sighed under her breath as she fished out her BlackBerry. She glanced at it and said, 'Okay, no charge. Which explains why you couldn't get through to me.'

Ruby looked ready to murder her mother now. 'Well, *charge* it then. God, I don't *buh-leeve* it!' she cried, throwing her pretty head back in despair.

'Okay, that's enough, Ruby,' Bubbles snapped. 'Bring your phone to my room and I'll call them. But no yelling if, by some chance, the boots aren't ready. They don't normally make that design in cherry red, as you know, so there may have been some delay in getting it from Milan. Besides, I have to get ready myself now.'

'Why, where are you going?' Mrs Raheja enquired suspiciously as Bubbles picked up her bag and prepared to leave the room.

'It's Karran Dilshaw's fundraiser at the Dorchester tonight, remember. The AIDS thing. Aren't you coming?' Bubbles asked from the door.

'Ooffo,' her mother-in-law exclaimed, falling back on her bed. 'No, no, I am not coming. I am having terrible body aches. You go,' she said. 'Someone needs to make sure your father-in-law doesn't drink too much.'

At midnight, Bubbles dolefully eyed the detritus on the table: soiled plates and wine glasses, and linen napkins with food and lipstick marks staining their thick snowy whiteness. She was now fading and in desperate need of her comfortable bed and a large goose-down duvet. She looked around the Dorchester ballroom, thronging with London's glitterati, and finally spotted Binkie. He appeared to have made up with James and was still joshing with him and some other friends at the far end of the room. He didn't look ready to leave at all, Bubbles thought, realising with further dismay that the auction was only just about to start. It would be at least another hour before she could make good her escape. Someone had said that Sting was doing a special performance later too. Binkie would surely want to stay for that, but perhaps he wouldn't mind if Bubbles slipped away.

Despite the presence of social luminaries like Jemima Khan and Richard Attenborough, Bubbles had had a dull evening, sandwiched between a raffish Swedish arms dealer and a doddering buffer who had opened their conversation with, 'So, do you manage to meet any of your own kind here in London, my dear?' Fortunately for Bubbles the old boy had swiftly lost interest in her soon after his opening gambit, probably worried she wouldn't be able to carry on a coherent conversation in English. The arms dealer had given up on her too, but not before the usual round of 'tests': pretending he couldn't hear her over the music and therefore putting his face far too close to hers, breathing single-malt fumes over her and, of course, inadvertently brushing his forearm against her breast . . . Bubbles wondered whether he'd had better success with the expensive-looking woman with the Arab name who was seated to his left.

Finally, at half past midnight Bubbles could not stand it any more. She muttered an excuse and got up from the table, picking up the Sonia Rykiel purse that contained her precious phone. The plan was go to the powder room and find a quiet corner to call Sam, who would hopefully not mind a late-night chat, seeing that Akbar was travelling. Looking back from the door, Bubbles saw that the auction had just started. She smiled as her father-in-law made the first bid: £10,000 for a weekend at Milan's seven-star Town House Galleria. Perhaps he had got a little drunk on all the Pol Roget he had been downing, and had forgotten that Milan wasn't his wife's favourite destination, but his beaming smile when he won the bid told Bubbles she ought to let him be.

'So how's the party?' Sam queried when Bubbles got through.

'Don't ask,' Bubbles wailed softly, sinking into a chair. 'The same boring faces, the same old meaningless chit-chat.'

'Poor Bubbles. How on earth did you ever come to share your life with London's great and good, huh?'

'The "good-goods" Binkie calls them. But then he loves all this. As for me, the last party I remember enjoying was your seventeenth birthday party, Sam.'

'I know, Bubs,' Sam said after a small pause. 'It was the last time we were all really happy, perhaps . . .'

Bubbles tried to quell the small rush of emotion she suddenly felt at that. The tall gilt-edged mirror before her showed an elegant woman dressed in black Chanel and Cartier, but, as far as Bubbles was concerned, the woman in the mirror could have been someone she bore no connection to at all.

Chapter Seven

DELHI, 1993

'I'm having a party on the last day of term,' Sam sang as she waltzed into the classroom one morning, 'and you're all invited! My mum's going to turn out a real spread, I promise.'

In the clamour of conversation that followed, Sam could hardly hear Zeba's whisper. It took a couple more attempts for Zeba to finally get her message across. 'Please, please, not Lily D'Souza,' she beseeched, looking over her shoulder to ensure that Lily was not in the room.

Sam looked at her doubtfully. 'I can't possibly *not* invite her, Zeb. It would look so bad if the whole class is coming. Besides, what would Lamboo say if she found out?'

'I find it hard to care what Lily thinks,' Zeba responded tartly.

'Lamboo need never find out. I'm with Zeba on this,' Anita said.

Sam shot a look around. Luckily Lily hadn't come in yet. In the month since she had joined the school she had taken to wafting in mere minutes before the bell rang. The fact that she lived on the premises was a privilege she apparently enjoyed reminding those girls who travelled in from far-flung areas like Sainik Farm and Gulmohar Park. Sam had

109

only heard this second-hand but, in the few weeks since Lily had joined the school, a fund of anti-Lily stories had already gathered that was so sizeable it was getting hard to keep track of what was likely to be true and what wasn't. Sam had given up trying to attribute Lily's behaviour to anything but plain nastiness too, not merely because nobody would even consider any other theory, but also because she too was gradually losing her characteristic patience in the face of Lily's stubborn unfriendliness.

'Besides,' Anita added a few minutes later, 'there's every chance Lamboo will actually heartily approve if we collectively send Lily to Coventry. Have you noticed how little she actually seems to like Lily?'

Sam looked at her friend in surprise. 'What's eating you? You're normally the last person to be so petty, Anita,' she scolded.

Anita sighed. 'I know it's petty, Sam. Of course Lamboo wouldn't approve of any of us ganging up on anyone else. And I know it's completely irrational to loathe Lily the way I do – I barely know her!'

'She tends to leave you alone mostly.'

'Nervous of Anita's braininess, that's all,' Zeba chipped in.

'Oh I don't know about that,' Anita responded modestly, shrugging off the rare compliment from Zeba. 'All I do know is that Little Miss High 'n' Mighty hasn't deigned to exchange even one word with me so far, even though I've tried all sorts of overtures. And I don't think it's because she's a shy, retiring wallflower somehow.'

'Well, maybe my party will help to break the ice. I think we should give her one more chance. A last chance,' Sam said pleadingly. Then she added carefully, 'You know, maybe Lily's not really that bad. Maybe there have been things that have happened in her past to make her a bit more . . .

hard-edged or something. It's pretty obvious from the way she suddenly landed up here that something's wrong, isn't it? We ought to be a little more understanding, I think.' Sam stopped and looked a little alarmed as a chorus of protest broke out.

'It's all very well for you to say that. You're the only one she'll talk to, Sam.'

'And that's only because she knows she has to have at least one person to communicate with.'

'Practically all of us have things in our past that might make us "hard-edged", but we don't take it out on our friends!' Natasha expostulated.

'This is just typical of you, Sam,' Nimmi said, 'you don't have to take your head girl role so seriously all the time, y'know. Please, please take a break from being nice so you can see the wood for the trees!'

But Sam, eager to bring the bickering to an end, raised her normally gentle voice to say loudly and firmly, 'All I know is that I told my mum I would invite *everyone* in my class, and that includes Lily.'

The class fell silent as the subject of their conversation walked in. Sam, nervous at the possibility of having been overheard, spoke up in a weak voice, 'I . . . I was just asking the others where you were, Lily. Didn't want you to be late and get into trouble with Menon, y'know . . .' She trailed off, covered in embarrassment as Lily nodded curtly, barely looking in her direction.

Sam used the opportunity of the drinks break to make amends with Lily. When the others had left the classroom to fill up their water bottles and buy ice-lollies at the gates, she turned to her desk mate who was still writing assiduously in her notebook. 'Hey, Lily, I'm having a party on the

111

last day of term. That's what I was talking to the others about this morning, actually. I'd really like you to come too,' she said.

Lily looked at her with a startled expression. 'Me? Come to your house?'

'Yes, for a birthday party. Well, not *exactly* because my birthday always falls in the middle of the hols. So, just an end-of-term party, I guess. My mum throws parties at the drop of a hat anyway. She's a great cook, you see, and has a catering business . . .' Sam stopped and bit her lip as she realised she was unthinkingly wittering on about her mother to a girl who may have been recently orphaned. She delved into her desk and emerged with a foil-wrapped piece of cake. 'Here, try some of her cake.' She shot an anxious look at Lily as she broke the wedge in half and pushed a slice across the desk on a piece of foil.

But Lily looked calm. 'It's good,' she said, having taken a bite. She then added casually, 'My mum used to make great cakes too.'

Heeding the past tense with which Lily had referred to her mother, Sam decided to use the opportunity to break the ice. After all, the girl had been her classmate for nearly a month and they should have become friends by now. Sam leaned forward and put a hand on Lily's shoulder. 'I'm so, so sorry, Lily, I'd forgotten and didn't mean to upset you at all.'

'Forgotten what? You haven't upset me . . .'

'You know, mentioning my mum like that . . .'

'So what if you mentioned your mum?'

'Well, haven't you just . . .?' Sam trailed off, dropping her hand back into her lap.

'Just what?'

'Just lost your mum,' Sam said finally, all in a rush. She had

112

found to her cost that wimping around just made matters worse.

'Well, if six years can be considered "just",' Lily said, still looking mildly puzzled.

'You mean you lost your mum *six* years ago?'

'Yeah, about that. Five years and ten months, if you want me to be exact,' Lily said unperturbed, taking another bite of Sam's cake.

'Oh God, I'm not getting anything right, am I?' Sam said. 'I'm so sorry, Lily, but I thought Lamboo said that you'd recently been orphaned . . . Was . . . is your dad . . .?'

Lily looked like she had been caught off-guard for one moment before she burst out laughing. 'Jesus, was that what the old bat said?! *Orphaned!* Good grief, what a bitch – imagine lying so blatantly! Perhaps she thought it would get everyone to like her more – presenting herself as the guardian angel come to rescue poor little Orphan Annie. Whatever else I am, I'm not orphaned, I'd have you know, so please don't start pitying me . . . Christ, *orphaned*, what next!'

Sam was nearly in tears by now, stuttering in her confusion. 'B– but I don't understand why Lamboo would lie . . . she would never lie to me.'

'Oh don't you believe it,' Lily snapped, her pretty blue-grey eyes suddenly narrowing. 'Okay, let me tell you something. You all wanted to know on that first day if we're related. Well, yes we are. There, I've said it now.'

'But you said you weren't . . .' Sam replied, covered in confusion.

'Only because she'd ordered me not to say.'

'But why?' Sam asked. But Lily only shrugged, wearing her mysterious look again. 'So how . . . how exactly are you related to Lamboo?' Sam persisted, not knowing what else to say.

For a couple of seconds Lily looked a bit uncertain. And then, taking a deep breath and with a steely expression on her face, she said, 'I'm her granddaughter.'

Sam looked in complete bewilderment at the girl sitting next to her. 'What do you mean, "granddaughter"? I don't understand . . .' she said, trailing off.

'Exactly that. Grand. Daughter. Which bit of that don't you understand?' Lily responded in her normal sarcastic manner. Her voice was composed but Sam could see two pink spots high on her cheeks.

'But Miss Lamb's never been married, has she?' Sam queried, still perplexed.

Lily emitted a short laugh. 'I can't believe you're naïve enough to have said that!'

Now it was Sam's turn to blush, but she recovered quickly, managing to defend herself. 'Well, one is usually married before . . . y'know . . . And you have a different surname from Lamboo too; that's confusing.'

'Yes, well, in this case procreation didn't follow marriage, unfortunately. Lamboo – as you so charmingly call her – had my father when she was sixteen, and unmarried, and gave him up for adoption. Hence the different surnames. Seems to suit her nicely, though, seeing the difficulty she's having in acknowledging me as her grandchild. Can't risk spoiling her spotless reputation in this school, I guess.'

Sam decided to focus on the least complicated part of the information laid so abruptly before her. 'Oh dear, we'd never have called her Lamboo in front of you if we'd known she was your grandmother . . .' she said apologetically.

Lily laughed. 'I don't care what you call her. I've thought up a few choice names for her myself, in fact.'

This time Sam did not even notice Lily's rudeness about Miss Lamb, struggling as she was to digest all this information. 'But why would Miss Lamb tell me . . .? Maybe it was *me*. Maybe I just misunderstood!'

'No need to blame yourself. I think you'll find that your Miss Lamb would do anything to preserve her good reputation. So don't just go swallowing everything she says. Orphaned, indeed! Well, let me tell you, my father's alive and kicking and still living in Mussourie. Wonder what he'd say if he knew this. First his mother disowns him, and then, fifty years later, she has him killed off in the eyes of the world too. What a laugh!' Lily sat back in her chair, twisting a pen around in her hand so furiously that she was leaving great ink-smudges on her fingers.

'Oh, oh, please don't tell your father!' Sam cried. 'I'm so confused and it was so silly of me to assume that you were . . . you are . . . Oh dear, it's all my fault! Now Lamboo will be upset with me and so will your father, and . . .' Tears rushed to Sam's eyes – this was a terrible conversation. She wished now she'd never started it at all and had merely gone with the others to buy ice-lollies at the gates.

'Oh, no worries about *him* finding out. We're not to speak ever again so there's no chance he'll get it from me. As for your beloved Lamboo, I won't tell if you won't.'

Sam stopped snivelling into her tissue to look gratefully at Lily. 'Oh, thank you, thank you, Lily. Let's keep it our secret – just you and me. No one need know any of this at all.'

'Oh, I don't care if they do, actually, it's all water off a duck's back for me. I'm keeping this quiet for your sake, so *you* don't get into trouble with your Lamboo. I don't plan to hang around here too long anyway. As soon as I'm old enough, I'm off back to Mussourie where all my friends are. I hate it here.'

Sam saw the determined set of Lily's chin and felt a shiver of something she couldn't put her finger on. It was a curious mix of fear and apprehension and puzzlement, for poor Sam was quite unaccustomed to disliking anyone at such early acquaintance.

When the bell rang, the girls of Class XII crowded back in to take their places for the next period, and Sam was careful not to catch anyone's eye, lest she inadvertently give away her agitated state. Peace descended slowly on the classroom as Miss Stella took her physics lesson and the afternoon sun filtered through the drawn bamboo blinds in the corridor. Sam could not concentrate at all, desperately trying to remember what exactly the school principal had said to her on the morning Lily had joined the class. Could it be that it was some kind of coded message and she had misunderstood it? Besides, why on earth was Lily not allowed to speak to her father and, even more intriguingly, why had Miss Lamb disowned her son? It was all very mysterious, and a bit exhilarating in a strange way. The year ahead had seemed so far to hold only the dull prospect of mock exams and preparation for the Boards, but now, suddenly, with the arrival of this strange new girl, things looked like they were about to take a turn. Sam felt terribly uneasy, but mixed in with that was a kind of illicit excitement as well. She stopped short, chewing her pencil as a new thought occurred to her. It was really important that she didn't tell anyone about Lily's revelations. It was *huge*, all that stuff about Miss Lamb. She imagined the consternation that would prevail if she did spill the beans. What a total bombshell it would be! Leading instantly, no doubt, to her own expulsion from the school for spreading rumours about the principal! It would be the first time a head girl would have been expelled, for sure. And then there was the possibility that it might not even be *true*. Lily could be the world's biggest fibber, for all Sam knew. In fact, thinking about it over again, she was getting more and more convinced that Lily's utterances were all nothing but lies.

Sam absorbed not a single piece of information from Miss Stella's class that morning. At lunchtime she kept a low profile, pleading period pains and going off for what Sister Carmel called 'a wee rest' in the sick-room. Sam had always liked the sick-room, a minuscule darkened chamber in the convent that was next door to the school. It contained nothing but a single bed overlooked by a picture of Christ, who had a bleeding heart nestled among the robes on his chest and blue eyes that seemed willing to weep for whatever sickness assailed the girl on the bed before him. Even as a seven-year-old, nursing a toothache and waiting for her mother to collect her, Sam had felt immensely soothed by the compassion on Christ's face and the distant sound of the nuns chanting their Mass in the chapel. But nothing could calm her turbulent thoughts today, and as she lay flat on the hard bed Sam glowered at Christ, who, apart from looking ready to cry at any minute, was unable to offer either succour or solutions.

Sam returned to her classroom late in the afternoon, her head still spinning. When the last bell for the day rang, she gathered her things and shoved them into her satchel. As she left the classroom and hurried away from the school building towards the buses, she heard someone hail her and saw Zeba and Natasha trying to catch up with her. Normally this was the time when the pair of them surreptitiously applied make-up behind their desk lids and rolled their skirts up at the waist-band. This was in readiness to perform their famous saunter that, rumour had it, sent waves of desire crashing through St Xavier's boys' school next door. But today they seemed to have other things on their mind, and Sam guessed it was Lily. Her heart sank. She had stopped lying at eight years old when she had first discovered how easy it was to get tied up in knots doing so, and was really not very good at it.

'What?' she asked in her least encouraging voice, looking pointedly at her watch.

'Oh God, you'd think she had a date with that Shah Rukh Khan, the way she's looking at her watch,' Natasha said.

'Well, if not Shah Rukh, it's definitely a *boy*, I can see it written all over her face. Don't tell me you've picked a puny Xavieran to romance, Sam! You can do better than those pimply young fellows next door, surely.'

Sam gave Zeba as frosty a look as she could conjure up. 'I don't know if *you're* in a position to say that, Zeba,' she said, trying to hold her nerve.

'God, you're not still going on about Gomesey, are you? I told you, I have all that stitched up nicely, so don't *worry*!'

Sam lowered her voice to a whisper. 'Well, your thing with your Gomesey is starting to look more than a little obvious.'

'Really?' Zeba suddenly looked nervous.

'Yes, really. And you want to watch that Lamboo doesn't find out or it's trouble with a big T for *both* you and old Gomes.'

'Actually, I've also been telling Zeba to be careful,' Natasha chipped in. 'I don't know what you see in him anyway, Zeba. He's so old, he must be at least thirty,' she added with a shudder.

'Well, it's not as if you get much choice in a girls' school, do you?' Zeba retorted defiantly, rapidly regaining her confidence. 'And there's only one thing I want from him. Once I have the Chemistry paper, I'm done.'

'Anyway, Sam, we wanted to ask you what you were talking about with Ice Queen Lily at break-time,' Natasha enquired, changing the subject.

'Oh, nothing much,' Sam said swiftly.

'Well, you looked really distracted when we came in after break.'

'No, I wasn't!' Sam hoped the tone of her voice was not overly defensive. 'It must have been my period pain distracting me. Look, I gotta go, really,' she pleaded. 'My mum's coming to pick me up today because we're going shopping to Connaught Place so she can get some sari blouses.' She realised that the more she elaborated, the more she would start panting and the more it would sound like the lie it was. And so, with a hurried, 'Okay, bye,' Sam turned and scampered towards the school buses. By the time her two classmates followed at their sexy, hip-rolling saunter, she'd hopefully be well hidden in the depths of the bus.

Also making her way out of the school that afternoon, Anita observed that Lily D'Souza was just ahead of her, going in the direction of the library. Her forehead furrowed in annoyance. The girl spent so much time there, was it any wonder she hadn't managed to make any friends yet, she found herself thinking uncharitably. She watched Lily disappear through the junior-school doors carrying a pile of books, not walking but sort of floating in, nose in the air, almost feline in her grace.

Anita had tried understanding her own reaction to Lily D'Souza, but, unusually for her, had come up only with blanks. Or theories she didn't especially like. Such as the faint physical attraction she felt for the girl, a reaction she had never had towards anyone before, male or female. Perhaps it was merely down to that hormonal high which prevailed in all-girls' schools, but Anita had so far not thought it necessary to partake of the collective angsting over matters of the heart that inevitably pervaded the senior school, Now she found herself not merely unable to ignore Lily's beauty but worse, much worse, Lily had also proven herself rather disturbingly to be a better student than anyone had thought possible. Anita found that aspect of the new girl most unsettling of all, not least because Anita had consistently held first place in her class ever since she had joined the school as a scholarship girl. It was, she knew, her scholastic prowess that had ensured her acceptance among girls much prettier and wealthier and sportier than her – all things that counted in a snobbish school like St Jude's.

Of course, Anita didn't mind a bit of academic competition. It made a change as no one else in her batch had ever bothered to take her on. However, there was the BIG scholarship that she had set her heart on the minute Miss Lamb had first told them of it. Instituted by the parents of an ex-student who had died of leukaemia many years ago, the Lalvani Scholarship was offered once every five years to an outstanding student of English to read Literature at Balliol College in Oxford. Everyone in the school had always assumed it would one day be Anita's – her own parents most of all, who had pinned all their hopes on their gifted daughter. Anita had grown up with the knowledge that she, as an only child, was the repository of her parents' dreams, of all the things they would never be able to achieve in their own lives. Which was why her father, determined to give his only child the opportunities he himself had never had, worked twelve-hour days in his lowly job as a lab assistant at the Pusa Institute, so that Anita could be given the extra tuition she needed and be bought all the books she wanted. The school scholarship she had won as a seven-year-old did not, unfortunately, cover the cost of these, nor the expense of school uniforms and winter coats and shoes. In the years of her growth spurt, her mother had painstakingly and skilfully taken out hems and cuffs, and turned frayed collars inside out. All so that Anita could continue to attend one of Delhi's most exclusive schools and not stick out like a sore thumb.

And now, here was this Lily D'Souza, landed on St Jude's so abruptly just when all that effort was about to pay off. Hard as it was for Anita to admit, Lily was clever, hard-working, and very, very good at English. Anita imagined how crushed her parents would be if she did not get to Oxford. It was imperative that Lily did not win the scholarship over her.

Chapter Eight

LONDON, 2008

Anita surveyed the grim grey building that was the BBC's White City premises. She had been chasing this placement at Television Centre for weeks, having been quick to spot a minuscule advert in *Ariel*, and ought to be totally chuffed at having jumped through numerous hoops to have finally got here. But all she could feel this morning, as she walked through the automated glass doors, was a flatness of spirit. A sense of utter futility of the stupid little goals she insisted on setting for herself that, in truth, really achieved no more than the faintest sense of smug self-satisfaction. Did anyone else care for one moment that she was about to start work at the biggest television studio in the world? Her colleagues back at the neanderthal World Service, her lazy bully of a boss, even Hugh? Did anyone care? Did they fuck! Even Ma, when she had mentioned it during her weekly phone call to Delhi, had merely delivered a bland Bengali version of 'Oh that's nice, dear' before telling her that yet *another* of her younger cousins was getting married. Anita's father would perhaps have been the one person who would have truly rejoiced, but he had died this past winter. It was still hard for Anita not to feel a push of tears behind her eyes every time she remembered that Baba was no longer there.

Having got a temporary security pass made, Anita walked towards the lifts. She had visited television centre once before, as a part of her training and orienteering with the Beeb, but could now remember only a vast space crammed with computer terminals and peopled by stressed-out journalists, none of whom had had the time or the inclination to make a bunch of rookies feel welcome. When she had found her way to the newsroom, it took only a moment to find that nothing had changed. That same vast space, only grubbier and noisier, and filled with, if not the same people, then just more of the same sort.

'I'm looking for Justin Hawke,' she said to a woman who was staggering past with a pile of newspapers.

'Him over there, red tie.' The woman gesticulated with her chin to a man talking on a phone held between ear and shoulder as he typed into his keyboard.

'Ta,' Anita muttered, wending her way over wires and cables before coming to a halt at the man's desk just as he put the phone down. 'Justin Hawke? Anita Roy,' she said.

'Who?' he asked in an unfriendly voice.

'Anita Roy from the World Service. I'm here for Kelly Hooper's maternity cover?'

'Ah yes. You're late,' he said irritably, loosening his tie to remove his top button.

Thanks, nice to meet you too, Anita thought before defending herself. 'Surely I can't be late?' she said. 'I was told quite clearly not to be here before ten on the first day as nobody would have the time to talk to—'

'Okay. Never mind. Editorial meeting's in five. Room sixty-seven. Coffees at the machine down the corridor.'

Not daring to ask where the toilets were, Anita made her

way out of the newsroom and in less than five minutes had found the toilets, coffee machine and Room sixty-seven. Feeling more sure of herself, she entered the room, coffee in hand, to find it already full. Justin, now divested completely of his red tie, was perched on a table and going through a sheaf of papers, scoring out some pages with a blue marker pen as though it gave him personal pleasure to trash someone's work. He looked blankly at Anita, making her imagine for one wild moment that he was about to ask her once again who she was. Luckily, he then merely nodded briefly and she slipped onto a vacant chair with relief. No introductions or welcomes then, which was perhaps just as well, given how disinterested everyone seemed in everyone else. It was the feature of some news-rooms, Anita knew, where the constant focus on war and other such significant world events led the people who worked there to be utterly scornful of their immediate surroundings, cosy first-world settings far removed from those places where *real* suffering lay.

She listened silently to the ideas that were being put forward. Not so much about distant wars but important first-world matters, oddly enough – Obama's Middle Eastern trip and the 'Israel for Obama' campaign, rumours that a Korean bank was looking to buy the Lehman Brothers, the WTO meetings in Geneva . . . Justin trashed most, with only one or two making it onto his scribbled list.

'You. Have you nothing to contribute?' he asked Anita suddenly.

She tried to maintain her composure and come up with something, despite being caught unawares. 'Umm, I read something about Hamleys opening up in India, with a company called Reliance . . .' Her voice started to waver as she saw a familiar look of condescension pass over Justin's face that she associated with some people who looked at her and saw only two things: 'Asian' and 'female'. 'Er, there may be a lighter story in there . . .' she trailed off, stiffening up in anticipation of a withering response from Justin. And, sure enough, in a few seconds it came.

'Lighter story?' he asked. Anita nodded, feeling stupid. 'And where do you think you've wandered into? Anglian Three Counties TV? In which case, of course, we could also do "Mrs Smith's cat got stuck in the laburnum again today". What do you think to that?'

There were a few small titters of laughter and Anita felt waves of mortification wash over her. So TV was as bitchy a place as Hugh had warned; filled with king-sized egos and drowning in testosterone. She waited until the meeting was over, noticing how little eye-contact or chatter there was among the people leaving the room. And she had thought Bush House was unwieldy and amorphous merely because you could sometimes sit in the canteen and not see one familiar face!

Without returning to the newsroom, Anita handed her pass back to the security desk at the door and walked right out of Television Centre within an hour of getting there. Her brush with television was over, and she hoped Justin Hawke was going to spend the rest of the day combing White Fucking City for her.

The disappointment of it hit her only as she boarded the tube and sat down on a tattered seat that was covered in grey chewing-gum stains. It would take her over an hour to get back home and, seeing that the charge on her mobile phone had run out, the first thing she'd have to do was call her boss and plead to be taken back. She'd probably have to offer to do a million night-shifts or – worse – the graveyard 2 a.m. slot before he'd agree. Even when he desperately needed every hand on deck, he was the sort of boss who managed to make his underlings feel he was doing them a personal favour when he assigned them work.

Anita suddenly felt totally defeated by her complete and utter failure to have made the right career decisions for herself, remembering with deepening regret how she had nearly gone into academia. But the traineeship offer from the BBC, unusually received while she was still in her final year at Oxford, had been so tempting. What had finally clinched it was the memory of being back in her Delhi home and going to sleep with her father's clapped-out transistor glued to her ear, the dulcet tones of the BBC World newsreader seeming then to represent a faraway world of immense privilege and honour.

The tube rattled along as Anita's thoughts travelled down an increasingly familiar path. What a terrible waste her two scholarships had been: the one that had put her through St Jude's, and the second, that much-coveted Lalvani endowment, that had despatched her to Oxford. What had been the point if that effort had merely culminated in a dead-end job where she had never felt valued? Where she would always remain a tiny cog in a massive machine that was, in fact, whirring on quite happily without her today. Where she worked ridiculous hours and got paid a pittance. Employment that afforded her a shoe-box flat attached to a gargantuan mortgage in a grubby part of one of the most polluted and crime-ridden cities of the world. Anita suddenly surveyed the empty tube compartment a little nervously. All she needed now was to be added to a growing list of crime figures already gathering in a police department somewhere! Luckily, however, the train had reached Shepherd's Bush and a couple with a pushchair were boarding her carriage.

She surreptitiously watched the couple coo at their baby, remembering to add her depressing record of failed relationships to the catalogue of disasters that her life was.

Even the fact that a nice guy like Hugh was coming around for dinner later tonight could offer no cheer. Anita looked away from the young couple and their baby, knowing without a doubt that real happiness would never, ever come to her – because she did not deserve it. Not after what she had done to Lily.

'*Fuck!*' Anita hissed, leaping away from the Le Creuset pot and sucking her scalded finger. She scrabbled frantically in her kitchen drawer. 'Dammit, I could've sworn I had a blasted thingy in here. Thingy, whatchummacallit! Wooden ladle, wooden ladle!' she yelled in frustration, knowing what a ridiculous picture she must make, bumbling about in her kitchen and shouting loudly to herself. 'Ah, there you are, you crafty little sonovagun,' she said, straightening up and wielding a pale pristine ladle that had clearly never met any form of food before. Keeping her distance from the pot this time, Anita prodded resentfully at the bubbling spaghetti. How long was she supposed to give the damn thing? she wondered. It looked like the whole mess was fusing now into one great wiggly lump. She had a vague memory of having once seen Sam throw a dash of olive oil into a bowl of pasta to 'separate' it, but couldn't for the life of her recall if that was after or before the water came out.

Anita, who usually survived on the offerings of the nearest Marks & Spencers' food hall, could think of many good reasons to never, ever, *ever* cook, but the truth was she owed Hugh this meal. In the two months since they'd been seeing each other he'd already rather expertly rustled up three delicious home-made meals for her in his flat, even turning out a pretty passable chicken jalfrezi on the last occasion, albeit using a bottled sauce and lots of Tabasco. It wasn't that she needed to compete or anything, and far be it for her to try and impress a man with feminine wiles. But she really had needed to demonstrate that she was capable of *something* after her shaming experience at White City that morning, and Hugh certainly seemed worth the effort. Yes, even this, Anita thought, casting a rueful eye around her tiny kitchen, which today looked as if a bomb had devastated it, with utensils scattered everywhere and the windows all fogged up with the heat. After placing the colander in the sink, she picked up a pair of kitchen mitts and gingerly approached her pot of bubbling spaghetti. Holding it ahead of her as far as she could, she staggered back to the sink and flung its load into the sieve with a frightened yelp. When the steam had cleared, she saw that apart from a small handful that had fortuitously landed in the sieve, the rest of the spaghetti was in the sink, clogging the drain, all over the draining-board and even trembling like startled worms across the coffee mug and muesli bowl that she had washed up after breakfast.

'Fuckety, fuckety, fuck, fuck, FUCK!' Anita yelled, trying to scoop the spaghetti lying in the drain back into the colander, thereby singeing her fingers again. Tears sprang to her eyes. If anyone did need a cook it was *her* – not Bubbles, who, despite her battery of chefs, only ever ate like a rabbit; and not, Sam who, despite having Masooma, could herself turn out the most delicious and complicated dishes so effortlessly. But Anita had been the clever swot when they were all young and she recalled now, with a twinge of shame, how she had used her intellectual prowess as a convenient excuse to avoid her mother's occasional half-hearted efforts to get her into the kitchen. Her father hadn't helped, of course, dear old Baba, so keen that his gifted daughter should not have to concern herself with such mundane and commonplace things as housework. That she would need culinary skills one day to impress a *man* would not even have crossed his mind, of course.

129

It was as the doorbell rang that Anita finally started to cry. Blubbering uncontrollably, she buzzed the entry phone and heard Hugh taking the steps two at a time up to her third-floor flat. When she opened the door he looked at her in astonishment as she stood before him, hot tears rolling down flushed cheeks, a length of spaghetti looped over her hair.

'Whoa, Anita, sweetheart, what's up?' he cried, concerned at first by the most uncharacteristic tears, but starting to grin as she narrated the sorry saga of her day between great gulps of air – her disastrous day at television centre and what now looked like an aborted dinner plan too. He stepped into the kitchen and in a glance took in the steamed windows, the upturned colander and the clumps of spaghetti solidifying firmly on the draining-board.

Seeing the look of helplessness on Anita's face, Hugh opened a few cupboards until he found a roll of bin-liners. Expertly using the kitchen brush to scoop the mess back into the colander, he tipped the over-cooked spaghetti into the bin before tying it up and tossing it to one side. Then he washed up Anita's breakfast things and stacked them back onto the rack before turning to her. 'You have a few take-away menus lying around, I imagine?' he said, his tone ironic but gentle.

Anita, considering how oddly sexy it was to behold a man performing traditional female tasks, nodded. Those she did not need to hunt for, luckily, and she quickly produced a pack from the drawer of her telephone table.

'Chinese? . . . Lebanese? . . . Thai?' she mumbled, shuffling through them, still snivelling.

Hugh covered her kitchen in three long strides and, first getting rid of the spaghetti that was still adorning her hair, grabbed her in a passionate embrace.

'Oh,' she said, dropping the take-away menus to the floor.

A few kisses had been exchanged on their previous dates but Anita wasn't one to rush these things generally, preferring to be sure she'd found an *intellectual* soul mate before leaping into bed for the messy stuff. This, however, was different, and she could feel her loins stir as Hugh's tongue parted her mouth hungrily, and then she felt the hardness form in his groin as his hands pressed into the small of her back.

'Oh,' she said again, as he took a breath, not usually at such a loss for words and conscious that she sounded like a Victorian miss being 'taken' for the first time. But Hugh's left hand had slipped up her tee-shirt and was now kneading her breast rather pleasurably, his thumb playing gently with one erect nipple. He steered her towards the futon in her living room and they fell onto it, yanking each other's tee-shirts off.

Hugh had joined the lunchtime news team from a satellite TV channel only two months ago, and Anita had liked him immediately for making the shift in a direction that was oppos ite to the one everyone else in broadcast journalism seemed determined to make. 'TV is an intellectual wasteland,' he had said in the Bush House café on his first day, adding wryly, 'and I figured somewhere along the way that I had exactly the right face for radio too.' Anita had once declared vehemently to her friends that she would never go to bed with a man who could not make her laugh. So it was just as well that Hugh had made her laugh on that very first day – as from what she could tell, she was now quite firmly in bed with him. Well, firmly on her futon, to be specific, but with no clothes on and busily yanking Hugh's belt and jeans off too.

'Let's open up the futon, be more comf—' she tried to suggest weakly, but he silenced her with another ardent kiss, the force of which pushed her onto the mattress. Hugh ran his hands down Anita's naked body, over her breasts and along the curve of her hip, before lifting her thigh upwards to meet him. She gasped as he entered her, remembering that it had been at least two years since her last sexual encounter, but soon she was accommodating Hugh's urgent thrusts, running her fingers up and down his back and buttocks and scratching him lightly. He groaned and buried his face in her neck as his speed increased and his entire body started to judder. Quite suddenly, and before she was ready, he had come with a guttural cry, slumping over her body as she felt his wetness seep slowly out of her. Anita, remembering too late that she should have at least enquired about condoms, lay quietly, playing with Hugh's back and shoulders, before he raised himself on one elbow and smiled down at her.

'Pardon me, but I couldn't quite help the haste, Ms Roy,' he said, cocking a faintly embarrassed brow at her.

'Mmmm, 's'all right, be my guest,' she mumbled, also a little discomfited suddenly.

Hugh ran his free hand over Anita's breasts and belly, examining her body before returning to her face and whispering, 'Your fault entirely – you're absolutely beautiful, d'you know that? Especially when you drape spaghetti so fetchingly all over your hair. Don't ever, ever, *ever* greet me like that again. I'm a complete sucker for women wearing spaghetti in their hair.'

Anita smiled and moaned slightly as she felt his hand reach her crotch. She closed her eyes as Hugh started to rub the tender point of her clitoris, leaning down to flick his tongue over her nipples, her navel, and then travelling further down to bury his face in her mound. She could feel the room around her rock and sway as evening sunlight played over their fused bodies. Usually it was exactly at this point, the moment she was ready to climax, that Lily's face would appear. The first time it had happened – years ago, in Anita's small student bedsit at Oxford – she had frantically pushed off her rather startled paramour, a final-year student from Nigeria, and told him later that she had just realised she was lesbian. But, later, with the passage of the years and some further sexual experimentation, Anita had realised that it wasn't some kind of latent lesbianism that was preventing her ability to orgasm freely, but merely guilt. Guilt over Lily and all that Anita had robbed her of. It was as simple as that. And as irretrievable. Which was why it was such a surprise to Anita that evening when Hugh, skilfully and unhurriedly, finally brought her to climax in a way she had not known before.

An hour later, Anita woke from the deepest post-coital nap she had ever had. Slowly surfacing from her sleep, she watched Hugh, still stark naked, wandering around her flat. He had found the bottle of Chablis that had been chilling in the fridge and had even managed to locate her corkscrew. As he sat down on her coffee table, holding the bottle between his knees to pull off the foil, she stretched her arms over her head and let out a yawn. He looked up at her and smiled, and Anita felt her heart do a small flip. She was not usually given to what she considered to be *corporeal* responses, but this tall grey-haired man – so comfortable with his body and seemingly rather taken with hers – was certainly having the strangest effect on her. Physically weakening her to the extent that she felt quite willing to simply lie on her futon for the rest of the evening, watching him pad naked around her flat.

'I was going to wake you with a coffee mug of Chablis,' he said. 'Couldn't find the wine glasses.'

'Up there,' she replied, pointing to a John Lewis box on the bookshelf above her head. 'Perched above Dostoyevsky. For easier reach,' she explained.

Anita sat up on the futon while Hugh put the glasses down on a side table and knelt next to her. Gently cupping the small globes of her breasts in his hands, he leaned down to kiss one and then the other, before dipping his finger into his wine glass and rubbing a bit of the liquid onto the aureole of both nipples. Anita groaned and thrust herself forward but Hugh picked up their glasses and, giving one to her, said, 'Now, now, that's quite enough of that, Ms Roy. Didn't think when I first laid eyes on you at the Bush House canteen that you'd be so . . . so *insatiable.*'

'Why, what did you think?' asked Anita, trying to make her query sound nonchalant as she took a sip of the wine.

'Ah, every new lover's first question . . . what did I think of you?' Hugh replied, frowning into his glass as though trying hard to remember. 'I thought – believe it or not – "prim" . . . I thought "sharp" . . . I thought, "cor, nice tight ass under such a staid pencil skirt"!'

Anita thumped him with a cushion before leaning forward to lick away the drop of wine that had landed on his chin. After they had kissed again, she leaned back on her futon and stretched her legs, quite amazed at how unselfconscious this man made her feel about her bare body. Especially at a time when she worried that she had started to put on weight around her bum. It sure helped that he seemed so genuinely appreciative of her, despite what she knew was not a perfect shape: legs too thin, breasts too wide apart, and a bum that was finally acquiring the right shape for saris at a time when she hardly got the chance to wear one.

There was always something very attractive about a man who found *you* attractive, she thought, watching Hugh over the top of her wine glass. But she'd have probably fancied Hugh even if he hadn't given her the time of day. She knew he was forty-something, possibly a good ten years older than her, but she'd always been attracted to older men, the ones her age invariably coming across as callow and self-obsessed. And Hugh looked rather good for mid-forties too – a full head of crisp grey hair and a face that crinkled into not unattractive laugh-lines when he smiled. His body was nice too: slim and toned (which, in Anita's book, was far preferable to muscular beefcake) and on the pale side, but with a small sprinkling of dark hair on his chest and arms. He certainly seemed completely at ease with his nakedness. Realising how much she was concentrating on Hugh's physical aspects when there was so much more, Anita felt suddenly very lucky. Men like Hugh didn't come by very often – she hoped there wasn't a catch in this somewhere. She'd already gathered that he was a divorcee, with two pre-teen children who lived with their mother in Milton Keynes. He said he saw them for a long weekend once a month, but Anita had not met them yet. But, apart from that, there seemed to be no skeletons in his closet – unlike hers. She crossed her fingers for nothing untoward to emerge now, when she was already smitten. Then, sighing, she put her glass down to go to the loo.

'You haven't told me much about yourself, y'know,' Hugh said, picking up a newspaper from the pile on Anita's coffee table.

'Oh, haven't I?' Anita asked, pretending surprise. She was often described as reticent, and had come to rather like that description, but this gorgeous man was worth a little effort. 'There's not a lot to say,' she said shyly. 'I grew up in India and won a scholarship to study English at Balliol, which was what brought me here to England.'

Anita paused, seeing the familiar look of admiration that always passed over people's faces when she mentioned her Oxford antecedents. And the scholarship. Never once had she told anyone of what a close thing it had been.

'And?' Hugh prompted.

'And not a lot more . . . I got onto the BBC's training scheme and chose radio for the same reasons that you recently did – more intelligent medium, more insidiously powerful, less inane, not having to dress up and put make-up on at 3 a.m., not having to work with people like Justin Hawke who think they rule the world instead of just some crappy department . . . you know.'

'I didn't mean the job. Think I know enough about the delights of that! I meant, relationships, marriage?'

Anita shook her head. 'No to the latter, a few of the former. Nothing too serious.'

'And family?'

'Oh, tiny. Just Ma and me. My father died last winter of a sudden heart attack.'

'Oh, I'm sorry to hear that. So your mother lives by herself?'

Anita nodded. It was still a painful thought. 'Yes, still in the old place in Delhi, although she's talking about packing up and leaving for Calcutta where her siblings live.'

'So you have no family here? I'd sort of half-expected that you came from one of those large spreading Midlands families with a crazy network of cousins and aunties and uncles. Like my old uni mate, Jaz. He was always dashing off to attend some wedding or birthday, come the weekend.'

'No, no extended family, thankfully,' Anita laughed, before hoisting herself up to make her way to the toilet. Pulling her tee-shirt on, she corrected herself. 'Oh, two actually – Sam and Bubbles. Childhood friends from Delhi and the closest I'll ever have to wanting a family. You'll meet them soon enough. Something tells me they'll absolutely adore you.'

Chapter Nine

DELHI, 1993

On the evening of the last day of term, Sam looked at the dining table with pleasure – her darling mother had done herself proud again. There were chicken kebabs and paneer kaathi rolls for the vegetarians, and an assortment of mini pizzas, veg and non-veg, thoughtfully separated onto two plates. Her mother, having recently attended a course in making confectionery at the Hyatt Regency, had gone to town on the sweet trolley. Sam saw walnut fudge and chocolate brownies and a bowlful of jujubes looking like small round jewels in an assortment of colours and sparkling with encrusted sugar. She popped a red one into her mouth and chewed delightedly. As Mrs Hussain came bustling in with a large pitcher of fruit punch, Sam darted across the room to give her a hug.

'My mamma is the cleverest, nicest mum in the world,' she said, as her laughing mother tried to prevent the drink from slopping over onto the floor.

Mrs Hussain put the jug down on the table and wiped its edges with a serviette. 'Well, seeing that we'll be up in Simla for your birthday, I thought it only fair that you should have a chance to celebrate with your friends before we go.'

'And it gives me the chance to look at some pretty girls too,' Haroon said, loping into the room. 'My mum's *so* considerate,' he added, kissing his mother loudly on her cheek. Mrs Hussain flapped him away with her serviette, turning her attention back to the table.

'Oh *bhaiyya*, don't spoil Mum's arrangement,' Sam wailed as her brother reached out to pluck a couple of pizzas off their platter.

'Don't worry, I'm sure there's more. Mum's always ready to feed the whole Indian army,' he drawled through a mouth full of dough.

Mrs Hussain was not amused. 'Sami's right, Haroon *beta*, don't take things from here. Ask Qadirbhai in the kitchen to get you a plate of food if you're hungry. He made chicken biriyani for lunch. Go now, stop troubling your sister. It's her day today.'

Sam exchanged a smile with her mother as she tried to hustle a reluctant Haroon out of the room. She had really hoped that her brother would have other plans for the evening, but he seemed quite determined to stay in tonight and cramp her style. He'd never shown so much interest in attending any of her birthday parties before, but then all her friends had been gawky and unattractive until about a year ago. She slapped her forehead, remembering that she *still* hadn't got around to telling Bubbles that there was no point moping after Haroon. She really should have done it before this party but there hadn't been the time today. Oh, what a bloody mess. And what a *pain* brothers were sometimes.

'Oh, I think they're here,' she yelped as she heard a car at the gate. Peering through the French windows, an inquisitive Haroon squashed up next to her, she saw the first of her guests – Natasha – sashay down the drive, looking sexy in a miniskirt and tank top. 'God, it's no wonder old Nats has so many Xavierans chasing her,' Sam said as she unlocked the door. 'She looks like a model when she dresses like that. I can't believe her mum and dad never seem to mind her wearing such skimpy clothes. It must be due to them having lived in America. And it sure makes girls like Zeba massively jealous.'

'Well, thank *God* for parents who don't mind their daughters in skimpy clothes,' Haroon said fervently, peering admiringly through the glass at Natasha's bare shoulders.

Sam giggled. 'Well, Nats' dad was India's ambassador to America before he retired, and that's the only reason why he's not like the other dads. Don't be expecting too many skimpy tops tonight, bro,' she threw over her shoulder as she skipped onto the verandah.

Sam and Natasha screamed in pleasure as they greeted each other at the door, which was perhaps a little dramatic given that they had spent all day at school together. 'Oh look, there's Zeba too,' Sam said as she spotted a grey Fiat pulling up on the drive. Unlike Natasha, who had come in a chauffeur-driven car, Zeba was escorted up the drive by her father, the rather dour and professorial Dr Khan, an Urdu academic at Jamia Millia Islamia University. Sam knew the score. Zeba came from an aristocratic Muslim family that was far more conservative than her own, and her parents seemed to live in constant fear that their beautiful daughter would somehow be led astray. Sam called out for her mother, knowing that Zeba's father would not depart until he had made sure that responsible adults were in attendance.

Finally Mr Khan left, duly reassured by Mrs Hussain's comforting assertions that she had no plans other than to supervise the party. When he had driven off and Sam's mother had returned to the kitchen, Zeba said, 'Thank God he's gone. Now this damn thing can come off.' Before Sam and Natasha's astounded gaze, she ripped off the loose tee-shirt she had come in, revealing a skimpy little halter-top underneath. Sam feared for the state of her brother's heart at the sight of all this female flesh.

As though on cue, Haroon sauntered onto the verandah. Sam resisted the urge to laugh at his efforts to look non-chalant as she started to introduce him. She knew he wouldn't recognise most of her friends from the last birthday party they had all attended at her house, seeing how much they had all transformed in the past two years.

As more of her classmates arrived, Sam was suddenly grateful for her brother's presence as she was finding it hard to keep up with who had had a drink and who was still waiting for one. She threw him a grateful look as he solici-tously started pouring out the punch. He certainly knew how to turn on the charm when required, and wasn't *that* bad really when she thought about it. He was even being extra-courteous to Bubbles, despite her persistently goofy air. Hopefully he wasn't overdoing it and giving the poor girl mixed messages again.

The last girls to arrive were Nimmi, Tanu and, a few seconds later, Lily, by which time Sam's mother's capacious living room sounded as though a screaming match was being held inside it. Sam greeted the newly arrived group warmly with a hug each, noticing that Lily looked at first startled and then a bit pleased at the unexpected embrace. Haroon ambled across in their direction with a tray of drinks, and Sam introduced him to her final guests.

'Of course, yes, I remember meeting both of you at the Residency Club recently. One of their Sunday lunches, wasn't it?' he said to Tanu and Nimmi, adding cheekily, 'Do you two always hang out as a pair?'

While they giggled, he turned to Lily and shook her hand

as Sam said, 'You wouldn't have met Lily before, Haroon *bhaiyya*, so you can stop racking your poor brain now. Lily joined our class recently from a school in Mussourie.' Just as she would have wanted, there was no clever repartee from her brother for Lily, which was just as well for Sam would have hated the uppity Lily to think she had a gabbling moron for a brother. But the reason for his sudden silence was clear. Sam could see it straightaway. It was written all over poor Haroon's face in that very first moment he laid eyes on Lily. A dazed look overcame his normally twinkly eyes and colour rose almost imperceptibly over his collar. His Adam's apple bobbed nervously as he wordlessly lifted the drinks tray and held it out towards Lily.

For some reason she couldn't comprehend, this knowledge distressed Sam terribly, even though she was not unused to the often capricious nature of her brother's silly crushes. Here one day, gone the next, she thought angrily to herself as she tried unsuccessfully to join in the cheery chatter swirling around her, her heart beating curiously fast. She could barely hear Natasha screeching with merriment as she narrated some inane joke about a man suffering from 'kneesles, toelio and smallcox', so loud was the crashing inside her head.

Sam looked around the room, filled with celebrating friends and classmates. She watched all the girls her stupid, annoying brother had his pick of – sexy Nats in her mini-skirt and sleek, helmet-like hair; beautiful Zeba with curly brown tresses falling over naked shoulders to her waist; innocent little Tanu who couldn't say boo to a goose; clever, sparky Anita; the clownish Nimmi who never failed to make everyone laugh; and poor, poor Bubbles, who had already silently given him her heart. Among that feast of beautiful girls, it was *Lily*, of all people, whom Haroon had fallen for that night.

Later, Sam would look back at her seventeenth birthday party little able to forgive herself for having led her sweet and trusting brother so unwittingly to the gallows of Lily's cold heart. That was how it felt to Sam for years afterwards; that the wheels of tragedy had been set in motion that night, and it was all her fault.

SIMLA, 1993

The Hussain family departed for their summer holiday early the following morning, but even on the drive up to the Himachal Hills, Sam could see that Haroon had started to mope. Gone was her brother's usual sunny chatter-box demeanour, and in its place was the kind of behaviour that Sam would have expected from a tormented poet. The hairpin bends usually made Haroon whoop with pleasure, especially as he watched Sam turning green and nauseous. But today her brother merely sat listlessly in the car as the plains disappeared gradually from view. To everyone's astonishment, Haroon even refused the party left-overs that their mother had packed to keep them going on their journey, when the car was stopped at Barog for an impromptu picnic. Sam exchanged an amused look with her parents when, after passing up his favourite mini pizzas, Haroon wandered across to dangle his feet in a nearby stream instead. 'As long as it is not a tummy upset,' their mother said.

After arriving in Simla, Sam tried all sorts of encouragement: admiring the splendid views from their aunt's new villa and remarking casually how pleasant the air in Simla was compared to that in Delhi. She read loudly from the papers a news item about the heat wave in the plains, so bad it was claiming lives. But it seemed nothing would budge her brother from his doleful position of already counting the days left until the Hussain family's return to Delhi. Simla was, quite simply, all wrong – because Simla was where Lily was not.

In the first few days of the holiday, and whenever they were by themselves, Haroon quizzed Sam furiously about her new classmate as they spent their evenings walking up and down the Mall. Despite her annoyance at him behaving like a mooning lapdog, Sam faithfully told her brother all she knew about Lily. Even the part about her being Lamboo's granddaughter and the mystery surrounding her absent father. *Especially* that part – because by now Sam was desperate to find something, anything, that would put her brother off his growing crush. Uncharacteristically, she even deliberately left out things about Lily that she thought might serve only to increase his approbation – Lily's cleverness, her fantastic command of English, her excellent grades – telling him instead about how cold she had been to everyone and how universally disliked she was in school. Sam was, in truth, terribly envious of the effect Lily was having on her adored brother, but she convinced herself that it was worry over how he was liable to be hurt. Haroon was, of course, merely scornful of her sisterly concern.

'You're all jealous of her,' he said when Sam tried to explain how even girls as tranquil and sweet-tempered as Bubbles and Tanu had grown to hate Lily D'Souza.

'Why on earth would we be jealous, Haroon?' she beseeched.

'Because she's more beautiful than the whole lot of you put together.'

'That's not true at all! Zeba and Natasha, those two are beautiful at least, and . . .'

'Not a patch on Lily,' Haroon said firmly, and Sam saw the familiar clench of his jaw as he made up his mind.

143

'Then tell me why girls like me and Anita and Bubbles are not jealous of Zeba and Natasha. They're a lot prettier than any of us,' she countered.

Haroon pondered that for a minute before saying, 'I think it's because you have all known each other since you were kids. Whereas poor Lily's the newcomer. Everyone always hates the outsider. Especially when they're better than everyone else.'

'*Better?!*' Sam's voice rose to an indignant screech.

Her brother smiled his cheeky grin. 'See? Admit it. Even you're a little bit jealous of her . . .'

'I'm not!' Sam expostulated.

'Look, why are we arguing?' Haroon said, putting his arm around his sister's shoulders to calm her. 'We're still each other's best friend, aren't we?'

For a moment Sam contemplated defending herself further, but even though she recognised Haroon's flattery, she couldn't help softening at such open acknowledgement that she was, in the end, his best friend. Girls like Lily would come and go, but she was forever his sister. It was comforting too to remember that Haroon's crushes generally lasted no more than a month or two. She should try not to mind that it was Lily this time, instead of one from the usual line-up of distant Hollywood film stars. If she waited patiently, this new idiocy would surely pass.

'It's getting dark, they'll be worrying about us soon,' Haroon said presently. 'C'mon, upsy-daisy, let's go.' They walked through the tumble-down churchyard back to the road, crunching pine needles underfoot, arms linked. Sam could see the evening mists rolling in from the surrounding mountains and shivered, wrapping her arms around her body. Haroon yanked off his sweatshirt and put it over her shoulders. She threw him a grateful look.

'Thanks bro,' she said, 'I should've remembered to take mine.'

'Easy to forget how damp and cold even summer evenings can get up here in Simla. Don't worry, I'm not cold yet,' he said, rubbing the goose bumps that were showing up on his exposed forearms. 'It's no wonder the British built these hill stations if you think of the dust and heat of the plains. This was their capital, of course, but Mussourie was popular too.'

Sam sighed tolerantly. She knew Haroon had slipped in the name 'Mussourie' only to talk more about Lily, but she wasn't going to get drawn into that dialogue again. She would regally ignore this crush until it had blown over and *he* came to *her* for sympathy. Whether she would commiserate with him when that time came or merely say 'told-you-so' was a matter she would decide later.

They passed the old church and little wisteria-clad cottages with names like 'Windermere' and 'Ambleside' in companionable silence. After a steep walk uphill that robbed them completely of breath and conversation, they reached their Victorian villa, bought recently by their aunt from a reclusive Anglo-Indian widower to become the family's summer retreat.

The siblings were greeted by the fragrance of chicken pulao cooking as they walked into the house, and the raucous sound of their mother and aunt playing rummy. Sam's father was wandering around the front hallway, clutching a newspaper and wearing his spectacles on his forehead atop a hangdog expression on his face.

'Oh Dad, you look like you've been searching for a quiet corner all day,' Sam giggled, giving him a hug.

'How long have they been at it?' Haroon asked, gesturing to the two women who were seated before the fire and oblivious to all else around them.

'You know your Auntie Gul,' Mr Hussain said mildly of his formidable elder sister, 'and, I don't know what it is but something happens to your mother the minute they get together.'

'You mean Mum gets transformed instantly from Dutiful Wife to Screaming Teenager, don't you?' Haroon joked.

His father laughed and shook his head in resigned fashion. 'I just can't turn them off,' he said, dropping into an armchair in the hallway and opening up his paper.

'Oh don't sit here, Dad, it's so draughty,' Sam protested.

'Apart from the fact that you'll ruin your eyes – what is this bulb, twenty watts or something?' Haroon said, peering under a faded silk lampshade.

Sam left them to it, going upstairs to the dear little room she had been assigned under the eaves. She hadn't yet replied to a letter from Bubbles that had arrived yesterday. It was most unusual for Bubbles to put pen to paper unless she absolutely had to, and Sam knew she must have been in a severely anxious frame of mind. Two whole pages too, poor Bubbles!

She took the letter out of her bedside drawer and read it again before constructing a reply in her head. This was serious stuff. From the time she was sixteen, Bubbles had been besieged with marriage proposals from the conservative business community, and even though she had extricated a promise from her parents that they would not marry her off until she had finished school, it had always been a close thing. Their classmates had been horrified when Bubbles had first mentioned the M-word, but Sam had understood that in the world that Bubbles came from, marriage at sixteen or seventeen wasn't that unusual. Her father had come up from being a delivery boy at a wholesale warehouse in the back streets of Chandni Chowk, going on to own a string of glittering sari shops across Karol Bagh, recently even opening his latest showroom in Connaught Place. Even though Mr Malhotra had been proud to use his newfound wealth to send his three daughters to Delhi's finest convent school, he drew the line quite firmly at university education. 'What can college-vollege teach you, *beti*?' he had reputedly enquired of Bubbles in a tone of genuine bafflement. Sam knew that Bubbles wasn't particularly keen on putting herself through another three gruelling years of education – school was imposition enough – but marriage was a scary thought to them all. Poor Bubbles wouldn't know the first thing about running a house or bringing up kids – or even the birds and the bees, as far as Sam knew. Besides, to complicate things further, Bubbles was now in love with Haroon.

Bubbles' anxieties were evident in the massive babyish scrawl that seemed to have been written without pause:

Oh Sam, this time my parents are just determined. They are not even listening to me about the Board Exams. The Boy is living in London with his parents. He did his school and everything there. He will be like an Englishman and I am sure I will hate him and he will hate me and his parents will hate me. But mummy-pappa are this time not even hearing one word I say and rather keep saying what about your sisters, two younger sisters, you must think of them. Why should I think of them – this is my life!!! And you know where my heart is given (not using HIS name, you understand???) Oh, I don't know what to do, Sam. I wish you were here. When are you all coming back to Delhi? Please come back soon and save me from this mess before it is too late!!! I am not going anywhere for the hols as mummy-pappa want to measure me and get the clothes and all made for my troo . . . tru . . .

A few scratches and squiggles followed and Sam's soft heart bled for her poor frantic friend so far away. Not that the

147

presence of their daughter's best friend would have stopped Mr and Mrs Malhotra in what sounded like very determined plans, but at least Sam could have provided a shoulder for Bubbles to cry on, had she been in Delhi. And she could have explained properly to Bubbles too about Haroon, persuading her gently to extinguish the candle she so hopefully and foolishly held for him.

Sam took a pen and paper from her drawer. It would have been so much better to elaborate on all this face to face, rather than in a letter. But this, she had to admit, was easier. Sam could imagine the wounded look that would have overwhelmed Bubbles' normally soft brown eyes had she been sitting in front of her and didn't think she could have borne it. If one had to deliver hurtful news, this was perhaps the more merciful way, even though Sam knew she was being cowardly. She bent her head and started to write, trying unsuccessfully to shut out the boisterous noise of Haroon and Auntie Gul tunelessly singing a Hindi film duet downstairs.

DELHI, 1993

Back in Delhi, three days later, Bubbles had for the first time concluded that the summer holidays were in fact a terrible chore. They had descended extremely inconsiderately upon her just after she had mustered up the courage to tell Sam about her feelings for Haroon. For all Bubbles knew, Sam might even have communicated that to Haroon by now, and he too could be longing to be with her, rather than up in Simla with his family. It was hard to know for sure if Haroon loved her back in the way she hoped, as he'd always been nice to her. But he was nice to *everyone*. That was the problem.

Even that baby niece who had visited the Hussain household recently and clambered all over Haroon, pulling at his nose and hair, only got an indulgent smile and a comical little lecture as it was held up in the air by its armpits. One never saw Haroon being anything but cheerful and polite, even to old people and animals and babies. That was what Bubbles loved most of all about him.

She looked at the framed photo that had been taken at Sam's house recently and now took pride of place on her bedside table. It showed Sam and Bubbles in their school uniforms, flanked by Haroon and his mum, a burst of red roses on a creeper above them. Haroon's dad had taken the picture and must have said something funny as they were all laughing, Sam with her eyes closed and her head thrown right back. It was the last thing Bubbles looked at every night, loving the sight of Haroon's laughing brown eyes looking right out of the picture frame and into her room. No one had ever thought it odd that she had this picture by her bedside, as she had been a part of Sam's family since the start of their friendship in kindergarten.

Something told Bubbles that her instincts weren't wrong about Haroon's feelings for her. Why else would his eyes soften in that way when he glanced at her? And why would he call her 'gorgeous' or 'beautiful' and insist, as he had done outside school that day, on giving her a lift home when everyone knew that her driver would be waiting for her? Like her, he too must like the fact that they already knew each other so well. Besides, his parents would love to have her as their daughter-in-law, seeing that she was almost their daughter anyway. Of course, the Hindu–Muslim thing would come up, but both families would surely overcome that, given that no one was too hung up on such things these days and Sam's wasn't the most orthodox Muslim family anyway. Even if they were, Bubbles knew she would happily convert to Islam if it meant she could marry Haroon.

But here she was, planning so far ahead when, there in the next room, her parents were plotting to marry her off to some stranger in London. And Haroon – to whom she had not even been able to *say* anything yet – was far away in bloody Simla!

Bubbles got up, sighing in resignation as she heard her mother calling stridently for her from downstairs. She dawdled on her way down the steps, knowing that it would be something to do with this London family her parents were getting so horribly excited about. As if she was to marry the whole damn family and not just their son.

She found her mother sitting on the sofa in the lounge, an array of blue velvet boxes spread out on the marble coffee table as a hopeful agent from Tribhuvandas Bhimji Zaveri Jewellers hovered nearby.

'*Beti*, come and help me choose one of these *ranihaars*,' her mother said, looking in confusion at an array of ornate necklaces spread out before her. 'Also we need a ruby set. Or emerald set? Which do you prefer? Maybe you should have both. Those Rahejas will be expecting God-knows-what-all.'

Bubbles sat down heavily on the sofa. She didn't want to argue in front of the jeweller but this was all getting too much. 'Ma, I told you, I'm not getting married now, okay? I'm not even finished with high school yet!'

Her mother merely smiled at the man from the jewellery store and said, 'See how these girls always behave when you first mention the word "marriage". Then, three days later they will be whispering on the phone and giggling and whatnot with their fiancé!'

'Maaa, this is really not fuss and *nakhra*. I really don't want to get married now. I think I want to go to college instead. All my friends will be going.'

'All your friends will be going to college because all your friends will be getting the marks. What marks are you going to get, hanh? Zero, that's what. Marriage to a rich boy is the only scholarship you are going to get, *beti.*'

Bubbles subsided into silence. Her mother was right about that. All her classmates would probably end up in the posh colleges like St Stephen's and Lady Shri Ram while her marks would at best get her into the South Delhi Polytechnic to study textile designing or something lowly like that. She contemplated telling her mother about Haroon instead, doing some kind of deal with her parents whereby she would agree to get married but only if it were to Haroon. Then her mother could buy all the jewellery she wanted and her father could plan the biggest wedding in Delhi, and she would be the happiest bride in the world.

Bubbles looked dolefully out of the window, knowing that strategy wouldn't work either as it was really *The Rahejas* her parents wanted her to marry, not any old anybody. And certainly not a boy of her own choice, and most certainly not a Muslim! Besides, Haroon's parents would probably not be keen for their son to get married until he'd finished with college and found a job. Bubbles held her tongue, her heart filling with sadness. She couldn't very well announce in front of the Tribhuvandas Bhimji Zaveri man that she loved someone else and not this Raheja in London. Not when her mother was already telling him about their good fortune in landing such a fine catch.

Bubbles listlessly watched the gardener put his water-hose down to collect a bunch of letters from the postman at the gate. Almost instinctively, she knew there would be one from Sam. She got up from the sofa to race out of the house and collect it.

Grabbing the bundle from the startled gardener as he made

151

his way down the garden path, Bubbles sat down on one of the wicker chairs in the verandah, riffling madly through them. There it was, with a Simla postmark on the stamp! Impatiently tearing it open, Bubbles scanned the contents and then read them again more slowly. It couldn't be. Haroon in love with *Lily*? Bubbles looked at the wet potted plants on the verandah, the lawn being watered beyond, and suddenly felt the muggy heat of the July day climb into her throat and choke her. Crumpling Sam's letter in one hand, she got up, not seeing that the rest of the mail had fallen into a puddle on the verandah floor. Dragging her feet back into the house, she heard her mother's voice through a tunnel.

'See, I have narrowed it down to three sets, Bubbles *beti*, one ruby, one emerald and one zirconium which is looking just like diamonds. Now I need you to make the final choice. Come. *You'll* be the one wearing these, not me.' Mrs Malhotra threw a conspiratorial wink at the jeweller, who smiled sagely.

In a daze and still clutching her letter, Bubbles sat next to her mother, who excitedly held one set after another over her daughter's chest, angling her head this way and that, while the jeweller obligingly held up a mirror so that Bubbles could admire herself too.

What Bubbles saw in the mirror – as clear as anything – was a girl whose heart had just shattered into a hundred tiny little bits. It was shocking that she could see it so plainly while neither her mother nor the jeweller could spot her invisible heartbreak at all.

Chapter Ten

LONDON, 2008

Sam wandered through the basement of Selfridges, seeing nothing that could tempt her. She understood fully the way in which retail therapy helped other women, but found it never worked for her. For one, her kitchen was already overflowing with all manner of aspirational consumer durables; a whole rack of Le Creuset cookware in tasteful duck-egg blue, a top-of-the-range Heals cabinet stuffed full of wine and whisky glasses, and another just for plates and dishes. She turned a corner and wandered down another aisle – even that gleaming Rancilio cappuccino machine over there had been a recent purchase and now took up precious worktop space next to their six-slice Dualit toaster, much to Masooma's annoyance. Akbar liked being surrounded by stylish things and was always buying the latest gadgets for the house. Sam supposed it was better being married to someone acquisitive than miserly. It was just that, being such a perfectionist, Akbar preferred buying everything himself, quite often finding fault with anything she happened to pick up.

Sam idly took the escalator, watching people thronging the handbag department as she glided up to the second floor.

Buying her own clothes and shoes she could get away with, especially since she almost always wore black and Akbar consequently never noticed when she wore something new. She stepped off the escalator into the quieter section housing designer fashions and walked slowly past racks marked 'Herve Leger' and 'Richard Chai', stopping every so often to lift a cuff or hem, feeling the fabric between her fingers and glancing at the price tag before dropping it back and moving on. Sometimes she annoyed herself with her inability to buy something nice, if for nothing else than to raise her spirits and make herself feel better. It wasn't that they didn't have the money. There was always plenty of that floating about, she could never fault Akbar there. Why, he had once even encouraged her to go out shopping on Bond Street with the expensively groomed wife of a visiting French partner, pressing his platinum Amex on her before they left. The trouble for Sam was that she looked terrible in most things she bought, clothes stubbornly refusing to drape over her in the way they did on those pencil-thin mannequins that so disingenuously lined womenswear departments. Besides, Sam had her guilt to contend with as well. Perhaps it was something she'd absorbed during her more modest childhood, but there always seemed something faintly distasteful about spending more than she absolutely had to on herself.

Having failed to buy herself any clothes, Sam fought the urge to go down to the food hall and determinedly took the escalator up again, this time to the health section. She made a beeline for the massage chairs and flopped down gratefully on the largest of them. The girl behind the counter smiled at her. She probably recognised her as one of the 'regulars', who used the free trials to get a few minutes' respite and a back rub, but was too polite to say anything. Who knew, perhaps one day Sam wouldn't disappoint her by walking away, chair un-bought. A massage chair was the kind of acquisition Akbar might suddenly decide he must have. Well, the idea of him asking *Sam* for a back rub was downright laughable. They hadn't done that kind of thing in months.

Sam felt the hard fingers of the shiatsu machine dig into her spine as it ran up and down her back and neck. She closed her eyes, feeling the bright lights of Selfridges recede and fade . . . she was back home in Delhi and her mother was rubbing coconut oil into her hair as she did every Sunday morning. Her father was reading the papers, sunning his feet and awaiting their customary biriyani lunch. And Haroon was whistling tunelessly in his room next to the verandah . . .

Sam's eyes shot open. She felt her heart thud in sudden and familiar panic and got up from the massage chair in a fluster, earning a glare from the shop assistant for forgetting to turn it off before hurrying away. It was unlike Sam not to apologise profusely for her omission, but she couldn't stop now, feeling her legs suddenly go weak and wobbly beneath her. She steadied herself on the arm of the downward escalator, using her free hand to find her phone so she could call Bubbles, nearly dropping it in her panic. She should go to the basement café and ask Bubbles to join her there. It would only take her friend a few minutes from Belgravia in her car, and Sam knew that if Bubbles was free she would come instantly. The kind of comfort Sam needed at this minute could only come from her oldest school chum, who never judged her, never questioned anything. No amount of therapy, retail or otherwise, came anywhere near carrying the same value.

*   *   *

155

Bubbles was lying draped across a pilates ball when she saw Sam's name flash on her screen. She rolled carefully off and took the call, knowing instantly from the sound of her friend's voice that something was badly wrong. She sat up, straining to hear Sam's frantic mumble. Only one word stood out in her gush of words – a name that still carried the power to make Bubbles' heart skip a beat. Haroon.

But Bubbles kept her voice calm, speaking gently. 'Slowly, slowly, Sami. I can't hear you if you speak so fast.' Sam was still incoherent so Bubbles asked, 'Where are you?' adding a second later, 'I'm coming. Wait right there, okay. In the basement café. And get yourself a cup of tea in the meantime.'

Bubbles leapt up from her exercise mat and called for a car as she walked quickly to her bathroom. She pulled off her leotards and riffled through the laundry bin to retrieve the pair of jeans she had thrown in there less than an hour ago. She knew how bad Sam's panic attacks could be sometimes, and there just wasn't the time to go through her wardrobe. Swiftly leaving the house, she got into the car that had been summoned for her.

But once she was seated in the car and it slowly circumnavigated the square, Bubbles looked out of her window at the green of the trees and the blue of the sky and wanted to shout at the world to stop behaving as though everything was hunkydory. It wasn't, it was all a mask, a *front*, she wanted to yell. Like those listed buildings they pulled down leaving just the Victorian façade in place, which they later used to cover up a glitzy new building behind it. That was what Sam's and Bubbles' lives were like. Beautiful façades that did not fit with what lay behind. But, whatever her own pain, how much worse the sorrow would always be for Sam. Bubbles pursed her lips tight, vowing to stay in control for the sake of her friend.

* * *

By the time Bubbles arrived at Selfridges, walking much too fast down the stairs of the escalator in a pair of killer heels, Sam had calmed herself with a large mug of hot chocolate. She smiled wanly as they kissed each other, saying only, 'Thanks for coming, Bubs.'

'You better?' Bubbles queried as she sat down, not taking her eyes off Sam's face.

Sam nodded. 'I think I am now. This will sound so silly, but I was sitting on that stupid massage chair upstairs, remembering my mum's head massages, when suddenly there was Haroon, Bubbles, right there in his room.' She saw Bubbles flinch at the sound of her brother's name and reached out for her friend's hand. 'I know, I know, we both think of him often, Bubs. But this was different. A really, really lucid moment. So full of clarity, I was there, in it, do you know what I mean? And the thing is, that moment offered a vision so very perfect, so within my grasp, that I felt a kind of yearning that hurt . . . really physically hurt, here.' Sam thumped a fist onto her chest before trailing off. '. . . Well, that was sort of how it felt anyway . . . I think I'm okay now. It was knowing you were coming, I suppose.'

She stopped waffling and looked at Bubbles, suddenly concerned about her friend's welfare. Sam had never forgotten that Haroon's absence was deeply felt by Bubbles too. Anita had once rather unkindly dismissed it by quoting Nabokov: 'The more you love a memory, the stronger and stranger it is', she had said to Bubbles, who had remained typically silent. Anita had meant well and perhaps it was true, but Sam had not been able to figure out just how much Bubbles still pined for Haroon. They said people never forgot their first love, but Bubbles – despite her many gripes about Binkie and his parents – never talked about Haroon unless Sam brought up the subject.

'I didn't mean to upset you, Bubs,' she said softly, 'but in my panic I wasn't really thinking straight.' Bubbles nodded, patting her friend's hand while looking down at the floor. Sam decided to change the subject. 'I didn't drag you away from something important, I hope?'

Bubbles gave a small mirthless laugh. 'Is there *ever anything* important about the things I do, Sam?'

'Oh don't say that – you're such a terrific wife, mother, daughter-in-law – those are not *un*important roles to play, Bubs. No one in their right mind would complain about someone as sweet as you. You know that.'

'Hmmm, maybe complaints would at least remind me that I'm there, and not just invisible. So much for being the perfect wife, mother and daughter-in-law.'

'Well, imagine if Binkie were constantly complaining about you. That would be so much worse, wouldn't it?'

Bubbles tried to laugh but merely looked wretched. 'Binkie doesn't complain, that's true, but only because he doesn't really care what I get up to. It's like the more he leaves me alone, the more he hopes I'll leave *him* alone.'

'I know, I know,' Sam responded, 'but that must surely be better than someone who wants to control you all the time. Think about it.'

The two women exchanged a smile. 'Let me get you a drink,' Sam said, getting up. 'What do you want?'

'Oh, their biggest glass of orange juice, please,' Bubbles replied. She appeared to have recovered slightly as she took out her compact and examined her face. 'I must be ~ mess. I was halfway through my pilates routine. I just threw something on and left the house as soon as you called.'

Sam grinned at her. 'From anyone else, I'd have taken that with a huge fistful of salt, seeing how elegant you look in those skinny jeans and, oh God, are those *new* Jimmy Choos?'

Bubbles stuck out a leg to examine the sandals she had hastily slipped on without noticing. 'They sure are,' she said.

'They're *gorgeous*,' Sam exclaimed. 'Crikey, just look at *me*,' she wailed, looking down at herself and her own sensible square-toed pumps as she opened her arms wide, the voluminous arms of her kurta top flapping. 'Pure Karol Bagh, eh? Not an ounce of style. I've been wandering around the clothes section for an hour and haven't bought a thing.'

'Never fear, darling, Bubbles Raheja of Belgravia has come to the rescue. Let me have something to drink and then we'll stroll very slowly through that designer department together to find you something really nice.'

A few minutes later, Sam returned with a glass of orange juice and continued the conversation. 'I really don't think I can stand the thought of trawling through the clothes section again, Bubs. *Nothing* looks nice on me – and it's not the fault of the clothes. Oh, Anita texted me the "Prayer of the Fat Woman" this morning. Did she send it to you? No, why would she – it's sweet, listen.' Sam intoned on a droll voice: '*Dear God, please, please, please make me thin. And, if you can't make me thin, then make all my friends fat.*'

They laughed. Weight was becoming a bit of an issue even for Anita, who, until her thirtieth birthday, had been as poker-thin as she was at school. Anita, of course, blamed the amount of time she was forced to spend at her computer terminal, only refraining to blame work for all her ills when Hugh had joined the news team. Well, thankfully she had found herself a nice man before ballooning out of shape completely, Sam thought, casting a covetous glance at Bubbles' slender waist as she downed her orange juice.

'Anita and I were envying the way *you* manage to be so slim at thirty-one, Bubs. In fact, I think you're more beautiful now than you were at twenty-one!'

Bubbles shrugged. 'Maybe I'm still trying to make my hubby fall in love with me?' she volunteered with a wry smile.

Sam laughed. 'Well, it's true that you transformed yourself for him.'

'With a little help from my friends,' Bubbles reminded her.

'Well, the potential was always there, lurking just below the surface,' Sam said before sighing. 'Whatever Anita's text may say, she and I are pathologically incapable of being jealous of you and the way you look, Bubbles. Friendship is bloody forgiving, isn't it?'

'Maybe it's because you can remember the way I *used* to look,' Bubbles said, starting to giggle suddenly.

'Oh goodness, yes! "Bubbles Malhotra, *why* are you late *again*?"' Sam said, putting on a South Indian accent and a teacher-like demeanour before switching into a breathless little-girl voice, '"Oh Ma'am, Ma'am, I'm *so* sorry I got late but I had *three* pimples on my face that I had to burst one-by-one this morning so I *missed* the bus and then my papa had to drop me to school, Ma'am . . ."'

'Shut up,' Bubbles said good-naturedly, draining her glass. 'You can never mimic me as well as Anita can. She had years of practice as my desk-mate right up from Class II. Right, enough chit-chat. Get me to that clothes department. Now!'

Sam laughed, gathering up her things. 'In a strange way I'm actually looking forward to being back at the old school with both of you, y'know. It's not *all* bad memories, we must remember.'

'Have you told Akbar yet that we're going?' Bubbles asked as they walked to the escalator.

Sam shook her head. There was time enough for that. Akbar had been really quite sweet these past three or four days, coming home unusually early in the evenings and asking after her day. He had even suggested they have dinner in a restaurant together tonight – not something they'd done in a long time. Why spoil his mood unnecessarily? She took Bubbles' arm as they stepped onto the escalator together.

'No, I haven't said anything to Akbar yet, but maybe once I'm in a snazzy new outfit I'll feel more able to announce our plans to him,' she said, only half-joking. As the escalator carried her up again, Sam – now feeling stronger – hoped with all her heart that life with Akbar was starting to take a turn for the better again. She could not bear the thought of losing more than she already had.

Chapter Eleven

Sam heard the news of Bubbles' engagement on the day she returned to Delhi from Simla. It was Anita who got through first, calling up at the very moment the Hussains were carrying their suitcases into the house. After that, the phone would not stop ringing, one classmate after another calling to ask if Sam had spoken to Bubbles. Only Bubbles had not called. Sam knew why, and the most terrible guilt assailed her heart.

It was when the telephone rang for the tenth time, pealing insistently through the Hussain household, that Sam's normally mild-mannered father put his paper down and queried snappishly if St Jude's had been hit by an atomic bomb.

After the phone call was over, Sam finally explained. 'Oh Dad, that was Nats. She'd only just heard. It's *horrible* news! Poor Bubbles is getting married to some millionaire in London!'

Mr Hussain absorbed what was obviously earth-shattering news, his newspaper still in his lap, before saying – completely irrelevantly it seemed to Sam – 'Bubbles in London! London is a great city.' Then, perhaps when he too had recovered from the shock, he added more sensibly, 'But what do the

163

Malhotras want a millionaire for – they've already got millions from what I can see?'

Sam exploded in irritation. 'Oh *Dad*! As if it matters whether London's great or whether they've got millions. Bubbles doesn't *want* to get married and be packed off anywhere. She wants to be in Delhi with all of us, going to college next year and . . . you *know*!'

'Well, seventeen is rather early for marriage, I suppose,' Mr Hussain said thoughtfully, adding in a more optimistic tone, 'unless she's only getting engaged now and the marriage will be later. Maybe she will be able to go to college in London? There will be so many opportunities in a place like that.'

'But she wants to be in *Delhi*, with us!'

'Well, when I asked Bubbles recently about her plans for college, she had none,' Mr Hussain said. 'And don't forget that many of your classmates will leave Delhi after the Board Exams. This is the point at which you must all scatter, having spent the growing-up years together. It is just one of the rites of passage that one must go through.'

Tears pushed behind Sam's eyes at the thought that the girls she had spent more than ten years with would soon be scattering everywhere. And Bubbles as far as London! She tried to concentrate on what her father was saying. He was doing his best to comfort her, even if he was making a complete hash of it.

'As long as Bubbles' parents aren't forcing her, there may be no harm in her being married to a nice boy and *then* finding something to do.'

Sam digested this, knowing she couldn't tell her father about Bubbles' crush on Haroon. Or that it was her fault that Bubbles had agreed to this marriage. It was purely on the rebound. If indeed a 'rebound' was possible when not much had happened in the first place. Sam tried to remember the contents of the letter she had written from Simla. She'd crafted her words so carefully, trying to explain that it wasn't that Haroon found Bubbles *unlovable* – just that he had fallen hook, line and sinker for Lily D'Souza. It was just a case of bad timing in some ways. Perhaps Sam should have waited to tell Bubbles all this after she was back in Delhi, but delaying it hadn't seemed the best course of action then. She was as sure as anything that Bubbles' disappointment over Haroon must have pushed her into this rash decision. So there was only one person on whom Sam could take out her annoyance.

She let her father return to his newspaper and then stuck her head through Haroon's door without bothering to knock. 'You've done it now! I hope you're happy!' she yelled tearfully.

'What the –' Haroon, busy hurling clothes from suitcase to wardrobe, looked up, startled by his sister's red face.

Sam walked into her brother's room, wanting to hurl something hard at his head, but when she spoke there were more tears than anger in her voice. 'Oh, Haroon *bhaiyya*, Bubbles has gone and said yes to a marriage proposal and now she's *engaged*, and I think it's because I told her that you were not keen on her . . .' she hiccupped breathlessly.

Haroon looked at her in horror. 'What?! I know she's completely dippy, old Bubbles, but *marriage*? Is she mad?!'

'Well, her parents have been trying to persuade her for some time and she must have suddenly succumbed.'

'Can't you stop her?' Haroon asked, concern written all over his face.

'Yeah, right – me against all the Malhotras! Even Dad didn't seem to think her getting married was too bad an idea!'

'It's a *rotten* idea. The girl can hardly string three sentences together without running out of breath and they're sending her off to London with a stranger. How the hell will she cope?'

'I don't know! You could try rescuing her . . .' Sam trailed off, looking at her brother hopefully.

'Me?'

'By offering to marry her. Not right now, of course, but if you *offered* to, once you'd got a degree and a job, the Malhotras might just . . .'

Haroon walked up to Sam and put his hands on her shoulders. 'Sis, sis, I've already explained all that to you. Much as I like your ditzy friend Bubbles, I can't ever *love* her like that. You know there's only one girl for me and, thank God, I've finally met her. Which reminds me, Sami. I know you have a lot on your plate right now, but don't be forgetting your promise to put me in touch with Lily. As soon as school reopens. *Please.*'

'I'll see what I can do,' Sam muttered distractedly before leaving her brother's room, her mind churning. Why oh why was she so hopeless at saying no. 'N . . . O' she chanted, trying to practice, even though she knew she was wasting her breath. Haroon would get away with murder as far as she was concerned. But first things first. She had to ask her mother for some money so she could catch an auto-rickshaw to Bubbles' house. She couldn't really delay contacting her any more and a phone call simply wouldn't do. She had to sit before her best friend, face to face, and find out the truth for herself.

Bubbles was sitting with her parents at the dining table, surrounded by invitation lists, when Sam walked in. The girls hugged each other silently as the Malhotras made their usual fuss over Sam, asking after her parents and their holiday

166

in Simla. Sam answered all their questions politely, hoping Bubbles would soon find a ruse to get them somewhere private. She soon did.

'Let me show you my new jewellery, Sam,' Bubbles said. 'It's upstairs, in Ma's room.'

It was only once the girls were on their own that Bubbles started to cry. Sam put her arm around her friend's shoulder, murmuring words of comfort while wiping her face with a diminishing roll of bathroom tissue. But Bubbles was inconsolable. Perhaps this was the first time she had let it all out, Sam thought, dabbing the seemingly endless flow of tears. Perhaps it was the stress of this wedding thing, and not just Haroon. Finally, when Bubbles sat up to blow her nose, Sam said, 'I'm so sorry about Haroon. I did try, you know, but he's got his heart set on that Lily. I just can't believe it, Bubbles – *Lily*, of all people. Boys are such donkeys.'

'It's okay, Sam,' Bubbles snuffled. 'What can you do, it's not your fault. It's just that . . .' at this point she started weeping again '. . . I thought . . . I actually thought he liked me.'

'But he does like you, Bubbles!' Sam beseeched. 'He really does, Bubs, how can he not? But that Lily's done some *jadoo* on him. He's just besotted by her.'

'Such a witch,' Bubbles spat into her tissue. The expression on her face was one that Sam had never seen before.

'Are you properly engaged now, Bubs?' Sam asked tentatively.

'Yes, I think so,' Bubbles said with a miserable expression on her face as she tore off another square of tissue to wipe her nose, now red and sore. 'They flew in from London last week to see me and fix things. But the engagement ceremony will be in September. They said they needed to give notice to their friends and relations.'

Sam nodded. 'And the wedding?' she asked, whispering for some reason she couldn't fathom.

'Next year, after the Board Exams. I should at least have a school-leaving certificate, they said.'

'Thank God for that,' Sam said fervently. 'At least you've bought some time that way. Maybe you can still wriggle out before then or something?'

Bubbles gave her an agonised look and Sam realised how foolish her suggestion must have sounded when every single person on the Malhotra horizon would already had been told of the engagement. And the clothes and jewellery had been bought. Why, mile-long invitation lists were being drawn up downstairs even as Bubbles sat here weeping.

'Also,' Bubbles added, sniffing, 'they wanted me to reach eighteen before the wedding. They said they didn't want to go against the legal age as the media were always watching them.'

'The legal age in England?' Sam asked.

'No, the legal age in India. My mother found out from Natasha's mum that in England the legal age for marriage is sixteen. She thinks these Rahejas are just using delaying tactics as much as possible.'

'Why would they do that?' Sam asked, mystified.

'Because I don't think they're as keen on this wedding as my parents are. They're much richer than us, you see.'

'Goodness!' Sam responded, trying to get a measure of this. The Malhotras were, after all, one of the wealthiest families she knew. She paused before tentatively asking her next question. 'Bubbles, tell me the truth, did you agree to this engagement only because of Haroon?'

Bubbles thought long and hard. She had, in fact, thought long and hard about this very question ever since the Rahejas had been to see her and she had found herself mysteriously saying 'yes'. There was certainly a part of her that wanted to be able to blame Haroon for breaking her heart. It made things easier, it was tragic, it was romantic. But, when she thought about it really, really hard, as she did now for Sam's sake, the honest answer was this: 'No, Sami, I don't think so. I don't think my parents would have let me say "no" even if Haroon and I loved each other. Don't blame him for this. And don't blame yourself for it either, promise me that. This is totally and completely my own doing.'

Although she was trying very hard to be brave, Bubbles' voice cracked again as she tried to imagine her new life in a strange faraway place, where she would have no friends, no Sam, and no chance of ever seeing Haroon again.

Chapter Twelve

LONDON, 2008

Sam went through her entire closet twice over before finally plucking out a maroon kurti to go with the black trousers she had just purchased from Selfridges. Bubbles had tried to get her to buy a slinky Roberto Cavalli dress, but Sam had thought the décolletage just a tad too low and hey look-at-me for her. She also did not like the fact that the clingy fabric revealed her pot belly, unless she kept it sucked in all the time, which was of course impossible. Instead she pulled on the embroidered silk top that had been bought in a boutique on her last trip to Delhi. Although she had initially baulked at the price tag, in the end she had been unable to resist its clever cut, so flattering it made her look almost slim. For one, the length just covered her widening bottom and the darts accentuated her full bosom just enough to make her waist look . . . well, nearly small.

Akbar was using the en-suite shower and so Sam nipped down the corridor to use Heer's bathroom instead. She'd always wondered at couples who shared bathrooms, performing embarrassing ablutions side by side. There had been a time, long ago, when she and Akbar had got into shower cubicles and bath tubs together, albeit in pursuit of adventurous lovemaking scenarios rather than to have a shared bath. But, around the time she had started to put on weight and sensed Akbar's gaze turning critical, this had stopped. It was her fault, Sam knew, and she wondered if Akbar noticed the elaborate ploys involved ('Oh, I'll be there in a minute, just need to do something first, you start without me . . .') but only she knew how hard it had been to maintain Akbar's attraction for her without subjecting him to the acres of cellulite that had sprung up almost overnight on her stomach and thighs. And, soon enough, Akbar seemed to have forgotten there was ever a time they had been so intimate anyway.

She undressed and pulled on a shower-cap, her thoughts wandering back to that distant time. Her marriage to Akbar had been arranged by her worried parents after she'd finished her MA and shown no inclination to do anything but hang around the house with them. 'We don't need looking after, *beti*. We'll look after each other, your mother and I,' her father had said. She hadn't taken it seriously, of course – the very idea of ever leaving home and being separated from her parents was abhorrent to her. Until she had been introduced to Akbar, that was.

Sam turned on the shower, testing its temperature before stepping in. She remembered how Auntie Gul had been going on about Akbar for days, the son of her old school friend from Lahore whom she'd met after years: 'such a fine family', 'old money', 'corporate lawyer . . . in *London*', always dropping the 'don' of 'London' as though it weighed a ton. Sam tilted her face up, allowing sharp jets of water to tingle on her face and tap noisily on her shower-cap. London had seemed both the best and worst part of the marriage proposal to her – she would have Bubbles and Anita for company, but her beloved parents would be so far away. Nevertheless,

from the moment she had met Akbar, all other consider-
ations had flown out of her mind. Sam had, quite simply,
fallen headlong in love. No one could possibly blame her for
that; he was handsome, witty, urbane, sophisticated and had,
amazingly, seemed utterly charmed by her too. As she soaped
herself, she recalled how much prettier she had been at the
time, having lost weight travelling up and down to Delhi
University for her MA, even able to slip into those figure-
hugging churidar kurtas that were in fashion then. She and
Akbar had taken to each other so easily in those few short
meetings before they had married, finding delight in all the
qualities one had and the other lacked. How odd that the
mere passage of years could sometimes turn those very things
first considered attractive into annoyances instead.

The restaurant booking was for eight o'clock so Sam did
not linger in the shower, pulling on her clothes while still
standing in Heer's small bathroom. From the shoe cupboard
in the corridor she pulled out a pair of pewter Anna Sui
stilettos, a gift from Bubbles and hardly ever worn. Teetering
on the unfamiliar high heels, Sam returned to the bedroom
to find Akbar pulling his own clothes from the closet, a towel
wrapped around his waist.

Sam sneaked a glance at him. He was fanatical about his
early morning gym visits and had certainly kept his shape
over the years. Except for the silver wings developing over
his temples, Akbar was pretty much the man she'd instantly
fallen hook, line and sinker for ten years ago.

Sam sat down at the antique dressing-table mirror to put
her make-up on. This was luckily still a minimal require-
ment as her skin was creamily smooth and unlined – just a
touch of compact and blusher needed, and a smudge of grey
kohl pencil on her eyelids. Akbar seemed to be concentrating
on Mark Lawson's review of a play on *Front Row* and so Sam

173

finished her toilette silently, putting on a slightly darker shade of lipstick than usual to go with her top before brushing her thick black hair till it shone. It was unlikely Akbar would notice these little things but Sam was too delighted by the prospect of a rare evening out with her husband to worry about that right now.

He wandered across to where she sat at her dressing table, holding out his right arm, a pair of cuff-links in his left. Sam wiped her hands on a bit of tissue before slipping the links in, careful not to get make-up on Akbar's brand-new Turnbull & Asser shirt. When she had finished, he suddenly reached out and held her chin briefly for a moment. His eyes were unfathomable and he looked as though he were about to say something before he changed his mind and turned away. Sam felt a flutter of apprehension – Akbar so rarely looked directly at her to say anything these days that she knew it was probably something important. On the other hand, perhaps he was just about to compliment her appearance before remembering suddenly that they no longer did spontaneous things like that any more.

'Ready?' he asked, and she nodded, getting up.

'Let's leave through the kitchen door so we can say good-night to Heer on our way out,' she said, picking up her purse and clicking off the lights.

They walked downstairs together, Sam wobbling precari-ously on her vertiginous heels. Perhaps it would have been better to wear a pair of her more sensible shoes, rather than risk being an embarrassment to Akbar by tripping and falling on her face in the middle of the restaurant. Too late now. It wasn't worth incurring Akbar's irritation by suddenly going back upstairs. She would soldier on in these ridiculous stilts, even though her absent-minded husband probably hadn't even noticed that she was suddenly three inches taller than usual.

Heer was eating pizza, her eyes fixed on the television, barely noticing as her parents came in. 'No troubling Masooma, baby,' Sam mumbled in her daughter's ear as she kissed her. 'When she tells you to go to bed, you go to bed, okay?' Heer nodded, busily chewing while her eyes stayed fixed on the screen, and Sam turned to Masooma. 'We're not very far, Masooma, call if you need anything.'

The maid smiled and, as Akbar kissed the top of Heer's head, said, 'You don't worry about Heer, Madam. She's with me so you go, just have nice time!'

As they left the house, Akbar looked up at the late summer sky that was just deepening to a soft indigo. 'Fancy walking there?' he asked.

Sam was dismayed. 'Oh Akbar, I'm so sorry I'm wearing silly shoes! But I can go in and change if you like . . .'

Akbar glanced at his watch, 'No, never mind, I have the car keys here, let's drive.'

Sam got into the passenger seat of Akbar's car, feeling illogically that she had let him down in some way, but he seemed unconcerned, humming along to the car radio as he zapped the gates and pulled out onto the road.

'We haven't been to Julie's in such a long time, I'm so looking forward to this,' Sam said, aware that she must sound as gushy as a girl out on her first date.

Akbar smiled and patted her knee. 'I'm sorry I've been so preoccupied of late, Sami,' he said suddenly. 'Just had rather a lot to deal with at work.'

'Oh don't worry, I understand completely,' Sam replied, looking out at the colourful bustle of Notting Hill Gate, her heart singing. It had been so, so long since she had last heard Akbar sound so warmly affectionate, she felt quite giddy with pleasure.

At the restaurant they were ushered to a cosy table for

two and Akbar ordered a bottle of his favourite Barolo. After their glasses had been filled, he looked at Sam and lifted his glass. 'To a lovely, patient wife, who doesn't always get what she deserves,' he said lightly.

'Oh, how can you say that, Akbar? I've got everything a woman could possibly want!' she protested, embarrassed and also a little anxious at where the conversation might be heading.

'Well, I know. But if I've been a bit abrupt sometimes, you should know it's nothing to do with you.'

'Has work been very stressful lately?' Sam asked, looking concerned.

'Well, not stressful exactly, but . . .' Akbar stopped to take his phone out of his pocket. He frowned as he read the name on the silently flashing screen and got out of his chair as he usually did to answer it. Sam settled back into the silk cushions, casting a happy look around at the other diners. There were a few other couples dining quietly like them, and a rather raucous group who had just broken out into a tuneless song for some odd reason that she couldn't fathom. As she caught the eye of one of the women in the group, they smiled at each other. Happiness like that was quite infectious, although Sam wasn't sure what Akbar would have thought of such drunken revelries spoiling their tranquil evening.

Sam looked around for Akbar, whose call seemed to be taking a long time. He was standing at the door to the far balcony with his phone held close to his ear, listening more than speaking. From his profile, and the way a muscle in his cheek was working, Sam could tell he was stressed. She looked worriedly across at him, hoping it wasn't another crisis at work. To give herself something to do, she beckoned the waiter and asked for a bottle of water. After he had poured a glass for her, she alternated between her wine and the water, and had perused the contents of the menu card twice over by the time Akbar returned to the table.

'Is all well, darling?' she asked anxiously.

Akbar nodded, but his lips were pursed and his face had lost the peaceable look it had worn earlier in the evening. He made no eye contact with Sam as he sat down.

'Was it someone from work?' she persisted.

'Yes,' he said, picking up the menu.

'Oh dear, there's some problem, isn't there?'

Akbar ignored her worried question, his eyes running over the menu instead. 'If you've decided what you want, then let's order without delay,' he said brusquely.

Sam felt her heart slide into her stomach and settle there. The magic had left the evening just like that, in one fleeting instant. She wasn't surprised to hear Akbar add, 'I might need to nip back to the office to collect some papers after I've dropped you home.'

So much for her longed-for new start, Sam thought, the lettering on the menu blurring as she blinked back sudden tears. When Akbar talked of 'nipping back to the office', he was usually gone for most of the night, coming back in silent and exhausted, long after Sam had turned in. His more loving behaviour these past few days had been no more than a temporary aberration, and now – after one short phone call – it was apparently gone for good.

Chapter Thirteen

DELHI, 1993

When school reopened for the autumn term, Victoria Lamb called Bubbles to her office. The previous occasions on which Bubbles had visited Miss Lamb's room had, without exception, been tense affairs, caused either by Bubbles' poor attendance or appalling grades, so she was naturally petrified when the summons came. It fell on Sam to calm her friend's apprehension by reminding her that, as she had only just returned after the summer hols, Lamboo was very unlikely to have already gathered negative intelligence on her. It was probably only to enquire about the engagement. Even though Bubbles – in deference to school rules – was not wearing the enormous rock that was her engagement ring, the news had already spread like wildfire through the school and many a cheeky junior had popped up before them as they had walked to assembly, congratulating Bubbles, nudging each other and giggling wildly as they did.

Victoria Lamb was, unusually, not seated behind her massive polished teak desk but had occupied one of a pair of velvet armchairs near the French windows that led to the school's garden. A small vase of purple flowers was on the table before the chairs and the principal was, much to Bubbles' astonishment, pouring steaming tea from a blue teapot into a pair of striped mugs. There was even a platter of assorted biscuits neatly arranged on a plate. With the sunlight pouring in through the windows, Bubbles thought that Lamboo wore an almost motherly look, her silver hair glowing like a small cloud around her head.

She looked up as she heard Bubbles coming in and called out in a brisk voice, 'Ah, my dear girl, there you are.' Bubbles shuffled along and stood obediently behind the second armchair. 'What are you standing there for, child? Stop gawping like a goldfish and do sit down before your tea goes cold.'

Bubbles edged gingerly around the chair and parked herself on the edge of it. She accepted the mug of tea that was being held out for her on a small tray and collected two Glucose biscuits from the plate in front of her. 'Good holiday?' the Principal asked, and Bubbles nodded, chewing. 'Did you go anywhere, outside Delhi, I mean?' Bubbles shook her head. Miss Lamb clicked her tongue impatiently. 'For heaven's sake, child, has the cat got your tongue?'

This time, instead of shaking her head, Bubbles swallowed the last of her biscuit and whispered, 'No, Ma'am.'

'Well don't look so miserable then. It isn't this engagement worrying you, is it? Your mother came in here to tell me of it this morning.'

So that was it. Sam hadn't been too far wrong. And the expression on old Lamboo's face was so sympathetic that, for a split second, Bubbles was tempted to burst into tears and tell the principal everything: about her heartbreak, her sorrow, her fears. She even wanted to confess her worries about the new life abroad that her parents were planning for her – but then that would have involved confessing her terror of English people, people like Miss Lamb herself, in

180

whose presence she invariably found herself sweating and tongue-tied. And now her parents were marrying her into a family living in London, whose son – her future husband – talked as if his mouth were full of pebbles like all those people in English movies. So little had Bubbles understood Binkie Raheja at their brief meeting, she had even had to ask him to spell something he had been trying to say and had received a supercilious expression and a string of letters that had all sounded like 'Euo Euo Euo'.

'What is it, child?' Miss Lamb asked, her voice turning gentle as she leaned forward to take Bubbles' hand in her own. 'You're not being forced into this marriage, are you? You know that I would much rather see all my girls leaving school for university, but sometimes I come up against parents who feel they know what is best for their daughters. Perhaps that is so . . . who knows.' She stopped, still looking searchingly into Bubbles' face and waiting for a reply, but she got none, for Bubbles was now pondering the reason why the two choices had to be either marriage or university. In truth, she was interested in neither, but the lesser of the two evils, at this point in time, did actually seem to be marriage.

'It's fine, Ma'am,' she whispered finally, one hand still in Miss Lamb's, the other clinging to her lukewarm mug of tea. 'My parents checked that everything was okay with me. I said yes.'

'With full knowledge of all that marriage entails?'

Bubbles was silent again, so Victoria Lamb rephrased her question. 'You have met the boy?' Bubbles nodded and the principal smiled, her voice turning oddly tender as she released her grasp on Bubbles' hand and leaned back in her chair. 'And you liked him, yes?' she asked.

Bubbles thought for a moment about that. She wasn't sure yet what she thought of Binkie Raheja. He seemed like a creature from another planet, with his funny accent and buttoned-to-the-top shirt and spectacles. More worryingly, he had seemed rather scared of his parents, his mother in particular; sneaking glances at her impassive face every time anyone asked him anything. It was obvious that he had accompanied his parents to the Malhotra household only because he had been dragged there, barely even looking at Bubbles as she had brought in the tea-tray, a job she had never performed in her life before, thanks to the army of domestic help employed by her mother. After handing out the teas, Bubbles had talked a little bit to Mrs Raheja about school, warming to her a tiny bit more when the subject turned to Hindi movies (and it turned out that Mrs R liked the new actor Shah Rukh as much as she did). After that, she and Binkie had been despatched to the Chesterfield lookalike sofa in the far corner of her parents' drawing room, where they had conducted a short conversation in two completely different versions of English. On the plus side, though, Binkie looked neat and tidy, quite unlike a lot of the rich Delhi boys who roared around on noisy motorcycles and wore their shirts unbuttoned to their navels exposing gold chains lying on great big mats of chest hair. That was the kind of boy her parents would probably have come up with if they hadn't stumbled upon this Binkie Raheja. It certainly wouldn't have been Haroon.

Bubbles smiled forlornly at Miss Lamb and uttered what was not a complete untruth: 'Yes, Ma'am. I think I am okay about this marriage.' She meant okay about the clothes and the jewellery and the heart-rending happiness of her parents. But Lamboo wouldn't understand that. The principal seemed satisfied, however, and was now telling her to return to class, which Bubbles did with relief. One more test passed, she thought, as she hastened back down the corridor, the eyes of past principals seeming to look sadly at her from their framed photographs on the wall.

After Victoria Lamb had seen Bubbles out of her office, she poured herself another mug of tea and sat back in her armchair, taking a sip and sighing in a resigned manner. Perhaps it was best for girls like Bubbles – who was not exactly endowed with high intellect, the poor dear – to be married off into decent families while they were still young and fresh and pretty enough. It was amusing, though, how parents like the Malhotras always assumed that she was completely incapable of empathising with their motivations. Mrs Malhotra had even nervously requested that she refrain from reporting them to the authorities for Bubbles being underage! Why, if the police did start rounding up the parents of all the seventeen-year-olds who were engaged, that would be most of West Delhi's business community behind bars in one fell swoop, given their predilection for using marriage as a way of strengthening business ties.

Miss Lamb could hardly blame Mrs Malhotra for her apprehension, though. After all, she knew she must come across to all the parents as the archetypal stern spinster who had made being principal of a convent school the very mission of her life. What would they know? Although she couldn't very well *encourage* them to hustle their daughters away from schooling and into marriages, she understood perfectly what they were doing. At one level, perhaps she would even condone it. Why, she knew better than anyone else that education and careers did not always bring the anticipated insulation from heartbreak.

She put her cup down and, pushing her glasses up onto her hairline, rubbed her eyes gently with the balls of her forefingers. They felt heavy again this morning, as though she'd suffered another sleepless night, which she didn't think she had. Perhaps she ought to consult the school doctor about this uncharacteristic fatigue, although she doubted very much whether sleeping tablets and tranquilisers would help. There was no point pretending that Lily had nothing to do with it. The arrival, so suddenly and out of the blue, of a grandchild she had not even known of could have been turned into a reason to rejoice. After all, the winter evenings *had* started to get terribly lonely in her little cottage at the edge of the deserted school compound. But Victoria could not discount the shock of it all – nor the problems she and Lily were having adjusting to each other. Despite her best efforts, the girl hadn't uttered a single civil word all through the holidays. Victoria normally prided herself on being able to get through to even the most difficult girls, but here, with her own grandchild, she seemed to have come up against a brick wall. It was natural Lily should want to take out some of her bitterness on whoever was nearest, and maybe time would slowly heal these terrible rifts. But, until they did heal, the odium of one's own flesh and blood was the worst pain anyone could have inflicted on them. Sharper even than a serpent's tooth. That line, repeated *ad nauseam* to batch after batch of schoolgirls poring over King Lear, suddenly made terrible sense to Victoria.

It was only at break-time that the class got their chance to quiz Bubbles on her engagement.

'Let me get this right – you actually had the opportunity to say no and you said yes?!' Nimmi queried disbelievingly.

'You didn't!' Anita said when Bubbles nodded, throwing her head back and closing her eyes as though unable to cope any more with the depth of her friend's stupidity.

'Bubbles Malhotra, you're mad,' Natasha declared. 'Imagine getting married at eighteen and never having any fun again. I'd rather *die*.'

Only Zeba – flatteringly for Bubbles – was impressed.

'London,' she breathed. 'A millionaire businessman, you said? What sort of businessman?'

'They started off in textiles like us – that's how Papa knows them. But now they do other stuff too, like chemicals and fertilisers, I think.'

'I *think!*' Anita said disbelievingly. 'Christ, girl, isn't that the least you should know?'

'What was HE like?! Did you talk?'

'Is he nice?'

'Handsome?'

'Did you go out? Like on a date?'

Bubbles' head was spinning from all the questions. She wasn't used to being the focus of everyone's attention, generally preferring to let Sam and Anita do the talking for her. But she held her nerve, surprising even herself with her composure. Oddly, Bubbles found their collective enthusiasm curiously infectious, even though she knew that her classmates' excitement was mostly for what they knew would be a massive party.

'I'll take charge of your grooming, Bubbles,' Natasha volunteered.

'Grooming?'

'Yeah, me and my mum. She's great at that stuff, she'll know exactly where you need to go for your hair and skin and things.'

'Good idea, you certainly can't go to London looking like that,' Zeba said tartly.

'Oh she's fine, leave her alone,' Anita growled.

'What, in her skin-tight polyester bell-bottoms and hair in a pigtail?! They'll think you're one of those sweepers when you land at Heathrow, darling.'

Sam intervened. 'I think your idea is lovely, Nats. Your mum will be the best person to choose a trendy haircut for

Bubs. And Bubbles will be able to do something adventurous with this beautiful thick hair. It's wasted tied into joodies and plaits. Your mum won't mind, will she, Bubs?'

And so it was arranged – with the grateful acquiescence of the Malhotras – for Bubbles to spend the following month visiting Natasha and her mother at their classy Maharani Bagh house straight after school. A trip with Mrs Walia (erstwhile first lady at various Indian High Commissions across the world) to the very clever Mario's at the Mughal Hilton resulted in bounces and highlights that Bubbles had always thought her greasy tresses incapable of. A subsequent visit to Delhi's best dermatologist had resulted in promises that her skin would be 'clear and creamy' by the engagement. That done, Mrs Walia revealed some mysterious western ways with table-settings and cutlery and crockery to Bubbles, who thought some of the stuff about milk-before-tea in cups (not to mention what one did with pinkie fingers) very odd indeed. Mrs Walia drew the line at kitchen work, of course, being quite sure that a London-based business family (who could afford to send their son to *Eton*, goodness gracious) would surely have at least one cook.

It was only at night, when Bubbles was alone in her room, that she felt the excitement of others slowly abate. In those rare quiet moments she would pick up her bedside picture of Haroon, standing laughing with the sunshine glinting on his hair, and shed a few private tears. She imagined what it would have been like to marry the boy she loved, becoming part of his warm and affectionate family. But that was not to be. For there was a strange bespectacled stranger awaiting her in London, and she had lost Haroon forever to Lily.

Chapter Fourteen

LONDON, 2008

It was not usually like Bubbles Raheja to take charge of her friends, but by October the plans for Delhi had been firmed up and the tickets booked. It had been no trouble at all for her, as she had merely asked James about the possibility of getting three seats on Raheja International's new airline when he visited the house one morning to collect some papers from Binkie's study. Within two hours of his departure, a motor-cycle courier had delivered the tickets in a manila envelope.

The new butler, recently poached from Clarence House, brought them in just as the family were sitting down to lunch. Everyone looked a little surprised when he walked around the large mahogany table to hand the envelope to Bubbles on his small silver tray. Perhaps, being new, he did not know that she never received anything, certainly not in those smooth manila envelopes that carried the official Raheja crest.

'For me?' she asked, as startled as everyone else.

'Yes Ma'am,' he muttered in his cut-glass accent, bowing respectfully as he held out his tray.

Bubbles took the envelope and used the accompanying paper knife to slit it open, conscious of her mother-in-law's

187

eyes boring into the letter as the butler obsequiously accepted the returned knife and slid away silently.

'What is the office sending *you*?' Mrs Raheja asked, the inflexion indicating her extreme displeasure at Raheja International's temerity in making direct contact with the lowly daughter-in-law of the family.

Bubbles grinned in delight as she upturned the contents of the envelope onto the tablecloth and three tickets fell out. She couldn't resist a small squeal of pleasure. 'Oh Binkie, you were right after all, what a sweetie your James is! I just mentioned it so casually and look – three tickets to Delhi!'

Binkie nodded indulgently but his mother squawked, '*Delhi?!*'

'Oh Mama,' Bubbles said, turning to her mother-in-law and trying unsuccessfully to sound contrite. 'Sorry, I didn't mention it before because . . . well, because I didn't know I was going until just now! Oh Binks, do thank James from me! Or was it *you* who told him?'

'Well, he did call to check a few minutes ago,' Binkie replied with a casual shrug, popping a blini into his mouth. 'Don't worry about it – first-class traffic hasn't quite picked up on that sector yet.'

'Who are the other two tickets for? Are Ruby-Bobby also going? You know that they are not keen on Delhi . . .' Mrs Raheja sounded confused, obviously still assessing whether she should be cross or not.

'Well, the pair of them will be on that Galapagos trip that Binkie's organising for their Christmas hols, so I thought I'd go to Delhi . . . erm, with Sam and Anita. I'd mentioned my plans to go with the girls, hadn't I, Binkie?'

Bubbles looked at her husband for reassurance and Binkie nodded again, this time with a little less certainty, shooting a slightly apprehensive look at his mother.

'But what is happening in Delhi *so* specially?' It looked like Mrs Raheja wasn't ready to give up.

Bubbles sighed quietly. She would have to follow Anita's careful instructions now. 'Well, I have not visited my parents since last winter and my father has been asking to see me,' she said as firmly as she could.

While Mrs Raheja glowered silently, holding her soup spoon aloft as though it were a sword, Mr Raheja, sunk amid the papers at the other end of the table, spoke up in loud Punjabi. 'Let the girl go and see her parents if she wants to.' He spoke slowly and significantly, his words seeming to make his wife almost visibly subside like a punctured balloon. Bubbles contemplated blowing a kiss at her father-in-law from where she sat and quelled a sudden attack of giggles, careful not to let her mother-in-law feel vanquished. Mrs Raheja opened her mouth to reply – she wasn't normally one to let a war remain unwaged – but her husband gave her a meaningful look over his paper that caused her to give in sulkily. She clattered her spoon into her spinach soup and slurped belligerently instead.

It was an old game. Bubbles had figured out a very long time ago that the mere mention of her father often had Binkie's parents hastily back off. Bubbles had never quite worked out what it was but reckoned that her father held some information on her in-laws from their early days in the textile industry that the Rahejas still remained nervous about. Bubbles even suspected that her canny old father might have used that very information to twist Dinesh Raheja's arm into getting his only son married to her fifteen years ago, which would explain the disparity in their social standing and their reluctant but eventual acceptance of her. Even at the time of her marriage, the Rahejas were already a wealthy family – far wealthier than hers – but they had certainly not reached the stratosphere they now occupied, making it to *The Times*' Asian Rich List ten years after she had married Binkie, and last year even slipping almost unnoticed onto the list of the UK's 100 wealthiest people, right up there, much to Bubbles' amazement, alongside the Duke of Westminster and the Queen!

She wanted to grab her mobile and call her friends straightaway with news of the tickets but she stayed at the table, decorously sipping on her soup and pretending not to notice her mother-in-law's sullen glances. To give herself something to do, Bubbles helped herself to a freshly baked wholemeal roll and deliberately cracked it open to butter it, even though she had not touched butter for years. Putting a piece of the buttered roll in her mouth, Bubbles savoured the unusual taste on her tongue. Perhaps it was due to their Rich-List ducal connections or her son's predilections picked up from boarding school, but Mrs Raheja insisted on western food at least once a week, much to her husband's dismay. He looked mournfully at a large portion of goat's cheese and trompette galette that was being served onto his plate, followed by a portion of sautéed girolles with oyster mushrooms and rocket leaves, shiny with truffle oil and dotted with pine nuts.

'I don't want this kish-vish, ghaas-poos,' he growled sulkily.

'It's not a quiche, Papa, it's a galette,' Binkie said.

'And salad is good for you, Papa, you mustn't call it "ghaas-poos",' Bubbles giggled. 'You really need to eat more greens, you know.' She tapped her own washboard stomach. 'Good for your system.'

'What is so unhealthy about Punjabi food, hanh?' Mr Raheja retorted. 'Good maa-di-daal and sarson-ka-saag, for example. My naani, who ate nothing but that, lived till ninety-two. She would race me in the compound at Ludhiana when I was ten and still beat me. And all her own teeth at ninety-two also!' He obediently swallowed a mouthful of the tart and winced. Suddenly shoving his plate away, he bellowed at no one in particular, 'What bakwaas is this! Bring me a paratha! Aloo! And some daal or saag. I cannot eat this rubbish, I tell you. Is this what I have worked so hard for?'

As everyone fussed around her father-in-law, Bubbles wolfed down her tart, barely tasting it. She was desperate to call Sam and Anita and give them news of the tickets. Not that either of them needed monetary favours from her, but it just felt wonderful being able to do little things for her two best friends. And Sam could certainly do with some cheering up, given the way Akbar had been behaving recently.

Bubbles excused herself from the table, and saw that Binkie was also escaping back to the office, swiftly exiting the noisy dining room. His father was increasingly leaving the day-to-day running of the business to him and had even been taking afternoon siestas these days, something that was previously unheard of. Bubbles, following Binkie out, waved joyfully to him from the hall windows, but he seemed not to have noticed her as he got into his Bentley to be driven off. She saw the car indicate left as it turned out of the square and wondered briefly why her husband was going in the opposite direction to the office. Perhaps he was going to pick James up from somewhere. She shrugged, turning away. For a long time now she had stopped questioning Binkie about his movements because it never got her beyond a few noncommittal replies anyway. 'Hers was not to wonder why' had become a sort of motto to Bubbles. Just occasionally, she panicked a little bit at the thought that perhaps Binkie was not up to the task of maintaining his father's empire for long enough to keep their children in the style to which they were now accustomed. All that talk on TV about the credit crunch was a bit worrying too. One really did have to give it to the old man, Bubbles reflected, having built such a huge business without a flash foreign MBA, or an Indian degree even. 'Generations will rest on my efforts,' her father-in-law sometimes proclaimed proudly, which was probably just as well given how little of his business chutzpah Binkie seemed to have inherited.

Bubbles, walking back to her room, decided that the reason she found it hard to be equally confident of Binkie's business abilities was on the basis of how poorly he kept track of the unlimited credit and debit cards that she and the children had use of. For all his attempted controlling, he had no clue as to who was buying what and for whom. And the family's accounts at Harrods and Liberty were completely beyond him, of course. She entered the sanctuary of her bedroom, mulling over how easy it was for her to order just about anything she wanted, often without even having to pull out a credit card. Like three first-class tickets to Delhi, with a mere snap of her manicured fingers.

It wasn't, therefore, without a touch of shame that Bubbles found herself inexplicably wishing for something more. She looked at her toned figure in the three-way mirror that occupied her walk-in dressing room. The new personal trainer's regime was doing her a world of good, making her fashionably lean and also bringing out some interesting shadows in her face. Additionally, every single item of apparel on her person had cost at least a few hundred pounds; even the diamanté Alice band sparkling on the top of her head was Chanel. Bubbles knew she ought to be grateful for the endless luxury of time and money that she had to lavish on herself. So why then did she find herself, every so often, wishing for inexpensive but completely unachievable things? Such as – not power exactly, but confidence. The kind of confidence that Anita, for instance, had in such abundance, a result of the authority she enjoyed to be herself and do what she wanted, without seeking permission or needing approval or, as Anita would have put it, 'caring a fucking monkey's uncle' for anyone or anything.

Bubbles looked at her watch. Sam would be picking Heer up from school at this time so she would call Anita first. It was her afternoon off so she would be at home.

'Hi there – it's me. Good news, I have the tickets.'

'Gratis?'

'What?'

'Free?'

'Of course, free, what did you expect?'

'Gosh, I should really be eating my words for having given you such a hard time when Papa Raheja bought his little airline!' Anita laughed.

'You're a complete monster sometimes, Anita,' Bubbles replied affectionately, 'but I think I'll forgive you.'

'I have to say I'm really grateful to you, Bubs. You can imagine the gaping hole my little sojourn in Barbados has left in my bank account.'

'Hey, I haven't cut in on anything . . . er, romantic, have I?' Bubbles asked. Anita hadn't had a boyfriend for months before Hugh had come along and Bubbles had consequently grown used to calling her rather inconsiderately at all times of night or day, depending on her work schedule.

'Nah. Hugh's working today so no afternoon delight, if that's what you mean. No nookie tonight either by the looks of it, as he's doing an extra shift at the World Service to make up for Barbados,' Anita replied.

'Sounds like it was worth every minute, though?' Bubbles asked, trying not to sound envious. Anita had come back from a week in Barbados earlier this month to tell her two

193

dumbfounded friends about the travails of midnight sex on a beach ('Sand up the cooter ain't exactly the best lubricant, darlings,' she had warned, forgetting that there was not the remotest possibility of either Sam or Bubbles getting anything up their respective cooters for the foreseeable future.)

'So what are you up to this evening then?' Bubbles asked. Both she and Sam derived a strange vicarious pleasure from hearing tales of Anita's chaotic life.

'Oh, nothing tonight, thankfully. It's been just manic this past week. We went to the movies on Tuesday to see the new Cronenberg, as Hugh and I both had the afternoon off, then Ronnie Scott's with a bunch from work on Wednesday night and dinner with friends last night in Chinatown – you remember Chrissie and John, you met them at mine once . . .'

'Oh yes, I remember them. Mostly because that was the first time I'd heard of tree surgeons!' Bubbles sighed. 'Feels like I only ever meet interesting people through you, Anita.'

'How on earth can you say that? You, who gets to dine with Elton John and David fucking Furnish!'

'Yeah, but only because Binkie dragged me to a fund-raising dinner at Elton John's that he'd paid thousands for! Yours, Anita, are the only parties I go to where I meet *real* people. Oh, and don't hear the word "Prada" uttered once.'

Anita laughed. 'Funny, though, that it's still you and Sam I'd turn to if I really needed anything important, not my tree surgeon mates.'

'Well, they weren't around when you were seven, were they? That must count for something.'

'Too right, there's no point in being pretentious with someone who's seen you lose your teeth and whose teenage zits you've helped burst, eh?' Anita yawned loudly. 'What are you up to later today then, Bubs?'

194

'Oh, nothing much actually. Papa and Binkie are busy with meetings every evening this week and Mama has her cards set over later today. I'll be helping with the tea.'

'What do you need to help with? What are her army of cooks and maids doing, for fuck's sake?'

Bubbles smiled – good old Anita, always outraged on someone else's behalf. 'It's no big deal, I don't have much else to do,' she said, before changing the subject. 'Have you eaten?'

'I'm treating myself to a proper lunch today actually, having been up since four bloody a.m. Picked up a Waitrose meal on the way home. Not that you would know what that is, of course.'

'Of course I know what Waitrose is, how dare you!' Bubbles exclaimed. 'In fact, there's one recently opened round the corner here in Belgravia, you know. I go past it every day on my morning jog to Hyde Park. But if you think *that's* proper food, it's no wonder you're putting on weight, Anita! My dietician was telling me how much sugar they put in those ready-made meals.'

Anita laughed, yawning. 'Even worse, there's half a bottle of left-over Sauvignon Blanc beckoning from the fridge! I'm afraid a day that's lurched between realpolitik in Pakistan and this fucking endless American election deserves more than a few dry oatcakes.'

Bubbles imagined Anita all by herself in her messy little flat bursting with books and plants. No one to report to and no one whose permission she needed for anything. She felt a strange twinge of – what was it? – not envy, surely? Bubbles felt faintly ashamed as she looked around her own palatial bedroom, quite probably half the floor area of Anita's whole flat, seeing its ivory pile carpet and the pair of mauve silk Rococo chaises longues that Binkie had had specially ordered at Linley's this summer. They were meant to match the enormous curtained four-poster bed acquired last year that, despite being the size of a small tennis court, hadn't yet seen much . . . well, nookie, as Anita had put it.

'Hello?'

'Yes, I'm still here,' Bubbles replied.

'Are you all right, sweetie? You sound a bit down . . .'

Bubbles could hear the wary tone in Anita's voice and recognised that, although she had asked a genuine question, she really did not want to know. Anita had never been as good a listener as Sam and, even when they were all much younger, Bubbles had tried never to burden her with too many of her woes. Her old friend and desk-mate was just incapable of understanding certain things, her brain being intended for other, more complex issues, or so Bubbles had concluded long ago.

'No, just a bit bored with my life, that's all, Anita. But, as you so often remind me, it's mostly my own fault, isn't it. Well, I'd better let you get on with your lunch,' Bubbles said, sitting up on the silk chaise longue and sinking her toes into the soft pile carpet. 'Let's get together one of these days, you, me and Sam, and make the final plans for Delhi. We don't have that much time, you know. Two months.'

'Oh fuck. Apart from being with you two and seeing my mum, I've never *not* looked forward to a holiday as much as this, you know, Bubbles.'

'Hey, did Sam tell you she had another call from Zeba the other day? Seems she's coming too and wants to know our dates. You'd have thought she'd have more exciting things to do than visit an old school principal.'

Bubbles did not notice Anita's moment of silence before she replied in a sober voice, 'Yes, Sam mentioned that Zeba was coming too.'

'Strange, that. She must have been the one who hated Lily the most because of that whole Gomes affair,' Bubbles said. 'Even though Lily never did tell on her, did she?'

'Perhaps Zeba hated Lily all the more for *not* telling on her actually. But that was Lily's way, wasn't it? Slow torture. How she must have loved it when she found out about Zeba. I mean, knocking off a teacher to get the exam paper, for fuck's sake.' Anita sounded as livid as though it had all happened yesterday, Bubbles thought.

'Isn't it curious, though,' Bubbles pointed out, 'that none of us really tried to stop Zeba from getting into that mess with Mr Gomes . . . well, we sort of tried, but not as hard as we should have done, I think.'

'You're right. Despite being right little prudes at the time.'

'Maybe we were just too frightened ourselves. I mean, if Lamboo had found out, Zeba would've been expelled from school on the eve of the exams, and Gomes . . . well, he would have gone to jail for having sex with a student. It's a jailable offence in India too, isn't it?'

'Heavens, yes! I think you'll find that sex with a minor is an offence in most countries, Bubs. Oh God, how it's all flooded back these past few weeks . . .' Anita paused for a second before adding quietly, 'Although, in the hate-Lily stakes, I don't know whether Zeba came out tops, or whether it was me, Bubs.'

'Well, in Zeba's case it wasn't just the Gomes thing . . . remember the annual play?' Bubbles couldn't resist a sudden giggle.

'Oh Christ, of course, *Saint Joan!* Of all the bloody things Zeba could have got her knickers in a twist over, it was Shaw's *Saint Joan*! What a laugh. From the sublime to the ridiculous, *Saint Joan* to Bollywood Queen!'

'Well, at the time she *wanted* to be a stage actor. She was always going on about trying to get a scholarship to RADA. I don't think being a Bollywood superstar was Zeba's plan then.'

'Strange how she managed to behave like a diva even back then, though. Almost like she was practising the role before occupying her throne in Bollywood. Saint Fucking Joan!'

'I thought Zeba's hatred for Lily was total after the auditions, but then it just doubled after the Gomes thing, didn't it?'

'I have sometimes wondered whether that was really the only basis for Zeba's friendship with us that year. Y'know, our shared hatred of Lily.'

'C'mon, Anita, how can you say that? We'd all been friends since we were tiny, even Zeba!'

'Actually, you're right, Bubs. Old school friends do seem to make the strangest couplings when you look back. I guess you just don't think of judging people you've known since kindergarten. We were close enough, all of us, and then Lily's arrival pretty much bonded us like glue.'

Bubbles knew they were both thinking of the same thing as she said in a soft voice, 'The truth is we all hated Lily, Anita. Even poor Sam, who always tried so hard to like everyone . . . but how could one blame her, poor thing?'

'How indeed,' Anita muttered in response. 'The last time Sam came back from Delhi she was saying that her mum was still completely heartbroken over Haroon.'

Bubbles was suddenly silent, realising that Anita had never completely understood the depth of her own feelings for Haroon. Especially as she had been married and whisked off to London before she had even had the chance to *say* anything. But that was exactly the point, Bubbles thought to herself, only half-listening to Anita now. It was because the young and foolish Bubbles Malhotra had never had the gumption to fight for the things she wanted that she had spent the rest of her life, as Mrs Bubbles Raheja, thinking about what might have been had she only been more determined.

Typically unaware of her listener's feelings, Anita was ploughing on and Bubbles didn't try to stop her. After all, it had been years since they had talked of all this. 'Do you remember, Bubs,' Anita was saying, 'how desperately Sam wanted to believe it was something else that led Haroon to do what he did?'

Bubbles had found her voice and managed to keep it steady. 'Maybe it would have been less unbearable if it had been something else, Anita.'

'You could be right, Bubs . . . but, hey, I don't think we should talk about this or there'll be no sleep for either of us tonight.'

Bubbles nodded vehemently with silent relief. She hadn't been sleeping at all well these past few weeks and really wanted this conversation with Anita to end now.

'Listen, thanks for the tickets,' Anita continued, 'and thank Binkie from me too. When all's said and done, I think I'd rather be in Delhi with all of you than not. Let's face the music together, huh?'

'You're right, Anita, we'll face it together. Listen, you go and feed yourself now. And sleep well.'

After hanging up, Bubbles lay back on the silk cushions of her chaise longue for a long time, looking up at the elegant Regency-style ceilings but seeing instead the cheap pink plaster of her childhood bedroom. She remembered weeping for days after those ghastly events, looking at that pink ceiling as though one day the answers would be miraculously written there for her to see. Even after Lily's death, fifteen long years ago, she had not been able to cleanse her system of the guilt and the blame. Bubbles had tried explaining it to one of her therapists once: how she could just about accept that Lily had come along and stolen Haroon (after all, even she had to admit that Haroon was never really hers to steal). But then Lily had gone on to break his heart. That was the bit Bubbles had not been able to forgive both Lily and herself for. For how differently things might have turned out had she had the conviction to fight harder for Haroon's affections. But Bubbles had never fought for anything all her life, never demanded, never stomped her foot and seized what other people took without a second thought. Why oh *why* had she not tried harder than she had?

She covered her eyes with her forearm as she felt the first tears roll down the sides of her face and gather in her ears. What a fool she had been as a girl, not even recognising her first surge of feelings towards Lily as being jealousy. Too innocent to understand emotions she had never experienced before. Up until that point, Bubbles had thought that it was only characters in movies who indulged in emotions as strong as jealousy and hate, when they competed for love or money and it became a matter of life or death or 'rozi-roti', as her father said. She had thought that it was only in books and movies that people plotted to do awful things. But seventeen-year-old girls could love and hate, Bubbles had found to her own horror that winter, with the same ferocity. Enough to want to kill, even.

Chapter Fifteen

DELHI, 1993

While Bubbles was swept up in preparations for her engagement, Sam was keeping her promise to Haroon by diligently planning a trip to an ice-cream parlour with some of the girls from her class including, most importantly, Lily. Haroon's cunning plan was to stroll in about halfway through, pretending confusion over Sam's pick-up time. Then he would be persuaded to join the girls in having a sundae and Sam would discreetly vacate the seat next to Lily so he could work his charm on her. 'Easy,' he had said, and Sam had to agree that it sounded beautifully simple. Sam had little doubt that her popular brother would succeed in charming the pants off even stand-offish Lily D'Souza.

One problem was that no one else from class would come if they knew that Sam was inviting Lily. So, discretion being the better part of valour, Sam asked her when no one else was around.

'Me? With you all? To an ice-cream parlour?' Lily queried, clearly surprised.

'Well, you enjoyed it when you came to my birthday party before the hols, didn't you?'

'I don't think your friends like me very much,' Lily said, her voice still suspicious.

'Oh, that's not true at all!' Sam lied recklessly. 'They're still sort of getting to *know* you, Lily, that's all. Friendship takes time, y'know, and maybe it would help if you met us outside the school. One sort of bonds better that way, if you see what I mean . . .'

'Well, we certainly haven't bonded so far!' Lily laughed nastily adding, 'just yesterday that Natasha nearly bit my head off when I used her protractor by mistake. She'd never have done that if it was any of you. Not that I care particularly. Just making a point.'

'Nats? Oh ignore that. Nats just has that sort of American brashness, she means no harm. She likes you, really. She was saying so the other day, in fact, that she feels she doesn't know you very well and must stop thinking of you as the "new girl" . . .' Sam blushed, aware she was now over-egging the pudding, but, to her surprise, Lily suddenly nodded.

'Okay, I'll come,' she said, and Sam tried not to whoop with delight at the ease with which she had kept her promise to Haroon.

'Great. Saturday afternoon – say, four-ish – at Nirula's in Connaught Place,' she said using her best poker face.

In the end, everything that could go wrong did.

First of all, Bubbles – whom Sam had deliberately not invited out of consideration for her aborted crush on Haroon – was bitterly upset to hear of the outing through a chance remark from Zeba as they left school that afternoon. Sam, unable to tell Bubbles that she was helping Haroon get to know Lily, tried to save the situation unsuccessfully on the telephone. 'I *wasn't* leaving you out, Bubs!' she pleaded,

202

'I just thought you'd be busy with the engagement stuff and wouldn't want to come!'

'What engagement stuff? How can you think that, Sam?' Bubbles wailed. 'Mummy-Papa are doing everything. I have nothing to do, you know that. I know why you are doing this. Just because I'm engaged now, you all think I'm already out of here and don't want to know me any more . . . oh . . . oh . . .' And with that, Bubbles burst into tears before hanging up.

The second thing to go wrong was when Haroon, in his eagerness to reach Nirula's from his college, arrived so early he got there even before Sam had. Sam's bus, stuck in a traffic jam, had crawled its way to Connaught Place, and by the time she had loped into the ice-cream parlour, out of breath from having run all the way from the bus stop on Outer Circle, she found her brother already deep in conversation with Zeba and Natasha, both of whom were too polite to express surprise at being presented so unexpectedly with Haroon's company rather than Sam's. Luckily no one seemed to mind very much as Haroon had already chivalrously bought the first round of ice-creams.

There was one more thing that could go wrong, and so, of course, it did. And that was that Lily arrived early too, getting there before Sam had had a chance to explain her presence to her two friends.

'Oh God, look who's here – it's Lily D'Souza!' Nats said, looking in wide-eyed wonder at the girl coming through the swing doors at the far end of the ice-cream parlour. She looked disbelievingly at Sam as it dawned on her. 'You called *her* too?'

Zeba echoed the sentiments less leniently. 'How *could* you, Sam!' she hissed, looking at Sam as though she had just committed a minor felony. She had just been getting up to join Haroon at the counter to help him carry the second round of ice-creams to the table, but sat down again with a thump. 'Oh well, she can get her own ice-cream,' she said picking up her bowl to scrape its empty bottom so that she could pretend to see Lily only when she was right upon them. Finally, when she couldn't feign lateral blindness any more, she looked up and smiled coldly at Lily, mumbling a luke-warm hello.

Sam pulled up a stool, trying to make Lily welcome in the face of Zeba and Natasha's chilliness. After all, she'd invited the girl here, she hadn't just turned up on her own! And where the hell was Haroon? she wondered. He was taking his bloody time! Perhaps, unable to cope with the sight of Lily in the same room, he had passed out on top of the ice-cream counter – that was all Sam needed to deal with now!

Haroon had indeed spotted Lily the minute she had walked into Nirula's. But Zeba's order was a complicated one and he now shifted from foot to foot impatiently as the man behind the counter took what seemed like forever, scooping and measuring and shaking a syrup bottle interminably before squeezing its pink goo over the ice-cream mound. Haroon groaned inwardly as the man then started chopping straw-berries for the garnish, leaving them on the chopping board as he went through the entire boxed contents of the fridge before emerging with a single mint leaf. Finally, *finally* it was done and he looked anxiously across at Sam's group of friends as he made his way back to them, trying to prevent Zeba's massive platter of Very Berry Strawberry from sliding around on the plastic tray.

'Oh, hel-lo, Lily!' Haroon said, hamming up the surprise element terribly it seemed to Sam. He could stop pretending now, she thought to herself, seeing that it was so bloody obvious to everyone that all this had been no more than an elaborate drama.

'Hello,' Lily replied without too much warmth. Perhaps she too could clearly see through the clumsy Hussain ploy. Sam felt about two feet tall.

'What will you have, Lily?' she asked, seeing that the other two were certainly not minded to be hospitable and were already tucking into the ice-creams Haroon had bought.

'Don't worry, I'll get it,' Lily said, starting to get up.

'No, no, I will, you stay sitting,' Haroon said eagerly. 'Just tell me what you'd like.'

'A scoop of Jamoca Almond please,' she replied.

Haroon left with the order, returning a second later. 'On the other hand, you could come with me and choose your flavour at the counter, Lily,' he said weakly. 'They have a lot of new ones in . . .'

The doting expression on her brother's face made Sam curl her toes inside her sneakers. He was *such* an embarrassment! She hoped inwardly that Lily would leave the table for a few minutes so that she could explain matters to her friends, but the girl shook her head at Haroon and repeated politely, 'No, Jamoca Almond's fine, thanks.'

Sam looked at the hubbub at the counter, which was crowded with office workers and schoolchildren, calculating that Haroon would be at least another ten minutes. That would be ten minutes of her having to keep a monologue going to cover up the awkward silence that had fallen over their table at the unexpected arrival of Lily. Both Zeba and Natasha were behaving as though they'd never had such delicious ice-creams in their life, scooping and licking and savouring so as not to have to make conversation. Despite Nirula's powerful air-conditioning system, Sam could feel the sweaty semi-circles sitting stubbornly under her arms.

'Hey, you should have called the rest of the class too, Sam, why just stop with us three,' Zeba said, looking at half a strawberry balancing delicately on her spoon. Sam glanced at her, trying to assess if the remark had been sarcastic, but Zeba wore a perfectly innocent look on her face as she popped the fruit into her mouth and started chewing it.

'Anita had to be somewhere with her parents and couldn't come,' Sam replied.

'Well, Bubbles was really upset when I mentioned we were meeting here. I hadn't realised it was a *secret*,' Zeba said.

'Don't be silly, it's not a secret at all,' Sam replied, all hot and flustered. She turned to Lily, trying to change the subject. 'Did you go anywhere for the hols, Lily?'

Lily shook her head, taking a sip of water from her bottle.

'So you stayed on the school premises *all* through the summer?' Natasha asked in a horrified voice. Finally, someone other than her was engaging with Lily, Sam saw with relief.

Lily nodded again, but before she could say anything they were rescued by Haroon's arrival with her single scoop. 'Thank you,' she said, as Haroon pulled up a stool and Sam made room between herself and Lily.

'Hey, did I tell you guys I'm off to London to attend a wedding during the Christmas hols?' Natasha said.

'Wow, London!' Haroon exclaimed. 'I plan to go there one day.'

'Oh I've been many times, got cousins there,' Natasha replied. 'It's quite boring actually, rains all the bloody time. London has lots of dusty old museums and nothing else really. And *so* grimy! Just like Washington. I prefer Los Angeles any day. Californian sunshine and sand and surf, the best combo one can ask for,' she added, tossing her shiny hair like a Hollywood temptress. A knowledgeable, well-travelled, well-heeled temptress that could entice anyone but Haroon,

Sam thought. She watched her brother, seated at the table with two of St Jude's most acclaimed beauties, but with eyes for no one else but Lily D'Souza. How could Lily fail to notice his stupid puppyish adoration? Sam eyed the generally disdainful look on Lily's face nervously and thought of how Lily would now hold her in even lower esteem, seeing that all her scheming had become so obvious. Sam slumped on her bar stool, hunching her shoulders miserably and spooning her sundae into her mouth without tasting it. There was no point even trying to keep the conversation going. Zeba and Natasha were determined to continue chatting with each other without giving Lily an opening. Haroon was so star-struck he'd lost his stupid larynx at the crucial moment. Bubbles was upset with her and would probably never speak to her again. Sam did not normally use profanity, even in her deepest thoughts, but today she could not help asking herself what the fuck she'd thought she was doing.

Lily, leaving Nirula's an hour later, was more or less asking herself the same question. She should have known better when Sam had invited her out so unexpectedly. But, foolishly, she had actually imagined that Samira Hussain, the school's most popular girl, had taken a genuine liking to her. 'What a fine ass you've made of yourself again, Lily D'Souza,' she muttered to herself. Stopping at a shop window and seeing her reflection in the glass Lily remembered that she, more than anyone else, ought to understand the business of reading people's motives. Especially when they were being overly *nice*. She had worked out long ago that people were nice only when they wanted something from you, and quickly turned nasty once they'd got it.

Did Sam seriously think Lily was fool enough not to see that this trip had been set up purely for Sam's brother to slaver all over her? And what a slobbering idiot he was, all mooning eyes and breathless 'Lily this', 'Lily that'. As for those other two – the Dodgy Duo, as Lily had already mentally dubbed Zeba and Natasha for their god-awful flirty behaviour – they couldn't have been more snotty if they'd tried. Rubbing her nose so horribly in the fabulous lives they led, compared to her own lonely one. She'd had it with their persistent cold-shouldering and meanness, she thought. 'You will not cry, Lily D'Souza, you will not cry,' she hissed sharply to herself, keeping one hand on her clogged throat. A sales assistant materialised from the dark interior of the shop. 'You are wanting some help, baby?' he grinned. 'Come, come inside. I will show you everything. Come, na?'

Lily saw red paan-stained teeth and a lascivious expression and turned tail. She fled as fast as she could, running down the corridors of M-Block and out into the sunshine where an auto-rickshaw nearly careered into her, screaming its tinny horn angrily as it drove on. What was it with this world? she thought. Either they wanted to exploit you or they were trying to kill you!

She looked over her shoulder and saw that the shop-man wasn't following her. Taking a deep breath, she spotted what looked like a gift shop in the next block. 'Giggles' it said over the door. The shop next door was a card shop called 'Sniggers'. Well, if those didn't cheer her up, nothing would. She was damned if she was going back to the cottage straightaway. The Old Bat had been tickled pink at the idea of Lily being invited out by Samira Hussain and her gang. 'Oh that's marvellous, they're such a lovely bunch of girls, I'm so pleased for you, darling,' she had said.

'*Maahvellous! Lahvley!*' Lily mumbled mockingly. What did *she*, her so-called grandmother, know? And who was *she* to decide who was of worth and who wasn't? Lily wondered what her grandmother would say if she went back and told her that the faultless, chaste Samira Hussain had invited her only to pimp on behalf of her brother. That would no doubt make Principal Victoria Lamb keel right over in shock.

Lily wandered through the gift shop, inspecting the small clay trophies marked 'For My Best Friend' and 'World's Greatest Mum'. She stopped next to one that showed a figure in a tartan dressing gown and slippers, pipe in his mouth and goofy expression on his face, with the words 'World's Best Dad' written on the pedestal beneath. Lily shot a look over her shoulder and, when she saw that the woman behind the till was busy serving a customer, she picked up the small figurine and, with all her might, smashed it against the wall in a swift blow. Wiping a bit of crumbled plaster onto the back of her jeans, she then quickly exited the shop. Her action was both puerile and futile but Lily felt much better for indulging in such mindless violence, closing her eyes as she turned her face up to the sun and swallowing back the inevitable tears.

Chapter Sixteen

LONDON, 2008

Sam anxiously scanned the members' room at the Tate Modern. It was buzzing as usual, people carrying trays of drinks and salads to the tables lining the room as autumn sunshine lit up the dome of St Paul's in the distance. She was five minutes early but that was preferable to being late, in her view, especially when meeting Anita and her new man. She wondered if she ought to first visit the toilet to touch up her lipstick. The last thing she'd want was to let Anita down when meeting Hugh for the first time, especially since her friend was increasingly sounding – for the first time ever – quite genuinely in love. She wondered whether Hugh had heard as much about her and Bubbles as they had of him, but thought not. Journalist couples probably spent all their time discussing world affairs and other high-minded things. Hugh was, Sam decided, very unlikely to notice if she had put lippy on or not. It had been far more imperative to pore over the papers all morning in order to practice intelligent things to say – which Sam had diligently done, even voicing aloud to her mirror her views on the credit crunch and Obama's chances of success in the forthcoming US election, formulating her thoughts this way and that as she had got dressed.

There they were, around the corner, seated on one of the sofas overlooking the river. Sam's heart gave a little lurch as she saw Anita, oblivious to all around her, exchange a lingering kiss with a grey-haired man. She was clinging with both hands to the collar of his fleece jacket while he tenderly held her head on both sides, his fingers laced into her hair. Sam couldn't even remember when she and Akbar had last kissed like that, their entire beings smouldering with longing.

She made her way past the bar and chairs laden with shopping bags and coats, slipping off her own duffle. Autumn had come early again and, without waiting for it to get too cold, Sam had already pulled out her bulky jackets and boots with relief. Being able to cover up was one of the good things about the approach of winter, summer fashions being the bane of her life – all those skimpy spaghetti-tops and minuscule shorts making her feel positively elephantine.

She was spotted as she reached their table and Anita reached out for a hug, laughing and extricating herself from Hugh's embrace.

'Hugh, meet my dearest friend in the world, Samira Hussain,' she said, and, turning to Sam, added just a tad shyly, 'Sam, this is Hugh Appledawn.'

Sam laughed as she shook hands with Hugh. 'Do you know, she insists on using my maiden name, even after ten years of marriage!'

'I don't see why not,' Anita said, 'that's the name I knew you by for nearly twenty years until Akbar came along.'

'Oh, Akbar sends his apologies, by the way, couldn't get away from work. He'd sure have liked to have met you.' Sam smiled at Hugh, hoping her white lie wouldn't be obvious to him, even though Anita was rolling her eyes behind his back.

'Likewise,' Hugh replied. 'Anita tells me he's a corporate

212

lawyer. I recognised the name Koehler & Gunn from a story I did in the City once.'

Sam hoped he wouldn't mention the details for she was very unlikely to know anything about it. Luckily, Anita was gathering their orders – a pot of tea and scones for Anita and Hugh to share, hot chocolate and a slice of coffee-walnut cake for Sam.

'There's no point waiting for Bubbles, I suppose,' Sam said, looking at a group of people coming through the door.

'I'm happy to wait,' Hugh said.

Anita waved their concerns away. 'She'll be late, for one, and then when she does turn up all she'll want is Perrier with lime. We might as well get on with our drinks. Hugh's booked us tickets to see a movie at the BFI so we won't be able to stay too long, unfortunately.'

'I noticed that the posters were carrying warnings about "strong real sex", whatever that means, and it convinced me that it was a must-see!' joked Hugh.

Anita responded in a hammed-up posh accent, 'Darling, would you care for some strong real sex tonight?' making both her companions smile.

'I get the "real sex" thing on the poster – as opposed to pretend sex, I suppose – but what's "strong"?' asked Sam.

'Hmmm, maybe it's drawing out the difference between the sort of passionate sex a new couple would have, to the kind of gentle, languid stuff that a couple who've been together for years are more likely to have. I'd call the first "strong" and the second "mellow" or something, you know,' Anita said, adding, 'three ardent thrusts and it's strong!'

'How the hell did we get into this conversation anyway?' Hugh smiled. 'Sam, my apologies, I don't usually launch into a full-scale discussion about sex when in new company. I'm so sorry.'

'I know,' Anita concurred as Sam pursed her lips and shook her head in mock-disapproval. 'But you must be warned, Hugh, Sam's one of the few people privy to my darkest thoughts. Even . . .' she dropped her voice to a droll whisper, 'even my confession that I do actually have sex on the brain a bit these days!'

Sam was suddenly faintly embarrassed but saw Hugh and Anita exchange a private look that seemed to silently speak volumes. They were far too lost in each other to even notice her discomfiture. She took a sip of water, wondering briefly whether Anita had forgotten that Sam and Akbar had no sex at all these days, let alone 'gentle, languid sex' night after night.

Bubbles arrived alongside the tea and cakes in her usual breathless head-turning style, loudly demanding a glass of Perrier with ice on her way to the table, quite forgetting that the Tate Modern bar was self-service. She looked scrumptious, Sam thought, like an iced cupcake in a cream Chanel top with a peach mohair cardigan thrown around her shoulders. She wore Gucci glasses perched on her glossy hair and was trailing clouds of her favourite Amouage perfume. She threw her arms around Hugh exuberantly.

'Oh, what a cutie you've found, Anita! I approve totally,' Bubbles cried loudly, flinging her bag and packages down on a chair before delving into a Harrods bag to emerge with a small exquisitely packaged gift for Hugh.

As she pressed it into his hands, Sam could see how over-whelmed the poor man was. He'd soon need to get used to Bubbles' extravagant generosity if he intended staying with Anita. Sam looked at his face, now reddening slightly with all the attention Bubbles was lavishing on him. She certainly hoped he *would* stay with Anita. He seemed absolutely lovely and was now throwing a helpless look at Anita to check the propriety of accepting a gift from someone he barely knew.

'It's fine, sweetie, take it. Bubs will never speak to you again if you don't,' Anita warned.

Bubbles' gift turned out to be an exquisite woollen Louis Vuitton scarf, for which she earned a warm kiss from Hugh before he promptly wound it around his neck, now barely able to conceal his delight, though still glancing at Anita for approval. When she nodded appreciatively, Sam noticed how chuffed Hugh looked. He seemed oddly boyish for forty-something, but sweet and kind and rather nice looking too with all that crisp grey hair – Sam hoped with all her heart that Anita would have the sense not to lose him. Anita's love life so far had been tumultuous to say the least, or non-existent, which was probably worse, and made Akbar refer to her derisively as 'lesbo'.

As teas were poured and forkfuls of cake and scones passed around, the girlfriends quite effortlessly drew Hugh into their circle. And Hugh, for his part, despite never having laid eyes on anyone even remotely resembling Bubbles before, felt that vast quantity of love wrap around him as snugly as his new scarf. Unable to keep up with the rapid-fire conversation full of reference points he didn't entirely get, he leant back on the sofa, sipping his coffee, marvelling at the easy dynamic that seemed to operate between these quite dissimilar women. Even he could tell from this very first meeting how unalike the three were. Of course, he too had kept in touch with a few classmates from his grammar school in Dudley who were now working in London, meeting up with them for an occasional jar or game of squash. But what Anita and her friends shared apparently transcended normal friendships. He could see it in the way they effortlessly anticipated each other's tiniest needs - like a spoon or a glass - without a word being exchanged. He'd only ever seen his parents do that kind of thing before, and they'd been married over fifty years!

'My personal trainer will kill me,' he heard Bubbles say as she waved away Sam's offer of a bite of her cake. 'Hey, did I tell you about him? He's Italian. Giovanni. He's Jude Law's personal trainer actually, recommended to Binkie by James. He was actually employed for Mummy-Papa to try and lose some weight, but they couldn't be bothered so I'm using him now.'

'What do you need to lose more weight for, Bubs?' Sam asked, mildly remonstrative. 'You'll just disappear.'

'What is important is to be fit, not merely lose weight,' said Anita.

'Yeah, exactly,' Bubbles said. 'I might be thin, but I really do think I should up my fitness. Well, so Giovanni says.'

'Well, he would, wouldn't he?' Anita growled. 'I mean, the Raheja millions won't exactly be a turn-off to a penurious personal trainer.'

'Exercise can do no harm, I say,' Bubbles insisted.

'I worry that you're getting rather addicted to this whole business of fitness, Bubs,' Sam said. She turned to Hugh. 'Do you agree that it's all too easy to get hooked on exercise, Hugh? I think it can work almost like a drug sometimes, taking over your brain a bit. You're not an exercise junkie, I hope?'

'Nah,' Hugh replied, 'although I wouldn't mind being a small junkie in that regard. I really should be doing more than just the occasional weekend jog around Clapham Common.'

'I think Sam's right,' Anita put in. 'You meet these people sometimes whose chief source of conversation is their latest faddy exercise machine or the PB they achieved in the morning. Crashing bores who refuse to drink and still look ready to pass out before the entrée is served because they've been at the gym since 5 a.m.'

216

'They're even worse when you get them as couples,' Sam observed, 'like Dippy and Tilly – remember those two we met at the Asian Achievement Awards?'

'Heavens, I remember them and how, when pressed, they fessed up to being Dipankar and Tillotama actually!' Anita grinned. 'God, yes, I do recall them describing their epiphanous bonding moments while jogging on Richmond Common.'

'Like listening to a couple talking about a shared orgasm, wasn't it?' Sam giggled.

'Ooo, I can take it from Anita but it's not like you to be catty, Sam!' Bubbles said.

'Honestly, those two really did manage to get my goat that evening,' Sam said. 'It's not just the way they were but that they operated like brand ambassadors for their lifestyle, telling me essentially that I should aspire to be like them.'

'My word!' Hugh chuckled. 'Perhaps they mistook your politeness for interest. I've never met anyone – after my parents, of course – who'd tell me how to live my life. And even they gave up on that in my teens.'

'Parents, spouses and teachers are the only people allowed to tell you what to do,' Anita said emphatically, 'and even that only within reason.'

'And only nice old teachers, like Lamboo,' Sam added.

'Lamboo was Victoria Lamb, our school principal,' Anita explained, turning to Hugh.

'That's not a very Indian name,' he queried.

'She wasn't Indian,' Sam clarified. 'But Irish, although back then we all thought she was English. She was a terrific teacher. How we adored her.'

'She could make even Shakespeare interesting, I remember,' Bubbles said, with a small shiver of disgust as she said 'Shakespeare'.

'Every school in India should rightly have a head like old

217

Victoria Lamb,' Anita declared. 'She *was* St Jude's. Had been there forever, too. I certainly can't remember a time when she wasn't there, and I joined the school aged seven!'

'And she's *still* at Jude's – isn't that amazing?' Bubbles added.

'Really?' Hugh asked. 'She must have been one of those that stayed on after India became independent, like the Greta Scacchi character in *Heat and Dust*. Well, what made your Miss Lamb stay, do you think?'

'Don't think we know the answer to that really,' Anita replied. 'Somehow we never got around to asking her.'

'Well, it would have been a bit rude to ask, wouldn't it? Like, what are you still doing here when all the rest have gone? And Irish nuns and teachers were not uncommon in Delhi schools in our time. Mostly because of the Catholic church's missionary work,' Sam explained.

'Lamboo certainly cut a lonely figure sometimes, I must say, despite being surrounded by girls all the time,' Anita recalled.

'Has anyone replied to her letter yet?' asked Bubbles.

Sam shook her head. 'We'll do a joint letter once I've told Akbar.'

'You are coming, aren't you, Sam?' Bubbles asked, looking worried. 'I won't go without you.'

Anita elaborated for Hugh's benefit again. 'We've all had letters from Miss Lamb inviting us to some sort of reunion.'

'School reunions are usually a hoot,' Hugh said, failing to notice the women exchanging quick looks as he was looking at his watch. 'Much as I hate to break up this jolly little gathering, I think we need to leave now, Anita, if we don't want to be late for our flick,' he said, smiling at Bubbles and Sam.

'We may stay for a bit, but you carry on. Don't be late for your movie,' Sam said. She got up and gave Hugh a warm hug, adding, 'It was truly lovely meeting you. My dear friend Anita has needed someone like you to sort her out for a long time.'

'What do you mean, "sort her out"?!' Anita spluttered before breaking into a smile and giving both her friends big hugs. 'Sorry to be rushing like this, my darlings, but today was the only day both Hugh and I had off this week and I didn't want to delay his meeting you any more.'

Anita yanked on her coat and Sam saw Hugh straighten its collar at the back as they turned the corner. She sighed before sitting down again and turning to Bubbles. 'He's *nice*, isn't he?'

'Very sweet,' Bubbles agreed vehemently.

'I do hope Anita doesn't drive him round the bend. He might be a bit too affable for her. She'll just gobble alive anyone who doesn't stand up to her.' She glanced at Bubbles who was still standing and now looked a bit distracted. 'You don't have to rush off, do you? Stay and have another drink?'

Bubbles shook her head. 'Sorry, Sam, but I need to go too. Have my appointment with Gio, you see. The personal trainer guy I told you about.'

Sam smiled. 'Oh, it's *Gio*, is it? Watch you don't let yourself get seduced by the attentions of an Italian Casanova, my sweet, they do love Indian women, you know . . .' She collected her things and got up, not noticing Bubbles' blushes as her friend hunted in her jacket pocket for her phone to call her driver. They made their way out of the members' room and went down the escalators to the ground floor. Bubbles' car and driver were waiting for her in the small alleyway behind the Tate, but Sam turned down Bubbles' offer of a lift. 'I'm okay. I should try to walk over the river at least . . . it's only at this point that I ask myself *why* I went and put all that cake in my tummy,' she said ruefully.

219

The two women kissed as Bubbles' white Mercedes drew up next to them, and Bubbles blew Sam another kiss after she had got into the car and it started pulling away. She felt a pang, watching Sam pull the jacket of her collar up as an autumn breeze picked up, blowing leaves around her ankles. Poor Sam, she'd probably hoped to kill another hour or so with them all until it was time to pick Heer up from school. Bubbles, plagued with sudden guilt, almost asked Rob to turn the car around before remembering again that Gio was probably already waiting for their session in the home gym. Besides, she didn't want to talk to Sam about that just yet. Well, there was nothing to *say* yet, but Sam – sometimes so *over*-perceptive – was sure to smell a rat. Much as Bubbles loved her, she didn't really want a granny-lecture until she had done something to deserve one.

At home, Bubbles hurried up the stairs and asked Humphries the butler if Giovanni had arrived as he held open the door for her.

'I showed him down to the basement about half an hour ago, Ma'am.'

'Any of the family at home?' she asked, allowing him to take her jacket and scarf.

She was pleased to hear the words, 'No Ma'am', and wondered why that was the case. It wasn't as if she was planning to *do* anything with Gio that would require privacy. Perhaps it was just nice to know that there would be no annoying interruptions if she did.

'Please send word to Giovanni that I'm here and will take just another few minutes to get changed,' she said, pulling off her ankle boots and trotting barefoot down the corridor in her socks. It was exactly the kind of behaviour Binkie disliked; even when the children were small they had not been allowed to run around the house in anything but the most immaculate clothes and shoes. 'One must never let one's hair down before the servants,' Binkie said. But Bubbles knew the staff had other things to do than examine the family's couture, and so had taken to quite determinedly letting her hair down when no one else was around. As though to emphasise the point, she now unpinned her chignon and set her cloud of auburn hair free.

In her bedroom, she changed swiftly. That was one thing that growing up with two sisters had taught her – the wisdom of getting dressed speedily. Mostly so that she could beat them to wearing the best clothes or newest pair of shoes, before one or the other would come crashing into her bedroom making some false claim that she would invariably succumb to. Today Bubbles was having difficulty choosing the right gear, though. She held a leopard-print leotard against herself before discarding it as seeming a bit too predatory. She chose a pair of shorts instead, pulling them over her black Lycra leggings. Then, freed breasts bouncing as she searched through her chests of drawers, she found a sports bra and her new coral Helly Hansen top. That was an easy choice as she'd purchased it just yesterday from Harrods when she'd gone to buy Hugh's scarf. Having pulled on a pair of gym shoes, she trotted out of her room and down the corridor again, yanking on a pink sweatband to hold back her hair. Gio had already lavishly complimented her hair once so she would leave it untied while she did her stretches. So far she had only met him three times, but already his hotly appreciative looks had conveyed to her that he found her rather sexy. How could she not warm to such open admiration? It wasn't that Bubbles ever suffered from a paucity of leering looks from men – she got those wherever she went, and frequently. This was something rarer and more unattainable: the piercing interest of a man who even seemed to care about the state of her hamstrings. And it helped too that he was good looking, though in that rakish sort of way. She had certainly not had that kind of attention from Binkie in ages, except for that time in Martinique during the half-term hols around six months ago when, flicking through the TV channels as the children frolicked in the pool outside, Binkie had stumbled upon a porn channel – specifically a scene showing two men with a pneumatic blonde – and had been overcome with a short, sharp burst of lust for her. She thought hard, trying to be fair to Binkie – after all, he wasn't a bad bloke, just a bit distant in that British sort of way – but, yes, that had definitely been the last time.

She bounced happily down the stairs and opened the door to the gym. And there was Giovanni, looking as though the very sight of her was enough to make him the most idiotically happy man in the world.

'*Mia bella*, Miss Bubbles!' Giovanni said with a flourish, running hot black eyes up and down her body before mumbling what sounded like, '*Sonotantoinamoratodite.*'

He had done this the last time too, switching every so often to Italian, a language of which Bubbles, of course, understood not a word. Her inability to understand what Gio was saying made her feel oddly excited and breathless, though, as if she were speeding along the edge of a precipitous chasm in a fast car.

'So sorry, Giovanni, I am late . . .'

'Ah!' he said, stopping her short with an upheld forefinger, 'I tell you already, *mia* Bubbles – Gio, Gio, not Giovanni! We must firstly be friends before I become your trainer. You must talk and I must talk. About everything. If we don't keep talking, you will not exercise. I learn that from whenever I work with the ladies.'

'Of course, Gio,' Bubbles said smiling, but feeling a small jab of jealousy deep inside her at the thought of all the other ladies Gio might pay attention to.

'Okay, so how is your body feeling today? Your back, your legs, your *thoorrso* . . . no aching and paining from last time's exercise?'

'My body . . . feels great, actually,' Bubbles said, although in truth her body sometimes felt terribly starved of the loving embraces of a man. She was aware, though, that Gio's elongated use of 'thoorrso' had provided him with an excuse to examine her curves all over again. She knew she really ought to mind his flirtatious behaviour very much and promptly sack him. Oh God, what would her in-laws say if they saw these hot, lusty looks. But, on the other hand, they were not likely to see them as they never came down to the basement, thanks to their varying states of arthritis. And it wasn't as if she was *doing* anything wrong – God, no, that she would never, ever do. Bubbles simply couldn't help adoring the way she tingled all the way up to her neck and ears when Gio's dark eyes looked at her. For years she had been married to someone to whom she was mostly invisible, and now, suddenly, here was a man who not only *saw* her when he looked at her but noticed and appreciated all her component parts. Besides, Gio reminded her terribly of Haroon sometimes, with his thatch of black hair and cheerful lopsided grin. *How* could she *not* help transforming into a gawky sixteen-year-old instantly, her knees turning to water in the glare of this handsome man's warm and sunny attentions.

Chapter Seventeen

DELHI, 1993

As the date for Bubbles' engagement neared, she found herself swinging from fear to excitement to near hysteria. She had long forgiven Sam for her exclusion from the ice-cream parlour trip, knowing that if she'd had a brother like Haroon, she would have done the same for him. Bubbles had even absolved Haroon for his crime of not loving her back, realising gradually the problems she would have faced in trying to convince her parents that she should marry him over Binkie. The only person it was still difficult to pardon was Lily, who had sashayed into all their lives and so unthinkingly stolen Haroon's heart. Without that happening, Bubbles reckoned she might have stood at least half a chance.

In school, however, anticipation over Bubbles' engagement party was at fever pitch by the time September rolled around. Class XII's teachers had to give up trying to keep the girls' attention on the forthcoming mock exams. The enthusiasm had even filtered through to the staff room as, a week before the ceremony, Mr and Mrs Malhotra had personally delivered a stack of silk saris and shirt pieces as gifts for Bubbles' long-suffering teachers. The girls had been given an even better treat, being invited en-masse to the new flagship

Malhotra shop in Connaught Place to pick out material for the salwaar suits and lehngas they would wear to the main ceremony. The entire class boarded the school bus that covered Connaught Place on its run, trooping into Malhotra Suit-Pieces & Textiles one afternoon. Even girls who normally never wore Indian clothes got into the spirit of things, holding bolts of material against each others faces and helping match up chiffon dupattas to their suits. Salesmen draped themselves in saris like an array of drag-queens as trays full of bottled fizzy drinks were passed around. Looking around at her celebrating classmates, Bubbles felt almost happy to have been the cause of so much bonhomie.

However, when the morning of 2 September dawned, poor Bubbles woke up in her bed shivering like a monsoonal peepul leaf. She turned her head and felt slightly reassured when she saw Sam asleep in the neighbouring bed, her friend's plump, sweet face seeming to be smiling even in slumber. Bubbles sighed – what was worst about this whole marriage thing was the thought of leaving such dear friends like Sam and Anita behind when she finally left for England. May was not that far away, really, and then she would be all alone out there in the world, in distant, unfamiliar London. Natasha hadn't helped by telling her how cold and wet and grimy it always was. Only the musicals were fun, Nats had said, but, much as Bubbles longed to see *Phantom of the Opera*, she knew life as Mrs Binkie Raheja was unlikely to involve visiting theatres every day. Finally, when the fretting was starting to give her headaches, Bubbles told herself that she would only really start worrying about the marriage once the number of months left could be counted on the fingers of one hand. As things stood, she had – she counted them off on her fingers once again – nine months left, if she included the month of May. What was a more immediate concern was that the Raheja family would have arrived last night and taken up residence in the thirty-odd rooms that had been booked for them at Le Meridien. Bubbles was just starting to quail again at the thought of meeting them – the entire clan this time – when Sam opened her eyes and smiled at her.

'Heyyy . . . bridey . . .' she said softly.

'Ohhh, don't call me that, Sam. I'm trying to forget!'

'Forget? Don't be silly now . . . it's going to be so marvellous today and you're going to look just gorgeous in that beautiful orange lehnga.'

'Well, no pimples today at least. In fact, I haven't had one for two weeks now, Sam. That doc Nat's mum knows has been just amazing, no?'

'Strange how a little dose of zinc was all you needed.'

'See, *that's* the kind of thing they should be teaching in Chemistry class, what chemicals can do for your body and hair. Imagine, I always thought zinc was a poisonous metal!'

Sam laughed and swung her legs out of bed. 'God, don't talk of Chemistry, I haven't touched my books in days and feel sure I'm going to flunk every paper.'

'Well, at least Zeba is sure she'll be okay for the Chemistry paper, thanks to Gomes.'

Sam groaned. 'Stupid girl, such a high price to pay! Is he coming today too?'

'Who, Gomes? Yes, they're all coming in the evening, I think: Gomes, Moss, Menon, Lamboo . . .'

'Is Lily coming with Lamboo?'

'I suppose she will. The others will come in the evening, although Anita and Zeba have promised to come early.'

Sam started to brush her teeth in Bubbles' very pink bathroom. There was plenty of time to get ready before her own parents and brother arrived later in the evening but she still hadn't formulated a plan for keeping her promise to Haroon to ensure he got to spend some time with Lily. After that unproductive trip to Nirula's he had not managed much more than the occasional glimpse of Lily, gained by coming to pick Sam up and hanging around the school gates until his protesting sister dragged him off. At the gates, his chances were not good. Unlike the other girls who had to board the school buses outside school, Lily only went there if she wanted to buy a kulfi stick or bread pakora. Haroon had spotted her once at the kulcha vendor and managed to hastily cut his way through the crowd, catching her just before she vanished back onto the school premises. She had frowned at first, seeing his red face and sweating brow, but had then thawed enough to exchange some small talk, asking him if he wanted her help to look for his sister. They had briefly combed the car park together for Sam, bumping into her as she emerged from the gates a little later. Sam remembered how Haroon had smiled all the way home in the car that day, humming a tune to himself and grabbing their mother to give her an unexpected kiss when they reached the house.

Both Sam's and Bubbles' spirits rose by the time Anita arrived for the engagement party, accompanied by Natasha. Natasha had brought a giant vanity case with her, filled with her mother's stock of imported make-up, and the sampling that ensued was accompanied by enough squealing and shrieking to have Bubbles' father despatch a servant upstairs to ensure all was well.

'Sshh . . . sshh . . . let's keep it down,' Sam said, still giggling at the unfamiliar sight of Anita's round Bengali eyes wearing green eye-shadow.

'Hey, listen, everyone, I forgot to tell you, the beautician's bringing a hairdresser to do my hair later on and Mamma has said that you can all have your hair blow-dried too. She's happy to pay.'

'No way! All of us? That's far too generous!'

'I'm telling you, really, she wants to do it. You will all look so fab.'

'You don't want us looking too fab, silly. What if Mr Binkie Raheja takes a shine to one of us instead?' Anita fluttered her sparkling eyelids coquettishly.

Bubbles threw a pillow at her. 'You wish!' she shouted, starting to giggle hysterically again.

'Listen, you all carry on with your make-up. I'm going downstairs to get some breakfast, I'm starving,' Sam announced. The aromas had already started emanating from the caterers who had set up shop in the Malhotras' back garden two days ago, and Sam could smell her favourite aloo-parathas. She reckoned she had put on a kilo in the past two days, but this was not a normal circumstance and there would be plenty of time to diet once this engagement was over. After all, she was sure to lose some weight once the stress of the exams kicked in.

She wandered downstairs, leaving Natasha and Bubbles experimenting further on Anita's face. Mrs Malhotra was looking worriedly out at the skies from her drawing-room windows. A thunderstorm appeared to be brewing in the west and the day had suddenly grown close and muggy.

'*Beti*, it won't rain, na?' she asked Sam, who joined her at the window to look upwards.

'No, I don't think so, Auntie,' Sam replied, trying to sound comforting just as the first fat drops of rain spattered down on the cement patio.

'Oho, all will be ruined!' Mrs Malhotra wailed, opening the French windows and running in the direction of the caterer's tent. Sam followed her – at least she was running

229

towards the source of food. As Mrs Malhotra engaged the head cook in animated and worried conversation, Sam found a pile of plates and, wiping one on her dupatta, walked up to a man who was assiduously puffing up a sizzling paratha on a frying pan.

Sam spent a few minutes in quiet absorption, finishing her breakfast in an empty corner of the tent. Mopping up the last bit of dahi and pickle with her paratha, she promised herself that this was really brunch and not breakfast, and that she would now eat nothing more until tea-time.

By evening the rain clouds had passed, leaving the Malhotra garden smelling pleasantly of damp earth and grass. As the fairy lights that had been draped over all the surrounding trees and bushes were switched on, the small gathered crowd let out a collective sound of appreciation. Only the closest Malhotra friends and relations had arrived at this point, including Sam's parents and brother. They sat on metal chairs that had been encased in pink satin with large purple bows at the back. The women tucked their saris and skirts under themselves to save their borders from getting wet on the lawn, while the men stood around awaiting turbaned waiters who had started working the still subdued crowd with their trays of drinks. Bubbles, by now resplendent in a brocade lehnga the colour of a deepening sunset, sat surrounded by her dozen or so friends, smiling shyly at all the compliments but keeping a wary eye fixed on the doors through which the groom's contingent would shortly appear. She cast a yearning glance at Haroon, sitting with his parents at the other end of the tent, but even Bubbles could recognise, not without a pang, that her sigh was more theatrical than heartfelt.

An hour later, thanks partially to Mr Malhotra's seemingly unending supply of Bacardi and Scotch, the party was in full swing, and Zeba, who had turned up looking fabulous in a slinky yellow crepe lehnga, was dancing on the makeshift dance floor with one of Bubbles' inebriated uncles. Sam watched her enviously; Zeba really did have the tiniest waist, accentuated further by her having pulled the skirt of her lehnga down to way below her navel soon after she had arrived. If Sam did that, her little paunch would hang right over the waistband, but Zeba's stomach was long and flat and smooth. Sam wished she hadn't eaten those samosas at lunchtime, or sampled the halwa at tea.

Some of the teachers had also arrived by now, and accompanying Miss Lamb was Lily. Sam, despatched by Mrs Malhotra to receive them, walked with them to where Bubbles was seated. While the teachers exclaimed over Bubbles' beautiful clothes and gave her their gifts, Sam took in the unfamiliar sight of Lily in a pale blue salwaar kameez and said, 'You look nice.' Lily, who had studiously avoided Sam ever since the trip to Nirula's, now gave Sam one of her rare smiles. 'Do you never usually wear Indian clothes then?' Sam enquired.

'I used to when I was younger,' Lily replied hesitantly, before suddenly blurting, 'my mother used to be a seamstress, you see.'

Sam awaited further revelation, but when none was forthcoming she added awkwardly, 'Anyway, the salwaar kameez really does suit you.'

'It seems to suit everyone,' Lily said, looking around.

'True, the world's most flattering garment,' Sam agreed. 'Don't know what I'd do without it!'

Sam was conscious of Haroon watching them from across the lawn, but she ignored him for now and hoped he would have the sense to hold back for a bit. The strategy seemed to work, for after Lily had exchanged a few stilted hellos with

Bubbles and the other girls clustered around her, she disappeared. A little later, Natasha leaned over to Sam and Anita and nodded in Lily's direction as she whispered, 'She's unusually chirpy today.'

Sam saw Lily on the far side of the garden, standing with Haroon. So he hadn't needed her help after all, Sam thought, noticing with some surprise that he was making Lily laugh by narrating some story, his hands gesticulating excitedly.

'Haroon does have such an easy way with people, doesn't he?' Anita remarked. 'I mean, have any of *us* ever seen Lily laugh like that?'

'Yeah, I was also wondering why we never get to see that nicer side to Lily,' Sam agreed.

'Because ... er ... maybe there *isn't* one?' Natasha said sardonically.

'But I've seen her with some of the juniors at school and they seem to adore her.'

'Juniors will take to any senior student who's either pretty or sporty,' Anita said, adding grudgingly, 'and she's both, if you think about it.'

'It's just the way that Lily picks people to be nice to seems a bit ... y'know ... *random*,' Sam observed, still puzzled.

'Oh Sam, you're so accustomed to being liked, you just don't get it, do you?' Anita said. 'It's Lily's way of controlling people. She knows she has you on tenterhooks because you're waiting to be liked by her. And getting more and more desperate while you wait. It's a *game*.'

'But why would she want to play games like that with me? What have I done to be played with like that? She must dislike me.'

'Oh silly, you don't have to *do* anything to be disliked by Lily, because I don't think she particularly likes anyone,' Anita comforted.

'Or anything,' said Zeba, who had just come off the dance floor for a drink of water. 'She's just an awful misery-guts, that Lily. The one good thing about leaving school will be not having to see her morose face again.'

The music was getting raucous and Zeba was called back onto the dance floor by the other revellers. A couple of the men looked completely entranced by her, dancing as close as they could get without actually touching her. Sam hoped Zeba knew better than to allow any of them to start pawing her. She looked a little inebriated herself, although Sam knew she was conservative enough never to touch alcohol. Perhaps she was just drunk on all the male adulation.

A sudden burst of high-pitched shehnai music announced the arrival of the groom's party at the gates. 'Oh goodness, the groom must have arrived!' Sam said excitedly, leaving her group of friends to make her way hurriedly back to where Bubbles was seated.

'Where have you *been*, Sam?!' Bubbles hissed frantically as she neared her. 'They're *here*! *Don't* be going anywhere now, okay!'

'Okay, okay,' Sam promised, squeezing her friend's clammy hand. 'I'll guard you from those evil Rahejas. Won't let them come anywhere near you tonight. Ravan's army has come to get our Sita.'

'This is no time for *jokes*, Sam!' Bubbles said, sounding close to tears.

'Oh, Bubbles, quit worrying. You look so beautiful tonight, you're gonna knock them all for six, believe me. That Binkie won't know what hit him when he sees your new hair and skin . . .'

'And veneered teeth.' Bubbles tried to smile to show off her new pearly-whites but was not wholly able to wipe the petrified look off her face.

Sam watched the Raheja clan enter the garden. They had the same sort of general look as the Malhotras, expensively clad and bejewelled, except that some of them possessed that 'foreign' sheen that set them apart. It was something about their cleaner complexions, perhaps, or a certain air of extra confidence that Indians who lived abroad carried about their persons when they were in India. Sam knew from the time she had taken her American cousins sight-seeing around Delhi that touts could spot that foreign element from a mile away. She now watched as one sophisticated-looking woman from the Raheja clan picked up a glass of Scotch almost as soon as she came in. As far as she knew, none of the Malhotra women drank alcohol, but these were the *baraatis* and everyone knew that the groom's party would get anything they wanted and not be eyed askance.

Sam waited next to Bubbles, still holding her damp hand as the Malhotras went through the *jai-mala* routine, garlanding the chief players among the Rahejas and presenting them with sari boxes and suit lengths. It looked to Sam as if Bubbles' parents had emptied the entire contents of one of their shops for this wedding. Oh, and now Binkie was receiving the diamond Cartier watch which Bubbles had told her had been specially ordered from the family's smuggler-bootlegger contact weeks ago. She felt Bubbles tense as her father started to lead the Raheja parents in her direction.

'Haanji, haanji, our bride, ji,' Mr Malhotra said loudly, as though worried they might not recognise Bubbles without an introduction.

Mrs Raheja dipped her hands into what looked like a really expensive Gucci bag (Sam had never seen one outside the pages of a magazine before) and emerged with a sparkly necklace. Goodness, it appeared Bubbles was going to get diamonds too, as though the stuff she already had weighing down her neck wasn't enough. Bubbles bent to touch a few Raheja feet and was rewarded with the necklace being dragged down over her head – just a bit too roughly, Sam thought, as she helped Bubbles pull it over her dupatta without snagging it on her nose-ring.

That done, a small bespectacled man was shoved in their direction, whom Sam presumed was Binkie. She took comfort from the fact that the man who was about to spirit her poor friend away from Delhi looked about as terrified as Bubbles, staring from behind his glasses with a wild-eyed look at the shenanigans unfolding all around him. Now Mr Malhotra was dragging him off to another part of the lawn to pay his respects to Bubbles' elderly grandmother.

A few more members of the Raheja clan came up to examine Bubbles – or her clothes and jewellery more likely – and a couple of the presumably less sophisticated ones were nice enough to indicate their pleasure by tweaking her cheek or chucking her chin. One or two of the uncles tried engaging her in semi-flirtatious banter, but by now the shehnai players had reached a crescendo, drowning out all but the most determined conversationalists.

Sam craned her neck to see how her brother was getting on at the other end of the garden and was pleased to see that Lily was still with him. They seemed deep in conversation, and Sam had to agree that they looked good together, framed by the soft light of the illuminated tree under which they stood. Lily's silky hair was falling about her shoulders as she looked up at Haroon. He bent his head towards her to hear what she was saying above the music.

Suddenly worried that Bubbles would spot them and feel a renewed heartbreak in the midst of her own engagement, Sam nudged her friend's arm, directing her attention to the dance floor on the other side of the garden. Most of the crowd had gravitated to it and Zeba was by now the cyno-sure of all eyes as she danced, arms raised above her head, hair tumbling about her slender gyrating waist. Sam and Bubbles exchanged a smile on hearing a couple of the younger male Raheja relatives whoop in loud appreciation as Zeba turned her back to them and cheekily swayed her pert bottom right in their faces.

'Good old Zeba,' Bubbles whispered to Sam. 'At least *she's* not scared of my new in-laws!'

Chapter Eighteen

MUMBAI, 2008

'So, looking forward to the National Film Awards, hanh?'
Shiv Mirchandani asked Zeba, who was reclining next to him
on the sofa, a sheer French chiffon sari draped lightly over
her plunging neckline. Zeba knew from long experience that
nothing excited Shiv more than her perfumed bosom, and
so she always made it a point to wear saris rather than cover-
all kurtas when he visited.

'The awards have become such a big bore, Shivji,' Zeba
replied in a tone of extreme ennui. Then she remembered
the special word Shiv had had with the jury on her behalf
and added quickly, 'But, I must say, winning the Best Actress
Award for the third time is a great honour.'

'Honour! It is the world's greatest achievement. Not even
Madhuri or Aishwarya have ever won it three times. You are
the one and only, Zebaji!'

Zeba inclined her head and did an elegant *adaab* in a
gesture of thanks. 'Apki badaulat . . . it is all because of you,
Shivji,' she breathed.

'I would have attended, Zebaji, but unfortunately I cannot
leave Bombay at this time.'

'I understand, Shivji, you are a busy man,' Zeba breathed,

aware that Shiv had stopped flaunting their affair in public
ever since his son had started work in Bollywood.

'Najma going with you?' Shiv enquired.

'No need for Najma,' Zeba replied. 'She knows exactly
what I need when I'm away from home and will pack everything for me.'

Zeba leaned across the glass table for the bottle of
Glenfiddich they were sharing, allowing her sari pallav to
slip delicately off her left shoulder as she did so. She poured
a tot into the lead-crystal glass Shiv was holding out, feeling
his sharp black eyes bore holes into the velvety undulations
that formed her cleavage. Then, putting the bottle back, she
slowly replaced the pallav in its rightful position across
Bollywood's most magnificent breasts and smiled at him
from under dark lashes.

Shiv dragged his attention back to Zeba's face and managed
to gather his thoughts. 'Why are you not taking Najma with
you?' he queried presently, looking mildly worried. Most
Bollywood heroines never travelled anywhere without their
entourage of maids and secretaries and pushy mothers,
although Zeba Khan had always been different in this matter.
Zeba had always been a cut above the other heroines, in Shiv
Mirchandani's view, sort of independent and smarter. It was
clearly a quality that also made her sexier, although Shiv
would have struggled to explain the connection between
brains and sex appeal. All he knew was that for ten long
years he had not lusted after anyone else, despite the dozens
of aspiring starlets he could have with a click of his fingers.

'Gupta has arranged my accommodation at the Mughal
Hilton. They always reserve their royal suite for me,' Zeba
replied, failing to mention that it was a hotel that anticipated her every need in a most attentive manner because
the chairperson of the chain had long been a devoted suitor.

Jealousy in a kindly lover like Shiv Mirchandani was to be judiciously employed.

'But the Mughal Hilton is at one end of the city, Zebaji, and the Film Awards are at the other end, at the Siri Fort Auditorium?'

Zeba shrugged. 'I have some family matters to attend to also and, after all, Delhi is my childhood city. It is in fact Bombay that I still don't know very well!'

'Ahhh, Bumbai, Bumbai,' Shiv said, swigging deeply on his Scotch and looking suddenly maudlin. Zeba knew that he had come up from the backstreets of Bombay, a teaboy in a jewellery shop who had arrived in the city with dreams of becoming a film hero. She studied his pock-marked face, able to see clearly why he had never become a star, but felt her usual rush of admiration for the pragmatism with which he had merely side-stepped his original ambition and become such a successful director instead. Even the arrival of the new generation of film-makers that included his own son had not, thankfully, caused Shiv to give up just yet. Only last week he had announced his grand new project: a remake of his very first superhit, *Dil*. The role that Ragini Devi had played in that version would be perfect for Zeba today, just perfect. Shiv had not yet promised her the part, but it would be foolish to doubt it. Or to put pressure on the old boy unnecessarily.

Zeba reached out and plucked Shiv's BlackBerry out of his hand to place it on the table. Then she lightly stroked his hand where it lay on his thigh, feeling the sharp edges of the enormous topaz ring he wore on his right pinkie finger for luck. 'Shivji, this city is like both of us,' she whispered. 'Dynamic, ambitious and more . . . more *seductive* the more you come to know it. Keeping one under its spell more with each passing day. Perhaps that is why it has been kind to both of us all these years. Twin souls always recognise each other, hain na?'

Shiv looked for a minute at the smooth, bejewelled fingers massaging his hand and felt his loins stir as they always did within minutes of being in Zeba Khan's company. There was only one problem with brainy women like Zeba: sometimes they talked too much. Which was annoying for simple people like him who only knew how to do one thing at a time. He picked up her hand and pushed it into his groin, the force of his sudden movement causing his rings and hers to pierce his testicles a little painfully through the thin silk of his kurta pyjamas. He drew in his breath sharply, but primal urges were now overwhelming all other concerns. Putting his drink down, he pulled Zeba towards him. Roughly pushing her chiffon pallav aside, he yanked on the buttons of her blouse. Good girl, she hadn't bothered with a bra, those nightmare garments with hooks and buckles in the most unpredictable places. Shiv feasted his eyes lovingly for a moment on the familiar pair of breasts that had popped out of Zeba's blouse and always reminded him of a pair of alphonso mangoes, magnified to twice their size and ripened to perfection. But enough of looking now. Shiva parted his lips, aiming for the nipple gracing Zeba's right breast like a rare pink pearl.

After Shiv had left her house that night, Zeba lay back on her jacquard couch, feeling the usual mixture of relief and regret. The business of having sex with men like Shiv Mirchandani, who had not the faintest idea of clitorises and g-spots, was invariably a rather gruelling affair, and usually Zeba was glad to see him off so that she could get her beauty sleep. But sometimes, just sometimes, she watched Shiv washing away the telltale smells and signs before he donned his clothes and returned to his wife with a faint sense of envy. After all, Kamla Mirchandani, an uneducated woman whom Shiv had married at twenty, knew about her husband's long-standing affair with Zeba. Who didn't? Nevertheless, Shiv washed himself fastidiously before returning to his wife out of some curious sense of respect or consideration for her that Zeba couldn't help being awed by. Kamla, for all her lack of sophistication and beauty, was, all said and done, the woman that Shiv *returned* to when he had finished with Zeba. And even though Zeba had never once asked Shiv to divorce his wife and marry her, something told her, as he hurried away from her bed in the dead of night, that it was perhaps the one thing he would not do for her.

Zeba got up to search for her panties and found the tiny scrap of lace draped over the potted ficus where Shiv must have flung it in his throes of passion. She didn't need to wear it again for the short walk back to her room but she buttoned up her blouse and pulled on her sari underskirt before loosely winding her powder-blue sari around her body, gazing contemplatively at the night sea through the French windows. Stray lights of a few fishing vessels bobbed among the black waves. Zeba thought for a minute about those poor fishermen doing their difficult and smelly work in the dead of the night before emitting a short, bitter laugh. 'Not that different from the dirty work I must sometimes do in the middle of the night,' she muttered in a low voice to herself, dropping to her knees to look for her slippers under the sofa. Pulling them out, she stood up and walked barefoot to the door, trailing both slippers and panties in her hand. This second lounge of hers was connected by a glass corridor to the dining room, beyond which lay the rest of the house, and she couldn't possibly have walked back to her room naked. Her vast entourage knew exactly what she was up to tonight, her affair with Shiv having long passed the stage of being gossip material in the kitchens and servants' quarters. Neverthless, some innate sense of conservatism – inherited, she was sure, from her father – kept Zeba from flaunting what was, after all, an illicit liaison.

Feeling curiously low-spirited, she made her way past the rosewood dining table, polished and cleaned since her cosy dinner with Shiv a couple of hours ago. She couldn't even remember when she had last seen this enormous table laid for more than just two. A family gathering had been out of the question for many years now, her strict professor father having cut her dead the minute he had first heard about her affair with Shiv. Why, he had barely been able to stomach her becoming a film star, let alone living the life of one. Occasionally she managed to sneak a phone call or a fleeting visit to her mother, but only when no one else was around. She had not seen her father, or two older brothers for that matter, since she had turned twenty-two.

'But, no regrets, Zeba Khan, you must do what you must do,' she said firmly to herself, closing the dining-room door behind her and walking towards the stairs that led to her bedroom. She had always used men to further her career; it was now almost second nature to assess a man by what he could do for her and how far she could push him to get what she wanted. She certainly owed Shiv more than she did her father and brothers and was grateful for the clout he had wielded with the panel of jurors to ensure she won the Best Actress Award again this year. But, God, had the gongs taken their time coming! Perhaps it wasn't so odd that she had only just started receiving critical acclaim, seeing that her early roles had all been song-and-dance chocolate-box ones, where she had mostly performed the function of a clothes-horse for Mumbai and Delhi's top designers. It was only as the years had passed, and directors had found her popularity 'evergreen', that more imaginative scripts had started coming her way. The timeworn graduation other long-haul actresses had all been subject to – of schoolgirl-collegestudent-younglover-youngwife-notsoyoungwife-sister-mother-oldmother-veryold mother – seemed to have bypassed her. Thus she had recently done a whole variety of roles: the temptress corporate boss ('Think Demi Moore,' the director had said) and the married woman who faces temptation (Meryl Streep) but deals with it in *Indian* not American style. Her most recent offer had, rather excitingly, been the role of Catherine Earnshaw in the Bollywood version of *Wuthering Heights*, a book she had been taught at school by Lamboo, which was fortunate as she suspected that the director had not managed to get past page ten.

Zeba opened the door to her dimly lit room and saw that Gupta had propped up a piece of paper under the raw-silk bedside lampshade. It was a suggested itinerary for her next shoot, which was to be a month in Johannesburg, followed by her trip to Delhi in December. She sat on the edge of her bed and picked it up to examine the dates, angling the piece of paper under the soft light. She had not been back to Delhi for so long now. The faraway city of her childhood. Now there was not even the attraction of sneaking a visit to her mother, as her parents had moved to Hyderabad to stay with her oldest brother after Abba had retired from the university. And yet, the city was beckoning her back with a force she could not comprehend. Crowded, polluted, aggressive, there were few reasons to remember Delhi with affection. Even film directors hardly ever shot sequences there these days, as it was easier now to take entire crews to Scotland or China where they worked without any other distractions and even got given subsidies for their pains. In recent times, Zeba's few trips to the capital had been made only to collect the occasional award. This was likely to be her last Best Actress gong, though, as no female actor over the age of thirty-five in Bollywood was ever awarded one. What lay next, perhaps some years down the line, was one of those 'Lifetime Achievement' things that usually meant one was either at death's door or that nobody wanted to cast you in anything but a cameo role any more.

She shuddered and rang the bell for Najma. When the woman came in, wiping her hands, Zeba asked, 'Have you spoken to Tanya about my clothes? I need something good for the awards ceremony?'

'As Madam said, two or three boxes have come from the Maleeha Malkani boutique.'

'Okay, good.'

'Maleehamadam sent the matching stiletto sandals also.'

'Yes, she said she would.'

'And Rajudriver will pick up the matching jewellery from Popatlalsons once Madam has decided.'

'Good. And for the previous day?'

'Previous day, Madam?'

'I told you, Najma,' Zeba clucked irritatedly. It was not like Najma to be scatterbrained. 'On the night before the awards I will be going to a family function and need to be soberly dressed for that.' The suitably vague 'family function' had been used to cover up other trysts before, but never a school reunion.

'Ah, yes, Madam said. Funeral, no? I will take out the white sari with silver mokash and long-sleeved blouse . . .'

'I never said funeral, Najma,' Zeba snapped. 'Memorial, memorial! I don't wish to wear white.' She could imagine it: turning up in white and seeming to be in mourning for the anniversary of Lily's death. Everyone, even Miss Lamb, knew that she had never liked Lily, and it would seem too much like . . . well, like acting.

244

'Pack me a sari – one of the designer crepe silk ones that shows the figure but in a subtle way.' (After all, it was unlikely there would be any men around who would be worth her while.) 'But not too much sparkle-warkle, hanh?' She had to get it just right – look expensive (after all, Bubbles Raheja was going to be there) and sober (for poor old Lamboo did not deserve what had come to her), but also sultry and sexy, as would be expected of a star. In some ways it was a pity that Lily was *not* going to be there, typically depriving Zeba of the chance to flaunt her success in her face.

Zeba shivered as she realised what she had just wished for. Not that she believed in ghosts and divine retribution and all that psychic crap. But the shivers had been returning these past few weeks, ever since she had received the letter from Lamboo. Even a hunky male model she had brought back from a party recently for a bit of nocturnal entertainment had not been able to sufficiently distract her from her dark mood.

Najma was still waiting so Zeba turned again to her. 'Don't forget to pack a couple of shawls, Najma. It will be cold in Delhi.'

'Yes, Madam. Also, I will put jackets in if you are wearing pants. And three shawls for the sari suits. Okay na?'

Zeba nodded and tried to smile, but as her maid turned to leave she called after her in an uncharacteristically small voice, 'Najma, please sleep in the dressing room tonight, okay? I am not sleeping very well these days.'

Chapter Nineteen

DELHI, 1993

It was the hardest job for Class XII to return to school after the revelries of the Raheja–Malhotra engagement party, but Victoria Lamb was determined that, in the six months left until the Board Exams, she was going to get the best out of her girls. The start of the grind was a stern pep-talk one morning in the school quadrangle after assembly.

'My dear girls, believe me, I don't tell every senior batch that they're the best I've ever had. But to you – to this batch – I have said it often enough because I genuinely believe you're special. You haven't been dubbed my *crème de la crème* for nothing, you know! I've watched you grow from children and come into senior school to now be standing where you are; on the brink of womanhood. Why, one of you will even be married soon!' Victoria broke off to smile at Bubbles but regained her serious look to carry on. 'Now, I want each and every one of you to make me a solemn promise that you will, from this day on, concentrate every pore of your beings on getting the best grades you possibly can in the forthcoming mock exams. You have three weeks left to December, which is time enough to be well-prepared. We'll think about the Board Examination after that because, as

247

I've often said, if you're prepared for the mocks then you're prepared for the Boards. But remember, the time for fun and games is now well and truly over. Yes?' She looked around and, as usual, there was one cheeky response.

'But Ma'am, what about the annual play?'

Victoria had not forgotten – the annual play in February was as much a source of pride to her as it was to the senior girls who took part every year. She had once even confessed to a past batch that old dream of treading the floorboards as a professional actress herself. 'Oh, too many moons ago to even remember now . . .' she had dismissed when pressed for details.

She now looked around at the small group occupying the quadrangle. 'Yes, of course, there's still the school play to look forward to,' she conceded, 'but I have to warn you that we may have to take most of the cast from the junior classes this year.' The principal raised her voice slightly as a murmur of discontent rippled through the assembled group, Zeba's voice loudest of all. 'Merely . . . *merely* because Bubbles' engagement took many days out of our syllabus. Come on, tell me you were all much happier attending those ceremonies than taking part in the school play. I'm afraid that's the sacrifice you're going to have to make. Remember, last year's play almost completely comprised girls from this class . . .'

'And what a great production, Ma'am!' Natasha said. 'My cousin tells me that the Xavierans next door still talk about our Jean Brodie.'

Victoria smiled at Zeba this time, who was trying unsuccessfully to look modest in the front row. 'Yes, indeed,' she said, 'one of the best we've ever turned out, I have to say. Of course, seeing that this year's play is Shaw's *Saint Joan*, we will need a really strong lead player again. I'm certainly not ruling out the possibility of at least one role going to this class. But that will be decided by Mr Moss at the auditions and, of course, you will all be given time to attend those.'

Sam saw Zeba shift slightly; everyone knew the part was already hers, even though Lamboo sounded as though she might be hedging her bets.

'And Ma'am, the school Social?'

'Ah now. How can we possibly forget the school Social?' Victoria smiled indulgently, looking around. 'As usual, that will be on the last day of the winter term, to celebrate the end of the mock exams. The last hurrah before the Board Exams, lest you think these final two terms in school are all cram-cram-cram. Yes? Come on, cheer up – lots to look forward to so let's see less of the glum faces. Well, off with you now. Back to class. Mrs Menon will no doubt be waiting.'

Victoria Lamb watched her girls file disconsolately out of the quadrangle. She always felt for them as the exams approached. Life at sixteen should rightly offer more pleasures than cramming for exams, for didn't she, more than anyone else, understand the transient nature of youthful happiness?

Victoria turned to walk to her office. Unfortunately, the syllabus left little room for extracurricular activities in the final year and it was always a struggle to know how much leeway to give the girls when it came to matters like their beloved annual play. She smiled as she opened the door to her room. Perhaps it was wise not to tell her students what an avid thespian she had been at their age, playing her heart out in her first major role as Desdemona when she had just turned sixteen. Victoria couldn't help remembering the exhilaration of that performance when she coached the girls.

Just as tenderly as she remembered the man who had played Othello – young Subir Shah, the only man she had ever loved. But these were not memories she normally indulged.

Sunlight was dappling the pile of papers awaiting her on the desk, but Victoria turned away from them. Her thoughts, usually so easy to discipline, had been on an unfamiliar rampage these past few weeks. Was it creeping old age or Lily's presence that had catapulted her back to a past she had wrongly believed to be quite firmly erased from her mind? Faces and names from days long gone were insistently surfacing like stubborn ghosts. Perhaps there was no point trying to fight them.

Victoria sat down at her desk and unlocked the lowest drawer. The envelope of photographs was quite deliberately tucked away right at the back. She considered it laudable that she had not had cause to look at them in years, but now she sat back in her chair and gently pulled them out, wondering if she ought to show these to Lily, to explain and assuage and perhaps, yes, to apologise.

Sepia images, frozen between tattered and yellowing edges, revealed smiling faces. Smiles summoned up for the flash of a camera that would forever belie sorrows that either shadowed the background or were cruelly lying in wait just around the corner. A few of the photographs were of Victoria herself as a young girl; trying to look grown-up in a black silk cocktail dress and dark lipstick, a martini glass in one hand. Here, wearing starched tennis whites, a racket under one arm, the other draped loosely around the neck of a now nameless friend. Strange how the setting for most of these jolly pictures were the old club – the Cawnpore Club, as it was then known by its mostly British patrons, army men and box-wallahs. Victoria stopped at a picture of her parents, taken on the eve of their return home to England, both looking too worried to smile. How it must have hurt them to leave her behind . . . and here the reason . . . her baby in blurred black and white, swaddled in a blanket, a hint of surprise on its tiny face. Victoria gazed pitilessly at the picture; half a century was long enough for the mourning to have ceased. But she searched foolishly for traces of herself and, indeed, of Lily. Something, anything that linked them and could perhaps unite them. So much reparation was called for, where could she even begin? And had it all been her fault?

Victoria carefully set the picture aside and picked up the next two, placing them side by side. She only had two pictures of Subir – one of him in his lieutenant's uniform, the jaunty angle of his cap at odds with the serious expression on his face; while the other was of them together, Victoria and Subir, their heads leaning against each other, making it hard to tell in the black and white of the photograph where one's hair ended and the other's began. She remembered the over-weening love and hope of that time. Had it been love or some kind of lunacy that had gripped them, as war destroyed other parts of the world while India's independence seemed ever nearer? There had been a kind of madness in the air in those days, Victoria could still recall it as though it were yesterday. A blend of despair and euphoria that drove people to love and to hate with passions so inflamed they bore no reason. So while men killed each other on distant continents, others rioted Indian streets, blowing up government build-ings and cutting electricity supplies. And – almost as a counter to all that hatred – Victoria had given her heart away to Lieutenant Subir Shah just before he had left for war-torn Italy . . .

She jumped at the sound of a timid knock on the door. Shoving the pictures back into their envelope, she quelled the sudden quaver in her voice as she called, 'Come in!'

Two small faces appeared enquiringly around the door, the school secretary behind them. 'Ah, birthday girls!' Victoria said, noting the colourful frocks and tins of sweets both children were carrying. She beckoned them in and helped herself to a sweet from each tin, asking the usual questions: 'How old are you today, child?' and 'Are you celebrating tonight?' One was going with her family to the Chinese restaurant at the Taj, the other was having a party at home with a cake from Wenger's. Victoria kissed both upturned faces gently before sending them on their way.

When the children had departed and the door closed with a click, Victoria sighed and opened her drawer to return the envelope to its hidden recess right at the back. Firmly turning the key, she muttered softly, *'Bliss was it in that dawn to be alive . . . but to be young was very heaven . . .'* Then she straightened her back and firmly pulled the neglected pile of test papers towards her. These students in her care would understand none of the passion and anguish that had fired up her own generation. The world around them had grown soft and cosy, leaving them with little to strive for. There were times when Victoria was thankful for it and other times when she worried that strong emotions – real ardour and real elation – would simply pass her girls by.

That evening, Sam trudged home from the bus stop in a horribly despondent mood. It really did feel as if there was nothing but the bloody exams to look forward to. The school play meant little to her because she wasn't really the type for the limelight, and, besides, everyone knew that Zeba would get the part of Joan anyway. The Social was small cause for excitement too. Inevitably it set off a flurry of exhilaration and endless talk about dressing-up, mostly because the boys from St Xaviers' Class XII were invited every year. However, Sam couldn't muster up much enthusiasm for all that. It was all very well for those girls who had already staked their claims to some of the boys next door: they could look forward to spending all evening wrapped in the weedy arms of their boyfriends, away from the eagle-eyes of their parents. But – despite the goofy looks that Iqbal Singh had been throwing her way at the gates all year – Sam had not acquired a boyfriend yet.

She sighed deeply, shifting the weight of her bulky schoolbag to her other shoulder as she neared her house. Even Bubbles, who could normally be relied on for an inane giggle, was all tense and preoccupied these days – not with the exams, of course, but with her impending wedding and her ridiculous terror of moving to London (*who* in their right mind would be terrified of moving to a glam city like that, for heaven's sake!). Moreover, Bubbles was still spending most of her evenings at Natasha's house, continuing the grooming sessions with Mrs Walia in the midst of joint study sessions. Sam could imagine how little studying probably went on in those sessions and had steadfastly refused to join in.

She pushed the front door open, wondering if she ought to ask Anita for help with the *Odyssey* notes. Then she scowled, remembering that Anita invariably went into some kind of weird hibernation three months before any exam, revising and re-revising every page three times over in that geeky little head of hers, while her parents fielded all her phone calls.

Sam thumped her bag down on the dining table and looked into Haroon's room. The bed was neatly made-up and the desk free of its usual clutter – Haroon obviously hadn't been in since the cleaner had come that morning. She wandered into her brother's room. Whitney Houston smiled perkily out at her from a poster above the bed, but Sam noticed that Haroon's recently acquired *Basic Instinct* poster had taken prime position on the opposite wall, a strategic point probably carefully chosen so his eyes could dwell on the sultry face of Sharon Stone just as he dropped off to sleep. Sam sighed. She barely got to see her brother these days, and the ignominy of losing his company was far worse because she knew it was to Lily. Things between him and Lily had apparently really taken off after Bubbles' engagement, although Sam would never have guessed it from Lily's attitude to her at school – still nose-in-the-air and behaving as though Sam was just a bit of algae that happened to be floating in her pond. All her clues had come, of course, from Haroon, who was terrible at keeping secrets and had confessed in an unguarded moment that he was now seeing Lily regularly. Last Friday evening it hadn't taken much to guess that he was preparing for a date when he had given himself such a close shave it had left his chin all pink and raw. Sam had pestered him until he owned up that it was Lily he was meeting, the confession made only because he had needed his sister's help to choose his clothes. He had sworn her to secrecy, of course, as though she would for one moment want to tell her classmates that her doltish brother had found no one better to date than Lily D'Souza. She had to concede that he was managing to maintain his reticence better than Sam would have ever thought possible. It must have been at Lily's behest, and Sam felt a piercing recognition of how much influence Lily must already exert over her brother.

There were sure to be lapses, though, and Sam smiled suddenly as she spotted one: a piece of paper lying under an old model aircraft that now served as a paperweight. It was a piece of poetry in Haroon's scrawly handwriting, entitled 'My Water Lily'. Sam cast an amused eye over his ramblings. This was neither Keats nor Wordsworth but pure Haroon Hussain, and, Sam had to admit, one of his worst. Sam read a verse aloud, trying to catch the hard-earned cadence.

> *I am but a goldfish*
> *Swimming aimlessly*
> *In water upon which*
> *Floats my lily*

A goldfish?! It was hard not to retch at that, however fond she was of her brother. Sam pulled open the drawer of Haroon's desk and slipped the scrap of paper in, glad to have spotted it before one of their parents had. Surely they would not be best pleased with their teenage son concentrating on a girlfriend rather than his studies. What *did* Haroon see in Lily that he was willing to risk even their parents' peace of mind?

Haroon licked his lips before opening the wicket gate that led to Miss Lamb's cottage. He had never been this far inside his sister's school before, and the guard at the main gate had asked him for chapter and verse, even calling the principal's cottage to be sure a visitor was expected before letting him through. But Haroon minded the humiliation not a whit, for this was, finally, his first proper date with Lily. Haroon simply could not believe his luck! It was as if his trainers were treading air, so jaunty was his walk as he made his way down the driveway of St Jude's.

Haroon had already met Lily once at Buddha Jayanti Park and, three days later, they had gone to see a movie at Rivoli. He could barely remember anything about the film now except for the fact that it was a period drama featuring women wearing flouncy dresses, so conscious had he been of Lily's presence in the seat right next to him, the light fragrance that emanated from her hair every time she tossed it back, and the electric charge that ran right through him when he passed her the popcorn tub and her fingers brushed his. She had seemed to love the film, though, her face shining as they had exited the cinema into the bright lights of Connaught Place. Later he bought her an ice-cream from a street vendor's cart, which reminded them of their chaotic meeting at Nirula's, and Lily even joked about Sam's ham-fisted attempts at bringing them together. 'She's nice enough, your sister,' she said, licking on her cone and adding, 'her friends are all pretty bitchy, though.' Haroon attempted a small defence of his sister's friends by saying, 'They're all right, really. You know how cliquey girls can be.' But Lily only shrugged at that and Haroon quickly changed the subject, not wanting to spoil the magic of the evening as they walked back to her house. She had not invited him in, bidding him goodbye rather primly at the school gates, and Haroon, of course, had not pushed his luck.

Today was going to be different, though. She had called him four days ago, suggesting another film, except this time she had not demurred when he had plucked up all his courage to suggest that he picked her up *and* took her out for dinner afterwards. By Haroon's calculations, this would mean at least two hours more than he had got with Lily last time round. Perhaps three even, if he stretched it out and they walked really slowly. Three whole hours to look at Lily's beautiful face and joke around until he was rewarded with one of her rare smiles. And she had called back and said yes – yes both to being picked up and dinner afterwards! Haroon could not help speculating that, by contacting him on this occasion, Lily might also have started reciprocating his feelings in some small way. After he had spoken to her on that day, Haroon had had to control the urge to go out into the garden and turn jubilant cartwheels on the lawn.

But now the date was finally here and he was horribly nervous, his lips and throat parched as he rang the doorbell of Lily's house, although he reckoned it was more likely due to apprehension of getting past Miss Lamb. As it turned out, Haroon had no need to worry, as Sam's school principal answered the door with what he would have described as an almost delighted smile on her face.

'Hello, do come in, son,' Miss Lamb said, holding the door wide open.

Before he was able to step in, however, Lily had emerged from the house, slipping past Miss Lamb with a hasty, 'Let's go.'

Perhaps she was embarrassed, Haroon thought, although Miss Lamb seemed unaffected, calling out, 'Have fun, you two,' after them in a cheery voice.

'I wouldn't have minded coming in for a bit,' Haroon said to Lily, trying to keep up with her as she cut speedily through the rose garden.

'No need for that,' she said. 'She's just being curious.'

'Well, that's natural, I guess. At least she's okay about us being out together. Not sure what *my* parents would say.'

'You mean they don't know you go out with girls?' Lily asked, looking at him in surprise as they reached the school gates and she finally slowed down.

'Girls?! You make it sound like I'm out every night with a different girl!'

'You're *not*?!' Lily asked in mock surprise, making Haroon laugh.

'Well, if you must know, Lily D'Souza, you're the very first girl I've ever dated.' Haroon felt suddenly gripped with shyness as he said this, but when he glanced at Lily she was frowning slightly, looking down.

'Just don't tell your sister, okay?' Lily said, looking up, her voice suddenly sharp.

'No, I won't,' Haroon lied. 'You've already asked that of me, Lily, so I won't. But Sami wouldn't tell anyone even if . . .'

'Just don't, okay?' Lily repeated brusquely.

Haroon lapsed into silence briefly but Lily did not seem to notice as she scanned the road, saying, 'Let's get a scooty or we'll be late. Sheela's that theatre on the other side of Connaught Place, isn't it? Don't think we can walk there.'

When they hailed an auto-rickshaw, Haroon got in after Lily, cheering up at the proximity the small cabin forced on them. He could feel Lily's thigh and shoulders knock against his as their vehicle bounced along the pot-holed road. She too seemed to have forgotten her earlier irritation with him, even grabbing his knee and squealing slightly when the scooty took a turn at reckless speed.

At the cinema, Haroon was elated to discover that the movie Lily had asked to see this time was even longer than the last one. Which, to him, quite simply meant more time sitting next to Lily and re-familiarising himself with the lovely smells of her shampoo and soap and perfume. Haroon felt like the luckiest man in the world – *and* he had the meal with Lily to look forward to later. He had scraped together all the money he had and stuffed it in his wallet before leaving home, deciding that a date with Lily was worthy of a trip to the coffee shop at the Taj for one of their famed club sandwiches.

Schindler's List made her cry, however, and Haroon, although initially dismayed to see Lily in tears, soon discovered the opportunity this unexpected occurrence presented to him. She appeared genuinely distressed with the events unfolding on the screen, at first using the back of her hand to surreptitiously whisk away a stray tear or two, before taking out a handkerchief to openly weep into it. When her tears continued unabated, Haroon finally put his arm around her, quite sincerely concerned at seeing her cry. Amazingly, she did not pull away or recoil at his touch, seeming to need the comfort he was offering and placing her head gratefully on his chest. Haroon sat as still as he could, keeping one arm wrapped around Lily's shoulders despite the pins and needles forming in his own, feeling protective and strong and quite unbearably happy. He had not a clue what was happening on-screen, of course, and hoped Lily would not want to critique the film in detail later.

Afterwards, they took another scooty to the Taj, their arrival at the hotel presenting Haroon with another opportunity to be manful and show Lily around a place she had never been before. She had apparently gotten over the trauma of the film and, when they walked into the Machan coffee-shop, she looked delightedly around at the wildlife paintings on the wall while Haroon explained how the décor reflected the Indian safari experience. Before sitting down for their meal she asked to use the bathroom, and so Haroon took her through the lobby again, hoping everyone was noticing him traipsing around the hotel with such a beautiful girl.

He waited contentedly outside the bathroom for Lily, looking at the expensive handbags and shawls in the windows of the hotel's boutique and imagining how happily he would have bought up the entire contents of the shops for his lovely new girlfriend if only he'd had the money.

'Let me show you the pool before we go back to the Machan,' Haroon said when Lily emerged. They walked towards the stairs that led down to the health club and pool.

and, opening a heavy glass door, they stepped into the quiet hush of an empty garden.

Haroon wondered why he should feel puffed up with pride when he heard Lily draw in her breath with pleasure at seeing the pool, shining dark blue and calm, emptied of swimmers at this hour. It wasn't as if he was the architect of this lovely building, or Ratan Tata even. But it was enough tonight to be Haroon Hussain, and in the company of such a gorgeous girl as Lily D'Souza. Haroon could not have picked a more heavenly night either, the early November night breezes carrying just a hint of the winter to come.

It was with all these heady and tumultuous feelings in his heart that Haroon took Lily into his arms that evening. Right there, where the pool segued into fragrant flowerbeds, under the deep violet canopy of the night sky draped with the most enormous stars. It was the sort of night that seemed specially created for young lovers the world over, readying themselves for a tentative first kiss. Holding Lily's shoulders, Haroon bent his head towards hers, feeling their mouths meet. They brushed softly at first and then, in keeping with his meticulous research into such matters, Haroon used the tip of his tongue to gently part Lily's lips. His arms went around her waist, his fingers brushing against a velvet strip of skin where her jeans parted from her top. For a second she seemed to melt against him before she suddenly broke free.

At first unsurprised – for wasn't that what any decent girl would do – Haroon smiled shyly at Lily, fully expecting that he would need to employ a little persuasion before she would allow him to kiss her again. But the expression on her face was furious. Gone in a trice was the pretty face that had laughed at his jokes, and in its place was cold anger. She shoved his arms away and forcibly ran the back

260

of her hand over her lips as though needing to wipe away something bitter and dirty. In the half-darkness, Haroon saw Lily's eyes glint, first with anger before tears started to roll, and then, in a flash, she turned from him and ran back into the lobby as if all the devils in the world were chasing her.

Haroon pursued Lily as she weaved her way through a wedding crowd that had just entered the lobby, pushing past photographers and video men and over-dressed women. Some people looked at them curiously but Lily was oblivious, nearly bumping into the startled turbaned man at the door before turning and running down the drive. A car was forced to swerve away from her and its driver stuck his head out of his window to yell briefly at Haroon, who was in close pursuit.

Lily got to the gate seconds before Haroon did, and while she frantically scanned the passing traffic for a scooty, Haroon tried to plead with her.

'I'm sorry, Lily, I didn't mean to upset you. I love you and I just wanted to show you how much you . . .'

But Lily's frenzied arm-waving resulted in her being spotted by a scooty driver who swerved across the road to stop before them. 'St Jude's convent,' she said to the driver, an old Sardarji who took one look at her distressed face and, arriving at his own conclusions, gave Haroon an irate glare. Haroon tried another passionate apology – to Lily, to the scooty driver, to anyone who would listen – but Lily would not even look him in the eye as she clambered on board and the scooty driver noisily revved up his engine as if warning Haroon away.

Lily was driven off, and while her scooty was swallowed up by the frenetic night-time traffic, Haroon stood on the pavement of Maan Singh Road, befuddled at the crime he had committed. It was only a kiss, albeit an inexpert one and conferred on a very pretty girl. As far as Haroon knew, it was a crime that countless young men before him had got away with. The pain in his chest at her sudden departure also told him that he loved Lily more than ever before.

Chapter Twenty

Sam felt herself tense as she heard Akbar's car driving through the gates. It was ridiculous that she had been on edge all day at the thought of finally telling her husband that she was going to Delhi with Anita and Bubbles. Hoping to distract herself, she had tried calling Francesca to suggest they spend an afternoon at the Sanctuary spa but Francesca's nanny had said she had gone to Paris for a wedding. Sam had subsequently spent much of the dull winter afternoon wandering around the shops on King's Road, trying to remember when she had lost every last ounce of her old confidence and reached this abysmal state of anticipating Akbar's disapproval all the time. Then she had taken comfort in a moccacino grande accompanied by a huge slice of chocolate cake at Bluebird and made herself feel even worse, imagining those evil little calories rushing through her body searching for her already ample bum.

It wasn't even really a girlie holiday, just a visit to her parents', but the mere fact of making such a decision on her own had felt a little audacious. Besides, Akbar had reverted to type since that unusual good mood he'd been in the night they'd gone to Julie's restaurant. Once again, he seemed preoccupied by work and sometimes miles away. It was mostly why she'd avoided mentioning her holiday plans to him, but now, with Anita having booked her leave and Bubbles ready with the tickets, it couldn't be put off any more.

Sam got up and hastily turned on the lights as Akbar's footsteps came up the front stairs. It wouldn't do for him to know that she had been sitting in the dark waiting for him. She turned on her upbeat voice, calling 'Hello' cheerily as he came in. They had long since stopped greeting each other with a kiss at the door – but now there were some days when he barely smiled at her as he came in.

'Oh, hello. Didn't see you there,' Akbar responded. His voice sounded friendly enough.

'I just came down to draw the curtains and turn on the lights,' she lied.

'Where's Heer?'

'Must be watching something in her room. She'd have rushed down if she'd heard you coming in,' Sam replied, tugging at the curtain pull.

'It'll break if you do it like that,' Akbar said, coming across to help.

Sam stepped aside for him. 'Perhaps we should go for those electric ones I've seen in Bubbles' room, with a remote control, very handy,' she said, immediately regretting allowing Akbar the opportunity to make fun of her friend.

'Mrs Millionaire couldn't be arsed to draw her own curtains, eh?' he snorted, closing the last chink in the curtains with a smart tug.

Sam let his remark pass with a small laugh. 'Hungry?' she asked.

'Hmmm, not hugely,' he replied, already halfway out the door. 'Had a working lunch. Sarah ordered in some rather nice sandwiches for our two o'clock meeting and I think I ate one too many.'

'Something light for dinner then? Soup?'

Akbar nodded, pulling off his tie as he walked towards the stairs. 'Yes, soonish. I'd like to be off early again in the morning. Try and squeeze in a swim before work.'

Sam nodded. She was getting used to Akbar's fleeting visits to the house these days, sometimes merely to pick up a fresh set of clothes for an evening appointment. And, when he did pop in, she felt sure it was more to check on Heer than on her. In Sam's lowest moments she reckoned that Akbar had loved her for precisely four and a half years. It was around the time she was pregnant with Heer that he had first started to get bored and irritable. The remarks about her weight crept in a few months later when, despite all the breast-feeding and exercise, Sam had been unable to budge those pounds she'd gained during the pregnancy. At first she explained away the longer hours he spent in the office as being crucial to his career. Anita had once suggested that perhaps he just wasn't the fatherly type and would start enjoying her and Heer's company once the baby had grown a bit ('Men are sometimes quite emasculated by the whole mother–baby thing, give him space,' she'd said, and Sam had desperately held on to that hope for a while).

With her right hand on the wooden balustrade of the hall steps, she listened now to Akbar and Heer's voices upstairs, struggling with her temptation to join them. She could hear the faint sounds of conversation through the closed door of Heer's room followed by a sudden burst of high-pitched laughter from her daughter. Anita's assessment hadn't been too far wrong; certainly Akbar had grown fonder of Heer as she had grown out of babyhood. But Sam had just been shunted further and further into the fringes of Akbar's life, eventually becoming someone who turned on the lights of an evening and arranged the flowers and drew the curtains on the world . . . and even such simple things she evidently didn't always do very well.

Sam took her hand away from the balustrade, wretchedly acknowledging that she should not intrude on the short time Akbar got with Heer on a rare evening like this when he was home early. She could try, but he would most likely look up from their shared activity when she went in and Sam would not be able to help noticing the flash of irritation that would momentarily overcome his handsome features. Sadness washed over her again – the worst thing about losing love was the realisation that it didn't depart in some grand dramatic manner, but instead slipped away in the tiniest and seemingly insignificant ways.

Sam made her way down her spacious, elegant hallway, which, despite the bright pink gladioli and bowls of scented pot-pourri, suddenly felt like a morgue. She ought to go to the kitchen and give Masooma instructions for the soup before Akbar came down hungry for his dinner. She walked into the warmth of her kitchen, fragrant with the smell of cooking rice. Masooma was busy chopping a bunch of spring onions and looked up to smile at her. Good old Masooma, always cheery, even though her own husband and children were five thousand miles away. Self-pity was such a terrible thing, Sam thought, resolving to speak to her GP once more about the Prozac prescription. Perhaps he was right and that's all it was, some kind of chemical imbalance that didn't deserve all this navel-gazing and angst. After all, even Bubbles had said the pills were doing her a world of good. But so far Sam had resisted the doctor's gentle suggestion, the idea of taking the easy way out somehow terribly repellent when she looked at hard-working women like Masooma who slaved to make her own life more comfortable.

'Masooma, Akbarsahib wants soup, no dinner,' she said, popping a blanched almond into her mouth.

Masooma's face fell as she clattered her knife down. 'Then for whom I am making all this pulao and chicken? Even Heerbaby only wanted pizza.'

Sam looked apologetic. 'Oh Masooma, I thought sahib would want dinner. But he had something to eat at work. Keep the pulao for tomorrow?'

'But now it is fresh and nice!'

'Okay, don't worry, put it out in a bowl. I'll have some and then maybe sahib will be tempted too. But make some soup also. We have mushrooms? Quickly. I will help.'

Sam watched Akbar as they had dinner at the kitchen table. He was in an unusually relaxed mood, joshing with Masooma and even sampling a bit of her pulao, much to the maid's delight. After dinner he wanted to try out the new coffee machine and they all pitched in, even Heer and Masooma, to offer suggestions and advice. To Sam's delight the machine turned out a perfect frothy cup of milky brew that she artfully dusted with ground cinnamon for Akbar. Once a beaming Heer had been despatched to bed with a drink of hot chocolate, Sam and Akbar sat at the kitchen table, Akbar finishing his second cup of cappuccino while watching the ten o'clock news on Masooma's small kitchen TV.

He drained the last of the coffee before putting his cup down, and Sam knew there wouldn't be a better time to broach the subject of the trip to Delhi. As he poured himself the glass of water he would take up to bed, she suddenly blurted, 'Oh, Akbar, I've been meaning to say; I'm thinking of a short holiday in Delhi this December.'

He looked at her over the rim of his water glass, surprised. 'Delhi?'

'Yes, we haven't seen Mum and Dad since last year. They must be desperate to see us.'

He drained his water, swallowing slowly and deliberately, before asking, 'Us? Nice, if that includes me, but I have work commitments, you know.'

'Of course, I would have asked you first, Akbar. In fact, that's what I'm doing now!'

'What about Heer?' he asked, putting his glass down carefully, as though it really mattered where exactly it was placed.

'It'll be her Christmas hols, she'll go with me, of course.'

'Well, she won't,' he said, his gaze directly on her now, his hand rocking the empty glass which made an irritated clicking sound on the tabletop.

'Won't what?'

'Won't go with you to Delhi.'

'Not go to Delhi . . . but why, Akbar?' said Sam, looking at her husband open-mouthed.

'Because I'm taking her on a Kenyan safari,' he said swiftly, getting up to refill his glass from the water-cooler in the far corner of the kitchen.

'What Kenyan safari? You never said . . .'

'Well, you know now,' he said, his back to her as he filled the glass.

'But, Akbar, you should've said. I'd never have planned on us going to Delhi if I'd known you wanted us . . .'

'Who said anything about "us"? It wasn't me who used that word, remember?' He had turned from the cooler and now Sam could see cold anger written all over his face.

She paused for one horrified moment. 'Oh. Oh, sorry, I thought . . .'

'No, you don't, Samira, you don't think. That's the

problem. You never think. It's fine. You go to Delhi and I'll take Heer to Kenya. There'll be a few others from work going so I'll have help.'

'Okay, Akbar,' Sam tried reasoning, 'I didn't tell you about Delhi but then you never told me about Kenya either! How was I to know . . .'

But Akbar was putting his chair back under the table with one hand. He normally did this cautiously, lifting the legs so they didn't scratch the scrupulously chosen terracotta flagstones, but today the chair scraped the floor with a screeching sound. Sam knew he was silencing her and watched his tall figure turn and leave the room.

She sat engulfed in the sudden silence following his departure, her lips remaining parted in surprise for a few seconds before they puckered and hot tears started to roll helplessly down her cheeks. She shot a mortified look at Masooma, who was trying to busy herself at the other end of the kitchen, obviously caught as unawares by Akbar's sudden rage as Sam was. Deeply embarrassed by the look of sympathy Sam could see on her maid's face, she got up and ran into the cloakroom next to the kitchen. Slamming the door shut, she stood with her face in her hands, unable to stem the flood of bitter tears that now overwhelmed her. Though trying to weep silently, she was clearly not succeeding as, after a few minutes, she heard Masooma knocking tentatively on the locked door.

It was impossible to ignore such persistent taps and eventually the maid's determination wore Sam down. She looked exasperatedly at the door, trying to steady her voice. 'Offo, I'm coming, Masooma, okay,' she said finally, pulling herself together and taking a deep wobbly breath. Sam looked at her face in the mirror with horror, seeing that her large brown eyes were now all puffy and red. Akbar would be even more annoyed if he saw her going upstairs looking such a wreck. She washed her face, splashing water over her burning skin over and over, even as more tears squeezed stubbornly out of her eyes. She had never travelled anywhere without Heer. And why was Akbar stonewalling her, not talking, not listening? If he wanted to go to Kenya, with or without her, she wouldn't have objected. After all, he travelled without her often enough on business, and she knew that she had long ceased to be important in his scheme of things. She would eventually have found joy in the idea that Akbar loved their daughter enough to take her on such a wonderful holiday, and would have merely used the time to visit her parents and attend the school reunion. It just needed to be talked over and planned properly, that's all. Why did Akbar think that things could only be achieved with brusque words and angry expressions, as though their very life together had become one of his court cases?

Sam wiped her face roughly on the hand-towel. She was no fool. Akbar's reaction had given her the uncanny impression that Kenya had been planned all along – minus her – and that she had unwittingly provided him with an excellent opportunity to break the news to her. Perhaps she had imagined it, but Akbar had looked almost relieved that she already had other plans in December, so he could go on this safari with his colleagues. But why would the thought of taking her be so unbearable for him? Had she really become so hateful? Was she too fat, maybe, to haul herself easily into Jeeps? Why oh *why* had she allowed herself to become a figure of embarrassment to her husband, rather than someone he could be proud of?

Sam opened the cloakroom door with a soft click. Masooma was standing right outside, wearing an anxious expression on her face, and Sam patted her cheek gently before turning away and pretending her hands needed another wash at the sink. Luckily, Masooma was the type who never pried, although Sam was not sure how much of their conversation the maid would have understood, as they had been speaking in English. She saw the maid return to the table and scrape the remaining pulao into a Tupperware bowl, muttering under her breath. Sam switched the television over to Zee TV. That would perk up poor Masooma, Sam thought, although she wondered what she could do for herself. The occasional cheesy Bollywood song and dance sequence sometimes made her smile, especially if Zeba came on-screen, sexily swaying her hips like in the old days at St Jude's. It always tickled Masooma pink to know that Sam had been childhood friends with the Queen of Bollywood, and Sam sometimes regaled her with funny stories from that time. But tonight, none of that was likely to cheer either of their spirits.

As she gazed blankly at gyrating dancers on the screen, Sam wondered just how it had happened that she had lost her idyllic marriage when Heer had arrived, in much the same way that she had lost her idyllic childhood when Haroon had gone? She had been cursed, that was it. Cursed, she was sure, by the spirit of an old classmate who had not even been given a chance to experience marriage and motherhood. Because she, Samira Hussain, had wished with all the desperation of a grieving girl's heart for poor Lily D'Souza to die. And had secretly rejoiced when she did.

Chapter Twenty-One

DELHI, 1993

It was when their parents were out one evening that Sam overheard Haroon's phone call from the study. She had not intended to eavesdrop but could not resist listening in when she heard her brother utter Lily's name. He had been moping around since his big date with Lily two days ago and she wanted to know what was at the bottom of it. Standing just beyond the door to their father's den, Sam then heard him say, 'Please, please, Lily, don't say that . . . how can you . . .' He was silent for a few minutes, listening to Lily, before he spoke up again, his throat clogged with emotion. 'But I can't live without you, Lily, you know that . . .' At this point Lily must have hung up on him, for Haroon suddenly went silent before breaking down in noisy tears.

Sam couldn't believe it. She had last seen her brother crying when he was about ten years old, and even then it was only over his lost Scalelectrix car. She ventured to peer beyond the door and could just see the top of Haroon's head over what they called their father's leather 'big boss chair'. He had his back to the door and was holding his head in his hands as he wept – coarse guttural sounds emerging staccato from his throat.

'*Bhaiyya*,' she whispered, quite unsure of what to do or say. She was astonished when he turned around and she saw that his face was red and suddenly angry.

'What do you want?' he shouted, making her jump.

'Sorry, Haroon *bhaiyya*, I couldn't help . . .'

'What do you mean you couldn't help?! How dare you stand there listening . . .'

'Haroon *bhaiyya*, please, I wasn't!' Sam yelled frantically as her brother pushed roughly past her and ran to his room. She heard him bolt the door against her as she burst into tears herself.

If Sam wasn't depressed enough by the approaching exams, Haroon's remote behaviour set the seal on her unhappiness. And, as if all that wasn't enough, the fracas in class the next day made her want to scream with rage. After an uneventful morning of Physics and Botany, a handful of girls were quietly spending the last of their lunch hour studying their books when Zeba came bursting in.

'Would you *believe* it?! The *bitch*, the bloody bitch!' she yelled as she flounced across the front of the class, hurling the bound script she had in her hands across the room.

'What the hell?' Anita exclaimed, jumping out of the way as the fragile binding came apart and photocopied A4 sheets scattered across the floor.

'*She's* put her name down – can you imagine! For Saint Joan! *Lily*!!' Zeba's voice was getting higher with each successive word, the looks of incomprehension from her classmates seeming to enrage her further.

Natasha patted her shoulder, 'Calm down, Zebs, Lily'll never get the part. You're just too good at this acting lark.'

But Zeba could not stop her rant. 'She even got all dressed up in a white robe for the audition, while I just turned up in my bloody uniform. And you should've seen the way Moss was salivating all over her on stage! As though she was . . . *Julia Roberts* or something. *Aaargh!*'

'But Moss adores you,' Anita reminded her calmly, 'always has.'

'*Before* that little minx came along,' Zeba reminded her. 'Oh, I'm so *angry*! Why doesn't she just go back to wherever she came from, hanh? Who does she think she is, coming here and just taking over? Thinks she can ride over everyone else because she's the Princy's relative. *Bitch!*'

'Oh come on, Zeba, Lamboo would never expect Lily to be given preferential treatment over one of us. You know that,' Sam intervened.

Zeba turned on her, enraged. 'This is Delhi. In the end it always comes down to *connections*, everyone knows that!'

'C'mon, Zeba, Sam's quite right,' Anita drawled. 'What Lily does, Lily does with no reference at all to Lamboo. We can all see that they don't even like each other very much. If Lily does get the part, it will be on her own merit.'

Zeba turned to Anita in a fury. 'Yeah, like when she trumps you for the Lalvani Oxford scholarship. I'd like to see you being so cool about Lily D'Souza and nepotism then!'

'No way!' Bubbles breathed in awe. Anita was the cleverest person she had ever met and no one could possibly beat her to the school scholarship.

'Well, let's just wait and see, huh,' Zeba said, satisfied to see a strange pallor come over Anita's face as she silently returned to her book. 'Let me tell you one thing, though, Anita Roy. *You* may meekly roll over when it comes to the Lalvani Scholarship, but I am certainly *not* going to hand anything over to Lily on a platter. I promise you, if anyone plays Saint Joan this year, it will be me.'

*   *   *

275

The atmosphere in class did not improve at all in the days following the audition, although Lily seemed completely oblivious to the numerous pairs of eyes glowering at her back. Sam knew that the general foul mood was at least partially due to the forthcoming mock exams. The timetable had been announced and the countdown had already started. Exactly a month to go until the first paper, which was English. Then all the others would follow with two-day gaps between them, until the final paper, which was most people's worst (Maths), which fell on the third Friday in December. The Social was the following day – 19 December – after which Class XII would disperse for the study holidays until the start of the practical exams. No one had even mentioned the word 'Social' for weeks now, as though even thinking of jolly things would somehow bode badly for the exams.

When the bell rang for the last period that day, the class got up with a scraping of chairs and slamming of desk lids to troop across to the Chemistry lab. Despite the beautifully crisp November afternoon, spirits were still low as the girls tramped slowly across the yard, dragging their heavy satchels along as this was the last period of the day.

Old Gomes was his usual toadying self, sliding snake-like around his lab and grinning sideways at all the girls one by one. Sam watched him fawn exaggeratedly over Zeba's work, using every opportunity to peer down her blouse – which turned out to be a fairly frequent occurrence, thanks to a little assistance from Zeba.

'Oooh, the little minx,' Anita whispered to Sam as they poured assiduously from test-tubes into flasks. 'And look at him! Pretending to be so interested in Zeba's notes rather than her cleavage. If he carries on like this, he might actually steal the best actor role from under both Zeba's and Lily's pretty noses.'

Sam mustered up a smile. 'I'm worried about her, Anita,' she said softly.

'Don't be. I think Zeba Khan's perfectly capable of taking care of herself,' Anita dismissed.

'No, no. She told me earlier that today was the day she was going to get the Chemistry paper off Gomes. She's staying back after the bell goes.'

Even Anita looked alarmed at this information. 'What in heaven's name is that stupid girl going to do?'

Sam shrugged. 'She didn't say. But I don't think you could put her off any plan of action once she's set her mind on it.'

'Ohh, the fool, we've got to stop her.'

Sam shook her head. 'I tried. She won't listen. She'll be absolutely furious if we do anything. She's sure she's going to fail Chemistry without it. Apparently, she put away the textbook the minute Gomes promised her the paper.'

Anita wrestled with the problem for a few moments before making up her mind. 'Well then, I guess we just have to leave her to her own devices, Sam. Just make absolutely sure you have *nothing* to do with this paper if she does get her hands on it. You can imagine what Lamboo would do if she ever found out.'

Sam nodded. She had already tried imagining what Lamboo would do and had veered from the thought of mass expulsions to the more likely prospect of their Princy's genuine pain and distress, deciding eventually that the latter would be a lot harder to bear.

When the long bell rang, indicating the end of the school day, Sam picked up her bag and walked out of the lab without another look at Zeba, thereby missing the big wink Zeba was significantly throwing in her direction.

Zeba couldn't fail to notice Sam's uncharacteristic coldness, nor Anita's meaningful glare as she followed Sam out of the lab five minutes later. It was too late for any of these warnings anyway. What would girls like Sam and Anita understand of the kind of effort involved in working her charms on someone like Gomes, harder in some ways than sitting down and learning the Chemistry textbook by heart! Gomesey wasn't exactly her dream man, but he had something she needed and she was willing to set aside silly notions about romantic love in order to get it. Once she'd got her hands on the Chemistry paper tonight, of *course* she would have nothing to do with him ever again. Not a touch, not even a little flutter of her eyelashes. But right now wasn't the time to think of that. She had a task at hand. While all her classmates left in ones and twos and the lab gradually emptied, Zeba – still pretending to be making notes from her earlier experiment – stayed seated on a stool at the counter, sensing Gomes's impatience across the lab too.

Finally, they had all gone, and Zeba saw the Chemistry teacher getting up from his table to peer out of the lab and ensure that the last of her classmates was well on her way across the yard. Then he shut the door and slid its rusty bolt into place before walking back to her. At least he was tall and thin, Zeba thought to herself, and – whatever Nats said – not *that* old, well at least not compared to Mr Moss, their only other male teacher, who was positively prehistoric. She parted her legs on the stool, just far enough for Gomes to see that she had taken off her panties when she had gone to the loo just before the bell rang, stuffing them into her schoolbag under all her books. She saw beads of sweat break out on his upper lip as he neared her, certainly not caused by the sudden temperature drop as evening was drawing in on this cool November day. She rapidly unbuttoned the top few buttons on her shirt as he stood between her legs, slipping one hand into her blouse and the other between her legs. She felt her nipples spring obediently to attention and a pain crystallise deep in the pit of her groin as he started to push his finger into her. He then lowered his head, pushing his lips down on hers and shoving his sour-tasting tongue into her mouth. She felt it move around, counting her teeth and then searching for her tonsils, making her want to gag. She allowed him his thirty seconds before wriggling her head away as though eager to get on with the task of unzipping him. This she did expertly, but it was exactly at the moment when his penis had popped out, standing brown and shiny amid the folds of his trousers, that the door crashed open, its ancient bolt giving way. It now swung wildly on creaking hinges, revealing a lone figure standing against the pale evening light.

Lily.

Lily D'Souza, of all the people in the world, standing and watching them with their hands frozen on each other's privates, a knowing look on her face. Zeba yelped and dropped Gomes's penis as though it had suddenly burnt her, allowing him the chance to struggle frantically with it, stuffing it back in and zipping up his flies. Zeba hastily buttoned up her shirt and, leaping off the stool, bent over to pick up her school bag, thereby flashing her pert bare bottom briefly at Lily, who watched their struggles with undisguised disgust.

Zeba hoisted her bag over her shoulder, then loped out of the lab and across the schoolyard as fast as her long legs would carry her. It was only much later that she realised that she had not seen even a trace of surprise on Lily's face. She had known. Somehow the little rat had known what was going to happen . . . and she had deliberately timed her arrival at the lab to catch them in the middle of it. Most other girls would have slunk off and gossiped about it later behind her back; but not Lily D'Souza, that was not her style at all. *Why?* Zeba wondered. What was it she thought she'd achieve by confronting them like that?

What Zeba did not see was that Lily, having stopped Zeba and Gomes in their tracks, had stumbled with equal haste out of the Chemistry laboratory, running in the opposite direction. The two girls dashed as fast as each other – Zeba towards the gates and Lily back to the main school building. Even though Gomes had darted to the door to catch Lily and offer some feeble explanation, she had vanished in seconds behind the peepul tree before scrambling through the kitchen door.

Running alongside the gleaming steel shelves, Lily pushed past a pair of kitchen helpers and the head cook, all three of whom were startled by the redness of her face and the tears rolling down her crumpled features. The men looked at each other in consternation. The cook recognised the girl who had been staying with principal memsahib, and wondered why she was weeping so grievously. Such a pretty girl, but today with a face so twisted it was as if the world's worst anguish had been thrust on her. He had heard that it was some horrendous tragedy that had brought her to Delhi, but no one had liked to ask principal memsahib what it was. Perhaps it was the memory of that misfortune which was making the girl cry today, he thought, shrugging his shoulders and turning back to his helpers. He smiled at them and passed on a truth he had learned in his many years of working at the school. 'Girls', he said ruefully, shaking his old head, 'will be girls. Always agonising over some silly small things.'

Lily burst into the cottage through the back door, startling Lakhan who was singing along to his favourite Choli ke

280

Peeche while mopping the kitchen floor. 'Out of my way, you idiot,' Lily yelled, nearly tripping over his bucket as she ran for the stairs. Taking them two at a time, she ran into her bedroom and slammed the door shut, pulling the latch across. Then she bent over double and started to moan, an agonised cry rising up from deep in her stomach to emerge in one long bestial wail.

No one heard her, as Victoria Lamb was still in her office back at the school, and Lakhan had cranked up his radio so as to pretend deafness if that awful girl called him upstairs for something. Only for Miss Lamb's sake had he put up with all Lily's bad behaviour these past few months.

Alone in her room, Lily fell to her knees and started to hit her head on the stone floor. Once, twice, thrice, harder and harder and harder, the pain shooting through her head somehow preferable to that which had carved a great big hole deep inside her years ago. She hit her head, thinking of what she had just seen and remembering every little detail of what had happened to her. The look on Gomes's face, his hands slipping under Zeba's skirt . . . it was the very same thing, like being trapped, forced to watch herself in a hideous tableaux. She already felt besmirched by Haroon pushing his tongue into her mouth the other night, a terrible revisitation of her pain and guilt. And now this; as if she would never, ever be allowed to forget her terrible sin, however hard she punished herself. Finally, unable to take the agony any more, Lily rolled over onto the floor and lay there, weeping and shaking as she whispered repeatedly, 'I hate you, I hate you, I hate you . . .'

Even Lily couldn't have told of whom she spoke – it was everyone, a whole litany of people who had let her down in different ways: her mother, her father, her foster parents, that wicked old witch who called herself her grandmother, the girls in her class who hated her for no reason at all; even Haroon, for he too was surely only after one thing, like all men were. Lily hated *everyone*.

She was still lying there on the floor two hours later, curled into a ball and moaning softly, as night fell and crickets started to call from the rose garden outside.

Zeba waited till the safety of the following morning to tell her friends what had happened.

'Oh, I just can't believe Lily saw you and Gomes together, Zeba,' Sam wailed, sinking her head into her hands.

'I think this time you've really, really messed up,' Anita intoned.

The three of them had broken away from the others to have their discussion in private before the bell rang at the start of the following day – it was best that as few people as possible knew about the appalling incident Zeba had just recounted.

Zeba had spent a jittery night, jumping every time the phone rang, expecting it to be Miss Lamb calling with her suspension orders. She had concocted a tale to trot out to Miss Lamb if summoned to her office – some psychological claptrap about seeking affection from an older man in the face of her own father's coldness. But that did not sound too convincing even to Zeba, which led her to imagine her parents' reaction; her mother's tears, her father's shock. They'd never understand about the Chemistry paper. Never. Their concerns would be all about family honour and her father's professional reputation in the university. Zeba would not even have been too surprised if one of her brothers whipped her for this.

But Miss Lamb hadn't called. And so Lily hadn't told on her by the looks of it. As the assembly bell rang, Zeba followed

Anita and Sam to the back of the hall, filled with trepidation. Lily, as always arriving only in the nick of time, slipped past them, and Zeba saw that they were being treated with the usual disdain. Lily did not even turn to look at the group huddled at the back of the hall, three pairs of eyes watching her carefully. A new thought struck Zeba: perhaps Lily had spared her only to tell on *Gomes*. She leaned towards Sam, whispering this new theory urgently.

'But he's still here, I saw him coming into school as usual this morning,' Sam said.

'Zeba's right. It's strange that Lily hasn't told on him either. Seeing that she's not exactly the *kindly* sort,' Anita hissed.

'True . . . why would she protect him? I mean, Zeba is a classmate after all, but . . .' Sam pondered.

'Do you think I should go and thank her maybe? Y'know, for not telling on me?' Zeba asked.

Both her companions spoke with one voice: 'Don't be bloody stupid!' said one and 'Of *course* not!' said the other.

'But why do you think she's let him off the hook? Gomes, I mean . . .' Sam continued puzzling, the end of her pen by now a chewed-up mess.

'To get the Chemistry paper?' Anita volunteered suddenly. Both girls looked at her in shock and she continued slowly, 'She's got something on him now, so it should be relatively easy . . . well, easier than the route *Zeba* took.'

'God . . . the tart beat me to it then!' Zeba breathed, stopping short as both her friends glared at her. 'I know, I know – I'm not going after Gomes for it now, even if I flunk – *I promise!*'

In the principal's cottage, Victoria Lamb sat looking in tearful exasperation at the door Lily had exited through five minutes ago. She had been even more unbearable than usual the previous evening, coming downstairs for dinner only after Victoria had spent half an hour trying to coax her out of her room from outside its locked door. Lily had finally emerged with a sulky, puffy face, and had sworn dreadfully at poor Lakhan when she burnt her lips on his soup. Without bothering to finish it, she had then locked herself away again for the rest of the night, and this time Victoria had let her be. She had hoped the storm would have passed by morning, but the girl had appeared, red-eyed and taciturn, just ten minutes ago, pulling on her school blazer and stomping angrily out of the house with nary a word to anyone. Victoria looked at the slice of toast that long-suffering Lakhan had carefully buttered for Lily, left uneaten on her plate, her undrunk glass of Bournvita forming brown skin on its surface. What was eating the child now? Victoria thought, fury rising uncontrolled within her. Just when she'd hoped Lily's demeanour had been turning more pleasant, thanks to that nice boy she had started dating, Samira Hussain's brother.

Yes, of course, poor Lily had been put through the most dreadful ordeal last year, but, thanks to the wisdom of the nuns, she had been rescued and taken safely into their care. A year on from all that, and placed now in the happy atmosphere of St Jude's, everyone had hoped she would slowly start to blossom again. But, months down the line, there still seemed no chance of that at all. The girl would insist, it seemed to Victoria, on carrying her torment about her like a banner.

Victoria got up from the breakfast table, wincing at the pain in her knee. In the distance she could hear the school bell clanging. In five minutes she would have to take assembly and pretend to the world that she was her usual calm, collected self, ready at all times to absorb the woes of her girls and teachers like a sponge. But she paused for a moment, holding the edge of the dining table, waiting for the pain to recede. Uncustomary tears filled her eyes. Victoria Lamb loathed self-pity more than anything else and blinked them back angrily. She reminded herself that Lily had been through much worse pain than anything she had ever known. Much worse than losing a child and a lover in the space of a month.

Victoria raised her grey head and straightened her cardigan as she walked slowly to the front door. Lily needed her to remain as steadfast as a rock if she was ever to find her way through life again. She was determined to help the girl exorcise all her demons, however long it took. All that was required was time. Indeed, Victoria could not recall having failed to resurrect a single child, however troubled (and the school had certainly received a few of those over the years). She remembered one seven-year-old who turned up every morning at assembly with a hunted look on her face and bruises on her legs. And another, a skinny, sickly waif whose mother was found to be suffering from Munchausen's Syndrome. Victoria had, with the help of the school counsellor, managed to resolve all those seemingly intractable problems, revivifying family bonds where they were flagging, restoring love when everyone thought it was lost. Indeed, under her stewardship, the St Jude's credo had been not just the education of its girls but the enhancement of their very lives. She could not fail Lily, her own flesh and blood.

Stepping into the early winter sunshine, Victoria briefly touched a rosebud that stretched, gleaming and new, right towards her front door. It almost seemed to be begging for affection, she thought, feeling its tender petals under her fingers. She trod gingerly onto the garden path, still feeling the pain in her knee, and started to make her way slowly down towards the school building. The rose garden was ablaze with colour, she noted with a semblance of comfort, with dozens of blooms in different colours vying madly with each other for attention. Yes, life certainly had subtle little ways of offering compensation; one only had to look for them.

Chapter Twenty-Two

Bubbles led the way to the first-class lounge at Heathrow. She was filled with a new kind of confidence – born, rather oddly, from having done something wrong for the first time in her life. It was so wrong that she knew she wouldn't even be able to tell her two best friends for a long, long time. But, yesterday, in the dark depths of the gym and with the whole family wandering the floors upstairs, she had let Gio kiss her.

It had happened just as she was getting up from the rowing machine and he had given her a hand. Of course, they had touched many times before – he supporting an arm while she stood on one leg or holding her ankles as she stretched – usually without too much self-consciousness or embarrassment, but on this occasion, Bubbles had found herself suddenly standing inches away from Gio, her head right under his chin. She had looked up, laughing, expecting one of his usual jocular remarks, but had noticed a strange expression on his face as he looked down at her and failed to move away. Her breath caught in her throat as he raised his hands to place them on her upper arms. Then, he had bent his face towards hers, moving one hand around her shoulders while the other slipped down to the small of her back to propel her firmly towards him. For a millisecond she struggled, but it was a token gesture because she was turning rapidly to mush in Gio's arms as his mouth came down on hers. Binkie's rare kisses – even in the first few days of their marriage – had been decorous and fleeting, barely a brush of his dry lips on hers. But this kiss was straight out of a Hollywood movie, those '15'-rated ones Bubbles sometimes watched wide-eyed on her own in the dark solitude of the home cinema, sometimes coming close to groaning aloud with desire. This deep, lingering kiss was exactly like that. It reached right into her, seeming to suck every ounce of emotion up and out of her body, leaving her limp and shaking in Gio's arms. Until she had suddenly realised who she was, where she was and, crucially, in whose arms she was, where-upon she pulled herself away and bolted up the stairs.

Even now, the memory of that kiss was making Bubbles feel weak, although she could not tell if it was from guilt or excitement. If she knew how to write poetry, she would have said that the feeling was like Christmas and Diwali all rolled into one. Like the blinding starburst of fireworks she had seen one New Year's Eve over Sydney Harbour. Like the first mini-explosion of Cristal in her mouth. If she was to be completely honest, it was exactly like the kiss she and Haroon had shared in a million hopeless daydreams. She snapped out of her reverie as she realised that Sam was saying some-thing to her.

'D'you know, Bubs, I last visited this lounge when I was accompanying Akbar on one of his business trips – God, at least eight years ago. Hard to imagine now that there was a time when I regularly used to do that!'

Bubbles sobered up as she heard the sorrow in her friend's voice. She knew Sam never travelled with Akbar now, Heer being her usual excuse. Well, Akbar used Heer's schooling as the reason he would never take Sam anywhere, and Sam obediently used the same excuse to anyone who asked. Bubbles took her friend's arm and said cheerily, 'You're not to think of all that now. Forget Akbar. You're with me, and *I'm* sure as hell taking you first class, honey!'

The three women were ushered through dark glass doors that, when closed discreetly behind them, hushed the hubbub of the airport instantly. The pair of Raheja attendants who had accompanied them from the cars left with the luggage trolleys while an attentive BA ground staffer helped them with their coats. The sudden silence that enveloped them was as smooth and luxuriant as the finest malt whisky, Anita thought. Rather ludicrously, it was making her want to whisper.

'Binkie's dad's got a tie-up with BA,' Bubbles explained as they sank into the roomy sofas. 'So his first-class passengers use this lounge.'

Sam discreetly kicked off her pumps under the table and eased her feet onto the soft carpet underfoot before saying, 'It's really generous of him and Binkie, I must say. I hope you've thanked them nicely from us, Bubs.'

Bubbles waved the gratitude away, blushing slightly. She was always a little embarrassed by the knowledge that she could so easily be a benefactor to her two friends, but today – a mere twenty-four hours after That Kiss – she couldn't help feeling embarrassed at her own indulgence in Raheja munificence.

'Was Akbar okay about this trip in the end?' she asked, changing the subject.

Sam thought for a minute, remembering the chilly silences in the house ever since Akbar had announced his trip to Kenya with Heer. They had been so unbearable that Sam had even, in a moment of terrible ignominy that she now deeply regretted, pleaded to go with them, quite willing to sacrifice the Delhi trip to be with her husband and daughter. But Akbar had refused, saying something that had made her reel. 'There was a time when you were fun to be with, Sam,' he had said, with an air of genuine sadness that was oddly more hurtful than if he'd spoken in anger. Sam, having thought about his remark endlessly for the past few days, had to agree that it was true. The laughter that had left her life when those dreadful events had occurred fifteen years ago had returned in some measure when she'd met Akbar – then, somewhere along the way, it had dissipated again.

'I don't know for sure, Bubs,' Sam replied, managing to keep her voice steady, 'he was all cold and silent for a few days, as you know, but he actually started getting nicer as our departures approached. Almost jovial.'

'When are he and Heer off on their safari?'

'Later tonight. Heer was so excited, you should have seen her face when I did her packing yesterday,' Sam said, trying to quell her resurfacing wretchedness on seeing how little it mattered even to Heer that she wasn't going with them.

'Will Akbar manage her care, Sam? Y'know, bath and stuff,' Anita asked, accepting a glass of sparkling water from a hovering attendant.

'Well, apparently there's a few people going from the law firm, it's not just him and Heer. So he'll have help, should he need any.'

'And Heer's now grown-up enough to manage herself very well, isn't she?' Bubbles said comfortingly.

'Yes, I guess.'

Anita, noticing Sam's trembling lower lip, changed the subject. 'What about your two?' she asked Bubbles.

Bubbles rolled her big brown eyes. 'Oh God, right little

devils both. You wait till your Heer's a teenager, Sam, and thinks everything you do is so *boring* and so *naff*. I can't help feeling quite relieved that my two are not with me on this trip. The last time I took them to mummy-pappa's, they complained incessantly about everything and were so damn rude and demanding that I spent all my holiday apologising to my parents for their behaviour.'

'Well, when your folks married you off to a millionaire, they never quite bargained on dealing with millionaire grand-kids, I guess,' Anita laughed.

Bubbles nodded. 'Too right – my kids must be the only kids in the world who expect their tea-time biscuits to come with their names iced on them!'

'You don't say! Is that how biscuits are served in the Raheja household these days then?' Despite her socialist leanings, Anita couldn't help looking impressed.

'God, no! That was when we were at the Four Seasons in New York last year. So, when I took the kids to Delhi straight after that, Ruby was insisting that everything be served with her name on it, even the aloo-mattar. I think she was doing it just to irritate my mother's cook, though. Poor old man was driven quite batty with all the pea decorating!'

'Good thing her name's Ruby and not Rubaina Begum then,' Sam giggled.

Pleased to see Sam smiling again, Bubbles hammed it up a bit more. 'Oh God, who knows if it's millionaire behaviour or just general teenage behaviour, but it's almost impossible to find anything that will please Ruby any more. I mean, Binkie's arranged for them to go to the Galapagos Islands this Christmas, to see the giant turtles, y'know, and do you know what Ruby says? "I hope they've got air-conditioning there, Lakshadweep last year was just *gross*".'

'Well, at least your Bobby's losing his pampered air of

late, isn't he, Bubs?' Anita said, recalling a recent meeting with Bubbles' son, who, in response to her jolly greeting, had parted the curtain of hair covering his eyes to peer out and grunt something unintelligible. Although it had taken a little prodding on Anita's part, he had finally roused himself and even grown animated when she had pressed him for details on his new drum kit.

'He's okay,' Bubbles said, unable to hide her gratification at having managed to wrest a rare compliment out of Anita. 'But, God, my Ruby is something else altogether.'

There were murmurs of general agreement. On a recent visit to the Raheja household, Sam had looked on in horror as Ruby, a haughty young miss who had inherited her mother's sleek looks without the hard graft that had gone into it, had barely acknowledged Sam's presence, before haranguing her mother who was refusing to let her hire Mahiki as a venue for her thirteenth birthday party.

Anita swirled the bubbly water in her glass. 'Well, let's hope they've put out a turtle-alert on the Galapagos letting the poor critters know that Ruby Raheja is due to arrive,' she said drily.

Sam took up Anita's cue. 'Oh, those poor turtles will surely not have met anyone like Ruby Raheja in their hundred years on earth!'

Bubbles laughed good-naturedly. Only these two women were allowed to say what they liked about her kids. She waved her Salvatore Ferragamo in the air, joining in the banter. 'Nor seen an Anya Hindmarch handbag on their islands – and she's taking two!'

When Bubbles and Sam departed to use the ladies' room at the other end of the lounge, Anita took a book out of her handbag. It was the new Booker Prize winner, but the novel lay unopened on her lap as her mind wandered to an increasingly familiar thought. It was one that occurred to her only when she was in the company of her two old school-mates, hardly ever arising in her normal workaday life or when she was out with her English colleagues and friends, and she had worked out that it was very likely to do with the fact that most of her non-Indian friends were, like her, childless. Out of *choice*, of course, they tended to reassure each other on the rare occasions that the subject came up. But her childlessness was a fact that Anita was starting to focus on with more regularity than she cared to admit even to herself, especially when Sam or Bubbles mentioned their offspring so casually.

It had first come to Anita in a moment of shocking clarity when her father had died last year and she had rushed to Delhi to comfort her mother and help conduct the funeral rites. That act had suddenly made her realise she was busy carving a future out for herself that deliberately excluded the presence of someone who would do the same for her. On the other hand, however, the idea of shaping a child to become a decent human being quite terrified the life out of her. What qualifications did she possess that would allow her to take on such an important task? None, given how flawed she herself was.

She'd never discussed the subject with Hugh, of course. He already had two children from his previous marriage anyway and would no doubt take fright and scamper right over the horizon if she ever mentioned children. Anita sighed deeply, remembering that Hugh had in fact just bounded away and out of her life, thanks to her rapier-sharp tongue and their ghastly row last night! Anita closed her eyes for a minute, trying to pretend she didn't really mind the humili-ating departure of yet another nice man from her life. Was there any point in investing any more in a relationship that wasn't likely to be the final one? Experimenting was all very well in one's twenties, but now, speeding headlong into the mid-thirties, there just wasn't the time for dummy-runs any more.

She sat up as her two friends returned and a Raheja Airlines employee materialised to announce that it was time for their flight. Anita shoved her unread book back into her bag while Bubbles and Sam fussed around gathering up their things. A nine-hour flight would give her enough time to finish the book. If she could stop herself brooding on the showdown that had finally finished things with Hugh yesterday, that was.

In the end, the unusual luxury of a bed in the first-class cabin combined with the anxiety she had been fighting in the run-up to this trip, put Anita to sleep minutes after the flight took off. Like her, Bubbles got into a pair of flight pyjamas and soon nodded off over a glossy magazine. Only Sam stayed awake, gazing at her own face in the dark window and feeling the metal capsule she was travelling in hurtle her further and further away from her husband and daughter. At this point in time she would not have known which frightened her more – the uncertain future that awaited her on her return, or the past that she was returning to at such reckless speed.

Chapter Twenty-Three

DELHI, 1993

For Sam, the dreary December days, with the mock exams now just around the corner, had become unbearable. Delhi was encased in a grey fog that some said meant snow in the hills and others said was just pollution choking them all slowly to death. Sitting at her desk, Sam looked out of her window at the leafless jacaranda in the darkening back garden, feeling more morose than she had thought possible. Even Haroon had stopped bothering with her these past few days, seeming to have grown away from the whole family due to whatever stupid love-pangs he was suffering from. He had taken to spending more and more time locked away in his room, appearing only occasionally for a meal, unwashed and unshaven, and then toying disinterestedly with the food on his plate, much to their mother's annoyance.

After Haroon's initial anger with her had passed, Sam had tried worming it out of him, without success. 'Why has Lily broken up with you? Did you say something stupid?' she asked, by now quite genuinely concerned about his unusually stubborn despondency.

Haroon shook his head. 'She's just a bit stressed-out with the exams, I guess,' he replied shortly.

'Well, I'd hardly blame her if she has ordered you away for a while. The syllabus is huge, you know, and we have just a few days now for the mocks . . . I'm glad *I* don't have a boyfriend to distract me!' But Haroon hadn't smiled at that unlikely prospect, continuing to look melancholic. She tried another tack. 'Look, Haroon *bhaiyya*, Lamboo keeps telling us that these are the most important exams we'll ever face in our lives. And Lily's terribly competitive . . . Anita thinks she's after the Lalvani Scholarship. Maybe she'll cheer up once the exams are over.'

It was no use. Her brother continued to gaze sulkily out of the window as though incensed by something that lay in the gathering gloom outside. Sam suddenly felt sympathy for Lily, stuck with an asinine suitor like Haroon to distract her when she was aiming for those top grades. If he was going to mope about her having to study for the exams, then Sam would fast lose patience with her brother too. Moreover, she had tried warning him of Lily's cold-heartedness long ago. Whatever it was, their parents – who had no clue of Haroon's infatuation with Lily – didn't deserve to be treated so dismissively.

Later that night, Sam heard her father knock politely on Haroon's door and get no response. He knocked a little harder, to be heard over the loud music that was playing inside, but there was still no reply. She looked up from her books as her father wandered into her room, spectacles perched as usual over his furrowed forehead.

'He must be asleep, Dad,' she said, even though she had also been met with silence when she had tried Haroon's door earlier in the evening.

'Is he okay, *beti*?'

'What do you mean?' Sam responded guardedly.

'You know, he's not himself these days . . . bit quiet, you know . . . I don't want *you* worrying in the middle of your revision but your mamma and I are a bit concerned . . . Haroon talks to you . . .'

'*Used* to talk to me, Dad. Doesn't really any more.'

'Is there a problem?'

'Not that I know of . . .' Sam contemplated telling her father her theory about Lily and love-pangs but considered how furious Haroon would be with her when he found out she had tattled. Her father, luckily for Haroon, was typically following a completely false lead.

'You hear about drugs and things on the campus . . .' he said, forehead creased with worry.

Sam couldn't help laughing at that. 'Oh Dad, I'm sure that's not it. Come on – drugs? Haroon? He doesn't need drugs, he's high without them as it is!'

But her father's face failed to break into one of his usual smiles. 'That was before, beta. He's *not* his usual fun-loving self these days. Something is wrong.' Sam nodded, turning serious, and her father, seeming suddenly to realise that he was distracting her, wandered across to drop a kiss on the top of her head. 'Anyway,' he said, trying to raise his voice to sound a bit jollier, but, as ever, saying the wrong thing, 'you have much bigger things to worry about, Samibeta. You know, these school-leaving exams are perhaps the most important ones you will ever sit, affecting your whole future life and career. How is the revision going?'

'Okay, I guess. These logarithms drive me crazy . . .'

'Ah now, in this house, remember you are the only one with a mathematical mind. Even Haroon could never understand logarithms so your battle will be a lonely one tonight. But, *beti*, why are you struggling with logarithms now? The exams start with the English paper tomorrow, don't they?'

'Because I'm good at English, Dad. Tomorrow's paper doesn't frighten me at all. But *maths*, yuk . . .' she shuddered.

'Just like I was at your age,' her father beamed. 'How I too used to love English literature, poetry especially. I can still remember my favourite lines, you know . . .' He paused to put one hand dramatically on his chest before declaiming, '"*I come from haunts of coot and hearn . . . to sally down a valley*" . . . wah!'

Sam giggled. 'I'm sure that's wrong, Dad . . . "*sally down a valley*"! Sometimes you say "*bicker down a valley*" and sometimes you say "*sally down a valley*". Which one is it?' she demanded.

'Well,' came his reply, 'Tennyson wrote "*bicker down a valley*", you see, but I think "*sally down a valley*" sounds much better. Hear the rhyming in it . . . much better.'

Sam watched her father standing in the middle of her room, his expression turning maudlin, and realised that he was lost to the hills and valleys of his childhood in Kashmir. He was now raising one upturned hand in the air to deliver the punch-line she had heard at least a million times before. '"*For men may come and men may go but I go on forever . . .*"'

Mr Hussain stopped, enjoying the sound of his voice reverberating in Sam's small room. Then he heard his wife call out from the TV lounge, a voice that – however sweet – had an unerring way of bringing him back to earth with a bump. He cleared his throat. 'Your mother doesn't like me bothering you when you're revising, Samibeta . . . I'll go now,' he said, hastily shuffling off.

After he had left, Sam carried on studying into the night, stopping only for a quick bite in the kitchen while her parents watched the ten o'clock news on TV. A loud soundtrack was still thumping behind the closed door of Haroon's room when, an hour later, she stumbled to her bed and fell into an exhausted sleep.

Sam awoke to the sound of a blood-curdling scream. She sat up in bed, sweating under her blanket, imagining she had woken from a dreadful nightmare. Then it came again, her mother's voice, making the downy hair on her arms stand on end. It was the middle of the night and her mother was screaming . . . screaming and sobbing and yelling incoherently . . . Sam tumbled out of bed and ran through the dark, stopping for a few eye-watering moments as she stubbed her toe painfully on the leg of her table in her haste. She stood on one foot with her head spinning, clutching her leg and squeezing her eyes shut in agony. Mamma was still screaming and Haroon's music was still thumping loudly.

By the time she had hobbled frantically into the corridor, she realised that her mother's screams were emanating from Haroon's room. They were loud enough to drown the music but Haroon's voice was not to be heard, even though light from his room was spilling out into the dark of the corridor. Now Qadirbhai the cook was running towards Sam, a look of terror covering his wrinkled old face. He grabbed her, an action that, even in her panic, Sam found astonishing, seeing that Qadirbhai hadn't touched her since she was ten. She stood in confusion for a few seconds, wondering why her father was shouting gutturally as he ran out of Haroon's room towards the telephone. Qadirbhai's thin arms were cutting into her own and something he held in his left hand was piercing painfully into her waist. Sam looked down and saw that it was the big bunch of spare keys that was kept in a toffee tin in the storeroom. It came slowly to her as she started struggling to be let free . . . they had grown tired of waiting for Haroon to emerge . . . her mother would have wanted Qadirbhai to have his own meal and turn in . . . he would have refused to eat without feeding his beloved Haroonbaba first . . . her mother would have grabbed the spare keys in a temper and gone to confront Haroon about his inconsiderate behaviour . . . and now . . . now she was in Haroon's room, screaming and screaming as though she would never stop.

Sam struggled in Qadirbhai's arms, slapping at his hands and yelling to be let free, but still he clung on to her as though his life depended on it.

'Let me go, what is it, what is it?' she yelled, forgetting that Qadirbhai knew no English. '*Chodo, Qadirbhai, mujhe chodo!*' she shouted desperately again.

'*Nahin, nahin Samibaba,*' he replied, burying his grey head in her hair and starting to cry.

Sam had only ever seen their old cook cry once before, and that had been when she was seven and had brought in a telegram from his village. Her own terror was now making her feel weak and she no longer needed her mother's wails to tell her what was going on. Her father was shouting into the telephone for an ambulance. She stopped struggling to hang on to Qadirbhai's thin body, which had started trembling and shaking as if in a fever. Now he was moaning and slumping to the floor and she was free to go. Sam stood looking at the empty wedge of light outside Haroon's room before dragging her feet slowly towards it.

Haroon's funeral was the next day, the day of the English paper, which meant that none of Sam's classmates or teachers could attend. Sam – given special dispensation to miss the mock exams – preferred it that way as there was less sympathy to face, less thinking to do, less tears to cry.

After Haroon's body had been taken to the cemetery

overlooking the River Yamuna by her male relatives, Sam sat alone in her room, rocking herself with hands clasping her knees as she stared sightlessly at the walls. She did not dare shut herself into her room, knowing that closed doors would from now on be forever forbidden in this house. Someone – Auntie Gul perhaps – had taken over the house and the kitchen as, over the course of the day, regular trays of tea were despatched to sustain the visiting mourners and relatives, some of whom were arriving from as far away as their native Kashmir. Meals were being produced at all the right times too, food that had none of her mother's or Qadirbhai's magic ingredients, and turned to dust the instant Sam put it in her mouth. Someone must have picked up her mother from the floor of Haroon's room that night and taken her to her bed, but she had lain there since, weeping and moaning in a low voice, getting up only to go to the toilet and even then only if one of her sisters physically lifted her and took her there. Sam's father, never able to sit in one place for long, wandered around the house like a ghost, occasionally looking in puzzlement at the dozens of people crowding his living room, as if trying to recall what major event might have brought them all there. Every so often he would stick his head into Sam's room and she would try to smile reassuringly through her tears at him, silently promising that she wouldn't go and vanish overnight like Haroon.

Haroon. Sam had not been able to say his name out loud all day, although she was still half expecting him to come bursting in any minute with one of his inane jokes. She had tried making a pact with Allah that she would have her brother back even if he were returned permanently frozen in the shadowy despairing form he had adopted in the days before his death. Even that was better than no Haroon at all. How could he do it? she thought, wretchedly remembering the sight of her brother's pale face as he lay lifeless on his bloodied sheets. How had he not for one moment thought of her in the room next door as he had drawn his pen-knife over his wrists? Or remembered their disbelieving mother – the woman who had clung limpet-like to his ankles, refusing to let go even when the ambulancemen had come to take him away?

That evening, someone slipped into Sam's room and stood silently in the doorway. Drowsy from grief and exhaustion, Sam looked up and through blurred vision saw Bubbles. She reached out her hands and Bubbles rushed towards her, falling to her knees by the bed as she took her friend in her arms. They clung to each other and both girls started to weep in great shuddering sobs that could finally emerge from their silent hearts, filling Sam's small poster-lined room and spilling out into the living room, where someone said softly, 'The poor girl has not been able to cry so far. It is good, let her cry.'

Afterwards, Bubbles fetched a towel and a basin of water from Sam's bathroom and gently helped clean her friend's face, before arranging her pillows so she could sit up comfortably.

'Here, you take this end of the blanket, Bubs,' Sam said wanly, holding up the blanket covering her feet. 'Don't catch a cold. You have exams.'

Bubbles shrugged. 'We're all going to fail them. Even Anita said she sat looking blankly at the paper this morning for fifteen minutes before the first words would come. No one can stop thinking of you, Sam . . . and Haroon . . .'

Sam's eyes filled again but she plucked at the blanket, unable to stop herself from blurting bitterly, 'If only he had fallen for you, Bubs.'

Bubbles looked down, her lower lip starting to tremble, before she bit it hard, forcing herself to look at Sam. 'Did he really do it because of Lily?' she asked presently.

'What else, Bubs? There was no other reason. He was okay till she came along.'

'But what could she have done to upset him so badly, Sam?'

'Lily? Well, upsetting people comes pretty easily to her, doesn't it? And don't forget how crazy Haroon was about her . . . it wouldn't have been difficult to hurt a softie like him.'

Bubbles considered this carefully. These past few months had taught her many things about love that she had not known before: the terrible anticipation of a phone call that wouldn't come, the crashing in her heart when it did. First Haroon, then Binkie – it certainly didn't look like she was going to be lucky in love. After a lot of uncharacteristic reflection, Bubbles had concluded that hearts were no better than puppets in the hands of other people who did not always use their power kindly. From her few phone conversations with him, Bubbles had gathered that Binkie was not the kindest person in the world. So she understood perfectly what it must have been like for poor, gentle Haroon to have his heart tossed around in such careless hands as Lily's. If only, if only, he had given it to her, how tenderly she would have loved him back.

Bubbles wanted to wail again at this point but told herself sternly that she needed to be strong for Sam. She sat determinedly holding on to her friend's hands, but soon Sam, lost in her own thoughts, started whimpering again. 'Just think, Bubs,' she hiccupped, 'Haroon had probably never had anyone be nasty to him before Lily came into his life. He just wasn't used to being hurt. If it wasn't for her, we would still have Haroon here with us . . .'

303

Bubbles tried to shush her, but before she knew it she was dissolving into helpless tears herself. A few seconds later Sam pulled away, wiping her face roughly. 'I hate her so much, I wish she were dead, Bubbles. Really, I mean it, I could kill her . . .'

Chapter Twenty-Four

DELHI, 2008

The three friends stood holding their trolleys, the crowds and confusion of Indira Gandhi International Airport swirling around them.

'You forget how hot it gets even on winter mornings in Delhi,' Sam said, fanning her face with the in-flight magazine that she had appropriated for her father from the aircraft. He had by now acquired a shelf full of the glossy magazines, collected from Sam's visits home, which he steadfastly refused to give away, much to her mother's chagrin.

'Oh thank God, there's Papa's driver,' Bubbles said in relief as she spotted a familiar face beaming amid the placard-waving throng. The porters followed them to the car park, pushing their trolleys, as touts and beggars besieged them with a variety of pleas and offers.

Finally, having paid the porters far more than they were accustomed to, the three women ducked into Mr Malhotra's commodious Mercedes, heaving sighs of relief as the driver switched on the ignition and a blast of cool air from the air-conditioning vents ran over their faces and arms.

Bubbles leaned forward to give the driver directions to drop Sam off first at her parents' Hauz Khas house before taking Anita to Bengali Colony. Neither were too far from her route to the Mehrauli farmhouse her parents had moved to five years ago, and she had insisted it made more sense than Anita taking a cab and Sam dragging her poor father out in his old Fiat.

Anita looked out of the window at her childhood city, suddenly feeling strangely daunted by it. But, as the broad roads and big hotels flanking the airport gave way to the elegant mansions of Vasant Vihar and, soon after, the shabby working-class suburbs of R.K. Puram and Munirka, the familiarity of homecoming started to uplift her mood. She gazed at the unfolding scenes, wondering how this city of such huge differences managed not just to survive but also succeeded rather magnificently. The question had, in fact, led to the argument she had had with Hugh on the night before her departure for India, even though there were other, far bigger concerns lying just below the surface. It was the thought of confronting the memory of Lily that was plaguing her and poor Hugh had merely been in her line of fire. And, of all things, their argument had been about something as inane as multiculturalism! She positing scornfully that, for all liberal Britain's tall claims to multiculturalism, it was India that had long ago achieved it. 'You want genuine pluralism, you look at India, Hugh.'

'But there was no such thing as "India" until the Brits got there, admit it,' he had responded weakly and semi-jocularly, using that same old tired argument that no longer merely wearied Anita but flipped her mood instantly to irritation instead. She had not been able to help barking back, 'Exactly what imperialists like to salve their consciences with. Among the plentiful "gifts" you Brits conferred on India, you gave it its very identity too, sure. Never mind that the Romans and Greeks – Herodotus, for heaven's sake! – were referring to a sophisticated eastern land called the Indus at a time when your countrymen were running around in animal skins. But what was the other big one you so generously gave us? Oh yes, the railways! Railways that bled India of its raw materials and subsequently transported products made by those very materials around so they could be sold at inflated prices to . . . oh, to impoverished Indians, of course.' Anita had become aware that she was spluttering at this point but, unabashed, she had merely taken a breath and ploughed on, 'For that let's offer eternal gratitude, eh? At least you left it *behind* for us, rather than packing up the tracks and engines and taking them home with you. Glory be!' Hugh had sunk deeper and deeper into the futon as she continued to harangue him. 'It's only India that can lay genuine claim to pluralism, Hugh. It's nothing like your lily-livered brand of multiculturalism that quails and collapses the minute a 9/11 takes place in America. So that all previously unspoken barriers are given permission to safely spring up again. So we can make Islamophobia fashionable, for fuck's sake! Does anyone ever remember that that was exactly how Nazism started – just swap Jews for Muslims and it's the same thing happening all over again!'

Sitting in the cool of Bubbles' air-conditioned car, Anita now felt her face flush at the memory. Why had she flown off the handle like that? It wasn't as if kind-hearted, gentle and liberal Hugh (of all people, *Hugh*!) deserved a lambasting for Britain's colonial history. Especially when Anita's angst was certainly not over Britain's colonial history but merely her impending trip to Delhi. Hugh was, in fact, the sole reason why she *hadn't* gone potty with guilt as the departure date had approached. The argument that night had started off amicably enough, but she had been tense all day and it had so quickly ballooned into that preposterous full-scale barney. Ending with the pair of them screaming ludicrously at each other through the living-room wall until Hugh had eventually grabbed his fleece and stomped out of her flat into the cold night. For good, probably.

As the car idled at one of those interminable red lights that Delhi specialised in, Anita watched a woman in a nine-yard sari and with diamonds on both nostrils haggle spiritedly with a roadside Sikh vendor selling dates. 'See, that's what I mean,' she spoke up suddenly. 'A Tamilian woman takes on a Sikh selling a product that's most likely come from Rajasthan. And no one's even speaking their own mother-tongue. That's not just diversity but is accompanied by such a comfortable *certainty* that no one even notices!' Anita turned to see perplexed expressions on her two companions' faces. 'Oh, sorry,' she muttered. 'Just thinking aloud.'

Sam and Bubbles, both of whom were accustomed to Anita's occasional eccentricities, exchanged amused looks as she turned to peer out of the window again. Anita looked at her reflection in the smoked glass. There was no point trying to explain any of this to her two mates, who wouldn't get it and, furthermore, would be exceedingly cross that she had not only broken up with yet another boyfriend – one they both liked – but . . . and Anita could imagine Sam's horrified expression: 'You broke up with Hugh over an argument about *multiculturalism*?!'

Still looking out of the window, Anita reached out a hand for Sam's and squeezed it briefly. In a funny way, Delhi's progress, despite all its diversities and difficulties, was a bit like the unlikely friendship she had maintained with these two women, surviving and flourishing not in spite of but perhaps because of their glaring differences. She would never have been able to make this trip back to confront her past without them by her side.

When they reached the Hussain household, Bubbles and Anita disembarked to pay their respects to Sam's parents. Sam's mother was standing on the verandah looking anxiously out as they arrived and, as they went through a round of hugs and greetings, Sam's father emerged from the house. Anita tried to hide her shock at how much the poor man had aged in the few years she had not seen him. Perhaps it was the memory of Lily, but her visits to India were not as frequent as Sam's or Bubbles' and she had never fallen into the habit the other two had inculcated of looking in on each other's parents whenever they were in Delhi. Anita hugged Mr Hussain gently, feeling an emaciated shoulder through his cotton kurta.

'Look at all three of you,' he said, pushing down the bifocals perched on his forehead to get a better look. 'Three such beautiful women,' he said proudly. 'Not our little girls any more.'

Anita laughed. 'We were really very silly little girls once, weren't we? I remember parties at this house where you put up with all our screaming so uncomplainingly.'

'Never silly,' he replied solemnly. 'Little, yes, and screaming sometimes, but never silly, never.' He shook his head, his grey eyebrows bristling in indignation at the very suggestion. 'In fact, I don't think they make girls as beautiful as all of you any more,' he declared.

Anita laughed again, 'You're too kind – but girls just get more and more beautiful if you ask me, Uncle. Look at Heer. Prettier than a china doll, in my opinion.'

She bit her lip as she saw Mr Hussain's face cloud over and realised her gaffe. Luckily the other two were deep in conversation with Sam's mum and had not heard. 'Ah yes,' Mr Hussain was replying, 'Heer. Heer is not coming this Christmas holiday, you know. She has gone on a safari holiday with her father,' he said despondently.

'Yes, I know,' Anita said regretfully.

'I had told Sami she should also go with them,' he said, dropping his voice as he saw that Sam's attention was on something her mother was saying. 'Families should take holidays together, you know. But you know what your friend is like. She wants to come here every year and make sure we are okay. You should tell her she doesn't need to do that. She will listen to you.'

'Of course Sam needs to come and check on you,' Anita said remonstratively, patting a bony shoulder blade. 'We need to be sure our parents are behaving, just like you did once with us.' She hoped she had not sounded patronising and was pleased to see Mr Hussain laugh at her remark.

It was not that untrue, though. When indeed had this role reversal taken place, leading to her and her friends adopting a parenting role towards their parents – making sure they exercised and took their medicines on time and 'behaved', as she had put it, as though they were obstreperous little children. Vast changes crept up so slowly, they were upon you before you even noticed. She saw Bubbles trying to catch her eye. 'I think we need to go now,' Anita said apologetically to Mr Hussain, 'but I'll come and visit again before we return to England.'

'Yes, yes, *beti*, go now. Your mother and Bubbles' parents must also be waiting anxiously to see you. But tell me before you go: is your mother okay after your father's sad passing? We heard about it from Sami and so Sami's mother called and spoke to your mother. It is difficult for us to go anywhere, you know, the traffic being what it is . . .'

Anita nodded. Tears didn't come easily to her but suddenly she could not trust herself to speak. It had not been easy to accept her once sparky mother's rapid descent into grey-faced widowhood. 'Ma's as well as can be expected,' she said finally, 'but she's thinking of moving back to Calcutta where her siblings live. I'm too far away to be of much support, you see.'

'Wise decision, wise decision,' Mr Hussain said. 'It is in old age that one realises the value of one's siblings. Better by far to tackle old age alongside those you grew up with rather than impose one's problems on the next generation. My sister – you remember Sami's Auntie Gul? – she has also moved permanently to Delhi now. And we are a great comfort to each other, a great comfort.' Noticing that everyone was now looking at him and waiting patiently for him to stop rambling, he patted Anita's arm and said hastily, 'Go, *beti*, your mother will be waiting. You must not let an old man bore you like this. But come and visit once more before you go, okay? We just don't see enough of you girls . . .'

Mrs Hussain repeated her husband's instructions as they walked down the drive with the three girls. 'Come back soon, yes, both of you? I will make your favourite mutton biriyani and you can all scream with laughter as before,' she said. After Bubbles had got into the car, she leaned in through the window and patted her gently on the cheek. 'You don't look like you are eating properly, *beti*,' she said affectionately. Bubbles, who knew that the remark arose from love, smiled and kissed Mrs Hussain's hand before moving up for Anita to climb in next to her. The two women nodded as Sam reminded them of the visit to the school the following day. They waved as she put her arms around both her parents and made the gesture of a telephone call as they drove off.

The next day, Bubbles called Sam at midday. 'At what time has Lamboo called us to the school?' she asked.

'Six thirty, I think,' Sam replied.

'I'll pick you up at six, we should go together.'

'Make that half five, Bubs. The traffic around central Delhi will be bad at that time. Shall we get Anita too?'

'Of course. I was going to call her as well.'

'Do you have news of anyone else? Or is it just us?'

'Well, if there are others it's you they're more likely to contact, Sam. Zeba has your number, hasn't she?'

'Perhaps I'll give her a call and let her know we're here. She might want to come with us.'

'I don't mind who comes. I just don't want to walk back into the school again on my own.'

'For me, it's facing Lamboo that's the unbearable thought. We barely saw her after Lily's death anyway, thanks to the exams, and once I started college I just couldn't bring myself to go back. Now I feel so terrible about that.'

'Never mind, Sam, it was such a bad time, especially for you. I'm sure she's always understood.'

After they hung up, Sam thought of the school, its old redbrick buildings and their Princy. Then she thought of Lily and Haroon, and when her thoughts became too unbearable she got up and went in search of her parents. Her mother had put her father's chair out in the sun and given him a bag of peas to shell while she pottered about in the back garden, pruning her climbing roses. Mr Hussain beamed at his beloved daughter as she stepped out through the kitchen door. He promptly put his bag of peas away and called out to the cook to bring a round of sweet lime juice.

Sam stretched her arms, enjoying the feel of the sun on them. 'Using me as an excuse to sneak a break from your shelling, are you, Dad? Typical!' she joked, throwing her eyes upwards and flopping on a chair next to him.

Mr Hussain hastily picked up the bag again, throwing an exaggerated look of fear over towards his wife who was still busy at her rose bush. 'Ssshhh, I'm shelling, I'm shelling,' he said, peering through his glasses at a peapod and fiercely denuding it of its last pea as Sam laughed and reached out for a handful to help him.

They sat shelling in companionable silence until the cook emerged with a small tray of glasses tinkling with ice. Qadirbhai had died four years ago but he had, in that quiet, kind way of his, inducted his nephew to be the family's new cook when he first came to know of his cancer. Mrs Hussain walked over the grass towards them, putting her pruning shears down and taking the chair next to her husband. She sighed before picking up her glass. 'It's so lovely to have you here, *beti*. But I do wish Heer and Akbar had come too,' she said, sipping on her drink.

'I know, Mum,' Sam replied, stung slightly by her mother's unintentionally hurtful words. 'But Akbar had to go to Kenya – it was a company thing, you know. And an educational trip for Heer. I wanted to be here, of course, to see you two. I also felt bad when Miss Lamb's card came and thought I should make the effort to attend this reunion and use the chance to see her too. She's finally retiring and leaving the school, she says.'

'Poor lady,' Sam's father said. 'If we don't understand the pain of what she went through, who will? Fifteen years, both for her and for us. But she just carried on. What a great teacher your Miss Lamb was, dedicating her life so selflessly to you children.'

'They never did find out if her Lily was killed or took her own life, you know,' Mrs Hussain said sadly, shaking her head and putting her glass down.

'But I always say, maybe such *causes* are not so important.' Mr Hussain turned to his wife. 'After all, we never found out why Haroon did what he did. But we managed to accept it somewhere along the way.'

Sam's mother smiled gently. 'And we found another son in Akbar. We should count our blessings.'

'*Beti*, why don't you call Akbar and Heer so we can also talk to them?' Mr Hussain said suddenly. 'Is the time difference okay to call them? What is the time in Kenya?'

Sam looked at her watch. She needed to tell Akbar she had reached Delhi safely, seeing that he hadn't called. Suddenly, irrationally, she longed to hear his voice. She fetched her mobile phone from her bedroom and dialled his number as she stepped out into the garden again. After a few seconds she could hear the distant *brrr-brrr* and imagined it ringing in his hotel room or game-park cottage – she didn't even know where they were staying. Then it clicked and she heard Akbar's voice, far away and tinny.

'Hello, hello?' she called, worried he wouldn't hear her.

'Yes, I can hear you, Sami,' he called back. 'Have you reached Delhi?'

'Yes, last night,' she said, even though it had really been afternoon and she had waited all evening hoping he would remember to call.

'Are your parents well?' he asked, and she nodded stupidly, suddenly feeling choked. 'What did you say? Hello?'

'Hello, Akbar, I can hear you fine. Yes, they're fine, thanks, and send you their love.'

'Here's Heer,' he said, and after a small scuffling sound Sam heard her daughter's voice. She didn't know whether to rejoice or weep when Heer went into a high-pitched and excited prattle that she could barely understand.

'. . . we saw elephants and zebras and buffaloes,' she ended in a rush.

'Buffalo,' Sam corrected.

'What?'

'You say "buffalo" for one or many, darling, like "deer"

and "sheep". And don't say "what", say "pardon"! Have you forgotten everything?' she laughed. 'Tell me, are you being good for Daddy?'

'Yes, I'm being very, very good. Sarah didn't even have to help me with my bath today. I did it all on my own. *And* combed and tied my own hair!'

'Oh what a good girl. Now talk to Nana-Nani, okay,' Sam said, passing the phone to her father, who took it tenderly with both hands as though reaching out for Heer herself. She got up to make room as her parents pushed against each other to hear their granddaughter's voice on the minuscule mobile phone.

Her father's voice rose in excitement. 'Really, *elephants*?!' he exclaimed. 'My goodness, Heerbeta, and buffaloes too! What is it, *beta*, speak slowly, speak slowly . . .'

Sam walked back into the house. Which Sarah was it that Heer had referred to? she wondered. Akbar's secretary was called Sarah, but he hadn't mentioned she was going. Perhaps one of Akbar's colleagues or one of their wives was called Sarah too, it was a common enough name. She was not going to worry until she knew she had reason to.

Sam stopped in the living room and looked up at the photograph of Haroon that her parents had had enlarged and framed a few months after his death. His head was cocked to one side and the hair falling across his forehead had caught the sunlight, turning it brown. His grey front tooth was just visible through his shy sixteen-year-old smile. He had stopped smiling properly for a while soon after that cricketing accident, grimacing in a strange way with lips determinedly stretching over his teeth instead. Then, he gradually seemed to forget about it, showing all his teeth again in his lovely lopsided grin. Until, of course, Lily happened, and he had stopped smiling all over again.

Sam leaned on the dining table, recalling how her hate for Lily had dissipated so speedily after Lily's own death, being replaced instead by a gnawing guilt for the part she had played in it. At first her rapid transfer of feelings had seemed somewhat disloyal to Haroon, but, as Sam had grown older, she had found it was her brother she was more likely to feel angry with rather than Lily. Whatever Lily had done to Haroon, in the end it was Haroon who had not cared enough about his family to keep from hurting them as he had done.

Sam walked up to her brother's picture and placed her fingers on its frame. His bright smile seemed to be telling her not to mind so much about Akbar and the state of her marriage. 'What to do, Haroon *bhaiyya*,' she whispered. 'Like you, I too have inherited this ridiculous family trait of loving too much. And of not being able to accept painful truths.' She glanced out of the window and saw that the telephone conversation was over. Her parents were laughing at something, probably the babblings of their beloved granddaughter. Now her mother was leaning over to show her father a rash on her arm and he was putting on his glasses to peer worriedly at it. Yes, she had certainly taken the business of loving-too-much out of her parents' book, which was all very well for people who just loved each other back. Neither she nor Haroon had been blessed the same way. But perhaps poor Haroon had paid with his life to teach his sister that love was only worth so much anguish.

Chapter Twenty-Five

DELHI, 1993

On the morning after Haroon's death, Lily sat all by herself in the cottage by the school, staring sightlessly out of the window at the grey winter sky. Her thoughts were spinning unstoppably like shuttles on a loom gone out of control, unravelling madly this way and that. She could never for one moment imagine that something *she* had done could have had such a terrible effect. Or that words, mere words, could wreak such damage. So far it had always been the other way around – the words and actions of others marking *her* life so indelibly. Yes, Lily had seen – and relished – the expressions of confusion and hurt every time she had lashed out at people. It had given her power at a time when she had been so powerless against her fate. But this? Haroon going home after that stupid row yesterday and lying down on his bed to slit both his wrists? Twin gashes running all the way up his arms, she had just heard her grandmother exclaim to someone on the telephone.

The phone had first rung at dawn, pealing relentlessly in the slumbering cottage, waking Lily from a restless dream. She had heard her grandmother shuffling hurriedly to get to the instrument as it stubbornly sustained its ring, muttering and grumbling under her breath. A few minutes later, Lily heard her gasp loudly, a muffled shriek almost. At first, thinking it might be news from Mussourie, Lily had sprung out of bed to stand shivering at her door. Then, straining to catch the words as her grandmother hung up and made a few outgoing calls, Lily could tell it was nothing to do with her father at all, but with Haroon. Haroon . . . Who had turned up at the cottage just yesterday when she had been revising for her English paper. All unkempt and frantic. But alive. Pleading to be taken back into her life. Could he really have killed himself merely because she had said she never wanted to see him again? That was nothing! A mere rejection. Rejection was better than so many of the other things people did to each other; Lily would have told Haroon about that if she had only had the chance. But he was stupid, and unwilling to accept that she was done with him. At first, going out together had been fun – it had all been harmless stuff anyway: movies and walks in the park. But that night at the Taj, when Haroon had tried to kiss her and started pawing at her, Lily had realised with unbearable disgust that he was no different to other men.

At first she had tried to let him down gently, telling him on the telephone that she was breaking up with him, even attempting to explain that it was nothing to do with him really. But the stupid boy had continued to follow her like a hungry puppy, hanging around outside the school gates hoping she would appear and making silent calls on the phone, leading her to instruct Lakhan to answer all incoming calls. Lily had realised that, like those street urchins with their dogs, she would virtually have to kick Haroon to get the message across. But how incredible that yesterday, after she had ordered him to stay away from her, he had gone home and slit his wrists. Because of *that*? How could Haroon have been so weak, so quick to take refuge in death?

Lily started to tremble sitting on her bed, realising that she had known, even as she had tormented Haroon, that his was a more tender soul than any she had goaded before. More tender and more trusting and more – she squeezed her eyes shut, feeling her body start to shake terribly inside her thin cotton nightie – more *loving* of her than anyone else she had known since her mother died. She hunched over, holding her arms around her shivering torso, telling herself not to weep, because if she did she knew she would never, ever be able to stop. As ever, she felt her mind waft out of her body to watch herself from the ceiling above – a small, shivering form, all alone.

It took enormous effort, later that morning, for Victoria Lamb to keep from lashing out at the unconcerned expression on Lily's face when she was told about the tragedy that had befallen the Hussains. But she held her tongue in check, reminding herself that anger would be most inopportune at such a delicate time. It was also possible that Lily was merely using nonchalance to hide her own confusion and fear. Victoria tried another tack, keeping her voice steady as she buttered her toast.

'Did the boy not say anything to you, Lily? Was there no indication at all of his suicidal intent?'

Lily shook her head, slurping on her oatmeal porridge. 'He barely talked,' she said finally, when Victoria refused to lift her iron gaze.

'What do you mean, barely talked? You went out with him a few times, didn't you?'

Lily seemed to take forever coming up with a reply and Victoria felt her patience wearing even thinner. Eventually, scraping her bowl noisily with the spoon, the girl spoke. 'Three times exactly. We went to the movies twice, and I really do hate anyone talking when I'm watching a movie. So not much conversation there. And the third time was for a walk in Buddha Jayanti Park where I had to do the talking for both of us.' Victoria, sensing that Lily was lying, cocked a quizzical eyebrow at her, forcing her to add, 'Oh, about nothing, honest to God! Look, I'm sorry he went and did such an awful thing, but it's really got nothing to do with me, okay? For heaven's sake, one would imagine *I* was going to be blamed for this as well.'

Predictably, a remark like that could only melt Victoria's resolve to be firm with Lily. Much as she wanted to get the truth out of the girl, she had to remind herself not to ruin the painstaking progress that was being made, very gradually and day by day. Nevertheless, she protested mildly, 'Oh Lily, how can you say that? It's absolute stuff and nonsense to suggest that anyone's ever blamed you for anything. But I truly would like to help the Hussain family come to terms with their terrible misfortune and I did rather hope you might be able to throw some light on this. I've only met the lad briefly a couple of times and can't say I saw a depressive. That's the only reason I ask.'

'Well, you'd be surprised at how looks can deceive,' Lily said angrily, her face turning pink. Her voice sharpened as she got up from the table but she studiously avoided eye-contact with her grandmother. 'He certainly wasn't a barrel of laughs – a bit like his sister really, constantly moping about something.'

'Fiddlesticks,' Victoria countered, secretly pleased to be finally having a semblance of conversation with Lily even though they were arguing. 'Samira's a lovely girl – empathetic, thoughtful, and so full of compassion.'

'Compassion's just a step away from pity, and that includes self-pity,' Lily replied, flopping on the sofa to pull on her socks followed by the shoes that had been brought in by Lakhan, freshly polished.

Victoria sipped contemplatively on her tea. 'You make a very good point, Lily,' she said, surprised as the girl's perspicacity. 'But I do believe Samira stays on the right side of that line.'

'Wish I could say that,' Lily responded tartly. 'She's always looking at *me* in that false pitying way of hers, which I really do hate. If she did really feel for me she could try telling her bunch of friends and hangers-on to stop throwing spiteful looks at me all day long.'

'Nonsense, darling,' Victoria said comfortingly, 'I'm sure you're imagining it. What reason could they possibly have to be spiteful to you?'

Lily stood up and shrugged on her coat. She had now returned to her familiar glowering silence and Victoria recognised with a pang that their brief conversation was over. Still, it had been an unexpected pleasure not to have been snapped or growled at, as was Lily's usual wont. 'I'm going to visit the Hussain family today with a couple of the teachers. Would you like to come along?' Victoria asked hopefully.

Lily looked at her grandmother for a moment, as though briefly tempted by the offer. Then, shutters descending across her face again, she muttered, 'Think I'd rather not.'

Despite the exams, Sam's friends, classmates and teachers trickled into the Hussain household in two and threes over the following few days to pay their condolences. As Victoria Lamb said to Sam's father, reaching out to touch his shoulder while taking her leave at the gate, Sam was one of the most popular girls at school and everyone grieved deeply on her behalf.

Lily was conspicuous by her absence during these visits. Sam wondered whether there might actually have been enough humanity in that cold heart to feel at least a small twist of guilt over Haroon. She comforted herself with that thought, until Zeba confirmed there was no such thing.

'She was playing basketball in school today, Sam, leaping around the court and laughing like a maniac. Almost hysterical. Would she do that if she even for one moment thought of you and Haroon?'

'Who was she playing basketball with? Was it one of our classmates?' Sam asked, testing everyone she knew with how much *they* grieved for Haroon.

'No, of course not, none of us would even think of having fun when you're going through all this! No, it was one the juniors,' Zeba said, making Sam feel instantly infuriated with that nameless junior.

Sam saw Anita later in the week but she had even less news of Lily. In fact, she had barely spoken as they sat silently holding hands. It seemed that even Anita had lost her usual powers of logic and deduction in the face of Haroon's death.

It was on the conclusion of the last paper, the dreaded Maths, that Bubbles, Anita and Zeba took the school bus to Sam's house in order to spend some proper time with her. It was the Social the following night, and Miss Lamb had asked Sam's classmates to try to convince her to attend ('She has to come out sooner or later. We're keeping it low key this year anyway out of consideration for her. Her father would very much like to see the poor girl get out of the house, so do try to persuade her,' Lamb had instructed them, her blue-grey eyes cloudy behind her glasses.)

The three girls gathered around Sam, perching themselves on her bed where she seemed to have taken up permanent residence, sipping silently on mugs of tea. Already the winter evening was darkening outside, and so far Anita – who had been chief spokesperson of the group – had been unsuccessful at getting a 'yes' out of Sam for the Social. It was not just the Social, merely getting words out of Sam was hard enough. She seemed to have sunk even lower than the last time they had seen her, Bubbles thought, noticing the purple shadows under her friend's eyes and her lank, greasy hair. She put her arms around Sam, unable to bear her unhappiness any more.

'*Please* come, Sam, or we're none of us going, I swear,' she said.

Sam sat up abruptly and Bubbles' arm fell off her shoulder. She looked like she was about to say something, but stopped when Qadirbhai came in with a room heater. Waiting until he had finished plugging it in and turning it on, Sam spoke up only as he left the room. Her voice was low and trembling. 'I will come for the Social,' she said, looking around at her three friends gathered on her bed. 'I will come, but on one condition.'

'What? For you, anything. You know that,' Anita agreed quickly.

Sam's whispered reply was barely audible. 'I will come . . . I will come if you will help me kill Lily D'Souza.'

Her words hung in the silence as everyone froze in disbelief. Suddenly Zeba giggled a little hysterically. 'You're joking,' she said lamely, inviting a look from Sam that wiped the pleading smile off her face in an instant.

Sam continued speaking, her words getting swifter and more determined. 'I know you think I'm mad to even say it, but I've sat here these past two weeks and thought of nothing else but killing Lily, or at least hurting her so badly that she'll never hurt anyone again the way she did Haroon. Believe me, I'll do it. Even if I have to act on my own.'

She was still surrounded by silence, and the faces around her were getting hard to read in the half-darkness. Nevertheless, Sam looked at each of them pointedly, not giving them time to think as the words continued to tumble out of the recess of her mind where she'd kept them hidden all these days. In all the days of mourning Haroon, it was these words that had been her sustenance, and she had mulled them over countless times – carefully polishing and shaping them to perfection until she would use them. Now, however, they were tumbling out of her, all ugly and raw and beseeching. 'You all have good *reason* to help me,' she said. 'It's not just for me. Anita, think of the Lalvani Scholarship – with all that's happened to me, I'll bet you've been distracted from giving the exams your best. Could you say, in all confidence, that you think you're going to get the scholarship and that Lily won't beat you to it? And you, Zeba, have you really forgiven her for what she has made you go through over Gomes? Teasing you and playing with you as though you were a mouse and she had you trapped in your little hole. Think too about the school play. Moss has given her the part of Joan, hasn't he? I know, Bubbles told me. How unfair is that, tell me? Especially since you've always had the lead part in our school productions and needed this for your application to drama school. Please tell me you all want to hurt Lily as much as I do. You want to help me, don't you?' Sam's voice sounded more beseeching than determined by now as she fought to hold off the tears.

There was another heavy silence before Bubbles spoke up in a small voice. 'What about me, Sam?' she asked. 'What reason have I got to hurt Lily D'Souza? I'll be getting married and leaving for London and I'll never have to see Lily ever again . . . what reason have I got to kill her, Sam?'

Bubbles could, of course, think of many reasons for which

324

she would willingly kill Lily D'Souza. For having stolen Haroon, for having broken his heart, for having robbed Bubbles of the chance – however remote – of a future with Haroon. But far more urgent than all that was to stop Sam, the sweetest girl in Bubbles' world, from talking in such a scary way. To get rid of this haunted look on her face, to return her to the reliable friend she had always been; someone who, from childhood, had shown herself to be kind and generous to everyone who came her way, even those whom everyone else shunned. Bubbles knew that better than anyone else – for wasn't it Sam who, aged six, had steadfastly refused to be put off by the chicken pox pustules on her face, unlike everyone else in class who had run screaming in the opposite direction. How had it come to pass that the very same Sam was now talking about killing one of their classmates?

Sam looked up at Bubbles blankly. She had forgotten that Bubbles had never hurt a fly in all her life and probably never would. And now she was asking her to help her kill a girl, their classmate. Simply because . . .

'Because you're my friend . . .' Sam whispered, dissolving into tears again. She buried her face in her blanket and moaned at the sheer, awful, inexplicable cruelty of it all. Why her, why them, why her parents, who, like Bubbles, had never hurt anyone in their lives? Why poor, sweet, stupid Haroon?

She felt Bubbles put her arms around her again and almost couldn't believe her ears when she heard her say softly, 'I'm with you, Sam. I'll help. I'll do anything you want. Even kill Lily D'Souza if that's what you want me to do.'

Zeba was next. 'I'm in too,' she said firmly.

The three of them looked at Anita. Sam could see that Anita was rationalising and calculating as she always did, she could almost hear the whirring of brain cells trying to work out this new conundrum. After a couple of seconds, Anita spoke, her large eyes liquid in the half-light, her voice quavering with uncustomary doubt. 'How? How would we do it, Sam?' she whispered.

And so it was that, as night fell over the Hussain house, the four girls plotted out what they should do to Lily. It was a simple enough plan and Sam had already given it a lot of thought. All they had to do was get Lily away from the crowd at the Social, somehow tempt her into the Chemistry lab or the rose garden, hold her down and then throttle her using one of the skipping ropes that were kept in a pile at the back of the gym. Lily was a tall and athletic girl, but surely not stronger than the four of them put together.

'She may start screaming,' Anita pointed out.

'Well in a crime novel I read they used chloroform but I don't know how difficult it is to get hold of . . .' Sam replied.

'Our lab may have some,' Bubbles offered. 'Do you know the chemical name for chloroform, Anita?'

Anita seemed not to hear the question, still focusing on all the possible pitfalls. 'We'll need a convincing explanation to get her out of the hall,' she said doubtfully.

'Won't be easy, seeing that she doesn't like any of us,' Bubbles acknowledged.

'Me, I'm just dirt under her shoes,' Zeba observed gloomily. 'You know she has not spoken one word to me since she saw me and Gomes that day in the lab . . .'

Anita ignored her, still thinking furiously. 'Thing is, Sam, Lily may smell a rat if any one of us suddenly cosies up to her. That's too risky . . .'

Sam, sensing the hesitation on Anita's part, said tearfully, 'Look, I don't want to drag any of you into this if you're so afraid. But I won't be able to rest until I've torn that bitch to pieces. Not after what she did to my brother. I promise

326

you I'll kill her with my own bare hands and all by myself if I have to.'

Anita put her arm around Sam as she started to cry again. 'You're not all by yourself in this, Sam,' she said. 'Not when you have us as your friends. Look, leave it to me for now. I'll think of something. And in the meantime, don't talk about it to anybody, okay? And I mean *anybody*. Not even Natasha, Zeb.'

'Well, I'm not likely to, am I?' Zeba responded crossly. 'She's flying to London tonight, remember?'

'Good,' Anita said. 'Not a soul should know about this plan but us four. Okay?'

All the girls nodded, relieved at someone else taking charge. But as they left Sam's house, travelling on buses and auto-rickshaws back to their own homes, their collective mood was sombre and scared. Not one of them slept easy that night, each plagued by strange dreams and uneasy thoughts as they tried unsuccessfully to convince themselves that the world would be a much better place without Lily plaguing it.

Chapter Twenty-Six

DELHI, 1993

On the morning of the Social, Sam woke up feeling strangely peaceful. It was raining ouside, a cold grey winter rain, but normal comforting noises were emerging from the rest of the house: the clank of Qadirbhai collecting the milk cans at the door, the thud of a rolled-up newspaper landing on the porch, her father gargling loudly in the bathroom down the hall. Then she remembered – and the familiar hole in the pit of her stomach widened a little bit more. Had Haroon still been alive, Sam would have heard him whistling tunelessly in the toilet, thumping around getting ready for college, popping into her room to borrow her pen or a tenner in that maddening way of his. Had he really been gone three whole weeks?

In a sudden, stabbing flash of guilt, Sam considered what Miss Lamb would be thinking this time tomorrow. They had all observed that Lily and Miss Lamb never showed affection to each other – maybe that was some peculiarity of English behaviour, or maybe it was Lily's coldness. It couldn't have been Lamboo, who, though sometimes outwardly stern, was unfailingly kind to her brood of girls. Supposing Lamboo had grown used to having Lily around in her house? Perhaps she too woke to the sound of Lily singing in the bathroom and felt happier for it. Like Sam's parents, Lamboo didn't deserve to have someone disappear on her just like that, vaporise into thin air without so much as a word. And from what Sam could see, Lamboo had no one else in the world but Lily to call her own. How strange and far away that day now seemed when Lily had told her about being Miss Lamb's grandchild. Had that been one of Lily's lies too? Sam had held onto that secret for Miss Lamb's sake, and now she squeezed her eyes shut, wondering if it may indeed be true. And, if it was, then how could she dare dream of robbing her beloved school principal of much, much more than a mere secret from her past. Lily would be Lamboo's last living relative.

Sam got out of bed, her mind in turmoil. As soon as it was a more decent hour, she should phone the others and call the whole demented plan off. She must have been out of her mind, suggesting they get together and kill Lily D'Souza, however much she hated her! She stood at her window, deciding to revert to Plan A, which had been to not go to the Social at all. There was a sudden thunderclap from the skies, which Sam, looking up at low, churning clouds, took as a form of celestial approval.

When Sam saw both her parents at the breakfast table, she knew they had rallied themselves for her sake. For the first two weeks no one had been able to cut past the sorrowful fog surrounding her mother, but now she was trying to force it off herself, determined to help her remaining child live.

'Ah, come, *beti*. Toast?' her father asked, setting aside his newspaper. 'The day of the Social, yes?' He said 'Social' as though grateful for the one certainty they could all cling to for the moment.

Sam kissed the tops of both her parents' heads before

sitting down. Her mother poured her a cup of tea and started to chop an apple. Sam watched her, wondering whether she had forgotten that the only reason the family had taken to eating their apples chopped rather than whole was because of Haroon's accident with a cricket ball that had left him with a permanently wobbly front tooth. Her question was soon answered when she saw tears start to flow down her mother's face again. When she could no longer see what she was doing, Sam's father silently took the paring knife off her to finish the task. Sam, who had been contemplating telling her parents that she was not planning to attend the Social after all, decided to hold her silence. She would go for their sake, whatever it took.

By the evening, Sam was feeling sick at the thought of leaving the house. There had been the expected round of subdued phone calls from Anita, Zeba and Bubbles, and the plan was set for the group to meet at the eastern portico of the old church that separated the boys' school from the girls'. Sam knew her friends were trying to protect her from the curious gaze of the others when she set foot in school for the first time after her brother's death. There was sure to be some elbow-nudging and murmuring, but Sam knew it wouldn't be malicious – it was bound to happen whenever she returned to the school, Social or no Social. At least tonight only her own classmates and teachers would be present – and a bunch of Xavierans who wouldn't know her at all. Facing Lily was, of course, her biggest fear, but Sam had planned for that as well. She knew that as a part of her own recovery she needed to hurt Lily in some way. How exactly she would achieve this was still a matter of the most awful uncertainty.

Sam picked out a pair of black trousers and a thick black sweater to suit both her mood and the cold wet evening.

The only concession she would make to the fact that it was Social night was a pair of silver earrings that Haroon had bought for her birthday last year. The others had offered to wear dark colours too, in Haroon's memory, although Sam felt bad on behalf of friends like Bubbles and Zeba who would normally have loved to use the chance offered by the Social to dress to the hilt.

Sam was the first to arrive at the church, as her father had insisted on driving her to the school rather than allowing one of her friends to pick her up. After waving him away, she made her way down the small path flanking the church rather than take the main driveway that led to the school. She stood shivering under a flickering yellow tubelight, feeling the damp of the December night creep in through her clothes to settle into her bones. Luckily Anita arrived soon after, and before long Zeba was hurrying down the path too. Bubbles came five minutes later, but Sam was suddenly rooted to the ground.

'I can't do this,' she whispered, white-faced. 'I can't go in there.'

'If Sam's not going, I'm not going either,' Bubbles said. 'We can go back to the car park. My driver will still be there and we can go home.'

'Nonsense,' Zeba dismissed the suggestion. 'You two are not going anywhere. Just walk behind me into the school,' she ordered Sam, 'and don't worry. *I'll* make sure no one looks at you.'

'Thanks, Zeb,' Sam muttered. 'I suppose we can't turn around now. But listen – I don't know what I'm going to do about Lily. I'll only know for sure when I see her. Just be there with me throughout, please, okay?'

Bubbles took Sam's hand in hers, then said; 'I'll be by your side all the time, Sam, I promise, and I will support you in anything you do. Anything. Okay?'

332

When they heard the distant rumble of thunder, Anita said quietly, 'We should go to the gymnasium now, it's going to rain again.'

They walked through the deserted school yard. Only a few dim lights in the convent were on, the rest of the buildings plunged in wet darkness. The beat of music was audible in the distance, but it was only as they walked around the library wing that the gym came into view, all its uncurtained windows blazing light. The doors and windows were closed against the December cold so the full blast of the pounding soundtrack hit the girls only when they pushed the doors open to walk in. Despite the lateness of their arrival, the party appeared to have only just made a tentative start: 'Oh Carolina' by Shaggy was blaring on the sound system and a couple of braver souls had ventured onto the makeshift dance floor. Sam saw a large table laden with half-finished platters of food at one end of the hall and a clutch of teachers scurrying about with bottles of squash and trays of plastic glasses. And there, leaning against the leather gym-horse in a sparkly white dress, was Lily, talking to a couple of boys in their dark green St Xavier's blazers. Her eyes flickered towards the group that had just walked in, and Sam knew she had taken in her presence.

Normally Sam would have at least nodded at Lily, but tonight, quite pointedly, she did what she had never done to anyone in school before. She turned her back on Lily and walked in the opposite direction. She was trembling uncontrollably, a red mist descending before her eyes as she thought of Lily dressing up in a pretty dress for the party while poor Haroon lay cold in the ground. Sensing her trauma, Anita steered Sam towards Miss Lamb, who was standing with Mrs Menon next to the old piano. The two teachers hastened across the room as soon as they spotted

Sam and, after an exchange of hugs, they talked for a few minutes about Sam's parents and how they were coping, their conversation calming Sam's feelings a bit. Bubbles returned with a tray full of drinks and Zeba found seats from where they could observe all the comings and goings in the hall. The girls settled themselves and a few others drifted across to talk to them, but Sam kept her eyes on Lily, who was now standing by herself near the door. Feeling a surge of anger so strong it almost made her giddy, Sam decided to try and stare Lily down. How dare she turn up at a party just three weeks after she had pushed Haroon into taking his life? How dare she show her face before his beloved sister as though his loss mattered not at all?

Sam was temporarily distracted by Mr Gomes, who had also sidled up to pay his condolences to her. She stood up and made polite conversation, seeing how nervous the Chemistry teacher was, sweating in his black silk shirt. Gomes was followed by a few other teachers and students, each of whom wanted to talk to Sam or give her a hug. By the time she was finally able to sit down again, Sam noticed that Lily had vanished.

A few awkward conversations later, Sam scanned the hall again and saw that Lily had indeed slipped away from the party. Perhaps she had gone back to the cottage, Sam thought, imagining with renewed anger how upsetting it would have been for someone as self-centred as Lily to see Sam sucking up all the attention tonight.

'Lily's gone,' she whispered to Anita.

Almost as though on cue, the four girls got up and left the gym hall as one. There was no need for affirmation of any sort, they simply knew that the time had come to find Lily. The party was by now so raucous that no one noticed their departure, all eyes on a pair of Xavierans doing a comic samba on the floor. The friends stepped out into the cold night air and followed Sam, who was purposefully walking in the direction of the rose garden as if she knew exactly where to go. She stopped as they reached the spreading old mulberry tree and peered over the hedge, but there was no one there. The flowers nodded dark heads under a sky clotted with clouds as a chilly breeze picked up again. The principal's cottage lay at the edge of the garden, its windows dark and empty.

'Let's try the Chem lab,' Anita said. 'If she was looking for the furthest point from the gym to hide from us, then that would be it.'

'I don't think she'll have gone there,' Sam said. 'She's more likely to be here, in the cottage.'

'But it looks empty. It must be locked. Even Lamboo's cook is at the gym,' Bubbles said, her teeth chattering from both fear and the cold.

'I'm sure as anything that Lily's come back here to the cottage. We may see a light at the back. I've got to find her. For Haroon's sake, please!' Sam's voice was shaking with a mix of anger and tears.

'Look, why don't you and Bubbles check the cottage while Zeba and I go down to the lab?' Anita suggested.

Sam nodded and took Bubbles' outstretched hand so they could pick their way through the rose bushes to Miss Lamb's cottage. Shadows were moving like spirits through the garden as clouds passed over the moon. In the distance a dog howled, making Bubbles cling even more tightly to Sam's hand. In her fear, Bubbles noticed all manner of things that quite terrified her: a dim light deep inside the cottage somewhere, a chink in the curtains on the ground floor, the madhumalati creeper above the front door that suddenly resembled a blackened claw.

The cottage looked more like its normal self as they neared it, shadows melting harmlessly and claws dissolving into creepers again. The two girls pushed at the front door but it was locked. Then, peering through the darkened windows, they saw only the reflection of their own frightened faces looking back. A few seconds later, both girls jumped as they heard the sound of the kitchen door being clicked shut followed by footsteps. It was Lily, who suddenly appeared around the corner. For a moment the two friends stood in the dark, still clinging to each other and staring at Lily as though she were a ghost and not the girl they had been combing the place for. Lily too looked shocked to see the girls she had been avoiding right at the door to her cottage, but before she could say anything Sam started to yell – loudly and hysterically and incoherently. All the words she had kept pent up ever since Haroon had embarked on his luckless venture with Lily now came tumbling out of her mouth. The years of having been brought up to be polite and kind and never use bad language were thrown to the wind as Sam shrieked every word of abuse she could think of at Lily until, finally, Bubbles, weeping and distraught, dragged her away.

Unaware of this, Anita and Zeba were crossing the playground to make their way through the buildings in the direction of the lab. But they found the lab door secured with a large brass lock. Looking through the windows into the murky interior of the lab, they saw bottles and implements shining in the pale gleam of light that was trickling in through the windows. Zeba clutched Anita's arm and said in a shaky voice, 'I don't like it here at all. Please let's go back to the gym.'

Anita, standing next to her, shivered. 'I agree – it all looks so different at night. So spooky.'

'Let's go back via the cottage and get the other two,' Zeba said.

By the time they returned to the moon-washed rose garden, Sam and Bubbles had gone, but there, sitting under the mulberry tree and leaning on its gnarled old trunk, was Lily. As they neared her, Anita saw that she was twisting the edge of her dress around and around in her hands as though in a fury. She looked up as she heard footsteps approach, and Anita saw that Lily's face was not wearing its usual uncaring mask, but instead an expression that seemed strangely beseeching. To Anita's astonishment, she noticed that Lily had been crying, streaks of tears and snot running down her face.

'I didn't want him to do it,' Lily whispered as the two girls neared her, looking at Anita as though only the school's most intelligent girl could offer some explanation for all that had happened.

But Anita felt a stony weight descend on her heart as she opened her mouth to respond. Later, in years to come, it was this she would agonise over: whether the last words she had uttered to Lily were spoken on behalf of poor, lost Haroon or poor, grieving Sam, or, selfishly, for herself. Because she so wanted that scholarship to Oxford. When she thought back, all she did recognise was that the words she spat at Lily were – despite her caustic tongue – the most hateful she had ever spoken to anyone in all her sixteen years, or would ever speak again. Even years later she could hear her voice and the way it trembled that night, full of stored-up fears and anger and resentment that she had never dreamed lurked within her at all.

'Do you really think it matters to us what *you* want or don't want, Lily?' Anita said. 'After what you did to Haroon? And Sam? And her desperate, grieving parents? They're dying of broken hearts, but do you for a moment even care? Do you ever think of anyone but yourself, Lily? Do you even know the meaning of the word "empathy"? You've been *nothing* but trouble since you came to the school, which was a really good place before . . . y'know. But you wouldn't know that, would you? You've never known the feeling of being in a good place, have you? Have you, Lily? *Malign*, that's what you are, a malign presence. Even to poor old Lamboo, who was kind enough to take you into her house. Even she has only looked wretched since you came to Jude's. And we all know what a contented person she was before. But, no, you wouldn't know that, Lily. You, who makes unhappiness your creed, your very mission in life. You just spread your own unhappiness around like a malaise. What everyone needs now is for you to *go*. Go back to wherever you came from. You should never have come here in the first place to ruin things for all of us. Just *go*, Lily, please, and leave us all to get on with our lives the way they were before you came and ruined everything!'

To which Zeba added, 'And, believe me, not one of us will miss you for one moment when you're gone. We just hate you, all of us. In fact, do you know of even one person who doesn't hate you, Lily?'

Without waiting for a reply, the two girls turned around and walked swiftly away from the rose garden to go in search of their friends.

Less than half an hour later, Lily's body was found.

At ten o'clock the party came to an abrupt end when the music was suddenly turned off. The sound-system man had been urging Mrs Menon since nine that it was time to start dismantling if he was to reach his home across the river before the fog descended. The teacher looked around the hall and, seeing that quite a few of the children were already leaving for their waiting cars at the gates, finally gave her assent. In the sudden silence, the last notes of 'Young at Heart' echoed briefly in the corners of the hall before dying away. The now depleted group of boys and girls on the dance floor stopped bopping to shrug in embarrassment at each other, as though the music had somehow made their proximity more acceptable. They awkwardly started to bid each other good night, some of the girls exchanging kisses and wishing each other happy holidays as they would now meet only after the Christmas break. Victoria Lamb knew it would be at least another hour before she would be able to lock up the gymnasium and told Mrs Menon she would be back. She needed to use the toilet and also thought it would be a good idea to nip back to her cottage so she could put the two bottles of leftover Cava served to the teachers in her fridge before they lost their fizz and went flat.

It was a few minutes after Victoria Lamb had left the hall that a scream was heard, for it was she who, picking her way across her darkened rose garden, first spotted Lily. At first she saw no more than a shadowed heap on the ground, but, as she neared, a horrified Victoria saw that it was a body . . . Lily's body . . . lying with her white dress spread around her like water. As she stumbled towards her, the first thing she noticed was how awkwardly the girl's arms and legs were positioned, like a rag doll discarded after play. Nearby was a broken branch from the mulberry tree and wound around Lily's neck was a skipping rope. It was only when Victoria saw the blood oozing from somewhere on Lily's head that she started to scream.

Miss Lamb's screams were loud enough to penetrate even the closed windows of the gym. Everyone tumbled outside and ran in the direction of the noise, reaching the periphery of the rose garden to see the principal kneeling in the mud, cradling Lily's head in her lap. Stepping closer, people observed in horror that blood was emerging from Lily's head and forming a huge red stain on the front of Miss Lamb's cardigan. The principal looked up at the assembling crowd, her face – normally so poised – twisted with shock and grief.

The first person to fall to his knees and help was Gomes. He grabbed Lily's shoulders, shoving his fingers past the rope wound around her neck to feel for her pulse. He looked up aghast, shaking his head. Then he laid her gently down on the earth before getting up and trying to help the weeping Victoria Lamb to her feet. She allowed herself to be pulled up, her hands covered in blood and mud, before she collapsed against the Chemistry teacher's chest.

In the chaos that followed, someone had the sense to call the police. They arrived to a scene of pandemonium: a school full of hysterical and panic-stricken children, a rose garden shrouded in fog, rain-softened earth over which dozens of pairs of feet had trampled, and the corpse of a girl which had been touched by at least five pairs of hands. The senior policeman at the scene noted at first that it could just as easily have been either suicide or murder. It was clear that there had been an attempted strangulation, given the ligature mark around the victim's neck, but the victim's neck was not broken and the tree branch nearby would indicate an unsuccessful hanging. What was probably the eventual cause of death was that, in her fall, the victim's head had hit a jagged piece of rock. The possibility could not, however, be entirely ruled out that someone had deliberately bashed a rock against the victim's head, as there were many such rocks ringing the garden, all of them covered that night in petals and rain and mud.

Chapter Twenty-Seven

DELHI, 1993

Technically, the cause of Lily's death remained unknown. Days after her body was found, police investigators were still unsuccessfully combing the now out-of-bounds rose garden for clues and attempting to interview distraught students and teachers. Victoria Lamb, aware of the appalling effect the investigation was having on her school, carefully weighed up the pros and cons before calling up Delhi's District Superintendent of Police, a man whose daughter had once studied at the school, to tell him all about Lily's troubled past and beg him to call off his search. 'My senior class has a Board Exam to sit in a month's time,' she pleaded. 'This investigation is not helping anyone concentrate and the futures of these children could be ruined by this. Please, sir.' And the DSP, a man of unusual good sense, mulled over the remote possibility of finding a murderer from among the 100-plus possible suspects, if indeed it was a murder at all. From what the principal had told him, he had gathered that the victim was a severely damaged young woman and suicide was a far more likely option. Besides, a boy with whom the girl had been associated had also recently killed himself. Perhaps it had been some kind of lovers' suicide pact. Perhaps she had been unable to cope with the boy's death. There was certainly no clear motive for a murder, although, in the DSP's vast years of experience of crime in a city like Delhi, he was aware that when the victim was a pretty young girl there often wasn't one. He sighed deeply and took a last look at the photograph he had been provided, seeing a heart-shaped face with blue-grey eyes and a sad smile that would have seemed, had he been a more fanciful man, to already convey hints of a tragic end. Reluctantly he scribbled next to the box marked 'Cause of Death': *Unknown/Suicide*, before closing his file on the Lily D'Souza case to move on to other things.

St Jude's class of '93 managed to pass their Central Board of Secondary Education examinations, maintaining the school's spotless record of no failures, but without the shining grades that had always been expected of them. Despite not achieving the anticipated high marks, Anita was awarded the Lalvani Scholarship and began her preparations for Oxford. Bubbles married Binkie Raheja one month after the exams and departed with her new family for England, tearfully getting Anita to promise she would be in touch the very minute she arrived. In the face of great opposition from her family, Zeba left Delhi to take up a place in the National Institute of Film and Television that she had secretly applied for. Samira scraped a place to study English at Lady Shri Ram College, which, being near to where she lived, meant less time away from her parents and home.

The girls met one last time – at Bubbles Malhotra's wedding – in order to confer and make a pact. No one had confirmed anything so far, but – in the confusion of the Social and the subsequent investigation and exams – it had occurred to

342

each of the girls that one or the other of them may have been directly involved in killing Lily. After all, she had died in the manner they had plotted and it went without saying that, if any one of them was culpable, they would need to close ranks immediately. They could not possibly have chosen a noisier venue than a wedding to make a pact of silence, but Bubbles would be leaving India the following day and the chance of the four of them meeting in the near future was remote.

Bubbles sat in her bedroom wearing a lehnga that had been specially tailored and embroidered at Ushnak Mal: blood red and covered in a profusion of rice pearls and Swarovski crystals that had been flown in especially from London. She felt her lehnga scrape against her skin with every little movement and wondered how she would cope with it weighing her down for the next six hours. Sam arrived first, and Bubbles was saddened to see her wearing a plain silk salwaar kameez, grown even tighter around her bulging tummy. Her own newly trimmed figure had inspired her to deliver anxious lectures to Sam about losing weight, but she decided to spare her friend today, given the heartbreaking expression on her face. She reached out a henna-covered hand and asked, 'Did your dad bring you, Sam?'

Sam shook her head and sat down. 'I took a scooty.'

'Is your dad all right? Seems unlike him not to insist on dropping you,' Bubbles asked, concerned.

Sam's voice was sad as she replied. 'Everyone thought it was Mum who would never recover from Haroon's death, but Dad – poor Dad, who seemed so strong at first – well, he's the one who seems to be sinking now.'

Bubbles squeezed her hand. 'I remember them all at my engagement, they were so happy,' she said quietly. 'Especially Haroon.'

Sam nodded. 'It was the last time we went out together as a family, Bubs. Somehow I'm glad it was here, in your house.'

Anita was the next to arrive, looking ungainly in her mother's best Dhakai silk. 'Ma insisted I wear this,' she said, casting a rueful glance at her untidily bunched-up pleats. 'She wants me to take a couple of saris to England too, but I doubt I'll ever wear the damn things.'

'Looking forward to Oxford? Not long now,' Sam observed, trying to take her mind off her troubles.

'You bet I'm looking forward to it, Sam. I need so desperately to escape this crass old city. Although I am quite nervous of England too, I have to say. Can't help thinking sometimes that an American university might have suited me better, the great melting pot and all that. One hears about racism still being rampant in English universities – even the finest colleges. Perhaps most of all in the finest colleges, actually.'

'Oh Anita, you'll be fine. You're so smart, you'll just zap them,' Bubbles said. 'Think of me stuck among all the snobby money-bags in London!'

'Just don't let any of them look down on you, okay?' Anita instructed, slipping back for a moment into the protective role she had always adopted towards her old desk-mate.

Bubbles wore a doubtful look on her face, although she nodded obediently. At that moment Zeba appeared at the door, causing all three of them to draw in their breaths in unison. 'Oh you look just great, Zebs,' Bubbles cried. 'That material's so slinky on you!'

'Didn't your parents mind the neckline?' Sam asked curiously.

'*And* the waistline?' Anita added, eyeing Zeba's long and sexy abdomen.

344

'Naah, they've decided I'm a lost cause now that I'm off to NIFT,' Zeba replied, kicking off her stilettos and sinking onto a floor cushion. 'My Ammi thinks I'll be sleeping with every single producer who'll offer me a role.'

'And might you?' Anita couldn't resist asking.

'Hmmm . . . I'll have to see about that,' Zeba replied vaguely. Sam tried to prevent herself from feeling a little scandalised by the knowledge that Zeba actually meant it.

A sudden silence overwhelmed the group as they realised that they had gathered not to make small-talk about their unknown futures but to acknowledge the great dark shadow that still loomed from their immediate past. They had not discussed Lily or the night of the Social in any detail so far, but this meeting had at first been Sam's idea. 'If we are to move on, we must try to achieve some kind of closure,' she had said to Anita on the telephone, although Anita – assuming Sam's guilt – added a more sensible reason: 'And we need to ensure we all maintain the same story. Just in case someone gets confused, you know.' Anita and Zeba had, on the day after the Social, even reflected on the possibility that Sam had killed Lily as threatened. It was not implausible, given that Sam and Bubbles had been missing when Anita and Zeba had returned to the gym after meeting Lily in the rose garden.

'Shall I call for some tea or Pepsi?' Bubbles asked, picking up the intercom phone. Sam wanted elaichi tea but everyone else asked for Pepsi, and they waited, talking about other things, still unable to mention Lily and the Social while the maid brought a laden tray in.

They sat looking at the plate of sticky yellow chum-chums covered in silver foil that the maid said Bubbles' mother wanted the girls to sample while they were still fresh. There was something faintly ridiculous about the festive air of the sweetmeats – and everyone's fine clothes, for that matter – given what they had gathered to discuss.

Sam knew she owed it to everyone to finally open the subject. Her voice was so low it was barely audible. 'It was my fault, what happened that night. And I can't even begin to tell you how sorry I am to have dragged you all into it,' she said finally.

'Come on, you could hardly be blamed for wanting to hurt Lily under the circumstances, Sam,' Anita said.

Zeba nodded. 'It was initially just your grief talking, Sam, and then we all got caught up in it one way or the other,' she said.

'Weren't we all grieving for Haroon in different ways, Sam?' Bubbles said, taking Sam's hand in hers again.

'And you were coping with the weight of your parents' anguish too, Sam. Something was bound to give,' Anita said. 'Good God, something like that would've plain destroyed me.'

'Don't blame yourself, Sam,' Zeba added. 'You weren't alone in hating Lily enough to kill her.'

Sam, remembering the sight of Lily's crumpled and bloodied body lying in the rose garden, pulled her silk dupatta around her shoulders with a shiver and insisted, 'Nevertheless, what a thing to even contemplate . . . killing a classmate . . .'

The words hung in the air between them as they sat silently for a few minutes, not meeting each other's eyes, listening to the distant blare of the brass band practising for the arrival of the groom's contingent. Happy shrieks of various Malhotra nieces and nephews playing in the garden came floating in through the windows.

'There are even days when I wonder whether we imagined it all . . .' Sam continued.

'What do you mean?'

'You know, about Lily. Whether she really was responsible for Haroon's death, for example.'

'What else could it have been, Sam?'

'Oh, I don't know – it could have been any number of other things, I guess. Maybe he was worried about his exams or something. Maybe it was drugs. *Maybe*!' she added as she caught Anita's sceptical look.

'Do you know, Sam, I've thought the same thing myself,' Zeba said hesitantly. 'Not about Haroon, of course. But about Gomes and all that. That I might somehow have misjudged Lily. It's *possible* that Lily did not tell on me – or on him, for that matter – not for her own selfish reasons or to get the Chemistry paper, but actually to save me. Maybe she deliberately came bursting into the lab like that in order to save me from Gomes. Do you think that's possible?'

'Practically anything's possible, of course,' Anita said. 'But the fact is that we *all* universally hated her – that strength of feeling couldn't have just come from nowhere.'

'Maybe we were just jealous . . . and our jealousy sort of rubbed off on each other?' Sam volunteered.

'Come on! We've never been jealous of each other – and don't tell me we don't have reason to be. I could be jealous of Zeba for her figure or Bubbles for her money or –'

'But that could be because we've known each other since we were kids, Anita!' Sam cut in. 'We grew up together, we're *used* to each other. But Lily was the newcomer, the interloper in our world . . . and she was better than us at most things too, we have to admit it . . .' Sam stopped, unable to speak any more for her quivering mouth, recalling a long-ago conversation with her brother in a Simla churchyard.

Anita cut in before Sam could start crying. 'I know one shouldn't speak ill of the dead and all that, but perhaps we're forgetting just how horrid Lily was, Sam. She was just so *nasty* all the time. I don't think we should be caning ourselves now for having been unable to like her.'

'There must have been a reason for her anger,' Sam insisted. 'I mean, she'd lived for a while with nuns in a convent somewhere and she once mentioned in passing not being allowed to see her father. Maybe he was in prison or something. So there were *things*, you see. It just didn't sound like she had the same kind of life as us.'

'Maybe Lily was brought up by nuns because she was poor. They do take girls from impoverished Christian families into the convent sometimes to provide food and education, don't they? Maybe that's why Lily didn't like us – because she was poor and thought we all had money,' Bubbles suggested.

'More than just money, I think. She did sometimes look sort of ... y'know, *upset* when the last bell rang and people mentioned things like their mums picking them up from school. And she always clammed up if anyone asked her about her past. I did try asking her once because I was feeling sorry for her, but ...' Once again Sam stopped short of mentioning Lily's claim to being Miss Lamb's granddaughter. There was no need to pass on what was probably a lie, especially now that Lily was dead. A scandal would be terribly unfair on poor Miss Lamb, who was already coping with so much.

They all sat remembering Lily for another few minutes, trying to fit her into other moulds than the one she had occupied in their minds for the past few months. Finally Bubbles piped up, the wobble in her voice matching everyone's mood. 'So weird and so ... so *horrible* that Lily died in much the same way that we had planned to kill her that night ... you know, the skipping rope and all ...' she said.

Zeba quickly volunteered a theory. 'You know, if it was murder, it could have been Gomes,' she said hopefully. 'I saw him leave the gym before Lily was found . . .'

'Oh come on, he was in the toilets!' Sam cried. 'Bubbles and I saw Gomes going into the school building as we were coming out of the rose garden.'

'Yeah, I clearly remember seeing him too,' Bubbles said. 'He was ahead of us when we went to the toilets in the main building. We were in search of tissues, weren't we, Sam?'

'But Gomes is definitely a possibility,' Anita insisted, 'given the information Lily had on him.'

'Well, he sure as hell got himself covered in Lily's blood as soon as he could after the event, didn't he?' said Zeba.

'Yes, he could have deliberately gone to check her pulse. Well, that would have been the logical thing to do if he wanted to ensure that his fingerprints would be all over the skipping rope,' Anita said, aware that she was scraping the barrel now, suddenly terrified of hearing what Sam might say.

Zeba wasn't giving up either. 'And he was wearing black too,' she pointed out.

'So were we all,' Sam said, 'for Haroon's sake, as you know.'

'And so were half the other people there. Everyone wears black at night anyway,' Bubbles agreed. 'Natasha's mother said so,' she added by way of explanation as Zeba gave her a withering look.

'Well, we could quite easily have been seen as the perpetrators,' Anita said, wrapping her arms around herself and shivering. 'I mean, there we were plotting to kill Lily the night before, so it would have been the logical thing to have been accused of it when it did take place. All I can say is, thank goodness Lamboo called the investigation off.'

Zeba shuddered. 'You're right – just think how easily

we would have crumbled if we'd been questioned. It wouldn't have been difficult for the police to be convinced it was us.'

'After all, Sam and I had only just come back into the gym before Lily was found,' Bubbles said, 'they could easily have thought it was us who killed her.'

Sam, whose head had been bowed for a while, finally raised it to look at her friends. 'But it was I who killed Lily . . .' Her whisper pierced the still air for a second before she continued. 'Sure, I didn't wrap a skipping rope around her neck and throttle her, as planned. We all know she took her own life . . .' Sam spoke softly but her voice broke as she added in a barely audible whisper, 'but it was I who drove her to it.'

Anita, overcome by a mixture of relief and guilt, spoke up, first. 'No, no, Sam, if Lily was driven to take her own life then it wasn't you at all, it was me.'

'And me,' Zeba said.

'What do you mean it was you?' Sam asked. 'You weren't even there when I screamed at Lily. Only Bubs was. And I have to thank her for dragging me off to the toilets before I did any worse.'

'You two saw Lily?' Anita asked, surprised.

'Yes, in the rose garden . . . just after you and Zeba went off to the Chemistry lab.'

'Then it must have been soon after you met her that we came upon her too, on our way back from the lab. She was in the garden, sitting under the mulberry tree. She looked quite upset but we didn't realise . . .' Anita trailed off. She looked confused but the pieces were slowly starting to fit.

'We wouldn't have said anything to her if we knew that Sam already had, would we, Anita?' Zeba asked. Her face by now ashen too.

350

'Why didn't you mention this at the time?' Sam asked Anita.

'When could we have? We'd split up and had only just come back into the gym before her body was found . . .'

The four girls looked at each other in horror before Sam whispered, 'Does that mean we *all* spoke harshly to Lily before she . . .'

The awful silence was shattered by a sudden cacophony emanating from the garden below Bubbles' room. Guests were cheering and the brass band was exuberantly striking up their version of tequila with a great clashing of cymbals and blaring of bugles. Footsteps came thundering up the stairs and a pack of children tumbled in. 'They are here, they are here, the baraat is here! The bridegroom is on a horse painted all gold!' they yelled excitedly, causing the girls to get up in consternation, straightening their blouses and pulling on their sandals. Sam, seeing the frightened expression on Bubbles' face, moved closer to her on the bed and took her hand.

'Don't worry, I'm right here with you, Bubs. Your mum's asked Anita and Zeba to lead the welcome party with flower trays but I told her I would stay with you,' she said, gesturing to the other two to leave so they would not miss the *jaimala* ceremony to greet the bridegroom and his relatives. In a while they would all be back, along with Bubbles' mother and sisters, to escort the bride to the *mandap* where the final rituals would be carried out; the final transformation of Bubbles Malhotra into Mrs Raheja Junior of Belgravia, London.

Sam and Bubbles sat in silence as the noise of the crowd slowly abated and the band's music turned reedy and sentimental in readiness for the arrival of the bride. The only light in their room came from the fairy lights draping the trees in the Malhotra garden, but neither girl wanted to get up to turn switches on, quite unwilling to let go of their terrified grasp on each other's hands. They clung to each other in the half-darkness, praying for each other and to be forgiven this most terrible thing they had done.

Chapter Twenty-Eight

DELHI, 2008

As their car pulled up outside the school, Bubbles clutched Sam's arm. 'This is awful. I really, *really* don't know why we're here,' she said, looking up at the old church building that fronted the school as though it might suddenly open its big wooden doors and swallow her whole.

'Don't be silly, we've only come here to meet Lamboo and say goodbye before she leaves.' Sam spoke firmly as they got out of the car, although her heart was thudding in her chest too. The old Edwardian church building loomed over them, majestic as ever, the figures in its stained-glass windows eerily coming to life as they caught the last rays of the pale winter sun.

'Isn't it weird,' Anita whispered. 'Put a bunch of women in front of their school and they're instantly transformed back into little girls again.'

'It's the church doing it to me, I think,' Bubbles replied, feeling far more like gauche, goofy Bubbles Malhotra of yore than Mrs Raheja of Belgravia.

Anita wrapped her coat around herself and shivered. The wrought-iron gates of St Jude's were shut and barred at this evening hour. The *chowkidar*'s guard-house too lay unlit in the gathering dusk, with no sign of the burly moustachioed man who had stood by the gates at school-leaving time, waving flocks of giggling girls on. Anita had always found the presence of the *chowkidar* a reassuring reminder of all the things a school was meant to be – safe, peaceful, stimulating – but today, absurdly, her fervid imagination was making her think of Cerberus at the entrance to Hades.

'Oh, look, that must be Zeba,' Sam said, her eyes on an approaching car. 'She asked me to look out for a Jag.'

A silver Jaguar rolled to a halt in the car park and Zeba emerged from the back seat, wearing a beautiful beige sari and with a shahtoosh shawl slung over one shoulder. To Sam, she looked far lovelier than she did on screen. Her hair, which had tumbled in unruly brown waves in their schooldays, was now groomed to perfection, lying shiny and smooth, rippling all the way to her waist.

'Oh, you look absolutely gorgeous, Zebs,' Sam said warmly, kissing both her cheeks and holding her by the shoulders to take in her old classmate's clothes and hair and stunning figure. 'But that's stating the obvious to India's top movie star, I suppose!'

Zeba looked momentarily surprised at what was clearly an honest compliment and responded by saying, 'You don't look so bad yourselves, all three of you. So it's true what they say about thirty being the new twenty, and there I was so conceitedly thinking it was just me!' She kissed the other two women as she said this, her cheeky schoolgirl smile still much the same as before.

Sam wagged her forefinger and said good-naturedly, 'Bubbles and Anita may look twenty. Me, I don't think so.'

'You only have a small problem around here,' Zeba said, patting Sam's tummy affectionately. 'But come stay with me a month and I'll get rid of it for you.'

'Seriously?' Sam looked impressed. 'Don't tempt me, Zeba, I might just take you up on that,' she laughed.

'I mean it, you'd always be welcome to come and stay. Do you ever come to Mumbai?' Zeba asked, looking at the other two.

'I've been a couple of times but only for a few hours here and there. If I'd thought of taking your number from Sam, I'd have called you for a chat, Zeb,' Bubbles replied.

'And I was treated to five hours at Chhatrapati Shivaji Airport once, trying to get across to Cal. Not an experience I'd want to repeat,' Anita said.

'You guys see a lot of each other in London, don't you?' Zeba asked. To Sam's surprise, her voice sounded a little wistful.

Bubbles replied vehemently, 'Yes, and thank God for that. If I don't speak to either Sam or Anita every day, I feel completely lost. But we try to meet three or four times a month at least.'

'Hey, we should go in now. Lamboo's probably still the stickler for punctuality that she was back then,' Anita reminded them.

An unfamiliar *chowkidar* emerged from the warmth of his guard-house when they knocked on its glass pane. He let them through the gates with no questions asked, obviously having been given instructions to expect them. Sam took in a deep, wobbly breath as they walked down the drive. The distraction provided by Zeba trying to catch up on a whole host of information was useful, and for another few minutes they talked briefly about their children, husbands, jobs and other surface details. The shared past that had brought them back here today – one they still found difficult to confront – remained unspoken.

They walked past the side door of the church where

355

Bubbles, by habit, did a small superstitious bob as though going in for an exam. Sam remembered the night she had shivered under its yellow tubelight, dreading having to face Lily at the Social. The memory was so vivid, she could almost feel the cold of that terrible night now leaching through the woollen fibres of her stout Burberry coat. Sam surveyed the old trees flanking the driveway: fifteen years hadn't changed them very much, nor the other outward trappings, such as the green sign that pointed the way to the school reception. Only the bougainvillea arch at the end of the drive had, with the passage of the years, become thick and woody, almost tree-like. The women walked under it, ducking their heads to avoid the low-hanging boughs, finally finding themselves facing the old school building, its red brick glowing in the evening light.

'Her letter said we were to go straight to her cottage round the back,' Sam said.

'I do hope there's others from our class coming,' Bubbles said in an attempt to be optimistic.

Anita shook her head. 'You know, I'm quite certain it's just us.'

'Look, I'm sure there's nothing to worry about,' Sam said, still trying to sound a lot more positive than she felt.

'Lamboo would never call us here to upset us,' Zeba reassured them. 'Our batch was really special to her, although I remember she especially adored you, Sam.'

'Haven't done much to deserve that these past fifteen years,' Sam replied.

'But does anyone know exactly why she's called us here? It can't be just that she wants to see us, can it . . .?' Zeba asked.

'Maybe she's ill and dying and wants to meet all her old pupils one last time?' Bubbles offered.

'Oh shit, I do hope it isn't something like that.'

'I heard she'd retired ages ago but they let her keep the cottage as she still helps around the school. Still directing the annual play, someone said, would you believe it!'

'But now she's finally leaving Jude's. Disappearing into a convent, her letter said . . .'

They stopped talking as they walked around the building and the principal's cottage came into view. It looked exactly the same as before, a twist of flowering madhumalati hanging over its front door, white lace curtains fluttering at the windows. Before it, the rose garden lay in its usual winter splendour, dotted with enormous evening blooms in a riot of colours.

Sam's stomach lurched, as it always did, at the over-powering smell of roses. Through the turmoil in her head she spotted a gravestone in a corner of the garden and guessed it might be Lily's – but then the door to the cottage opened and Miss Lamb was standing in the doorway, a huge smile on her wrinkled face, her hands stretched out in welcome to her girls.

Miss Lamb hugged the women one by one as they trooped in, and when she came to Sam it felt as if she clung to her a little longer than the others. Holding her by the shoulders for a couple of moments, the old principal looked search-ingly into Sam's features and laughed softly. 'I'd have known that face anywhere, with those two pretty moles gracing that little chin. My dearest Samira, how very splendid to see you again . . .'

Sam, too overcome to say very much, kissed Victoria Lamb on either side of her face before letting her move on to Anita behind her. Sam had been into Lamboo's neat little cottage a few times in her childhood and looked around its front parlour, crowded today with cardboard boxes stacked against one wall. Flanking the blackened, disused fireplace were the principal's once crammed bookshelves, now emptied of books but filled with hundreds of cards and pictures, all of smiling girls' faces, of varied ages, complexions and hues. At first glance, Sam could not see any familiar faces among them, not even Lily. She turned to look at the old principal, who was deep in conversation with Anita now. Lamboo looked well enough, but smaller, somehow. Perhaps she was simply not holding herself as ramrod straight as before.

Miss Lamb's old manservant emerged from the kitchen with glasses of wine and water arrayed on a tray. Sam greeted him affectionately; he must have been an oldish man even back then but now he was positively ancient, his Nepalese features creased into a face that looked like a crumpled ball of paper.

'Lakhanji, don't tell me you are also leaving the school with principal-sahib?' Sam asked in Hindi, accepting a glass of water.

'I also retire. Sunday is my last day at St Jude's,' the old man replied, beaming.

'Yes, Lakhan's looking forward to finally going home to Nepal, with a very deserving pension in hand,' Miss Lamb said. 'Thirty years of cooking for a batty old Englishwoman has, luckily, not robbed him completely of his sanity. Or his cooking skills!' She waved her arm around her half-emptied living room. 'My dear girls, do find yourselves somewhere comfortable. This weekend the sofas get taken away, so you would have had to sit on these cardboard boxes if you'd come this time tomorrow.'

'What happens to the cottage, Miss Lamb?' Zeba asked. 'Will they keep it as it is?'

'Ah yes, this old place stays, thankfully. After I leave this weekend, they plan to renovate it so they can move the library in here. It was my last plea to them, as the single room inside the junior school really isn't big enough. Certainly not now that they have to take in my entire collection of books as well!'

The four women had seated themselves by now, Bubbles tucking herself safely between Anita and Sam on the sofa. An expectant silence suddenly fell over the room as Miss Lamb took the armchair near the door and now squarely faced her old students. She took off her glasses and wiped them on a lace handkerchief, squinting slightly as she said, 'I know you're baffled by why you're here.' Smiling, she put the glasses back on. 'I *could* say I called you here only because I wanted to see you before kicking the bucket . . .' a small ripple of uncertain laughter went around the room '. . . and that wouldn't be entirely untrue. You see, I knew you four would probably never come back to the school unless I expressly called you here. Every single girl from your batch came back at some point . . . all except you.'

Sam felt the anticipated rush of guilt, but Miss Lamb paused for only a moment before speaking again. 'Don't get me wrong, my dear girls. I understood completely your reluctance to stay in touch, of course I did. I've never before or since had a class that suffered as much tragedy as you did in that final year.'

Sam shifted slightly on the sofa. Lamboo was using generalities but she felt she was talking directly to her. The principal was, however, looking at Zeba, who was nearest to her, carrying on speaking in her slightly quavery voice. 'But, when the time came for me to retire and leave Jude's for good, I wanted to call you girls here. To tell you a story. A story that perhaps one of you will go on to write one day. Or, indeed, make a film about!' She smiled at Zeba before taking a sip of wine and resuming her spiel.

'It's more of an autobiography than a story, actually. Do you know, I always found it strange that among all the questions my girls put to me, in and outside the classroom, no one ever asked why a British woman like me ever chose to live in India.' She laughed gently before taking a deep breath. 'But now I have to go all the way back to 1947 to explain it, and explain it I must if I am to tell my story properly. You will forgive an old woman some reminiscing, won't you?'

Bubbles nodded, but a strange stillness fell over Sam as Victoria Lamb recounted her tale, her gaze pausing carefully on each of the four faces before her. 'My dear girls, I was twenty years old – a lot younger than all of you are now – when India became independent and the British left. My parents wanted me to go home to Dublin with them, of course, but I couldn't. And the reason I desisted was because, four years before that, when I was sixteen, I had fallen in love, become pregnant and delivered a baby boy in a convent.'

A frisson of disbelief went around the group. No one made eye-contact with anyone else out of respect for their old principal, and Sam looked blankly down at her shoes. She could almost feel the heat of that May afternoon, suddenly, and hear Lily's voice telling her that she was Miss Lamb's granddaughter. Words that she had never repeated to anyone for fear they were a lie and would hurt Miss Lamb.

'Yes, I had a baby boy,' Miss Lamb continued softly, 'whom I had to give up for adoption. There seemed no choice. His father, a young lieutenant, had died in the war in Italy without even knowing that I was pregnant with his child. It was the forties and a pitiless time for a single unwed mother, you know. And, in the end, I accepted the need to give up my child without too many questions. How strange that now seems to me, but I was a different person then; perhaps you understand.' She paused for another sip at her glass before

360

continuing in a stronger voice. 'However, when my parents were packing up to return to Ireland, I knew that the one thing I could not do was go with them, leaving behind the only home I had known and, of course, the child I had given birth to, even though by that time I had no idea where he was. All that the sisters at the convent in Kanpur would tell me was that he had been adopted by an Anglo-Indian family living in one of the hill-stations. No more. But the sisters helped me train as a teacher and I ended up here, at St Jude's, aged twenty three.'

'Your boy, Ma'am? Did you ever see him again?' Anita asked, leaning forward.

'My boy . . .' Victoria Lamb repeated dully. Suddenly she looked a little confused before picking up her thread of thought again. 'Yes, I suppose I never gave up hoping that I would see my son again, if I am honest. Even though I knew adoptions carried out by the church didn't usually allow it. But I never heard anything at all . . . until . . .' At this point, the elderly Victoria Lamb stopped and looked, for the first time that evening, hesitant to carry on speaking. She took a breath and started again, raising her voice resolutely. '. . . until 1993, when the Mother Superior at Sacred Heart Convent in Mussourie called me and told me there had been an incident. A terrible incident. My son, Christopher, was by then a man of fifty with a family of his own – well, a wife who had died six years before and a daughter called . . . Lily.'

Sam felt Bubbles' hand clutching her arm. She looked across the room at the school principal and this time caught her quiet gaze as the other three shot surprised questions at her.

'So Lily was actually your *granddaughter*, Ma'am!'

'Was she told that she was your granddaughter? Heavens, it must have been such a shock for both of you to meet like that . . .'

361

'What was the incident with your son, Ma'am? Why did they call you after so many years and why was Lily sent to you?'

Sam looked at Miss Lamb in alarm to see that she was now weeping, taking off her spectacles so that she could dab her eyes with her handkerchief. Zeba got up to sit on the armrest of the principal's chair and put a comforting arm around her shoulders. After a couple of minutes, the elderly woman had recovered and looked gratefully up at Zeba, who now slipped down to sit on the floor before her. With an expression on her face that almost seemed to be begging forgiveness, Victoria Lamb continued softly, 'It had been a most terrible thing. Christopher had been bringing up his daughter by himself after his wife's death, but when Lily started to say strange things about her relationship with her father . . . some quite alarming things . . . the nuns knew they had to get her away from him before things got any worse . . .'

A wordless ripple went around the room as the import of what Miss Lamb had left unspoken sank in. Bubbles' fingers were causing indentations as she squeezed Sam's arm in shock. Even Anita was manifestly trembling, and Sam closed her eyes momentarily, breathing deeply as she felt a sickening tumult in her own stomach.

It was Zeba who broke the silence first. 'And you were contacted as Lily's closest relative, Ma'am?' she asked sympathetically from her position on the carpet. Sam momentarily marvelled at the calmness of Zeba's demeanour before remembering an article that mentioned Zeba's recently founded charity to help street children in Mumbai. Sam had not been able to help wondering if it was merely a publicity gimmick, but perhaps she had been wrong – as she was about so many things, she was starting to see.

'The Sacred Heart sisters tried a fostering arrangement for Lily at first, while attempting to trace relatives through her parents' records,' Victoria Lamb continued quietly. Sam could see that the old principal was trying to keep her own tone composed, but the strain in her voice was evident as she continued speaking. 'But Lily's fostering arrangement broke down in a matter of months – her foster parents being sadly ill-equipped to deal with the kind of ordeal she had been through – and that was when I was contacted by the Mother Superior. They had by then tracked me down from the details on Christopher's records and must have considered a girls' school like St Jude's as the best place for such a troubled soul as Lily. I was asked if I would take Lily in. Except that I wasn't allowed to say we were related – the Mother Superior insisted on that so that the reputation of St Jude's would not be compromised.'

This time it was Anita who spoke up. 'Did they press charges against Lily's father?' she asked.

Miss Lamb shook her head. 'Lily would never speak about the abuse, you see. They tried everything, mostly to offer her a chance to work through her own trauma, but she would not say a word against her father. Not one word.'

'Children are often like that, aren't they?' Zeba remarked, 'eager to protect their parents, even when they are the abusers.'

Sam threw an admiring look at Zeba. It was clearly her charity work that led to her having grown so understanding about such things. Miss Lamb seemed to realise that too, nodding in appreciation at Zeba's words and wiping her eyes before she spoke. 'Oh, there were days when I longed to go up to Mussourie, to track Christopher down and confront him about the damage he had done. But I suppose he would merely have turned around and made the same accusation

363

of me – perhaps claiming that the rot had set in with what *I* had done all those years ago. He could have been right too, but the burden of my secret was not just a heavy one but one I could do little about. Over the years I learned to exorcise my guilt. Who indeed does not make mistakes when they are young? The nuns would never reveal Christopher's whereabouts to me anyway, saying only that he was being dealt with by the church. What was important was that Lily had been brought to a safe place and, given time, would be able to put the past behind her and blossom and grow . . .' Miss Lamb's voice broke at that point, causing her to stop speaking again.

In the pained silence that followed, Bubbles spoke up, eager to fill the void. 'Oh Ma'am, Lily's death . . . not that we didn't think it painful for you, as she was living with you, but, oh God, she was your *granddaughter*. If we had only known . . .'

Miss Lamb appeared to have recovered her voice as she straightened her back and echoed Bubbles' words. 'Lily's death, yes. That was what I was referring to when I started my story. And the reason why I wanted to gather you all together again – to enable all of you to stop wondering and stop feeling guilty, as I know some of you did when she died. That was obvious from your refusal to return to the school.' Miss Lamb paused and the silence deepened around her, causing her voice to take on a strange reverberating quality in Sam's ears when she started to speak again. 'You see, we found Lily's diary six months ago when some furniture was moved. And in that diary were all those things that she had always kept secret. All the pain and all the rage the poor girl had felt in those years – it was clear that the abuse had brought her to the brink of suicide long before she even came to Jude's. Lily was a deeply traumatised, deeply damaged child, and I wonder now whether anything or anyone could have saved her from doing what she finally did. Despite the uncertainties at the time, I think we always knew Lily's death was suicide, but what I wanted you girls to know was that her death had nothing – *nothing* – whatsoever to do with you.'

It was now so quiet in the room that an owl could be heard hooting from the trees behind the Chemistry lab. Again, it was Zeba who recovered first, getting up to refill Miss Lamb's water glass.

Sam, hand in hand with Anita and Bubbles, sat in silence on the sofa for a few moments, feeling a mixture of emotions wash over her. What was it? Relief, remorse, overwhelming sorrow at all that poor Lily had been through? Fathers, to Sam's mind, had always been gentle creatures who bumbled around trying – often in ham-fisted ways – to make their daughters happy. Never abusers of that love and trust. She could feel Bubbles leaning her forehead against her shoulder, either seeking or giving comfort, Sam could not tell which. And a glimpse of Anita's face revealed tears rolling uncontrollably out of her eyes. Sam got up and walked across the room to Miss Lamb.

Kneeling before her old teacher, she said quietly, 'Miss Lamb, you said you knew that some of us have been feeling guilty all these years . . .'

The principal smiled gently down at her and took her hands. 'Perhaps it was the motherhood I was deprived of, my dear Samira, but I made it my business to understand my girls inside out. And I knew a little of what had been going on.' She glanced at the three women who were now comforting each other on the sofa, before saying softly, 'Your brother picked Lily up from here once, you see.'

Sam nodded, unable to speak, and Miss Lamb continued,

'He was a delightful lad. Such an open, honest face. And he would have been so good for Lily. But he wasn't to know the suffering she had endured before she had come here, of course, and the reason for which she too needed to hurt someone. But how terribly she must have wounded him for him to . . .' Miss Lamb broke off before looking searchingly into Sam's dark eyes and continuing, 'I understood completely that some of you hated Lily enough to want her dead. I could never blame you for that, my dear Samira . . .'

Sam gulped back the tears clogging her throat. Then she spoke firmly. 'What Haroon did cannot be blamed on anyone else, certainly not on Lily. He made his own choice, Miss Lamb. It was just easier at the time for me to blame Lily. You understand that, don't you?'

'Of course I do, my dear. Your own torment in those days must have been so dreadful that Lily's death could only have seemed like a gift. It's only natural. You didn't cause her death by wishing it, I hope you know that. But how the guilt must have followed you around. It was obvious that was why you never came to see me again.'

Sam could feel an enormous weight roll off her heart at these words. By now, the other three had joined them, clustering about their principal's knees on the faded carpet.

'How *did* you cope after Lily's death?' Bubbles asked in a kind voice. 'It must have been so hard . . .'

'Oh, I can now admit it was sheer torment, my dear. But, as I was just about to say to Samira, there were so many reasons to soldier on. Five hundred and twenty-nine at the time, to be exact. I sat down and counted once, at one of my lowest points.' Miss Lamb laughed at Bubbles' confused expression and added, 'I mean all of you – the girls who were studying here at the time Lily died. Don't forget I'd known you all a lot longer than I'd known Lily

366

and had watched some of you grow from seven-year-olds into adulthood. I lost her, yes, but then I did still have all of you.'

Anita spoke up next. 'I know you'll be honest if I ask you this, Miss Lamb . . . please don't mind my bluntness . . . but did you ever . . .' she took a deep breath '. . . did you ever think that any of *us* could have had something to do with Lily's death?'

Victoria Lamb looked at the four faces before her and took a few seconds to gather her thoughts before replying. 'I have studied little girls for many years, my dear Anita, and know them to be capable of as much cruelty as they are of tenderness. At the time, I suppose practically anything seemed possible. Yes, anything. And there was a part of me that was truly terrified when the police started their investigations. You never know what they might have come up with, rightly or wrongly.'

'And that was why you asked for the investigation to be called off?' Zeba asked. 'To protect us?'

'Yes, of course, I wanted to protect my girls. And the school . . . there was a lot at stake. And I knew in my heart why Lily did what she did. There was no doubt about that in my mind at all.'

'But you never wanted to question us about our behaviour towards Lily when she first came here? You must have been able to see our resentment towards her . . .' Anita persisted, her face screwed up anxiously.

Victoria nodded. 'I think I picked up on some of that. But isn't it just human nature to feel threatened by the outsider . . . to want the established order of things to remain unchanged?'

Anita gazed at her in silence for a few seconds before nodding. 'I think I sometimes see that in England, you know,

367

being the unwelcome "outsider" and all that. But I've never been as forgiving of it as you . . .'

'Well, acceptance can be an overrated virtue,' Victoria responded, smiling.

Bubbles cut in. 'I too was brought up to accept things with no questions asked, Ma'am. But sometimes you just can't help *wanting* things to be different, can you?'

'It's true,' Sam said. 'I mean, when all is said and done, you would rather Lily had lived, wouldn't you, Miss Lamb?'

'Yes, of course I'd have wanted her to live,' Miss Lamb replied. 'But, as Thoreau said, you make the most of your regrets and you use them to live afresh. Perhaps life here at Jude's would eventually have changed Lily. Perhaps one day you would have become friends with her. But, beyond a point, dwelling on such possibilities merely grows into negative thought, does it not?'

Sam agreed in a grave voice. 'Yes, indeed it does, Ma'am. But I can't help thinking that if we had only stopped to understand Lily better, and befriended her, we might have helped to save her.'

Anita nodded and said sombrely, 'We certainly would have tried to help if we'd known, I'm sure of that. But, dear God, how swift we were to judge . . . and condemn . . . poor, poor Lily . . .'

'Well, you were so very young,' Miss Lamb said, 'so don't beat yourselves up about what you did or didn't do when you were mere girls. You weren't to know what Lily had gone through and why she was the way she was. Believe me, it was hard enough for *me* to cope with her, and I knew exactly why she kept lashing out at everyone around her.' Victoria paused, before adding in a firm voice, 'And that was why I thought it important to tell you about her diary when it was found. You girls were not the reason for Lily taking her life.

It was much, much closer to home. It was her father and, in addition to that, it was me. It was her blood family who let her down, not you girls, and let that be absolutely clear.'

A short silence fell over Miss Lamb's living room before Anita spoke softly. 'Thank you, Miss Lamb,' she said.

'Whatever for, my child?'

'Oh, for writing and calling us here. I don't know whether you realise how much I've needed to hear these words from you.'

'Ah, and I don't know whether you girls realise how much I needed to see you all before I retired and left St Jude's.'

Zeba, who had been silent for a while, spoke up at this point. 'And I don't know whether any of you know how much I've needed this reminder of the really important things in life,' she said, before gesturing at the other three. 'It was these friends who constantly put themselves out to rescue me from myself, if you know what I mean, and for all sorts of stupid reasons I've so thoughtlessly cut that precious resource out of my life.'

'It's never too late, Zeba,' Sam said impulsively. 'Just get on a flight and come to one of us when you need to. With friends around, nothing will ever be too unbearable. Believe me, I should know!'

And so it was that four old friends from the Class of '93, Lamboo's *crème de la crème*, spent the rest of the evening finishing Victoria Lamb's wine stock, getting drunk and alternately tearful and maudlin and hysterical with laughter. Deeper secrets and sorrows were exchanged as the night wore on, as were addresses, with promises from Zeba never to lose touch again.

Miss Lamb added a last proviso: 'Just go on to lead happy and useful and productive lives and I will consider my job

369

done. Oh, and be there for each other, as Samira said. Life will continue to throw up the unexpected once in a while. And, strong as you might think you are, it's your friendships that will see you through.'

'So here's to female friendship then,' Zeba cried, waving her wine glass in the air.

'The power of the sisterhood,' Anita joined the toast.

And, to her astonishment, Sam heard herself throw in riotously, 'Yeah, and who needs men!' Before they all fell about laughing again.

It was only when Miss Lamb insisted that it was way past her bedtime that the four women could finally be persuaded to leave. They bade their teacher affectionate and slightly tearful farewells as they gathered together their coats and shoes and eventually stumbled out into the moonlit rose garden. The night air was cool and moist on their flushed faces as they inhaled deeply on the smell of wet roses. Sam turned to cut her way silently through the garden and, as had happened fifteen years before, the three others found themselves following her. They soon saw what it was she was aiming for as she stopped by a small stone grave nearly obscured by the night's shadows. Together the old classmates stood, arm in arm, remembering Lily, and remembering another such winter night when, instead of this precious peace, it was hate that had filled their hearts. Finally, turning away, they tramped across the damp earth, looking for their well-known old short-cut to the car park.

Chapter Twenty-Nine

DELHI, 2008

As the women stumbled into the car park, both chauffeurs spotted them and glided the cars in their direction. Zeba turned to the others. 'I don't know about you guys, but ten o'clock is way too early for me. Care to come to my hotel? Quick nightcap?'

Sam, who had been looking forward to going home and telling her parents about Miss Lamb, heard the beseeching note in Zeba's voice and nodded at the other two. 'Yes, why not,' she said.

While Bubbles gave her driver instructions to follow Zeba's car to the Mughal Hilton, Anita and Sam climbed in next to Zeba. 'Hey, wait for me,' Bubbles giggled as she clambered in after them.

'Ouch, I think that was a stiletto going through one of my metatarsals,' Anita yelped.

'Oh God, I hope you haven't broken my Jimmy Choos, Anita!' Bubbles said, sitting down and examining her shoe.

Anita turned to Zeba. 'I don't know about you, but Bubbles doesn't wear shoes, she wears bloody weapons.'

The banter continued as their silver Jaguar made stately progress through the night-time traffic that was still heavy around central Delhi. Steam from their combined breath condensed on the cold glass, and Sam, cooling her face against the window, thought how beautiful the world looked through the mist: the street vendors had winter fruit piled high on their carts and the haloes of their kerosene lamps were turning apples and papayas to jewels. People, hundreds of people, were jostling about on the streets, buying things, trying to get to their homes, living their lives. The girls drove thus through the city of their childhood, which looked as though it had been magically lit up that winter night just for them, pointing out old landmarks to each other and feeling sentimental. When they reached Zeba's hotel they walked swiftly through the lobby, hoping not to be waylaid by any of Zeba's fans. Fortunately, a member of the hotel's staff had already spotted her and swiftly escorted them upstairs in a private lift. When he had departed and they were alone in Zeba's penthouse suite, she said, 'Feel free, kick off your shoes, do what you like. I'm going to take my make-up off.'

Anita flung herself onto the capacious bed while Sam and Bubbles investigated the fruit basket and mini-fridge. Assiduously moisturing her face and neck with La Prairie at the mirror, Zeba said, 'Hey, would someone order whatever from room service please?'

Sam sat down next to the telephone and scanned the menu card. 'What would you like, girls? Shall I order something to eat? Is anyone hungry?'

'Darling, no one's *ever* hungry after ten,' Zeba said, adding, 'like it or not, Sam, honey, I'm taking over your diet and fitness regime from now on. By phone and email and remote control from Mumbai, if I have to. In three months' time you won't recognise yourself, I promise you that.'

'Here, have something from the fruit basket, Sam,' Bubbles offered in sympathy.

Sam looked regretfully at the menu before putting it away. 'Nuff said. But can I at least get a drink? Please, please, Mistress Zeba?'

Anita, lying on the bed with her eyes closed, said beatifically, 'I'm seeing you in my mind's eye, Sam, three months from now . . . all slim and long-thighed, a sort of PVC-clad dominatrix with a whip . . . and, oh look, there's Akbar on his knees, begging you to take him back!'

'But I haven't left him,' Sam laughed.

'Yet!' Anita said, her eyes snapping open and throwing Sam a challenging look.

Bubbles asked, 'You aren't seriously thinking of leaving Akbar, are you? I know we talked about it a bit on the plane but I hadn't realised it had got that bad.'

Sam considered the question. 'To be honest, I'm not sure myself exactly how bad it is just yet but I'm as certain as anything that he's in Kenya with another woman.'

'Well, I just don't think you should wait to find out,' Anita said, sitting up. 'You have enough reason to leave him anyway, given the way he behaves sometimes.' She turned to Zeba, 'What do you say, Zeba? If a woman suspects that her husband might be bonking someone else, should she do the polite thing and wait to be told – as our lovely and decorous Sam would seem to prefer – or should she accost him with it instantly?'

Zeba's shapely eyebrows arched upwards. 'Ouch, that's a bit of a challenge . . . let me think. I'm personally the accosting type myself, but that approach could be very damaging if the man *hasn't* been . . . er, bonking someone else, as you put it.'

'Hello, it's my *life* you're talking about here!' Sam said, but suddenly even she was smiling. She turned to Zeba. 'You're right about not accosting Akbar when I'm so unsure of what he's up to. That's what I've been saying to these two. I think I have no choice at the moment but to wait and see.'

'Hey, being on holiday together can put a real strain on a relationship, right?' Bubbles said. 'So, even if Akbar is having an affair, it'll probably all be over by the time he gets back from Kenya.'

'Yeah, like *that'll* make it all fine and acceptable!' Anita replied.

'It's odd, though,' Zeba said, as she stroked a pad of cotton-wool over her neck, 'that Akbar insisted on taking Heer with him. I mean, would a guy do that if he's off having an affair?'

'Well, piecing the bits we know together it could be that the affair has been going on for a while now. Perhaps this was Akbar's opportunity to be sure this woman can cope with a kid. Which means he's at least fond enough of Heer to factor her into his future plans,' Anita said grudgingly.

'Is that right, Sam?' Zeba asked.

Sam smiled wanly. It was much more of a relief to be talking about this than she had thought possible. 'Anita could be right,' she nodded. 'That's certainly my gut feeling too. Nevertheless, can one make accusations without more than a *hunch* to go by?' Sam picked up the phone to call room service and added, 'One thing I do know is that I'm actually having rather a good time in Akbar's absence. I thought I'd be moping endlessly, but, hey, look at me! This single life might be more fun than I'd have ever thought.'

'Well, make sure you tell him that, girl! *Nothing* drives men crazier than realising you can have a first-rate time without them!' Anita agreed.

'The only downside to the single life is that you have married men hitting on you all the time,' Zeba warned, laughing, while Sam wandered to the other end of the room, phone to her ear as she called for some chilled champagne.

'Yeah, married men with beautiful wives waiting loyally for them at home – *why?!,*' Anita said, her voice turning kinder as Sam returned to the sofa. 'If you ask me, the big question is: do *you* still want *him* enough to stay, Sam?'

'Well said, Anita,' Zeba applauded. 'All said and done, the choice should be *yours* to make, Sam, not his.'

'Easier said than done, my darlings,' Sam said. 'What the hell would I do with myself – and Heer? I don't even have a bloody job.'

'Would you do that, Sam? Take up a job?' Bubbles asked, her eyes like saucers. She pronounced 'job' as though it were an outer-galactic planet she was extremely unlikely to ever visit.

'I don't see why not, actually,' Sam replied, 'if anyone will have me, that is.'

'Which . . .' Zeba said, putting her forefinger in the air '. . . which brings me to something I've been meaning to say all evening actually. I've just started a charity to help Mumbai street kids and I could really do with some help . . . fund-raising events, that sort of thing.' She looked hopefully at both Sam and Bubbles.

'In Mumbai or London, Zeba?' Sam asked.

'Both. It might involve a bit of travel.'

'You know what . . .' Bubbles said, 'having heard about what happened to Lily, I think I'd like to do something for abused kids too.'

'There's enough to be done. Think what we can achieve together!' Zeba cried.

'And Anita knows loads of journalists, so publicity should be easy too,' Bubbles said.

'We can get Anita and Hugh to do a programme on BBC World to highlight the issue too!' Sam added, her eyes shining.

Anita fell back on the bed again as the conversation whirled on excitedly around her. She hadn't had the time to tell her friends about her spat with Hugh and now she was glad she hadn't. 'Hey, Zeba, you wouldn't happen to have internet access in this room, would you?' she enquired, sitting up again.

'Use my BlackBerry,' Bubbles offered.

'Oh no, I hate those fiddly things – not for a long email.'

'Who're you writing to at this time of night? Hugh?' Sam asked.

Anita nodded. 'I'd like him to get it first thing. Won't be long, I promise.'

'You'll find everything you need in there, sweetie,' Zeba said, waving in the direction of an alcove.

Anita wandered through the silk curtains and found an entire office equipped with a scanner and a fax machine. She switched on the computer before settling herself on the chair. She had a big apology to make to Hugh and she was going to make it as humbly as she knew how. Why had being irate become such a habit with her, she wondered, while watching the small bouncing yellow icon trying to connect. There were times when she behaved almost as though it was *au courant* to be in a state of some outrage all the time, vainly hoping people would mistake aggression for assertiveness and self-confidence. She pulled the keyboard towards herself, feeling a rush of shame at the thought of how she had flailed out at poor Hugh on that last day in London. There was a fine line that divided being intense with being tiresomely angry, and perhaps she hadn't always understood that in the way she did now. It was people who'd suffered real anguish – like Lily – that had the right to be angry, not her.

By the time Anita had finished writing her email to Hugh, her friends next door had cranked up the Latin

American music as loud as it would go. She walked back into the bedroom and saw a large drinks trolley in the middle of the room. The others had kicked off their shoes and were dancing and hooting and behaving maniacally. Zeba's long tumbling hair, left loose, was swinging around her curvy hips as she and Bubbles held hands and did a passable salsa, moving towards each other and back again with short quick movements of their bare feet. Sam, standing in the middle of Zeba's bed, was crooning with a glass of champagne in one hand, ice-tongs masquerading as a mike in the other. Grinning delightedly, Anita leapt up to join her. After a few more energetic twirls, Zeba, dissolving into giggles, held her waist and bent over to catch her breath.

'The hotel will throw me out . . . throw us all out,' she panted.

'Not if the Chairman's in love with you,' Bubbles dismissed, looking at herself in the full-length mirrors with arms held above her head, her shapely bottom moving slowly and seductively to the strains of 'Girl from Ipanema'.

'Not *in love*, dear Bubs – God, you're still the hopeless romantic you always were, aren't you! For heaven's sake, the man's just trying to get my knickers off,' Zeba said, falling onto a sofa and knocking back a slug of water.

Sam climbed off the bed and, putting her flute down, accepted the glass of water from Zeba. 'Another married man then, I take it?' she asked.

'Of course,' Zeba replied. 'Is there any other sort? It's true what they say: when you meet those that aren't hitched, you can instantly see why not.'

'For God's sake, keep away from the married men, Zeb,' Anita cried. 'Surely the sisterhood must count for something!'

Sam nodded. 'You know, if I did leave Akbar it would

never be for another man. It would be purely and solely and very definitely for myself.'

Anita collapsed on the edge of the bed, facing them. 'Have you decided that's your course of action then, Sami?' she asked.

'Oh stop nagging her, Anita!' Bubbles remonstrated from across the room as she turned the music down.

'Not nagging!' Anita yelled back. 'Just trying to ensure she finally stops doormatting herself to Akbar, that's all.'

Sam looked solemn. 'It's okay, you two,' she said, 'I know you want what's best for me, and I think I'm beginning to see what's best for me too. It's just taking a little time, that's all.'

Suddenly Zeba looked worried. 'It wasn't anything I said, was it, Sam? I mean, singledom's all very well but sometimes it can get bloody lonely too,' she warned.

Sam made room on the sofa for Bubbles to sit down next to them. 'She'll never be lonely as long as I'm around,' Bubbles said firmly, putting an arm around Sam.

Sam smiled. 'And I'll never stop thanking whoever's responsible for my being so rich in friends. I'm truly blessed in that department at least.' She turned to Zeba. 'No, it wasn't anything you said, my darling. But in fact it was something Lamboo said about guilt and blame.'

'About not blaming ourselves for Lily's death?' Zeba asked.

Sam nodded. 'It's been terrible, I can now admit it – my guilt over Lily and the way I yelled at her the night she killed herself.'

'Oh Sami, it wasn't just you, it was all of us!'

'And, for God's sake, who could blame you for being so distraught? Haroon had only been dead for three weeks! We were all distraught.'

'I know, I know, but, believe me, it's haunted me something

378

awful all these years – the thought that Lily went and killed herself because of what I said.' Before her friends could respond, Sam raised her hand to continue. 'And consequently it seemed rather logical then that Akbar should behave so shittily to me sometimes. Do I make sense?'

'Oh God, I don't understand what the connection is!' Bubbles wailed, but Anita slid onto the floor to get closer to Sam.

'*Every guilty person is his own hangman,*' she muttered, looking around to say, 'Seneca, not me.' She then reached out for Sam's hand. 'I do know what you mean, Sam. I haven't exactly been impervious to remorse myself, y'know. It wasn't just what we said to Lily on the night she died. Consider how we all were to her that year – it was a form of bullying, I think now. And maybe we were merely avoiding our own guilt by refusing to talk about it for all these years. But, Sami, you *knew* you'd tried to befriend Lily before finally turning against her. And who'd blame you for that after what happened to Haroon?'

'True, but all I could remember later was how I accused her of killing Haroon. And over the years I convinced myself that my words must have been the sole reason for her going and killing herself. So, in the end, what I did to her seemed no better than what she did to Haroon. Was it any wonder I've been so depressed all these years?'

'I think we've all felt the same way at different times about Lily. But today Lamboo said something quite crucial about refusing to feel guilty. Remember?' Zeba asked.

'Yes!' Bubbles cut in. 'About making mistakes and learning lessons and moving on.'

'Well, that's what this night is for then,' Anita concluded. 'To remember Lily with the kindness that we didn't know she deserved. To atone for the terrible mistake we made as girls . . .'

'To be bloody sure we never judge anyone again without trying first to understand,' Zeba cut in.

'Absolutely,' Anita agreed, 'and then, when all that is done, to close that fucking door and move on.'

Chapter Thirty

DELHI, 2008

Sam awoke the following morning feeling the previous night's fearsome melange of drinks furring up her tongue and throat and head. And she'd promised to go shopping with her mother to buy Heer the sequined gharara she'd asked for – a trip to the heaving, crowded shops of South Extension – she couldn't bear the thought!

'Shit!' she mumbled out loud, trying once more to get up and feeling her room spin around her. Through blurred vision and propped up on one elbow, she tried to revive her addled brain. She saw the usual books and pictures on the desk, her wedding picture on the wall, the bunch of garden sweet-peas that her father had insisted would give her fragrant dreams. It was no use. The aroma of milk boiling in the kitchen was wafting all the way through the house, making her want to puke.

Her mother came bustling in with a mug of black coffee and Sam managed to conjure up a wobbly smile as she dragged a pillow behind her to sit up. 'Oh Mamma, I feel just wretched,' she moaned, clutching her head in both hands.

'Well, who asked you to be out so late? And drink so

much?' her mother responded unsympathetically as she handed the coffee to Sam before pulling aside the curtains. Delhi's weak winter sun trickled into the room.

Sam hastily closed her burning eyes again. She gingerly took a tiny sip of the scorching coffee, hoping it wouldn't eject itself instantly in a projectile across the room. She decided to change the subject and deflect her mother's imminent lecture. 'I don't know whether I like it or not that you've kept my room in virtually exactly the state it was in when I was in college, Mamma,' Sam said, trying not to slur and hoping she didn't smell of booze.

'Don't change the subject,' her mother said, before sitting down on the foot of her bed. She looked cross but Sam knew the grumpiness wouldn't last. 'Honestly, what would Akbar say if he knew, Sami? There he is, looking after Heer on holiday, and here you are, partying with your friends till one o'clock. You're not a teenager any more. You know, your father would not sleep until we heard you coming in.'

'Oh Mamma, I'm so sorry but it was just so wonderful to see Lamboo and Zeba again after all these years. You understand, don't you . . .?'

Her mother's expression melted. 'Oh, of course I understand, *beti*, but I'm just glad Akbar didn't call while you were out. What would I have said?'

'Well, he'd have probably called on my mobile anyway, Mamma. And Akbar wouldn't have minded that I was out with my friends. He goes out solo too with his work mates, you know.'

Mrs Hussain shook her head. 'Oh, I don't know what life you young people live these days. Separate outings, separate holidays. Your father and I – we have never been *anywhere* without each other in all these years!' Then she changed the subject to ask, 'So how is Miss Lamb? Retired life will not be easy for someone like her. So devoted to you girls.'

Sam thought for a minute, sipping her coffee. 'I think she'll manage her retirement very well, actually. Lamboo has reserves of strength that you and I can only marvel at. In fact, I got the impression that she's actually quite looking forward to a little quiet time on her own.'

'Maybe that is so,' her mother said, getting up again and flicking her duster over Sam's wedding picture. 'People often discover strengths and depths they never knew they had when they are on their own. Okay now, come on, *beti*, get up, enough dawdling in bed. We have *so* much to do today! Quickly, before Akbar calls!'

Sam watched her mother leave the room, feeling half amused and half sad. It certainly wouldn't be easy to shatter the happy fantasies her parents harboured regarding her marriage. Sam cast a glance at the wedding picture on the wall and thought suddenly of Akbar's elderly parents back in Lahore – they too would be pretty devastated if their son's marriage broke up. They had always adored Sam, referring to her as the daughter they'd never had, turning up in London for respite whenever Lahore got too hot, loving every minute of the fuss Sam made over them. It was quite unbearable, the thought of all the widespread heartbreak she and Akbar would cause if they split up. But then, deflecting pain from others was never a very good reason for continuing to punish oneself with it.

Sam pushed her quilt aside to drag herself out of bed and tottered to the bathroom. Her mother was right – people invariably found the strength they needed when there was no other option. There would be the most fearsome storm of tears all around, a veritable tidal wave stretching all the way from Delhi to Lahore, but, when all was said and done, it would be the old folks – her and Akbar's elderly parents – who would prove to be tougher than any of the rest of them. That she knew for sure.

The following evening, Zeba collected her Best Actress award at a dazzling function at Talkatora Gardens while her three friends applauded her noisily in the audience. They met briefly in the green room after the event as Zeba was catching a night flight back to Mumbai.

'I'll call one of you as soon as I've set it all up, yes?' she asked. 'Should be easy since I've already registered a charity, got the income-tax waiver, et cetera. The involvement of you guys will be invaluable. I can't wait to get it moving now, honestly.'

'We'll come as soon as you need us to sign up as board members, Bubbles and me,' Sam said.

'And we've decided we'll use the name of the existing charity, yes? Street Flowers?'

'I *so* like the name,' Bubbles said emphatically. 'Did you come up with it yourself, Zeb?'

Zeba nodded. 'Well, I was thinking "wild flowers" initially . . . you know, "*heaven in a wild flower*" . . . but then I thought this would be more appropriate.'

'Bollywood didn't make you forget Blake then?' Anita observed.

'Don't forget to get the symbol done so it can go on all the letterheads and flyers – a single white lily, as agreed,' Sam said.

'Emerging through a crack in a pavement,' added Anita. 'Something symbolic of struggle and survival.'

'I really, really like that,' Bubbles sighed. 'God, you people are just so clever. I have *zero* imagination by comparison.'

Zeba kissed her. 'What you do have is enormous heart,

Bubbles, and don't you forget that.' While hugging the other two, she added, 'Listen, you guys have a safe flight back . . . and think of me every time you meet. Like saying grace – mutter my name religiously every time you're together and *before* the first drop of booze passes your lips!'

LONDON, 2008

After another week with their parents in Delhi, it was time for the remaining three friends to return to London. The tickets had been booked so that Anita could return to work just after the Christmas break and Sam would reach home one day before Akbar and Heer did. As the business of finally confronting Akbar loomed large in her mind, Sam focused fiercely on the hundred smaller things she'd have to do on her return   get the house aired and sheets changed, stock up on food supplies, collect Masooma, who was staying with her cousin in Tooting while the family had been away . . .

'You could really have stayed in Delhi another week, couldn't you, Bubs?' Sam asked her friend as they queued at the immigration counter at Delhi airport. 'You're not returning early for my sake, I hope.'

'No, of course not. True, Ruby and Bobby are only back next week. Not that they would even notice if I wasn't around, though!'

'Rubbish! There you go denigrating yourself again,' Anita said crossly. 'I don't think you even realise the extent to which the Raheja clan revolves around you, my dear.'

'Revolves around *me*?'

'I agree with Anita,' Sam said. 'Just observe the way the Belgravia household runs, Bubs. They might have all the serving staff in the world, but it's you they all turn to when

385

anything important needs to be done. Binkie, more than anyone else, would be totally lost without you.'

Bubbles looked unconvinced. Surely it was his dad, or James, that Binkie would be lost without. Not her. But they had reached their turn in the queue so she did not argue.

As was her wont, Sam was carrying all their paperwork in her calf-leather folder, and the other two waited while she talked with the immigration officer in Hindi. The man's impassive face broke into a smile at Sam's mention of visiting elderly parents. He nodded sympathetically. 'Mine live with me and are replacing my children now that the children have left,' he said, stamping the documents and pushing them back over the counter to Sam.

Once seated in the lounge, Sam returned her friends' passports to them. When Sam's folder slid to the floor, Bubbles picked it up for her and spotted a couple of photographs tucked behind a plastic window. One was a family snapshot: Sam's parents, with Akbar and Heer as a baby in her grandfather's arms. The other was a picture of Haroon that Bubbles had not seen before. As always, he was smiling – was there a single picture in which he was not smiling? – looking directly out at Bubbles, seeming to wink at her as the light caught the plastic. 'Hey, gorgeous,' she could almost hear him say, 'don't you go forgetting me now, huh? But you go out there and have a bit of fun. No harm in that at all.'

Bubbles ran her forefinger gently over Haroon's face before firmly closing the leather folder. Sam was busy chatting to Anita about something and did not even notice as Bubbles slipped the folder back into her bag.

Heathrow was heaving with its returning holiday crowds. There were at least ten times as many people as they had seen at Delhi airport, and not half the space required to squeeze them all in.

'And they call *that* the Third World,' Anita grumbled as she hauled her suitcase off the carousel. The queues at the trolleys had been so long, the girls had decided to do without them. 'Honestly, look at the grime on the floor and those wires hanging out of the ceiling,' she continued a little later as they trudged down an endless corridor, wheeling their suitcases after them. 'They have some cheek describing themselves as a developed country!'

'Oh Anita, stop muttering,' Sam laughed. 'Whatever happened to your plan to be less crabby?'

Sam was right, Anita thought, providing a timely reminder of her recent resolution. But it sure would have helped to know what was going on with Hugh. He had taken a couple of days to respond to her emailed apology and a few rather muted exchanges had taken place since. Perhaps he had just been occupied with other things, having gone with his kids to his parents' home for Christmas. But Anita found it impossible to tell from the tone of his brief emails if he had forgiven her for that row. Maybe he was still mulling over the wisdom of taking on a bolshy little bitch like her? Maybe he was trying to politely shake her off. They would, after all, still need to work in the same newsroom and couldn't very well cut each other dead. Bugger, bugger, bugger, Anita thought as she walked through the Green Channel, picturing being in the same room as Hugh and pretending they had never shared a life together, however briefly. Affairs in the workplace were such a bad idea because they invariably turned rotten and stinky and you had to continue working in the stench because you had no choice. Anita had heard horror stories of people who walked up seven floors in their office buildings rather than risk bumping into ex-lovers in the lifts, and cursed her stupidity as she walked into the waiting area on the exit side. Bubbles had called her driver to collect them and Anita scanned the throng for his familiar face. It was a grey head that caught her attention, though. Taller than the others around him, wearing a familiar fleece and a Louis Vuitton scarf around his neck and carrying an enormous bunch of roses in his hands.

After Anita had rushed into Hugh's arms, babbling a stream of incoherent words, her amused friends followed her. Completely unaware of the reason for Anita's ecstatic reaction to Hugh's presence at the airport, they kissed Hugh, pleased to see that he looked equally delighted to have Anita back. Bemused, they watched the exchange of a few more passionate kisses between the pair before they finally departed for Hugh's car.

'Well, one happy homecoming out of three is not bad going,' Sam said as she saw Anita leaning her head briefly against Hugh's arm while he wheeled her suitcase into the car park. Then, shivering in the cold as a wind whipped around them, they followed the driver to Bubbles' car. 'You don't really have to drop me, Bubs,' Sam grumbled. 'I could take a taxi from the rank – there's dozens idling there.'

'You mad or something?' Bubbles responded. 'I'm going almost all the way up to Kensington anyway!'

'Not mad exactly,' Sam smiled. 'Just trying to kick-start my new-found independence at some point.'

'However "independent" you become, you'll never be able to get rid of me, you do realise,' Bubbles warned, looking worried.

'I suppose when I say "independent", I only mean the kind of life where a lot of time would be spent considering ME, do you know what I mean? I think it's the Talmud that says, "If I am not for me, then who will be?" Nice, isn't it?'

'Yeah, I like that. A lot. Makes being just a tiny bit selfish a good thing rather than bad. Not at all what we were taught as good Indian girls.'

Sam laughed. 'Well, there's a huge gulf between being selfish and being stupidly selfless – I guess I'm aiming for some happy, comfortable place in-between.'

Bubbles waved a diamond-encrusted forefinger in the air. 'Just remember, it won't be selfish at all when we make our first trip to Bombay together. *Whatever* Akbar and Binkie think. Okay?'

They talked and planned excitedly as Bubbles' car sped them into London. Fashion shows, celebrity endorsements, corporate sponsors, the possibilities were endless in a city like this, Sam thought, glancing out of the window. It was one of those grim winter mornings in London, the sky low and leaden, but the V&A had fenced off part of its garden to become an ice-rink, and Sam could see the cheery colours on skaters' hats and mufflers dancing and bobbing through the trees as they whizzed past. Most of the shop windows on High Street Kensington were still festooned with Christmas decorations as well as red sales banners, and the pavement was thronging with bargain-seekers battling the cold. It was oddly both calming and energising to be back in this great old town that would accept her exactly as she was, married or single, Sam thought. Perhaps that was just one of the reasons why London had, at some point in the course of all these years, and without her even noticing, slipped into the category Sam had marked in her head as 'home'. As they passed the church at the corner of her street, Sam delved into her bag for the house keys.

'Do you want me to come in with you?' Bubbles asked as the car pulled in next to Sam's gate.

'Naaah, course not,' Sam responded. 'I'll be fine, Bubs.

You just carry on home and I'll call you in the evening. Got loads to do anyway.'

Before she disembarked, however, Bubbles grabbed her hand. She looked her straight in the eye before saying softly, 'Sami, I'm not going to be like Anita and tell you what to do about Akbar because I know that, left to yourself, you'll make the most sensible decision. The one that's best for *you*.' Bubbles paused for a second before adding, 'Just remember one thing, though: that whatever decision you do take, your grass is pretty green on both sides of the fence.' Seeing some confusion on her friend's face, Bubbles explained, 'You see, on one side, is your old life with Akbar and Heer, which – let's face it – was not a bad one. But on the other side, you'll have the freedom to be yourself and live your life the way you want. With friends like me and Anita for support. Green on *both* sides. See?'

Sam smiled and nodded, swallowing back a sudden lump in her throat. 'Thanks, Bubs,' she said, squeezing her friend's hand and releasing it. She kissed her before climbing out of the car and opened the electronic gate for Bubbles' driver to roll her suitcase through. 'And thanks for the lift too, sweetie,' she added, waving and smiling reassuringly at Bubbles who was looking at her anxiously through the window.

After they had driven off, Sam let the gates click shut behind her. First she needed to clear out the post-box, which was stuffed and overflowing as expected. Her breath formed little puffs of mist as she fumbled with her key-bunch, ungloved fingers already starting to go numb in the cold. For one wild moment she imagined Akbar springing the kind of lovely surprise Anita had received from Hugh at the airport, hiding in wait just behind the door, holding a bunch of flowers in one hand and going 'Ta-da!' with a corny expression on his face as she walked in.

Sam unlocked the door with a wry smile and stepped into her silent house. Of course there was no Akbar behind the door – how silly of her to have hoped, even for one moment. She put her suitcase down and leaned on the door, sighing as it clicked behind her. Life generally wasn't full of lovely surprises. And Akbar had never been given to that sort of conduct anyway. She remembered, with some embarrassment, how she had caught herself feeling stupidly envious when Francesca from next door had once shown a group of them holiday pictures she had taken of Tom doing something silly. Striking the kind of poses Akbar would never have allowed himself to be caught in, let alone have captured for posterity on a camera! So highly strung and unbending and conscious of his image, poor Akbar. And so very difficult to love. Sam realised with a start that she was, perhaps for the first time, laying the blame for Akbar's behaviour not at her own feet but merely where it was due.

The house had the musty smell of disuse, even though it had been closed up for only two weeks. A bunch of gladioli that Masooma had obviously forgotten to clear sat smelly and rotting in a vase. Sam picked it up and wandered downstairs into the kitchen to turn the heating on. Fancifully, in the silence she could hear their voices from that horrible day when Akbar had told her about going to Kenya. She glanced at the calendar on the wall and realised it had been only two months ago. Two months! It felt like years had passed since. And somehow that the conversation would have traversed a completely different path were they to have it today.

Sam threw the flowers into the bin and then opened the fridge to peer in. Except for half a tub of full-fat Greek yoghurt and a couple of bottles of salad dressing, there wasn't much else. It would be good to make a leisurely trip to Waitrose later this afternoon and stock up afresh. Not with cakes and muffins, but with all manner of low-GI, high-fibre foods, as promised to Zeba.

'So, Sam Hussain,' she said out loud, closing the fridge and throwing the tub of mouldy yoghurt into the bin. 'Ready to take the bull by the horns and start a brand-new life, huh?'

The house was still cold, so she leaned against the tall kitchen radiator, feeling its slowly growing warmth against her back. She ran through her head the words she would use to confront Akbar about the state of their marriage. 'Confront' was not quite the word, though, as she would stay calm and peaceable, both for Heer's sake and their own. There was every chance he would get agitated, of course, and perhaps storm off to wherever it was that he disappeared to every so often. But, suddenly, Sam was far from terrified at the prospect of being alone. She savoured the feeling, on her tongue and skin and in her head. There was a difference between loneliness and solitude; she knew that from something Miss Lamb had once said when, as eight-year-olds, they had pestered her about her life in the cottage at the edge of the school. She hadn't understood Lamboo's evasive reply then, of course, but now it was making a lot of sense. Dear old Bubbles, blessed with an unlikely pragmatism, had put it rather well: green on both sides. She was absolutely right. There was nothing to be frightened of at all.

Sam walked to the window, thinking it strange that she had never before noticed how pretty the honeysuckle looked hanging down over the kitchen windows. Nor heard that bird chirruping madly on the cherry blossom tree; did it live there and was it always so stridently cheerful in the middle of winter? With palms placed on the freezing window pane, she looked out at the tree. Its branches were bare and knotty now, but Sam knew that inevitably – however harsh the cold – it would soon be ablaze with the most generous profusion of blooms.

Three miles away, Bubbles' car was pulling up outside the main entrance of Raheja Mansion. She too was in a tranquil frame of mind as she walked slowly up the stairs to where the butler was already opening the door for her.

'Hello Humphries,' she said, smiling at him. Bubbles had never seen the man look anything but solemn before, but today her warm greeting elicited a flash of yellow teeth. She hummed under her breath as Humphries helped her slip off her coat and then took her scarf.

Bubbles put her serene mood down to a combination of Miss Lamb's advice in Delhi and, of course, the prospect of finally having something useful to put her energies into, alongside friends she loved and trusted well. She had subsequently done a lot of thinking and had arrived at a few firm decisions regarding her life. First of all, she was henceforth going to be the person *she* was most comfortable being, even if that annoyed anyone else, especially if that 'anyone else' happened to be one of the Rahejas. After all, they hadn't given a toss when she'd done everything possible to fit in with them. She was also going to tell Binkie that he would simply have to pull his socks up and be more of a husband to her and, unless he accepted that, she would hereafter lead a completely separate life to his. And she meant separate.

Which brought her to Gio . . .

Contemplating her final resolution, Bubbles kicked off her boots and started to walk to her bedroom in her stockings. She stopped when one of the maids materialised in the corridor. 'Ah, Evelina,' Bubbles said, 'Rob will be bringing my suitcases up from the garage. Would you unpack them for me please? Only the Valentino jacket is for dry-cleaning, everything else can go to the laundry.' When the maid nodded, Bubbles asked, 'Is my mother-in-law at home?'

'No, Madam. She and Mr Raheja have gone to Milan for a week. They are back on Tuesday.'

'Ah,' Bubbles said, trying not to show how pleased she was at the news. She turned to Humphries, who was still hovering behind her. 'Didn't they want you with them, Humphries?' she asked. 'Papa normally can't manage anything without you.'

Humphries cleared his throat and inclined his head in acceptance of the compliment. 'Mr and Mrs Raheja are at the Town House Galleria in Milan, Ma'am,' he explained. 'Their suite comes with a private butler service.'

'Ah,' Bubbles said again, remembering the Dorchester fund-raiser where her father-in-law had made his winning bid for the Milan holiday. She remembered too how bored she had been at that event, sneaking out to the ladies' room to call Sam. How different it would be when she organised her own fund-raising ball for Zeba's Street Flowers charity! Bubbles turned to Humphries, beaming. 'Well, if there's no one home then I'm going downstairs for a swim,' she said. 'What better way to get rid of flight fatigue, eh?'

It was a rhetorical question, and Bubbles would not have expected an answer. However, she failed to notice the look that passed between Humphries and Evelina.

Bubbles did not need to go to her room as the cabinets in the pool-house had everything she needed – towels, caps, lotions, and her collection of swimwear. And so she walked across the vast octagonal hallway, still resplendent with the massive Christmas tree that was specially ordered from Harrods every year. Tugging off her solitaires, Bubbles went past Binkie's prized David Hockney collection, illuminated on a dark day like this by the vintage Belgian chandelier shimmering magnificently on the ceiling. Still humming, she skirted the Steinway that was only ever played by musicians hired for Binkie's parties before taking the stairs down to the pool-house, unbuttoning her cardigan in readiness for her swim as she got to the bottom of the stairs.

And that was when she first heard them. At first, it was distant laughter alongside the popping of a champagne cork, followed by their actual voices.

When she neared the door to the pool-house, she heard James cooing, 'Mmmm, this is heaven.'

To which Binkie replied, 'There's a pot of Keta caviar in the mini-fridge, to go with the Cristal. And some chilled langoustines. But if you want any of that, you've gotta come here and give me a kiss first.'

Bubbles did not really need to stand in the curlicued doorway, flanked by a pair of gold-nippled nymphs, to know what she was about to see. Nor did she actually need to see her husband frolicking naked with James to understand what she had in fact deduced many years ago: from her in-laws' reluctant choice of a girl like her, from the silent sympathy that sometimes emanated from the staff, but, mostly, from her husband's curious inability to fall in love with her. It was from all these things that Bubbles Just Knew. It wasn't really her fault that she had been too polite and kind and *considerate* of everyone else to prefer shoving it to the back of her mind rather than openly suggesting it as a possibility before.

Now, seeing it laid bare before her – the shared bottle of Cristal, the clothes strewn on the Italian glass mosaic, a towel flung carelessly over a plastic palm and her husband looking much, much happier than she had ever seen him before as he kissed his boyfriend – Bubbles did not really need to be so considerate any more. Nevertheless, unseen by the two men, she silently spun around on her stockinged heel and left the pool-house to return upstairs.

Perhaps because at some level she already knew, Bubbles experienced none of the head-reeling and shock and angry tears one would have expected. What she did feel, on the other hand, was the relief of acceptance finally settle over her shoulders like a warm winter blanket. The time was indeed ripe for her first two resolutions to kick into place, and at least she now knew with certainty what to do about the third. Bubbles took out her BlackBerry from her purse and, pushing open the door to her room with one foot, she scrolled down the list of names until she got to Gio's.

Epilogue

That same weekend, Victoria Lamb left her cottage on the grounds of St Jude's Convent in Delhi for the very last time. Some of the nuns who had come to see her off stepped back respectfully as she made her way across her beloved rose garden in the direction of Lily's grave. As Victoria picked her way slowly through the riotously flowering bushes, she found herself following four sets of footprints that had frozen into the winter earth: a set of sensible pumps, wedge heels, and a pair each of Louboutin and Jimmy Choo shoes. She would not have recognised those, of course, but what she did see was the poetry of girls who had left their impressions indelibly on each other, and on her, over the years. The footprints had tracked all the way across to Lily's grave before they made their way out of the garden in the direction of the car park.

Wrapping her shawl around her throat, Victoria stood on the dew-crusted mud that was scattered with fallen petals. She tried to imagine what the girls would have felt while standing before Lily's grave. As she had guessed, they certainly needed the comfort of last Saturday night's assurances, without which the poor girls would, in years to come, have no doubt continued to flay themselves unnecessarily with guilt. Everyone made mistakes in their youth – Victoria understood that better than most – but a girl like Samira Hussain had always been the sort who would wait for someone else to let her off the hook before she would stop punishing herself.

Victoria's eyes ran over the words of Housman that she had carefully chosen for Lily's headstone. Housman had never been her favourite poet but, for the epitaph, Victoria had quite deliberately picked a verse that acknowledged not just Lily's youthful end but the equally tragic death of the Hussain boy only a few days before. Victoria had never been to the riverside Muslim cemetery where the lad had been buried, but often, very often, she had mourned him too while laying flowers at Lily's grave. How could she not muse over what those two young lives would have become?

Victoria clutched her shawl around her shoulders and took a deep breath. She was glad she had finally got around to calling her girls back to the school before she had left for good. By never coming back, those four had certainly made it obvious that they were the ones who had most needed the comfort of knowing exactly what had happened to Lily. Just as Victoria had predicted, the girls had remembered Lily lying here in the cold before departing the school and, perhaps, in the quiet of the night, they had finally made peace with her too. It was never meant to be that women should bring anguish on one another. That, Victoria hoped, was one of the lessons she had taught all her girls well.

Read on for an exclusive extract of
Jaishree Misra's new novel, coming in Summer 2010.

Reva

She sneaked another look at the time on her mobile phone, holding it under her pashmina so that the light would not disturb the person sitting next to her in the darkened BAFTA theatre. Eight o'clock. Her heart sank. She would need to leave soon as Ben was expecting to meet her by nine at the restaurant.

The film had started half an hour ago, soon after the chair-person of BAFTA had announced that their chief guest was running late, 'held up by the inclement weather'. Reva had smiled at that, remembering what a wimp Aman, a regular Bombay boy, had always been about the English weather. But what did he have to worry about the snow in London now, given the fleet of cars and drivers he probably had at his disposal whenever he visited?

The printed programme had stated that the evening would begin with the Aman Khan interview, followed by the screening of 'Afterwards', his most recent film. Reva's plan had been to watch the interview before slipping out of the hall to make her restaurant rendezvous with Ben. She had seen 'Afterwards' a month ago at the London Film Festival anyway. Although she'd enjoyed it, and was quite accustomed to watching some of Aman's films twice, even three times over, she was finding it hard to concentrate on the screen today. Reva cast a glance around the half-darkened hall, wondering if others in the audience were similarly distracted by the imminent interruption that would be caused by the arrival of its lead actor. But all she could see were rows of half-lit faces intent on the screen.

Aman Khan's handsome face was filling the screen now in an extreme close up. It was the scene in which his character first spots the love interest as he looks over his garden wall and Reva recalled how something indefinable had caught at her heart when she had first seen the sequence at the NFT festival screening. A mellow trumpet piece played in the background and Reva, leaning her head on the backrest, remembered the young Aman with sudden sharp clarity. The years had been kind to him. Although she had observed his on-screen persona filling out in his thirties, an obviously new health regime in what would now be his forties had made him leaner and brought out interesting shadows on his face. Oh yes, still the old Aman, and still quite, quite gorgeous, Reva sighed softly, sinking down in her seat, trying again to concentrate on the movie.

But the next few minutes brought a flurry at the door – Aman Khan must have arrived as a wave of excitement was passing through the front rows of the audience. The picture on the screen was frozen before it dissolved away and, suddenly, there he was! The real Aman, being escorted onto the stage by Siddharth Jose, the young director who was due to interview him. The crowd erupted into a crescendo of clapping, some people even leaping to their feet to applaud. The BAFTA chair had popped up at the podium that had been lit again. He smiled indulgently, waiting for the seemingly interminable ovation to abate before tapping the mike lightly and asking for silence. When the crowd finally settled, he performed what Reva thought was a polished introduction, pronouncing all the Indian names with panache, while star and director took their places on two armchairs that had been hastily brought out from the wings for them.

Aman looked into the crowd as the house lights brightened and Reva's heart surged as she felt his eyes looking into hers. She reddened as his gaze moved on, telling herself to stop being so fanciful. For heaven's sake, she was sitting about ten rows away from the stage and Aman's long distance vision had never been very good anyway! On the other hand, it was entirely possible that he'd had that fancy laser treatment performed on his eyes, in which case he may actually have spotted her. He certainly knew she lived in London. She had told him that on the last occasion they had met. His attention was now, however, on the interviewer who was asking his first question.

'Why London, Aman?' Siddharth was asking, 'It's a city you make it a point to visit every year, I'm told. For someone who lives and works in this grimy old city, I can't help wondering why anyone would leave balmy Bombay for London, certainly when it's in the grip of winter like this!'

Aman laughed and settled back in his chair, 'I love it here, especially in the grip of winter,' he said in his familiar deep voice, one that always succeeded in making him seem like he meant every word he uttered. The crowd around Reva sighed with happiness. 'You forget how sultry it gets in Bombay – and how unrelenting. There's something very . . .' he searched briefly for the right word '. . . very *appealing* about the changes of season when you live in a place that doesn't have them. And London's so full of energy, it's such a great city. I love being here, in any season really, and so do my children. But a winter trip is compulsory so that my wife can wear her Burberry coat and Prada boots which otherwise never get the chance to be worn.'

He paused as the crowd laughed affectionately. Salma Khan's shopping penchant was much written about in the gossip magazines and Aman had hit just the right note of affectionate exasperation in his voice and facial expression. His English had improved considerably too, Reva noticed, trying to remember whether she'd have heard him use words like "unrelenting" before. Of course, they had been mere freshers when they had first met but there had been a couple more occasions, the most recent being in 1998 – Reva remembered it well. They had both been invited to the National Awards in Delhi and found themselves on the same panel discussing film adaptations; Aman to talk about his award-winning role of Heathcliff in an artful Hindi version of '*Wuthering Heights*' and she as a novelist whose debut book had been made into the film that had won the Best Film award that year.

The audience around her was laughing again and Reva realised with dismay that she had missed something amusing. Aman was looking relaxed and responding to a question he had just been asked about his early life in England. 'It was only for a year, although it gets mentioned quite a lot – as though I spent all my college years in Oxford or Cambridge or some grand place like that! Actually it was at Hull University and I only spent first year there – in the English Department. You see, my uncle was working in Hull and, because my parents were worrying that I was just hanging around not doing anything after school, he sponsored me to come here for my studies. Not that it lasted! I just wasn't good enough and so, at the end of that first year, I upped and went home.'

'Ah, but that was what took you to the Film Institute, was it not?' Siddharth Jose cut in. 'So, if you had been "good enough", as you say, for Hull's English Department, Bollywood – and all of us – might have missed out on one of our best actors!'

'Indeed, who knows – Bollywood's loss may have been Hull University's gain!' Aman joked, making the audience laugh again.

And mine . . . maybe? . . . Reva thought, recalling that long ago time up in Hull. How torn she had been between Aman's attentions and Ben's for six months. Before she had made her decision. And how strange fateful decisions like that could look in retrospect! Irrationally now, she tried willing the interviewer to quiz Aman more on the decisions he had made as a young man. Such as, 'Why, Mr Khan, had you not thought to fight just a little harder for Miss Reva Singh's affections before upping and leaving Hull University?' Annoyingly, however, interviewer and interviewee had already moved on to something else.

When the interview ended, Reva used the short break before the film restarted to get up and slip out of her seat. She tugged on her coat and gloves as she hurried through the foyer. It was a quarter to nine and, even if she now took a cab to the restaurant, she would be late. Ben did so hate being kept waiting, he would not be amused at all, she thought with a sense of slight panic as she ran down the stairs towards the main entrance. She drew in her breath at the sudden cold outside, annoyed that she had forgotten to carry her woollen cap. As had been predicted, snowflakes were drifting against the neon lights of Piccadilly while a bitter wind stung the tips of her ears and nose. A small gaggle of people were huddled against the railings and Reva heard one of them cry Aman's name out. Unthinkingly, she too joined his crowd of fans, quite forgetting her lateness and the no-doubt steadily growing impatience of her husband awaiting her in the restaurant. Standing on tip-toe, Reva saw that Aman had emerged from BAFTA's entrance – perhaps he had been just a few steps behind her! He was now getting into a long black limousine along with a couple of other people. As it pulled away from the kerb, the group of fans started waving and blowing kisses at the car. Reva joined them, running a little way down the pavement where the crowd was thinner. The car pulled away and Reva felt sure she had been spotted by Aman, his head turning around to look back at her as he was driven away.

WIN A TRIP TO BOLLYWOOD!

To celebrate the launch of *Secrets & Lies* by Jaishree Misra, TransIndus are offering one lucky winner the chance to win a trip to Mumbai - the home of Bollywood – for 7 nights! This prize includes an international flight from London Heathrow airport, arrival and departure transfers and at least 4* accommodation in Mumbai with bed & breakfast for departure anytime between 15th April 2010 to 22nd September 2010 *(subject to availability)*. TransIndus are governed by CAA and ABTA.

For more great award winning holiday ideas from the leading India specialist, TransIndus, visit www.transindus.co.uk

TransIndus
Holidays to India & beyond

To enter this free prize draw, simply visit www.avon-books.co.uk and answer the question below or send your postal entry to Avon Secrets & Lies Competition, HarperCollins Publishers, 77–85 Fulham Palace Road, Hammersmith, London, W6 8JB.

In *Secrets & Lies*, in which city did Anita, Sam, Bubbles and Zeba attend school?

A) Dakar
B) Delhi
C) Dublin

4. Closing date for the promotion is September 30th 2009 and entries must be received by the Promoter by 23.59 hrs. No entries received after this date will be valid. Proof of sending an entry via email or post is not proof of receipt. No responsibility can be accepted for entries that are damaged, lost or not received by the Promoter.

5. The winner will be drawn at random from all correct entries by an independent adjudicator. The prize draw will take place on 1st October 2009. The winner will be notified by telephone by 9th October 2009. The Promoter's decision as to who has won the competition shall be final.

6. To obtain the name of the prize winner after the closing date, please write to AVON/HarperCollinsPublishers, 77-85 Fulham Palace Road, Hammersmith, London, W6 8JB.

7. The prize consists of an international flight from Mumbai to London Heathrow airport, arrival and departure transfers and at least 4* accommodation with bed & breakfast anytime between 15th April 2010 and 22nd September 2010. This prize is only for one person. No warranty is given as to the quality of the prize.

8. The Publishers will pass the booking contact details on to the winner who will be solely responsible for booking this trip with TransIndus.

9. This prize is non-transferable. No cash or prize alternatives are available.

10. By entering this competition you are agreeing that if you win, your name and image may be used for the purpose of announcing the winner in any related publicity with AVON, without additional payment or permission.

11. HarperCollins Publishers reserve the right in their reasonable discretion to substitute any prize with a prize of equal or greater value.

12. Entry instructions are deemed to form part of the Terms and Conditions and entry into the promotion is deemed to signify acceptance of the Terms and Conditions. Any breach of these terms and conditions by an entrant will void their entry. Misrepresentative or fraudulent entries will be declared invalid.

13. Under no circumstances will the Promoter be liable for any loss, damages, costs and expenses arising from or in any way connected with any errors, defects, interruptions, malfunctions or delays in the promotion of the prize.

14. By entering the competition all participants will be deemed to have accepted and be bound by the terms and conditions and by any other requirements set out in these terms and conditions or any promotional material.

15. HarperCollins excludes all liability, so far as is permitted by law, which may arise in connection with this competition and reserves the right to cancel the competition at this stage.

16. These terms and conditions are governed by English law and are subject to the exclusive jurisdiction of the English courts.